SAINTS & SPIES

SAINTS & SPIES

SAINTS & SPIES SERIES
VOLUME ONE

JORDAN McCOLLUM

DURHAM CREST BOOKS

SAINTS & SPIES © 2015 Jordan McCollum

First printing, 2015

Published by Durham Crest Books
Pleasant Grove, Utah
Set in Linux Libertine

ISBN 978-1-940096-18-6

PRINTED IN THE UNITED STATES OF AMERICA

AUTHOR'S NOTE

For the purposes of this story, I have created a covert classification of FBI agents. To my knowledge, there are no covert FBI agents—but, then, would we know if there were?

This book is about an LDS FBI agent who goes undercover as a Catholic priest. As such, there is religion in this story. If you prefer not to mix religion and reading, this may not be the best choice for you.

Otherwise, enjoy!

1

FATHER PATRICK LAY ON THE PAVEMENT outside the parish office, his skin ashen, his trim graying hair disheveled, his purple stole wrapped around his throat. Numb with shock, Molly willed herself to look away again, to ground herself with the limestone cobbles, the smell of fresh-cut grass, the echo of the officers' measured footsteps. But the details only made the horror more surreal.

To her right, her coworker Kathleen sobbed again. Molly slid an arm around her shoulders and wished she felt the same surge of grief—or anything beyond shock.

Uniformed officers cordoned off the area near Father Patrick and the open office door. She always locked that door. Molly checked the doorframe: no scratches or other signs of forced entry. Had she forgotten?

Her stomach slowly sank. Had she left the office subject to some crime of opportunity, and Father Patrick stumbled upon it? With all the rumors of a criminal organization at St. Adelaide, they always expected a tragedy. But not this, not robbery, not one of their priests, not random violence.

Kathleen's crying broke into jagged gasps. Someone had to talk to Chicago PD, give the gruesome scene context. With Kathleen in hysterics, it had to be Molly. Because this was her fault.

Father Patrick might have thwarted the robbery, but he'd paid dearly for her negligence.

A policewoman gently towed Kathleen, still weeping, down the hallway. Another officer led Molly through an arched portal to the car park.

"Name and occupation?" he asked.

She took a deep breath and opted not to give her nickname. "Mary Malone. The parish secretary here at Saint Adelaide."

The policeman noted that in his pad. "You know the victim, then?"

"I do. Father Colin Patrick. Are you sure it was a robbery? I mean, I know there are no signs of forced entry, but—"

"A CSI fan, huh?" The policeman smirked.

"I used to be in law enforcement." Molly let her tone rebuke his lack of professionalism.

The officer missed the reproach. "Oh yeah? Whereabouts?"

"Ireland. Now, about Father Patrick?"

"Explains the accent. And yeah, looks like a robbery. So you found your pastor—"

She shook her head. "Father *Fitzgerald* is our pastor. He should be in the confessional." Confession had brought her here on a beautiful Saturday afternoon. She never expected to find . . . She didn't have to see the supine figure to remember the sickening pallor, the dead set to his eyes. "Father Patrick is his assistant." Molly winced and corrected herself. "Was."

She looked down. The first change of many they'd have to make now.

From the steps of Holy Name Cathedral, Special Agent Zach Saint scanned the downtown street corner. His boss's meeting with the archbishop was taking too long. Hadn't the archbishop agreed to this idea three weeks ago when Father Patrick was killed?

Zach turned back to the building and brushed the grit from the bullet hole in the cornerstone. Eighty years ago, the head of the Irish mob was gunned down here. Now, the archbishop was making the final call over whether Zach could join a parish across town—and the battle against organized crime so infamous in Chicago. But he'd be the first to do it in this capacity. He tugged at the white plastic collar insert.

"Quit playing with that."

Zach looked to find Assistant Special Agent in Charge Reginald Sellars glowering up as he reached the base of the cathedral stairs. "You see other pastors messing with their collars?"

"You try. It chafes."

Sellars rubbed one temple, like he was massaging away the headache that was Zach Saint. "Aren't you used to it?"

"Um, no." Some misunderstanding about the nature of his LDS mission must've convinced the Bureau he'd make the perfect Catholic clergyman with an intensive course at a Chicago seminary. Pity a real Catholic would be excommunicated for this scheme without a papal dispensation. "Now the archbishop is okay with a Mormon pretending to be a priest?"

The heavyset African American shrugged. "He liked your little reference to Matthew."

"Mark. And if he liked it, he shouldn't have kicked me out."

"Whatever." Sellars held out a manila folder as Zach ambled down the stairs. Zach held up a hand to refuse the files. Alongside his crash course in catechism, canon and communion, he'd studied the profiles and pictures of the parish's criminal contingent since Father Patrick's murder. If he didn't have the suspects memorized by now, it was too late. He traded Sellars the contents of his wallet for a license and credit cards in his cover's name: Timothy O'Rourke.

Father Timothy O'Rourke. After three weeks of playing a priest, he was prepared to root out the priest-murdering mob in St. Adelaide parish. Sort of. Tomorrow, he'd be helping to give Mass—if his cover passed muster with his immediate superior in the parish. "Did the archbishop say anything about the other priest?"

"Fitzgerald's staying in the dark. Apparently he's got 'ardent probity.' Whatever that means. Probably better this way—in case he's with them, too. Oh, and apparently he's a control freak. Likes to run the whole Mass show." Sellars jerked his chin toward the cab at the curb. Zach loaded his suitcase in the trunk.

"For the record," Zach said, "I still don't think this is a good idea."

"Then back out. I had a guy hand-picked for this job till D.C. came up with this crazy scheme."

Zach narrowed his eyes. Sellars harped on his pet agent every time they'd met. Like they weren't all part of the same Bureau. "You know I was made for this job." Zach meant the FBI, but Sellars could think what he wanted.

Sellars ignored him, still sneering. "Your best bet is the office. If they're laundering money through the church, the parish office has to know—so cozy up."

What did he look like, a rookie?

"Archbishop says you have eight weeks," Sellars continued. "And from what Patrick managed to tell us before they got to him, could be less."

Eight weeks? Agents could spend eight months—eight *years*—infiltrating a mob and still fail. The archbishop wasn't giving them half a chance. Zach shook his head and got in the cab. "Where to, Father?" the driver asked.

As Zach gave the address of the parish across town, he could only hope the parishioners would accept his cover that easily.

Molly stepped into the church vestibule behind a tall man clad in black, surveying the chapel interior. The chill settling over her wasn't only from the cool of the building. Three weeks to prepare, and she still wasn't ready for the change she dreaded most. The new priest was early.

"Sorry?" she called in greeting before remembering the Irish convention only served to confuse most Chicagoans. Even after five years, lifelong habits died hard.

"Yes?" The man turned, and Molly froze. It wasn't just his strong jaw or deep-set blue eyes. Wasn't there canon law against ordaining a man handsome enough to stop a woman's heart at a glance?

The white square of his collar confirmed her initial assumption. "Father O'Rourke?"

"Yes." His laugh made his response a half-question.

"Oh, but you're so . . ." She searched for some word to explain her surprise. Other than handsome. Or attractive. Or— "Young. Did they just drop you here?"

"Yep." An enticing gleam warmed his knowing gaze. "And what was your name?"

"I'm sorry. Molly." As she'd feared, her pulse quickened at his firm handshake.

"Nice to meet you. Is there something I can help you with?"

Now that was amusing. "I should be askin' you that—I'm the parish secretary."

The spark in his eyes flickered. "Right. I guess this is all kinda new to me."

"I'm here to help." She moved to pick up his backpack, but he beat her to it. He grabbed his suitcase and she led him out, careful to keep a sensible distance between them. She'd never swooned over a priest before; she wasn't about to start.

Molly paused at the arched open-air hallway to the office. She should get his keys. But that would mean walking through the place she'd found Father Patrick, and she still couldn't bring herself to approach that spot.

The parish house it was. Father O'Rourke fell in step with her in the car park, and she suddenly appreciated just how tall he was. Molly was far from short, but the priest was nearly a head taller than she, and broad enough in the shoulders that, despite his height, he wasn't the slightest bit gangly. Not many men made a woman of her stature feel delicate.

"I take it you work in the office?" he asked.

"I do. Have you spoken with Father Fitzgerald yet?"

"Not yet. What part of Dublin are you from?"

"Father O'Rourke, are you assumin' because I'm Irish, I'm from the only Irish city you know?" She winced mentally—she shouldn't tease a priest who made her heart beat a slip jig on sight.

He returned the codding tone. "No, I assume that because of your Dublin accent."

"Good ear." Molly stuck to a more neutral answer. She showed him into the nondescript brick cottage and set his backpack on the table. "Father Fitzgerald's out now, but he'll be back soon. Father Patrick's room is over there. Was." She lowered her gaze at the slip before gesturing at the now-vacant room. "You could start gettin' settled."

The silence stretched long enough that she dared to meet Father O'Rourke's eyes again. "Molly, I'm sorry. I know it's hard to lose someone."

"Thank you." Molly made herself flash a smile. She had yet to find the "proper" time to mourn the parish's loss—her loss. She changed the subject. "Father Fitzgerald's mobile number is there." She pointed to the message board by the kitchen telephone. "And the office number, and mine. Give me a ring if you need anythin'."

"I will, thanks." Father O'Rourke grinned, and yet again there was something teasing, something tempting in his eyes. Something more than friendliness?

Molly turned away. "I'll let you settle in." She hurried to put distance between them. He was a priest, after all. It wouldn't do her any good to go forgetting that.

Zach forced himself to look away as Molly left, her dark curls bouncing around her shoulders. Meeting a beautiful—no, gorgeous—woman first thing didn't bode well for his cover. And of course she had to be Irish. Like they were setting him up. How closely did a priest work with the parish secretary? He was supposed to cozy up to the office staff, after all.

Flirting with the parish secretary probably didn't fall under his priestly duties. He had plenty of experience *not* flirting with Irish girls after two years surrounded by them, and as an experienced FBI agent, he knew how to focus on the case at hand—even if his last assignment had entailed a *lot* of flirting to get what he needed.

Hadn't he seen enough James Bond movies to know sometimes the beauty was also the villain?

Then again, maybe that was the perfect reason to flirt with her. He resisted the urge to peer through the yellowed lace curtains to watch Molly's graceful, springing step. She could be the key to his success.

The government didn't normally get involved in the affairs of any church, or in any run-of-the-mill murder. But when a priest, having possibly laundered money through his church for the mob, was murdered hours before an appointment with the FBI, the Bureau would make an exception. Between threats of racketeering charges and losing tax-exempt status, the archdiocese had to comply with the FBI's wishes. They had no choice. And neither did Zach.

Now he had to lie to innocent people and look like the perfect patsy to take Patrick's place with the mob. Maybe meeting Molly was the first step. Sellars said to get in with the staff.

But flirting with her first thing might seem suspicious. Zach sank onto the threadbare couch with its tacky afghan and dug through his backpack for a distraction. Dog-eared and well-worn, the secondhand Bible was a last-minute find. His real scriptures weren't suitable for a Catholic priest, with the Protestant King James Version between the covers, "Zachary Tyler Saint" on the front, and "The Church of Jesus Christ of Latter-day Saints" on the spine. But the New Testament was basically the same, even with a stranger's notes and the lingering mothball scent from the thrift store.

He flipped open the Bible, but instead of reading the words, his mind wandered back to the memory of Molly's deep blue eyes.

Flirting with her could backfire. It could mean big trouble.

He knew Fitzgerald and the parishioners would test his cover, but would the parish secretary be the real danger?

Zach tried to concentrate on the Bible until a Catholic priest—a real one—walked in. "Father O'Rourke," Fitzgerald greeted him. He had to be in his mid-sixties, his hair fully gray and his gut fully round. Something about him seemed familiar . . . "Sorry we didn't meet during the interviews. Been hectic here. I'm Bruce." He offered a hand.

"Tim." Zach set the Bible on the old coffee table and rose to give his heartiest handshake.

"You finished the paperwork at the cathedral pretty quick—faster than we expected. Everything's in order?"

"Yep."

"And you've already met with your spiritual director?"

His what? Zach frowned and hoped that was an appropriate response. "I knew we were forgetting something."

Fitzgerald shook his head. "Chickens with their heads cut off downtown. We'll get that fixed, but in the meantime, feel free to come to me. So, is this your first parish?"

"Yeah, and I really want to do this right." On more than one level.

"Naturally," Fitzgerald said. "But the hardest part is understanding your calling. Once we accept God's will, He shows us the way."

"Absolutely," Zach agreed. "I mean, our will is the only thing we have that we can give over to God. Everything else comes to us from Him."

Had he just paraphrased an LDS apostle? Zach tried to keep his expression steady as the other man squinted, thinking. Finally, Fitzgerald nodded. "Very true—but try not to give over more than you can handle. It's easy to burn out before you learn your limits. Ready for Mass in the morning?"

"Hope so." Good thing Fitzgerald was the pastor and Zach only an assistant. He wasn't excited to deceive honest parishioners—though he'd do what he had to—but stumbling through Mass alone? No thanks. "Should I go ahead and unpack now?"

"Your room's over there." Fitzgerald gestured to the same door Molly had. "And the office has your keys."

Zach collected his suitcase and backpack, but before he could start for his room, Fitzgerald placed a hand on his arm. "Did they tell you what happened to Colin?"

"Only that he died."

"Then you should probably know he was murdered."

Zach schooled his features into an appropriate portrayal of shock. "Who'd kill a priest?"

Fitzgerald shrugged dismally.

"Any idea why?"

He stared at the rickety coffee table. "Apparently he interrupted a break-in. The office door was open when Molly and Kathleen found him."

"Did they catch the guy?"

"No." Fitzgerald sighed. "Just . . . be careful."

Zach waited a beat. "I'm sorry." When the older man said nothing, Zach carried his bags to his new quarters.

Then Fitzgerald hadn't connected the murder to the mob, either. With the parish and even Chicago PD buying the break-in story, Zach could appear just blissfully ignorant as the other priest.

A memory in the corner of his mind clicked into place—that was why Fitzgerald seemed familiar. He reminded Zach of his neighbor when he lived in Cork. Owen, that was his name. Like Fitzgerald, Owen was in his sixties and had even been a Catholic priest, until he gave it up to marry Fionnuala.

The former parish secretary.

Zach smiled. Fionnuala herself said they'd fallen victim to that old Catholic cliché. And if it helped him look like he was more susceptible to the mob's influence, even better.

Right now, his job *was* getting close to Molly.

Molly locked the office door, turning her back on the spot where she'd found Father Patrick. The only other place to look was the parish house. Was Father O'Rourke settling in all right?

No, she didn't need another opportunity to gawk at a handsome priest. Molly shook her head to clear her mind. As soon as she left the shade of the arched portal, a movement to her right drew her attention: Father O'Rourke leaving the brick cottage. He waved to her, and she waved back.

"Father Fitzgerald said you have my keys?" he called as he approached.

"Of course." She took him back into the office, retrieved Father Patrick's keys from her desk drawer—and hesitated.

Somehow, handing over these keys carried more finality than the funeral. Now Father Patrick would truly be gone. Molly lifted her gaze to the new priest's blue eyes. She wasn't ready for this, not at all. She squeezed the keys one last time, the metal biting into her palm like the guilt still needling her conscience, then opened her fingers and deposited the keys in his hand.

"Thanks." Oblivious to what the gesture meant to her, Father O'Rourke pocketed the keys. Time to move on. She ushered him out of the office, but he stopped in the door. "So what *does* a parish secretary do all day?" His smile seemed almost canny, as if he already knew the answer.

She caught herself smiling back a second too long. She laughed nervously, then ticked off her responsibilities on her fingers. "Direct people to resources, collect announcements and put the bulletin together, keep the records and the books—whatever needs done."

"You're the bookkeeper, too?" His grin dimmed a watt. "And stuck here by yourself all day?"

"There's the office manager, Kathleen Carver."

"Ah." Father O'Rourke started for the car park with her, but he soon slowed to a stop. Molly followed suit, watching him. Did he need anything more?

He squinted up at the belfry, an uncertain wrinkle in his brow. "You know, when I came to Chicago, I expected to end up in the inner city, not a place like this."

He scanned the whole scene, surveying the squat brick school, the parish house and the Gothic chapel's stone façade flanked by blazing red maples in a carpet of lawn. The dismay in his expression dissolved with his satisfied nod. St. Adelaide must seem like a suburban oasis to him.

Three weeks ago, Molly had been disabused of that notion. Now the idyllic scene carried a sinister undertone so strong she couldn't bear to look at it. She hadn't even noticed when the maples turned red.

Father O'Rourke sighed and looked to her. How could she tell him the truth and shatter his illusion? "It'll get to feelin' like home soon enough," she murmured.

"Hope so. I guess none of this is what I expected."

He couldn't already know the truth about his parishioners, could he? "I can imagine."

"It's very . . . different. From this perspective." He hooked a finger over the white insert at his collar and adjusted it.

Was that all he meant? Molly reached up and removed his hand from his collar. "Give us a chance. You'll get used to it—to us."

A secretive smile danced in his eyes. "I dunno. Having a secretary will definitely take some getting used to."

"You'll take some gettin' used to as well." She realized what she'd said and shifted, the gravel crunching beneath her feet. "I mean, it's an adjustment for all of us."

"I can't imagine what it's like to lose a priest like this."

She pulled her jacket tighter, as if to soften the chill at the thought of Father Patrick. If she'd done her duty, he'd still be here, and she wouldn't have to worry over Father O'Rourke.

"G'night," he bid her after a long silence.

"You too." Molly watched him return to the parish house.

Perhaps she couldn't help Father Patrick now, but there was one priest she could protect from the truth about their parish—one man who could keep his illusions as long as possible.

A T THE SOUND OF CHAIR WHEELS on linoleum the next day, Molly glanced up from a donation receipt for the school trust. Apparently, Kathleen was done primping her short, frosted hair for the fourth time. Rolling her chair over meant she had juicy gossip to foist upon Molly, something Kathleen hadn't done since Father Patrick died.

Father O'Rourke's arrival yesterday wasn't the only way things were returning to a semblance of normal around St. Adelaide.

"What's the new priest like?" Kathleen leaned over Molly's desk, the older woman's musky perfume invading the air.

Molly squinted at her computer to appear busy and give herself time to think of the appropriate response. Her coworker wasn't wondering how handsome he was. "Em, he's nice. Tall."

"Do you like him?"

Molly felt her neck flush and tugged the cowl neck of her cobalt sweater higher. Kathleen couldn't guess that. "He's grand."

"Grand? What are you, eighty?" She shook her head and rolled back to her desk. Kathleen's efforts at reforming Molly's Irish habits and vocabulary were well-intentioned, sure, but the constant corrections had mostly helped Molly cultivate a reservoir of patience deeper than Lake Michigan.

Before Molly could find another subject to occupy Kathleen, Father O'Rourke walked in and saved her the trouble. "Hello, Molly."

"Hi, Father." She tried to tamp down the nerves attacking her stomach. She didn't need to act like this over a handsome man; she wasn't a teenager. "Have you met Kathleen?"

He introduced himself and shook Kathleen's hand. His smile

seemed less disarming aimed at her. Kathleen directed him to the cardboard box in the corner by her desk. "Could you carry these books over to the school for us? Usually they're all okay, but you might want to check them first."

"Donation?" He knelt to rummage through the box.

"The Gallahers bring in their building's charity box every few weeks."

Molly held her breath. The Gallahers—and the other "heroes who cleared the punks out of the neighborhood," as Kathleen called them—were among her favorite gossip topics.

"Don't know how they go through so many books." Kathleen settled at her desk as Father O'Rourke rolled up the sleeves of his clerical shirt.

Molly watched her coworker. Kathleen rolled her chair closer to Father O'Rourke. "Funny thing about the Gallahers—"

Molly spotted the perfect change of topic. "Have you read that?" She nodded at the pulp spy novel Father O'Rourke was holding, *Catch Me in Zanzibar*, grateful for any distraction from Kathleen's gossip.

"No, have you?"

"I have. A bit of a James Bond knockoff, but it has its fans." She laughed sheepishly and pointed to herself.

He glanced at the cover. "I'll let you know what I think. If it's all right if I borrow this?"

"Sure now." Molly waved her permission.

He tucked the book into his back pocket and stood. "What were you saying, Kathleen?"

"Well, the Gallahers aren't just—"

"Sorry," Molly tried again, "but those books need delivered before the librarian leaves."

"Oh, sure." Father O'Rourke hoisted the box under one arm. "Afternoon, sisters!" He shot an all-too-charming smile at Molly on his way out. She settled back in her chair with a sigh. Crisis averted.

"'Sisters'? He does know we're not actually nuns, right?" Kathleen asked as soon as the door shut.

"I'm sure he does."

The wrinkles around Kathleen's lips twitched as if fighting her judgmental pucker. "He *is* pretty handsome."

"I suppose so." Molly turned back to the donation receipt to avoid the gaze of Kathleen the blond-tipped gossip hawk, ready to swoop down on her prey.

Molly replayed the last few minutes from Kathleen's perspective. Molly had monopolized Father O'Rourke's full attention. She could almost see the wheels of the gossip mill spinning in Kathleen's mind. But she'd take whatever rumor Kathleen might dream up if it meant Father Tim could keep his illusions about their peaceful parish.

Zach shook his head at himself as he carried the box through the school doors with a pack of students. He'd hoped to find Molly alone in the office. But Kathleen was the one who'd brought up the Gallahers—the mobsters. And the second she did, Molly changed the subject.

He didn't expect Molly to send him an engraved invitation to join the mob, but if she didn't even want their names mentioned, this would take longer than he'd hoped. Longer than he had. He'd have to step up his flirting game.

"Hey, Father Tim." Speaking of bringing his "A" game . . . Zach nodded at the familiar face—one of the basketball players who'd beaten him in a pickup game before school. DeWayne grinned. "Back for more?"

He held up the box. "Dropping these off."

"Thought so." The teenager stopped in the cafeteria door.

"Next time, I'm not going to go so easy on you." Zach rested the box of books on a table in the hall.

"Might as well give me the deed now, padre. I own that court."

Zach scoffed. "We'll see about that next week." He turned to the blond man standing between the table and the cafeteria doors. Paul, according to his name tag, was almost as tall as Zach—and definitely too old to be a student. A teacher or volunteer, then? "You play ball?" Paul shrugged. "Some."

"Free next Tuesday?"

DeWayne clapped a hand on Zach's shoulder. "Who's this white boy? Your contractor?"

Zach aimed an uncomprehending squint at DeWayne. "You're building a house with all those bricks you put up today, right?"

"After school?" Paul sized DeWayne up. "I'll bring some friends."

"Perfect. See you then." Zach patted the box. "Where's the library?"

"Oh, I can take that, Father." Paul accepted the books.

"Thanks." Zach took DeWayne by the shoulders. "In the meantime, you need to get schooled for real." He gave the teenager a friendly push toward the tutoring tables and hurried back to the parish house to grab his bus pass. He had to go downtown to report and get the full profile on Molly in a few minutes—enough time to stop by the office to test her again. A new priest familiarizing himself with his parish's financial status was normal, and he could see if she blinked. Or Kathleen. Shake up the office and see what tumbled out.

Molly was on the phone taking a message when he reached the office. The other two desks were empty. She finished her call and turned to him. "What can I do for you, Father?"

He took a moment to revel in the familiar accent, but stopped himself before he jumped into flirting. He should show at least a passing concern for his ministry first. Zach sighed. "How long did it take you to learn everyone's name around here?"

"Ah, you'll get it soon enough."

He frowned. "Hope so. It's a little overwhelming, you know?"

"The parish?"

"Everything." He gave a half-smile and studied her beautiful face—deep blue eyes, the slightest hint of freckles across her nose, all framed by her dark curls.

She squinted quizzically, then quickly turned away. Like she was hiding something. "I'm sure it'll all turn out fine."

"You're probably right." Zach glanced around the office for something to draw out the conversation. "Is Kathleen full time?"

"Well, she's supposed to be. She left early—holiday with her family."

"Does she work with the finances, too, or do you have to do that all yourself?"

Molly looked at Kathleen's desk. "Simpler to have one person handle it all."

"How're we doing in that department?"

"Grand. Why?" Molly's voice carried a teasing lilt. "Worried about your retirement?"

Zach laughed. "Who isn't?"

"We're all right. No need to worry yourself—that's my job." She fixed her gaze on her screensaver. Avoiding eye contact didn't help her case. Was she lying?

He tried to catch her eye again, but clearly that was all he'd get from her today, and he was late anyway. With a quick goodbye, he left for his bus.

Forty-five minutes later, Zach found Assistant Special Agent in Charge Sellars squinting up at the Water Tower downtown. The squat yellow castle seemed about as out of place among the skyscrapers as Zach felt in the collar.

"Father," Sellars greeted him. "Anyone grab your attention?" They started around the block, but a group of teenage girls in school uniforms cut across the sidewalk in front of them.

"I'll let you know Saturday after confession."

The teenagers covered giggles with their hands, staring at Zach. He nodded to them, but walked a little slower.

"We don't want you doing anything . . . inappropriate." They turned into the park to part ways with the schoolgirls.

"Don't worry, I appreciate the gravity of the priesthood." Better than most of the Bureau knew. "I won't do anything to keep them from asking us back."

Sellars shot him a cynical smirk and glanced back the way they'd come. The girls were gone. He gave Zach a folder. "Mary Margaret Malone," Sellars supplied. "You met her yet?"

"Parish secretary. Goes by Molly. Keeps the books." Zach flipped to a photograph of a beautiful woman with dark, curly hair and deep blue eyes smiling back. She even looked good in a driver's license photo.

"Parents were IRA." He said it like that should be enough probable cause for an arrest.

"So she's automatically involved." Zach snapped the folder shut.

The ASAC leveled him with a silencing glare suitable for a lion tamer and—once again—reminded Zach of stuff he already knew. "Generally, the bookkeeper's involved in money laundering. It didn't start until after she did. But I can always go back to my guy if this isn't your cup of tea."

Empty though it probably was, the threat was enough. "I'll get a keylogger on her computer."

"Warrant's in the file."

Zach shoved his personal qualms aside and the folder into Sellars's hands as they passed under a yellow-leafed tree.

"No sign of anyone else?" Sellars asked.

He shook his head.

"Wish we could get someone else in the school."

"No other covert agents in your division?"

Sellars barked a laugh. "Nobody we could spare full time."

"You could always recruit my little sister," Zach joked.

"She a teacher?"

Okay, that was taking the joke a little far. "Yeah, math. Or I could always sub at the school."

"I want you gunning for Doyle Murphy."

Zach suppressed a sigh. Sure. He only had to nab the highest-ranking mobster in the parish, the new second-in-command of the whole South Side mob. "That all?"

"If you have to, go through one of his captains."

Right. Murphy held a tight rein on his underlings, even living in the same building as his top soldiers to keep tabs on them. Gaining entry to that innermost circle wouldn't be easy—unless Molly could let down her guard enough to make the introductions.

If he could trust her that far.

Zach hoped three days' wait was enough time not to seem suspicious prying into the parish finances—or plying Molly—again. Now, armed with a suitable excuse, he could take this chance to catch her in the office alone.

When he walked in, Molly was poring over a computer spreadsheet. A ledger? Before he could get close enough to check, Molly killed the window. She smiled. "Can I help you, Father?"

"Actually, I had an idea I wanted to discuss—about the parish."

"What's that, so?"

It'd been a long time since he'd heard the familiar Irish version of the tag word "then." Zach launched into his readied excuse—a priestly duty he was comfortable administering. "We should have more social activities. I mean, we have a great youth ministry, but we could do more with the whole congregation."

"We have the Thanksgivin' service meal coming up, and we coordinate volunteers for the school. . . ."

"I know, I just want to get to know you better." Nice—flirting that could be construed as innocent. He shoved his hands in his pockets, pressing his wrist against the dial button on his low-tech spare phone in its dorky hip holster. "The parish, I mean."

Molly's laugh seemed forced, but her ringing cell phone cut off their conversation. As she pulled it out, Zach shifted to end the call. She frowned at the silent phone.

"Hey, I needed a new phone," Zach said. "Do you like yours?"

"Not if you're plannin' on textin'. If it were a person, it'd be functionally illiterate."

"What brand is it?"

She glanced at the phone. "Samsung. Not gettin' one of those again."

Perfect. He'd turn in her number, and the FBI could turn her phone into a roving bug.

"What kind of activity were you thinkin'?"

Zach tapped his hand on her desk. "We should see a movie," he proclaimed. She flinched slightly, and he shifted out of flirting mode again. "As a parish. Do we have money for that kind of thing?"

"Should be grand, as long as we're not plannin' to rent a whole theater."

"Are you sure? I mean, do we have an activity budget, or some surplus?"

"We're pretty creative when it comes to budgetin'." Molly pressed on before he could react. "And the school has a film projector. Know how to run one?" Her smile grew secretive.

"No, but I bet you do."

Her eyebrows shot up. He'd guessed right. Zach rounded the desk to see her monitor. No accounting programs open on the menu bar. "Do you keep our calendar on here?"

"It's the twenty-first century, Father. I keep just about everythin' on here."

That likely included the parish finances. Could he get her to open them?

Molly brought up the calendar. "We'll have to find somethin' on film, of course."

"Right. Think it'd be okay if we watched a spy movie?"

"That'd be fantastic—but it has to be family-friendly."

"I'll e-mail you some ideas by Monday." With a keylogger conveniently attached. They picked the twenty-fifth, a Saturday two weeks away, and she entered it on the calendar.

Zach turned around to lean back against the desk, and Molly rocked back in her chair. "Now, so," she said.

He smiled. "How long have you been in the States?"

"Five years—almost six now, I suppose."

"You never did tell me what part of Dublin you're from."

She lifted her chin as if rising to his challenge. "You never did tell me how you know I've a Dublin accent."

The sound of a throat clearing made them both jump. A figure silhouetted by the setting sun stood in the open door. One of the mobsters? Was his cover in jeopardy?

"Good evening, Tim. Molly," Father Fitzgerald said.

Oh. Zach straightened. Molly sat up, her chair creaking at the abrupt movement. "Evenin'."

"Thought you were out for the night, Bruce." He swallowed the rising guilt. He wasn't a missionary; there was no rule against his cover being alone with a woman. He was doing his job.

"The Baileys had to go to Jenny's recital. Just wrapping up, Molly?"

"I am." She shut down her computer. Fitzgerald gave Zach a hard stare.

"I'll walk you out," Zach offered Molly—but he focused on Fitzgerald. Molly stood and collected her jacket. The priest cast them another meaningful look, but finally turned away.

Zach followed Molly out of the office. Okay, he'd been flirting, but Fitzgerald's judge-in-Israel act really wasn't necessary.

And maybe flirting wasn't either. She thought he was a priest. They had no future in the real world. Unless terrorists' kids got Top Secret clearance in the near future, he'd lose his job or be blacklisted for telling her the truth. As a covert operative, he couldn't even tell his mom what he did for a living. But with how much time he spent undercover, he only had to avoid the topic with his family a few times a year. If even Mom wasn't safe territory, he definitely couldn't tell Molly.

Wait—had he just slipped into thinking about flirting with Molly for more than the case? Of course they had no future. They weren't supposed to, unless you counted testifying at her trial—if she was with the mobsters.

They reached Molly's car, a green Volkswagen hatchback. "Good night, Father." The sun's last rays lit her curls as Molly held his gaze, a faint smile on her lips.

Yeah, he'd really have to play this carefully. "Night." He opened her door, but didn't stand there to watch her leave. Once he was safe in the shadows near the office door, he glanced back to make sure she was gone.

And then he saw the maroon sedan across the street. Cars parked there weren't uncommon, but hours after school and tutoring ended, a man sitting in a car set the hairs at the back of Zach's neck on end. Had this guy been there before?

He made a note of the car, but tried to play it cool. Right now he had other work to do. He grabbed his keys. Normally, he liked to challenge himself with picking locks, but using a key was faster—and less suspicious.

Getting the parish's financial records would only take a minute. Zach started Molly's computer. As the computer slowly came back to life, he riffled through the desk drawers. Pens, compact mirror, hairpins. Nothing incriminating.

A noise echoed in the hall outside the office. Zach froze. Another noise. Outside the door.

An electric current sparked across his scalp. On training and adrenaline, Zach dropped to the floor, poised to draw his gun from his ankle holster.

As a priest, he probably had every right to be here. But skulking around in the dark—in the office where they laundered money—would be sure to raise the mobsters' suspicions.

He silently retrieved Molly's compact mirror from the drawer.

He flipped it open and held it so he could see the three small windows high on the door behind him, holding his breath as he counted to ten. No sign of a shadow. He reached twenty.

Nothing happened.

"Good job, Saint," he muttered to himself. "Eliminate the church mouse." Zach replaced the compact. He sank into the computer chair and found a password screen waiting.

Who would password protect a computer in a locked parish office? Sure, LDS office computers were password protected, but they had confidential files on—oh. Mormons weren't the only ones with church records. And if she was innocent, Molly believed the story that an attempt to break into her office led to Father Patrick's death.

But she'd also shut him down multiple times when the conversation came anywhere near parish finances or the mob.

He made two guesses at her password—it was neither of the most obvious choices, stadelaide or stadelaides—and stood in resignation. At the door, Zach made sure his pant leg covered his ankle holster. With a glance at the sedan still parked across the nearly-dark street, he headed back to the parish house.

He'd have to do a lot more flirting to get the "in" he needed with Molly.

WHEN ZACH WALKED INTO the parish house living room, Father Fitzgerald was waiting with arms folded. The old priest looked the part of judge from his condemning squint to his all-black attire.

Zach could've kicked himself. Walking Molly to her car shouldn't take ten minutes, and in this context, his usual stealth probably seemed suspect. Still, this did seem over the top for Fitzgerald. But whenever your cover was on the line, you had to play it harder. Zach kept his tone light. "How'd it go at the Baileys'?"

"Almost as good as your evening with Molly."

Zach shrugged with open hands, shooting for innocence in his wide eyes.

"I know whatever you were doing was probably fine, but we have to avoid even the appearance of impropriety."

"We were discussing an idea for a parish activity. That's all."

Fitzgerald relaxed his judging frown and shoulders a little and stepped away from the coffee table. "You know the priest and the parish secretary are always under scrutiny. How many times have you heard that story, ending with eloping or excommunication?"

Once, actually. "Bruce, we're not—"

"Do you know what that does to the parish?" Fitzgerald nailed him with an earnest stare and moved closer. Zach fought the urge to retreat. The archbishop wasn't joking when he said Fitzgerald was intense. "You've been given a sacred trust. Our parishioners just lost a beloved priest. Please—don't deprive them of another."

"I'll be careful."

Fitzgerald visibly relaxed and clapped a hand on Zach's shoulder.

"I'm sure you will. I don't mean to be too hard on you, Tim. Better safe than sorry."

"Definitely." This could even help with his cover. He was supposed to be a newbie, after all. "Feel free to let me know if I'm ever off track. Seems like I still have a lot to learn."

Fitzgerald nodded, and Zach went to his room and shut the door behind him. He shook the tension out of his shoulders. Almost a week in the parish and the closest he'd come to a confrontation was with Fitzgerald. Observing the church during confession tomorrow had better yield a target—one other than Molly.

With a sigh, Zach headed for his desk and the refuge of his secondhand Bible.

Molly arrived early, but Father Fitzgerald—at least she hoped it was Father Fitzgerald—was already in the other compartment of the wood-paneled confessional. She knelt on the worn velvet cushion and made the sign of the cross aloud. "Bless me, Father, for I have sinned. It's been three weeks since my last confession." She held her breath. Though she hadn't gone to confession this frequently since primary school, Molly still expected to do penance for less-than-weekly attendance. Or perhaps the priest would sense she was here mostly to keep her job.

But he didn't. "Tell me what brings you here, my child."

She allowed herself a silent second of relief. Not Father O'Rourke. But as she recounted her venial sins, she steered well clear of the topic of work and the new priest.

"Is that everything?" Father Fitzgerald's leading tone said he knew it wasn't.

"I suppose there's somethin' else." She focused on her white knuckles. "I'm a bit worried about workin' with Father O'Rourke."

"Do you mean a romantic kind of concern?"

"Oh, no, not at all, no. Well, I mean, I couldn't say I haven't noticed he's handsome." Molly snapped her mouth shut, but her mind carried on with the vivid memory of the knowing light in his eyes.

"My child?" Father Fitzgerald broke into her thoughts.

"I just haven't been completely honest with him."

"About what?"

Perhaps this wasn't something she was ready to confess—or discuss at all. "I'm only tryin' to keep him from worryin'."

"It's kind of you to be concerned, but we always want to be honest." He paused and Molly stared at the screen, as if she could read his expression through the shadows. "Are you absolutely sure it's not a more . . . personal-level concern?"

"I'm certain, it's only—" She swallowed a nervous laugh and rubbed her fingers against the wood grain of the kneeler armrest. "It's somethin' else. I don't know how to explain."

"All right. But please, be careful. I'd hate for anything to happen."

Molly's shoulders dropped. She was trying to be careful, but Father O'Rourke wasn't only handsome—he was asking the wrong questions if she wanted to keep him away from the parish's criminal element.

She'd have to work harder—on both of her problems with Father O'Rourke.

A few minutes after Fitzgerald left for confession, Zach staked out a place on the faded loveseat to watch the parking lot through the lace curtains. He was actually glad the archbishop had balked at the idea of Zach sitting in on confessions, and of course bugging them was out of the question. He might not believe in "mortal sins," and he was used to doing whatever it took to close a case, but Zach's stomach twisted at the thought of eavesdropping on innocent parishioners. Fitzgerald was right. This was a sacred trust, and he had no right to be here. And anything he discovered from confession wasn't admissible anyway as "fruit of the poisonous tree."

But anybody could see who walked into a church at a certain time.

As if on cue, a white car pulled into the parking lot. Zach searched his memory for a white car in the FBI's files on the mobsters. Gerald Flynn, maybe?

The car parked on the row closest to the chapel, and out stepped a barrel-chested man with red hair. Flynn, all right. The mobster shut his car door and hesitated there, tilting back his head as he took in the bell tower's full height. Tough to read him from this distance, but something about the set of his jaw said "grim determination" to Zach. The mobster trudged toward the chapel doors.

Was he just lucky, or did mobsters go through the motions at confession all the time? Zach waited until he was pretty sure Flynn would be in the booth—convenient that this church was built before they moved to face-to-face confession—before he headed over.

As he reached the top of the chapel stairs, the heavy wooden doors swung open to reveal—Molly. She drew a sharp inhale at the sight of him.

What should he say to someone leaving confession? He went for an Irish greeting. "How are you keeping?"

"Grand, you know yourself." She massaged her elbow, practically slinking past him.

Man, there was an Irish phrase he hadn't heard in a while—but what was with her edgy act? He'd missed something. Maybe Fitzgerald would fill him in, if he could. "See you at Mass tomorrow?"

"Of course, Father," she murmured. "Bright and early."

"Great." Zach stood in the door to watch her walk to her car. She glanced back once, her wide blue eyes full of chagrin.

On second thought, maybe he wouldn't ask Fitzgerald.

Once his vision adjusted to the interior, Zach surveyed the

chapel. No sign of red hair, but Father Fitzgerald was marching toward him, his bushy eyebrows pulled together like silver storm clouds. "Molly was just here," he whispered when Zach reached him.

"Saw her on the way out."

"You need to watch yourself with her."

Zach pressed his lips together and nodded. A priest wouldn't press for details—and a real priest couldn't give them. But whatever she'd said, Fitzgerald shot Zach a glare of censure. The man seemed to have a talent for blowing innocent details out of proportion. Would that end up blowing Zach's cover, too?

Before Fitzgerald launched into another lecture, footsteps sounded behind them, and he rushed to the confessional.

Zach rubbed a hand over his face. These next seven weeks were going to be too long and not long enough. He headed for the votives, the opposite direction from the confessional. He reached the candle rack in time to see a woman with wavy red hair slip into the confessional.

So Flynn wasn't spilling his soul to Fitzgerald, and he definitely hadn't left the chapel. Zach crept through the side aisle, rolling his feet to silence his shoes, scanning the whole room. Where was Flynn now? Would anyone notice Zach's search and think the new priest's zeal was suspicious?

A woman sat in the middle of the chapel, her head bowed. As Zach came even with her pew, he could see the rosary beads dangling from her fingers. Obviously deep in prayer, she didn't look up when he passed.

In front of the pews, the church widened to a smaller alcove to the side: the perpetual adoration chapel, where they kept the Eucharist and where parishioners sat vigil 24/7. Against the far wall, a white and gold altar topped by a gold sunburst sculpture stood beneath a stained glass window. Two men sat facing the altar, their backs to Zach.

Zach checked the sign-in book: Gerald Flynn was the last name on the list. He checked the men in the adoration chapel. One had red hair. Did unrepentant murderers make time to spend an hour with the body of Christ? This could be his "in"—or better yet, someone who could give them everything they needed. Zach quickly crossed to the other end of the adoration chapel to get a better vantage point.

The blond adorer, a man in his thirties, studied the Bible. Zach leaned down to see past him. Flynn's head was also bowed, but not over a rosary or a book. His face bobbed into view below the blond adorer's—jaw slack, eyes closed—before he jerked up again.

He was falling asleep. Zach swallowed a sigh. So much for that potential lead. He returned to the parish house to wait out Flynn's hour of adoration. Or naptime.

After ninety minutes with no sign of Flynn or any other mobsters, Zach headed back to the chapel. Confession was nearly over anyway. Halfway down the side aisle, he spotted Flynn coming toward him. Well, trudging toward him. They met in front of the picture of Jesus falling the second time as he carried the cross to Calvary. Zach introduced himself; Flynn didn't. "In for the weekend?" Flynn asked.

"No, I'm Father Patrick's replacement." Zach fell into step beside him.

Flynn looked him up and down. "Permanent? Thought they'd learned their lesson about St. Adelaide."

"Oh, we never give up on people."

"Hm." Flynn kept his pace deliberate. He was silent until they reached the end of the aisle. He slowed to a stop, staring at the painting of Jesus being led away from Pilate. "Never?"

Was he thinking about confessing? If this man was ready to come back to God, he might also be ready to talk to the FBI. The back of Zach's neck tingled. This was it. Six days in, and he'd found the key to this case. Who had that kind of luck? "Of course not. Never too late for Christ."

Flynn broke into a grin. "Good for Him."

Zach tried to push aside the disappointment and followed Flynn as he strode away. Across the chapel, a stout man lumbered out of the confessional—Cally Lonegan, another of Murphy's crew. He raked his dark, thinning hair across his forehead like the gesture brought order to his mind and his life. He saw Flynn and stopped short. Flynn, still a couple feet from the door, hesitated too. Zach tried to interpret the awkward silence, but Lonegan shuffled out before he could.

Zach hurried to catch the confessor in the vestibule, but Lonegan was quicker than he looked.

Flynn reached Zach again, clapping a hand on his shoulder. "Settling in okay?"

"I guess. Harder than I expected."

One corner of Flynn's mouth tilted upward. "Long week for me too, Father. They all are. You should join us for a drink tonight, get to know everybody."

Zach managed to hide the inward wince with a laugh that echoed off the walls.

Flynn finished his half-smile. "I gotta be home for dinner, but I tell you what. Come to Brennan's at eight and I'll introduce you 'round—and buy you a round."

"Eight it is." Zach grinned back. He had four hours to finish up his duties for the day and get to Brennan's prepared for just about anything. A week deep undercover and so far he'd found a gorgeous Irish woman who wasn't that involved—maybe—and only one interested mobster.

This lead had better be good.

The bartender placed fresh glasses in front of Zach and Gerald Flynn. Zach took a tentative sip of his, as bitter and alcohol-free as his last four drinks. Flynn had guzzled 90-proof gin as fast as Zach could down his tonic and limes.

Flynn reached for his tumbler, but looked away at the last minute. Distracted a split-second, Flynn knocked the juniper-based spirit in Zach's lap.

Great. Zach borrowed a towel from across the bar to mop up the mess. Oblivious, Flynn flagged down a friend. "Doyle!" Even with the crowd, his shout was twenty decibels too loud. But the shouting wasn't what captured Zach's attention—was this Murphy?

Before he looked around, the full case file flashed through Zach's mind. The crime scene photos of the last underling Murphy had had executed sprang to the forefront. He turned to follow Flynn's gaze.

Eyeing Zach, a man who carried his weight like he was used to being obeyed approached the bar. Just like his file photo. "What kind of company you keeping now, Gerry?"

"Who, this?" Flynn punched Zach in the shoulder harder than necessary. "This is Father Tim!" He roared with laughter, like the cover name was the punch line to a secret joke.

"Doyle Murphy." The newcomer—the ranking mobster in the parish—settled at Zach's left. Well, that was easier than he expected.

As long as he didn't end up like the last guy who Murphy didn't trust. The image of blood spatter on the sedate floral sofa hung in his mind. The Bureau believed the guy had been an hour late to deliver a shipment.

And then there was Father Patrick.

Zach fought down his pulse and shook the mobster's hand. He'd been this close to vicious killers before. Worked with them, even. But a nagging feeling in his gut said ingratiating himself to a control freak like Doyle Murphy over the next two months would be his career's most dangerous assignment.

M URPHY LEANED ACROSS THE BAR, scowling. "How much have
you two had?"

Flynn waved him off. "I'm fine."

"Sure you are." Murphy pointedly righted Flynn's overturned
tumbler. "And Father Tim poured his own G-and-T in his lap."

Zach glanced at his glass. Gin and tonic was the natural assumption, since he was drinking one and covered in the other. The bartender was too far away to correct Murphy, and Zach wasn't about
to, either.

"Oh, did I—sorry, Father!" Flynn clapped Zach on the back.

Zach shrugged and tried to maintain an affable air. "It happens."

"Hey, Doyle," Flynn called over Zach. "Remember that time you
spilled your drink on that accountant—the one who did the thing
with the city and the—"

"Shut up, Gerry," Murphy barked. Flynn jerked back, watching
his boss warily.

Though his hopes dropped an inch, Zach swallowed his disappointment with another bitter-sour gulp of his drink. He had to make
Murphy think he didn't know—or care—about their mob activities,
but he still had to look like the mob could get to him, just like Father
Patrick.

Flynn motioned to the bartender. "Whiskey sour and another gin,
Jimmy!"

The bartender checked with Murphy, who held up a hand. "None
for me tonight. Early morning Mass."

And there was the test of his cover. Zach laughed derisively,
matching Murphy's sarcasm. "Me too."

Murphy glowered. "Hitting the sauce pretty hard, then, aren't we?"

"Aw, lay off. He had a tough week." Flynn leaned over to defend him, but slipped off his stool, knocking Zach over, too. Zach grabbed the bar to keep from crashing into Murphy.

Murphy shoved Flynn away and hoisted Zach back onto his seat. "Really, how many have you two had?"

Flynn turned to Zach. "Do you know?"

Maybe Murphy would be more inclined to let Flynn talk if he thought the good father wouldn't remember the tales he told. Zach finished his drink and circumspectly regarded his glass. "This makes five for me. Six if you count the one I'm wearing." He frowned at his wet lap.

"And you've been here how long?"

"Since eight." Flynn squinted at the wall clock.

Murphy checked his watch. "An hour?" He shook his head. "No better than common drunks, the both of you."

"C'mon," Flynn protested. Apparently he was too drunk to correct Murphy's assumption, or he'd forgotten what Zach ordered.

"Next time you're thirsty, order water." Murphy yanked Flynn off his stool. "Let's go."

Puffing out a breath, Flynn took out his wallet and tossed some bills on the bar. "C'mon, Father, I'll give you a ride home."

His stomach tensed, and not because of the gin's Pinesol stench. "Think that's a good idea?" He could see it now: they'd get pulled for DUI and spend the night in the drunk tank. Then Flynn could regale him and the precinct's drunkards with tales about the city account-ant. Zach checked on Murphy. Would he offer a ride—if not to keep them safe, at least to keep Flynn quiet?

But Flynn was already blundering through the bar. Zach followed him to the parking lot. At his blue Ford, Flynn seemed to find oper-ating his key fob difficult. "You'll get to like Doyle," he said, hitting the lock button yet again. He tried the door handle and swore under his breath when it wouldn't open. "You know Doyle does the church's landscaping?"

"All by himself?"

Flynn snorted and shook the key fob. "He has a guy. And he gives . . . you know, members of the community a break on rent—like what's-her-name in the parish office."

Could he mean Molly? Zach moved to the other side of the car and leaned against it. That didn't change anything. He already knew she was a suspect.

For now, he had to focus on keeping Flynn talking and keeping up this bit. Maybe acting drunk could be advantageous in other ways. He slid down to the pavement—and slid his hand into his pocket for a GPS tracker.

"You okay?" Flynn shouted.

"Yep." Zach tried to get the tracker out, but he'd chosen an awkward position. Footsteps approached as he struggled with his stupid pocket. Finally, he pulled the tiny cylinder free. He planted the tracker on the car body in front of the tire just before Flynn arrived to help.

Zach regained his feet and spied Murphy approaching. "Gerald!" Murphy called.

Zach gave a mental sigh of relief. Riding home with a drunk, even for five blocks, could be the most dangerous part of his assignment's first phase.

Or maybe not. The specter of the bloodied couch returned to his mind. Murphy wasn't exactly happy to meet him, but to murder his new priest over talking with one of his soldiers? No, Murphy had shut Flynn up the moment he began to talk about something interesting. No reason to kill anybody yet. He hoped.

"Where should I take you, Father Tim?" Murphy asked.

Zach's mind went blank for a split second, but he hesitated only long enough for Flynn to jump in. "The church, of course. Where'd you think I picked him up? The local Priest Mart?"

"Saint Adelaide's?" Murphy scoffed. "Great, the new priest is a boozehound."

If the man hated drunks that much, he shouldn't hang out in a bar.

Wait. A sober man in a bar on a Saturday night. Either he took early-morning Mass too seriously to drink the night before, or

Brennan's was the mobsters' meeting place. That tidbit would please Sellars.

"You go to Saint Aledaide, too?" Zach asked, purposefully mispronouncing the name.

"Common drunks," Murphy repeated with the same tone of disdain he'd use for roaches.

Zach placed a finger to his lips. "Shhh—don't tell Fitzy." He leaned into Murphy's personal space. "I don't think he'd like it. I don't think he likes *me*."

"Can't imagine why." He turned to the other man. "Let's go." Murphy led the way to his black Audi.

Zach feigned sleep once he was in Murphy's backseat, in case they had anything to discuss. The short drive didn't afford him much time for eavesdropping. At the church, Murphy slapped Zach's leg. "We're here."

Zach pretended to startle awake and get his bearings. "Thanks for the ride." He opened his door and slid out. As he stood, something moving across the parking lot caught his eye. Careful to stay in drunken character for the mobsters' benefit, he slowly pivoted his entire body to see.

Molly. What was she still doing here? He groaned.

"You okay?" Murphy called from inside the car.

Would he have to play drunk for Molly, too? "We'll see."

Murphy grunted and climbed out of the car. "Let's get you inside." He walked around to take Zach's arm and start him toward the parish house—and Molly.

"Father?" she said.

No choice now. With Murphy here, he'd have to keep the act up for her, too. "Molly!"

She took another step toward him, caution in her eyes. "Doyle." She lifted her chin, her expression cryptic. Murphy nodded his greeting.

Molly was here well after hours, and the look she was giving Murphy meant something to him. She was involved.

Zach ignored the twinge at his gut and took the opportunity to lurch toward her. It hadn't been that long; he must still reek of

34

Flynn's piney drink. He expected her to back up at his approach, but she merely folded her arms. "Well, if someone isn't rather sloshed."

"Who? Murph? Doubt it." He sighed and took hold of her shoulders. "Oh, Molly . . . Molly, Molly, Molly."

"Hadn't you better be off to bed?" But she didn't try to shrug him off.

He released her shoulders and grabbed her hand. This was his chance: take advantage of the moment and ingratiate himself. For the case's sake. Zach met her gaze. Locked on his, her eyes held a mix of horror and hope.

He said exactly what he was thinking. "You are so beautiful, Molly." He waited for the inward wince that accompanied most of his lies. None came.

But not exactly the best pick up line for the mob.

Or a priest. Molly frowned and pulled her hand free.

"I almost wish—" He interrupted himself with a stagger.

Murphy stepped forward to catch him. "That's definitely enough." He towed Zach toward the parish house.

"No, I don't think—good night, Molly Malone!" He laughed. How had it taken him this long to realize she had the same name as the fishmonger protagonist of the Irish anthem?

She said nothing, but watched him go. Just one thing to do in this situation—burst into song. "Crying cockles and mussels, alive, alive oh!" Zach glanced over his shoulder one last time. Molly did not turn away.

He could only hope the trust he'd been working to build with her wasn't destroyed.

Zach was in bed by the time Father Fitzgerald got in that night.

At least he didn't have to worry about acting hungover for Fitzgerald.

He did have to worry about the morning's Mass, however. He'd helped to give Mass five days that week, but Sunday services brought the largest audience.

Zach smoothed the vestments laid out on the sacristy's low dressing table: the ankle-length white alb to cover his cassock like a sheet; the narrow green stole to hang from his neck; the green, poncho-like chasuble to go over them both. He was supposed to pray before donning them. God probably wouldn't bless him for this, whether he prayed or not.

Zach fingered the edge of the linen alb. He wanted to do this right, and not just for his cover—but to prove to himself that he wasn't mocking another church. It still felt wrong, but if the archbishop of Chicago—and the U.S. government—said it was all right, who was he to disagree?

With another sigh, Zach got down on his knees. He'd pray before dressing all right, but it wouldn't be the traditional vesting prayer.

Once he was ready, Zach took his place behind Father Fitzgerald, the deacon and the altar servers in the vestibule. In white robes, the altar girls carried candles, and the altar boy carried a gold crucifix on a pole. They had the hard part today—running around, getting the bowls and cups, carrying things. Today, Zach only had to look reverent until the Eucharist.

They started in: cross, candles, deacon bearing an ornate Bible, Zach, and Fitzgerald. Pressing his hands together and hooking his right thumb over his left was automatic after a month of practice—but that was about all he was comfortable with. And this was his first chance to really mess things up, to blow his cover.

His pulse accelerated until it was galloping at twice the pace of the procession's measured steps.

At the altar, he bowed. Or was he supposed to drop to one knee? No, bow and kiss the altar. When was he supposed to pray silently? He could hardly pray harder than he was already. Violent criminals didn't attend Mass, but here he was, faking this and deceiving a couple hundred God-fearing parishioners.

As Fitzgerald launched into a heavy-handed sermon on God's

judgment, Zach couldn't think of anything but his next duties—and the hum of nerves in his gut. He got away with mumbling the creed after the homily, but once Fitzgerald had prepared the Eucharist, it was time for Zach's toughest role.

The congregation rose, and he took his place with Fitzgerald. As the priest said the prayer, Zach had to recite his part quietly and gesture: stretching his hands toward the bread and wine at one point, his right hand only at another; bowing; raising both hands. Then there were the ones he did by himself—bowing, crossing himself and hitting his chest at certain times.

Finally, the Eucharist was ready and blessed. Zach dropped to one knee, accepted his wafer and returned to his place to wait. Fitzgerald showed the Host to the congregation. "This is the Lamb of God," he said, "who takes away the sins of the world. Happy are those who are called to His supper."

Zach replied with the congregation, asking Christ to heal them. Fitzgerald was supposed to say something softly there, too—something about Christ bringing him to everlasting life. But he ate the wafer in silence as he had every day.

Maybe Zach didn't have to worry so much about being perfect. All he had to do now was pretend to drink the wine and remember to bow to the altar on the way out, and he was set.

One week gone—and one job he'd rather not get good at.

After Mass, Molly followed the recessional and the rest of the parishioners out of the chapel, but she didn't make it past the votives. She wasn't the only one still lighting a candle for Father Patrick—but she might be the only one praying for Father O'Rourke.

He was already crawling pubs with Doyle Murphy and Gerald

Flynn. A week in the parish and the mobsters were closing in on him. What could she do? She pondered the votives a long time before depositing her quarters and lighting her candles.

"Molly?" Father O'Rourke's tentative voice ventured, as if tapping her shoulder would be too presumptuous.

She found a visibly chagrined priest behind her. "Mornin', Father."

"Did I see you here last night?"

"You did."

"What brought you by?"

She held up her bulletin. "Printer error." If they hadn't made a hames of the order, she would've missed him and Doyle Murphy—and never known how close he was getting to that outfit. Molly tried to wet her suddenly dry mouth and focused on his vestments.

Father O'Rourke leaned to the side until his face reached her eye level. Once he captured her gaze, he straightened again. "I didn't . . . do anything, did I? Or say anything?"

"Father, I'm Irish. I've been accosted by drunks more drunk and less polite than you were. But you might want to be a bit more careful with the gin."

The tips of his ears tinged with pink. He gestured to the votive rack. "Not lighting a candle for my eternal soul, then?"

Molly shook her head and lowered her gaze. "Father Patrick."

"I'm so sorry. I know it was sudden."

She could only nod.

"Could you tell me what happened? No one else will, not even Father Fitzgerald."

Molly caught herself rubbing her elbow and forced herself to stop and nod again.

"Shall we walk?"

"All right." Working up the courage to revisit that day, she followed him past the blazing red maples and around to the arcaded hallway outside the office.

The hallway she hadn't dared to traverse since the day they'd found Father Patrick here. Dead.

The Gardaí had trained her to handle things like this. She'd even worked a murder once. But nothing could have prepared her for a victim this close to her.

"Here," she murmured when they reached the spot a few meters from the office door.

Father O'Rourke stared at the cobbles as though the limestone would yield an answer. Molly glanced out at the car park. It'd been a beautiful late summer day just like today.

"It was a Saturday, and I must've forgotten to lock up the night before." Molly walked to the door and tested the knob. "I was comin' for confession." Emotion—guilt—strangled off her voice, and she covered her mouth. If only she'd locked the door that Friday night.

Father O'Rourke placed a hand on her shoulder. "If this is too hard—"

Molly folded her arms against her middle to allay the anxiety twisting into a coil of nerves there. She could tell this story. She relived it every day, didn't she? "He was here in the hallway."

Molly swallowed past the lump in her throat. She had to admit it; she had to tell the truth. "Someone tried to rob the office. Father Patrick must've tried to stop it, and the burglar—his sash." She finished the story with a gesture at her throat before turning away to rein in the emotion.

Within seconds, his hand was on her shoulder again. She faced him, and he pulled her close. She leaned against his shoulder and let unbidden tears slip down her cheeks. The church bells pealed in the silence, clanging as cheerily as if Father Patrick were ringing them himself.

Molly tried to calm herself with deep breaths thick with the woodsy scent of Father O'Rourke's aftershave. She shouldn't still be this upset. This wasn't her first violent crime, and she'd mourned Father Patrick with the rest of them, at the vigil, at his funeral.

No, she hadn't. Not really. Because letting herself feel this pain—admitting he was gone—meant accepting that his murder was her fault. An invisible clamp tightened on her heart. She was trained to protect others. And if the Chicago PD had been more willing to hire foreign nationals, she'd be doing that now. Instead, she ended up here, causing her priest's murder. If she'd only locked the office, the burglar—the murderer—wouldn't have been here when Father Patrick came.

"Molly," Father O'Rourke soothed.

She lifted her chin to see him, centimeters from her face. Her stomach dipped, and the vise around her heart squeezed tighter.

"It'll be okay," he continued in the same tone. "One day."

He didn't know the truth. She scrubbed at her tears and pulled away. "It's my own fault."

"How can you think that?"

"The door—if I had only locked the door, the burglar would've moved on to an easier target instead of bein' there when Father Patrick—" Molly broke off and turned away, but Father O'Rourke caught her shoulders again, leaning down to peer into her eyes.

"This was not your fault." The conviction in his voice took her aback. "You didn't make this happen."

She looked down, and more tears spilled over. "The door."

"Locking the door wouldn't have saved Father Patrick."

How could Father O'Rourke understand? Molly wiped her cheeks. He offered her a handkerchief.

"Thank you." Molly tried to clean the mascara from under her eyes, though she hated to stain his handkerchief. But she'd just been crying on his shoulder. She checked; black smudges marred his green vestment. "Sorry about your . . ." She waved a hand at the stains.

He hooked a finger in his collar to examine the splotches. "Won't be the last time." Father O'Rourke offered a small smile of forgiveness. "Now, have you heard if the police have any leads?"

"Not that they've told us." She knew the odds of finding a suspect now, so long after the fact: almost nil. Unless someone confessed, Father Patrick's murder would remain unsolved.

Father O'Rourke glanced behind her and did a double take. She followed his gaze. Father Fitzgerald stood beneath the red maple, waiting for them, arms across his chest.

Father O'Rourke took one step toward the other priest, but turned back to her. "Molly, this wasn't your fault. I'll do . . . any-thing—almost anything—to prove it to you."

Molly fingered the corner of his cotton handkerchief. "I don't think that's possible."

"Let me try."

"All right." She rubbed the handkerchief hem as Father O'Rourke left her.

He'd held her. Practically commanded her not to blame herself. And she hadn't had a priest hug her since primary school. Molly folded the handkerchief pensively. Last night he'd told her she was beautiful, and he almost wished—what?

But how much credence could she give the ramblings of a drunk?

She looked the direction he'd gone again. He hadn't seemed the slightest bit hungover.

5

FATHER FITZGERALD MARCHED through the chapel, shaking his head. Zach trailed behind, but his mind buzzed with the memory of Molly in his arms and her sweet floral scent clinging to his vestments. Molly smelled like home—like the flowering vine that had half the oaks in his parents' backyard in a chokehold.

Zach tried to shake off the memory. Head in the game.

"Tim, you've got to watch yourself with Molly."

Fitzgerald was more right than he knew. Flirting might help Zach get ahead in the investigation, but something about it felt . . . wrong. Besides, he couldn't rule Molly out as a suspect yet, even if she did fall apart over Father Patrick.

"You know she's struggling already," Fitzgerald continued his lecture.

"She was crying. Would you have left her there?"

Fitzgerald turned back to him midway down the aisle. "I saw you approach her."

Zach fought the urge to roll his eyes. This I'm-the-pastor-and-I-know-what's-best-for-you act was getting old. But at least it proved Fitzgerald was really buying his cover. "Do you have any idea how upset she is about Father Patrick?"

Fitzgerald deflated almost instantly. "Aren't we all?" He sighed. "Listen, it's natural to care about Molly because you work with her."

Zach nodded.

"Just . . . be careful." He searched Zach's face another moment, and Zach hoped his mask of penitence was convincing enough. Fitzgerald came closer. "Listen, I've seen this happen before, and—it would destroy you both. You've given your word to God."

"I know."

Fitzgerald cupped his hands together and stepped toward him again. "'When a man takes an oath, he's holding his own self in his hands. Like water. And if he opens his fingers, then—'" He held up empty hands. "'He shouldn't hope to find himself again.' Saint Thomas More."

"I'm not going to do that, Bruce."

"Good." He started down the aisle again, but quickly turned back. "I do think you can do this. And I think you're ready to start working with the school."

Zach channeled real enthusiasm into his smile. "Absolutely." Better than waiting on the mobsters to come knocking. Working directly with their children might be more successful than flirting with Molly, too.

Unless, of course, she was a mobster. The guilt she obviously felt over Patrick's murder might not have anything to do with locking a door, and either way, she could be involved in the money laundering. If she was, that also made her the most promising asset he'd found, unless Doyle Murphy came around soon.

Zach glanced at the crucifix high on the back wall of the chapel. Would it be too much to pray for Murphy to take an interest in the new priest?

Tuesday afternoon, Kathleen's first day back from vacation, Zach watched for her to leave for the school. Once she was gone, Zach poked his head in the open office door. He had to make sure Molly'd gotten the keylogger. And with Kathleen out, it was a good time to test Molly again. Maybe ask about her rent deal with Murphy. At her desk, she squinted at her computer, chin in hand.

"Hey, Molly. Did you get my e-mail?"

"I did, but I've never heard of those films."

Then the computer tracker was installed. Sellars would be happy. Molly turned her scrutiny on Zach. "What exactly have you been doin' all day?"

"You know, ministering?" Zach gave an innocent shrug.

She pinned him with a smirk that said she wasn't amused—but her eyes said she was. "Are you free for dinner?"

He raised both eyebrows. Was he coming on that strong?

"Father Fitzgerald promised some parishioners dinners this week," Molly rushed to add. "But he's overbooked."

"I'll do it." Zach rounded her desk to scan the calendar on her monitor. Only the name Lonegan was familiar—the parishioner at confession. "How about the Hugheses and the Lonegans? I've already met Cally."

She pressed her lips into a line. "I think the Lonegans wanted Father Fitzgerald."

He was taking that dinner whether she wanted him to or not. "I'm sure they all want Father Fitzgerald. Let's go get a sword."

"You're positively Solomon in all his glory."

"I know, right?" He grinned. "Oh, Father Fitzgerald wants me at the school, too." In the schedule, Molly assigned him to counsel students in the afternoons. And now it was time to test her. He leaned against the desk. "Found any deals on old film rentals?" he asked.

"I know where to look."

"But can we afford it? I mean, I could front the money."

She folded her arms, and a hint of annoyance crept into her voice. "Father, I've told you. We're all right on the budget. Can't you trust me? I'm the one that handles the books, after all."

That was exactly why he couldn't trust her. "Do the books take up most of your time?"

"And makin' sure your life doesn't fall apart."

"No wonder it's a full-time job." He let the topic drop for now—obviously she didn't appreciate his "fiduciary interest." Then again, she wasn't the only one in the office. Maybe her coworker did something else related to the mobsters. "And what does Kathleen do all day?"

"Um, get the mail, handle prayer requests, coordinate with the school and . . . gossip?" She laughed, but refocused on her computer, like thinking of her slacking coworker inspired her to work harder.

He was losing her. Zach shifted, subtly positioning himself between her and her monitor on the corner of her desk. "I read that book. *Catch Me in Zanzibar,* from the donations last week?"

"And what did you think?" A slight tremor shook her voice, a flash of fear or uncertainty.

"Katya should've killed Frank when she had the chance."

"Oh, that'd ruin it." Molly shook her head.

"Come on. He deserved it."

"Sure, he lied, but she loved him."

For a split second, Zach felt his calculated cocky expression slip. She had no idea what she was saying.

"Hey, Father Tim!"

Molly and Zach both jumped at the call from the open doorway. Two of the basketball players—DeWayne and that blond tutor guy, Paul—leaned in.

The teenager patted the ball under his arm. "Grab a notebook, padre. You're about to get schooled. Quit chatting up your girlfriend and let's hit the court."

"DeWayne," Paul chided. "Father Tim is a man of God."

"Whatever, man." DeWayne scoffed. "Even that won't help your weak—" He stopped short, obviously censoring himself as he eyed Zach's collar. "—moves."

As soon as Zach stood, DeWayne shot a quick pass to catch him off-guard. Zach caught the ball and glanced at Molly. "May I be excused?"

"I can see you have a very important meetin'."

Heading out, he passed the ball back to DeWayne. Zach turned back in the doorway. "I said I'd counsel the students, didn't I?"

From her desk, Molly gave him one last wry smile. "Go have fun, Father Tim."

Was it his imagination, or was there a certain spark in her eyes when she called him by his "first name"?

And did he care?

Maybe Kathleen would be a better route to Murphy. Or at least safer. For everyone.

Molly was still staring out the door after Father Tim when Kathleen returned. "How was your meetin'?" Molly asked, grateful for the distraction.

"Fine." She settled into her chair. "Father Fitzgerald's going to need eight hands to juggle all the counseling appointments, though. The teachers can't handle it anymore."

"Father Tim will be helpin' him." But if Molly had to hide every telephone book and parish directory, she wouldn't let Father Tim eat at the Lonegans' tomorrow.

"It's 'Tim' now?"

"Ah, it's what the students call him."

Kathleen gave her a look of *is that your best excuse?* Molly buried the urge to groan. She'd called plenty of priests Father Joe or Father Seán or Father Ted. When it came to anything that might be misconstrued into gossip, Kathleen was always on the prowl.

Molly turned to focus on the present task—the Lonegans. Wouldn't be too difficult to switch off the parish house Internet for a day or two. The spare paper directories were on top of the filing cabinet. She could hide those easily—but Father Fitzgerald must have a copy or two in the parish house. Could she claim she needed it to make more copies?

No, if she were going to lie to a priest, she'd just tell Father Tim the Lonegans cancelled.

She allowed a smile to steal across her face, lifted the receiver and dialed the parish house.

After basketball finished up, Zach headed for the parish house—and found Kathleen waiting on his front porch. He'd hoped to wait until he'd had a shower, but this was his chance to recruit a willing asset. "Hey, Kathleen."

"Father, I wanted to talk to you for a minute about an issue with . . . the office. Staff."

Zach sighed inwardly. Great. He'd have to settle some silly argument between Kathleen and Molly first. He showed her into the parish house, tugging on his shirt to fan himself. "What's up?"

"Molly is a good person, you know. We're friends, of course—we're very close."

Would Molly have agreed? "Is something the matter with her?"

"That's not what I mean. I just know her really well."

Maybe Kathleen was here to tell him about Molly's involvement in the mob. The anticipation of a case-breaker mingled with the residual adrenaline in his veins. He clamped down on the rising excitement. "What's up with Molly?"

Kathleen pushed past him to sit on the couch. "It's not exactly her. I mean, not just her."

Sellars would love this story. "Maybe it would be easier if we stopped dancing around this. What's going on with Molly and . . . ?"

"You."

Zach jerked back. "Me?"

"Well, Molly's a pretty young girl, and you're fairly good-looking, for a priest—"

"Thanks a lot."

Kathleen stood. The smoker's wrinkles around her lips drew

together—no, not smoker's wrinkles. Judgment wrinkles. "You know what I mean."

"Not really."

She shifted her weight onto one hip and crossed her arms. "You two just need to be careful."

Zach nodded slowly. Why did everyone assume he couldn't keep a vow with a beautiful woman around? Father Fitzgerald was one thing, but Kathleen hadn't caught him comforting her, or flirting with her. So much for Molly helping with the case.

He opened the front door. "Thanks for your concern, Kathleen, but I really think you might be reading too much into things."

She raised her eyebrow, nailing him with a patented mother-knows-better-than-you look.

Zach did his best to match her arch glare. "Did I cross a line?"

"I'm not saying you've done anything; I'm only trying to make sure you see you *could*, and avoid it, you know. Nobody's perfect."

He should've known she'd somehow backtrack and twist things around to make him the villain. "I see your point. I won't pretend like Molly's not pretty, but give us some credit. It's not like we're making out in the choir loft after work."

She set her jaw. "Is that supposed to be funny?"

"It's a little funny—but I take my vows seriously. I won't do anything I shouldn't." Zach gestured to the open door.

"Hm." Kathleen marched past him. "Pride goes before a fall," she tossed over her shoulder. Her light tone belied the threat lurking there. She probably thought it was her duty to make sure the "fall" part was very, very public.

Ten bucks said if he checked the choir loft at five, he'd find Kathleen waiting to pounce on their illicit rendezvous. He rolled his eyes at Kathleen's retreating figure—and then he noticed the maroon sedan across the street.

Time to get that license plate to Sellars. Maybe this guy could be his in. Zach grabbed a pen from by the kitchen phone, but stopped short when he saw the answering machine light blinking. He hit PLAY.

"Father Tim," Molly said on the message. "I just spoke to the

Lonegans and, em, they said tomorrow night doesn't work for them anymore. So scratch that off your schedule."

Zach deleted the message and headed out. But Molly's tone of couldn't-quite-put-his-finger-on-it evasiveness suddenly worried him more than the maroon sedan.

Molly had gone too far, and she knew it. At work the next day, she flinched at every knock, afraid it might be Father Tim come to call her bluff—or worse, one of those criminals. Could they possibly know what she'd done?

Of course not. They couldn't have bugged the parish house answering machine. Right?

Despite her own reassurances, Molly's nerves were near their breaking point by the end of the day. She was almost done balancing the books when the door swung open—and the lights went dark.

She clamped a hand over her mouth, but a single gasp slipped through her fingers.

The lights flickered on again. "Molly?" Father Tim stepped in, brushing raindrops from his hair. "I thought you'd left."

She steadied herself. "Still tryin' to finish up."

"Cooking the books?" he teased.

"What better cover than a church?"

Her joke tempered his grin a touch.

"Father, I'd never do such a thing." Molly tried to dispel the rest of her tension with a laugh, but it came out as shaky as her knees felt. "And I wouldn't still be here if I did, would I?"

Suddenly his smile left altogether. "No," he murmured. "You wouldn't be."

She let the somber silence stretch out. Had he believed her

message? "I'm sorry about the Lonegans."

"Yeah, me too." He chewed his lower lip. "Don't stay too late," he bid her on his way out.

Molly drew in the first deep breath she'd taken all day. She'd saved him—for one day.

As if on cue, the phone rang. Molly glanced at the caller ID— Doyle Murphy. Calling after hours. The walls seemed to jump a meter inward.

Did he know she was still there, or that Father Tim had been by?

She ironed all trace of fear and anxiety from her voice. "Parish office?" she answered.

"This is Doyle Murphy. I want an appointment with Father O'Rourke."

"Oh, Doyle, he's runnin' himself ragged just tryin' to meet everyone." She realized she was rubbing her fingertips on her desk and balled her hand into a fist.

"Great, then put me at the top of the list."

She managed two disjointed bursts of laughter. "He's booked out for the fortnight at least."

He scoffed. "There's not a single opening in the next week?"

There were no windows behind her, but she could almost feel Doyle's gaze on her. Molly tried to inhale, but the office's suddenly stale air wouldn't cooperate. "Two weeks. I'm sorry."

"We'll see about that." Doyle hung up.

Fantastic. She'd spared Father Tim from one dinner, but the mob was already poised to pounce.

S TILL WRAPPING HIS UMBRELLA, Zach stepped off the elevator at
the Lonegans' floor—and almost ran into Gerald Flynn, his
"drinking buddy." The oddly solemn mobster nodded to him.
"How's it going, Gerald?"

"Not so good." He brushed a hand over his red hair.

"Sorry to hear that. Anything I can help with?"

Flynn contemplated the elevator doors. "Doubt it." He rubbed his
tongue on his canine tooth. "But if you've got a minute—"

"Where do you think you're going?" a woman's voice shrilled
from the other end of the hall.

Flynn and Zach both looked that direction. A teenager sporting a
shaggy mane turned back to a woman with wavy red hair. "Ian's," the
boy said. "Math homework."

"Ladies and gentlemen, my nephew Brandon." Flynn made an
exaggerated *ta-dah* gesture for Zach. "Pride of the family, future of
the empire and teenager extraordinaire."

Brandon's mother thrust her hands onto her hips. "You think I
don't know Ian's failing math? You think I don't talk to Claire
Murphy?"

Brandon snorted.

"Get back here," the woman continued. "Father Tim will be here
any minute."

Flynn glanced back at Zach. "Guess Lisa and Cally probably need
you more."

"We'll talk later." Zach started for the mother and son. Down the
hall, the teenager turned away from his mom.

"Don't you need your backpack to do homework?" Lisa called

after him.

"Thought you said he was failing," Brandon snapped back.

Lisa shook her head. "He'll end up just like Cally," she muttered.

Apparently Zach should've angled for an invitation here sooner. He'd spent the last two evenings at Brennan's, but it wasn't like he could ask the bar's regulars about the mobsters. Plus, seeming like a drunk wouldn't get him in with Murphy—though it earned him another lecture from Fitzgerald.

Of course, actually getting this dinner appointment had been harder than necessary with Molly's "help." The evasiveness in her message had finally gotten to him, and Zach had to double-check. Lisa knew nothing about the appointment being cancelled.

Still shaking her head, Lisa stalked back into her apartment without noticing Zach right behind her. He stopped at the doorway, but her voice carried. "Couldn't you hear, Cal?"

"What do you expect me to do about it?" Lonegan stepped into view, glaring at Lisa. He noticed Zach in the doorway and turned away, scratching the back of his neck.

Well, this would be an enjoyable dinner. Maybe he could even teach them about Family Home Evening; they'd already mastered the part where everyone stomped off to pout.

Lisa returned to the kitchen, her flushed cheeks growing pinker at the sight of him. "Father Tim—I'm Lisa. Come in. We're ready to eat."

Just like at confession, Lonegan avoided Zach's eyes as he and the two younger boys filed through the kitchen. "Hi, Cally," Zach tried.

Lonegan barely nodded and pushed past him. He focused on the loud floral pattern on the vinyl tablecloth when Zach joined them at the kitchen table. Zach spoke to Lisa to dispel the tension. "Thanks for having me."

"Sure. We're so glad you called." Lisa swiped at the tablecloth with a rag.

"Me, too. Sorry about the mix up at the office." He pushed away the nagging worry about Molly's message. She was involved. Time to get over it.

"We're glad to get to meet you." Lisa offered a smile, forced but conciliatory.

"Oh, Cally and I have already met," Zach said. Though that might be a bit of a stretch.

"Cally, did you actually go to church?" She shot a look of mock-surprise at Lonegan. He rolled his eyes and served himself some lasagna.

Maybe Lonegan would be more apt to open up without Flynn around. "I've heard some great stories so far," Zach said. "Looking forward to more."

"Thanks. You follow the Bulls?"

"Sure." Zach tried to steer the conversation back to something material. "You know, Gerry was telling me about the city accountant and a spill. Sounded hilarious."

Lonegan's expression was dead serious, and he waved the topic away. "We don't talk business at home."

Zach nodded. So much for building on this relationship for quick inroads tonight. Maybe he'd have better luck with Flynn.

Molly hurried to lock up after work. Pausing in a portal of the arcaded hall, she scanned the car park for Father Tim—nowhere in sight. Not leaving for dinner at the Lonegans'. Of course he wasn't. He couldn't know she'd lied about them canceling. But every muscle in her shoulders was still as taut as a steel cable. She started for her car, dodging the car park's puddles.

If she went home to her empty condo, she'd relive that phone call from Doyle Murphy all evening, worrying herself past the point of usefulness. But was there anything she could do for Father O'Rourke now? Should she just tell him the truth so he'd know to steer clear of those families?

Molly braced herself and marched to the parish house. Her first knock was all but tentative. After waiting an eternity it seemed, Molly tried again. She watched the lace curtains in the window—no light, no movement. And no one answered the door. She slowly started back across the wet car park. Had he gone to dinner, so?

"Get out of my face!" The shout and loud splash to her left brought Molly up short. Doyle's son, Ian, stood in front of the school's brand new math teacher, Lucy. A few papers fluttered to join the stack already in a puddle between them. Ian pivoted on his heel and marched off.

Lucy dropped to her knees, muttering.

"Appears you've had a long first week," Molly said, coming to kneel next to her. "Let me help."

"Thanks." Lucy sighed as if this were the final act of the tragedy of her life and shifted her canvas bag to her other shoulder.

The brochures were smudged and ruined. "I hope these weren't too important," Molly said.

"Apparently not." Lucy frowned after Ian.

Molly shook off the last paper. "It could be worse. At least it's stopped raining. The entire car park usually floods ankle deep whenever I wear my favorite shoes." They both stood.

Lucy examined the spots of wet grime on the knees of her khaki slacks. "Story of my life. I've spent most of our class time getting my students excited for college, but a bunch of them—" She gestured after Ian. "—are *not* interested. And their parents are acting even worse."

Tension slowly strung Molly's shoulders taut again. What had Doyle Murphy done?

"I don't understand why they're even paying for private school." Lucy shook her head.

"They're not," Molly said, shifting her weight. "Their grandparents founded the school trust, and it provides legacy scholarships." And paid for the school, the teachers, and then some. Yet another example of Kathleen's "heroes."

"Figures. Free rides." Lucy shuffled the soaked brochures. "What about Tommy Mulligan? I might actually be getting through to him. Don't tell me he's a legacy scholarship."

Molly winced. "He is, sorry." The school only had a few hundred students, many of them parishioners—or, this case, former parishioners.

Lucy paused in rummaging through her canvas bag. "Doesn't he attend your church?"

For once, Kathleen's gossip was useful. "He did until his father died."

Lucy gave up her search. "Oh. His home life didn't sound so good—I had to counsel him once this week. Grief counseling, I guess."

They both paused solemnly at the allusion to the late priest.

Lucy hugged the soaked papers to her pale pink blouse. "How did his dad die?"

Molly couldn't proclaim organized crime in the parish killed Jim Mulligan. All she had to substantiate that was conjecture. And according to the *Tribune*, all the police had was Mulligan's severed hand.

"I heard it was work-related." Molly swallowed hard. Somehow, this was no less stressful than worrying about Father Tim and Doyle Murphy.

Lucy glanced down and did a double take. She groaned and pulled the wet brochures away from her blouse, now wet and dirty, too. "What did his dad do? Wholesale too?"

"I think so." Was no one safe from these people? "I don't really know, you know yourself. It was before I started here."

"A lot of my students' dads seem to work in wholesale. Does that have something to do with the church?"

"No." The answer came out faster and harsher than she'd intended. Molly loosened her grip on her handbag and added a tight laugh. Organized crime intertwined with the church was certainly not typical. No, not intertwined—even Doyle wouldn't dare. . . . Would he?

"I'm sorry. It sounds like I think Catholics are freaks or something. I really don't."

Molly waved away her concern. "Every church has its nutters. I have to work with ours."

"Kathleen?" Lucy glanced heavenward before digging in her

canvas tote again.

"Ah, I'm only coddin'. She's not that bad."

"Yeah, well, she hates me."

Molly pushed aside her apprehensions now that they were off the subject of Murphy's crew. They weren't after Lucy. Yet. "She probably just came off badly. What did she do?"

"I called for an appointment with the new priest, and she acted like I was propositioning him or something." Lucy pulled a plastic grocery sack from her tote. "Is he really that good-looking?"

Typical Kathleen. Why did everyone assume someone was after a handsome young priest?

But someone *was* after him.

Molly realized she was clenching her jaw. She willed every muscle from her shoulders up to relax. "Kathleen thinks she knows what's best for everyone else."

"Guess you don't have to worry about someone corrupting him with that bulldog!"

"She's always eager to 'help.'" Molly let the sarcasm ring in her tone. Kathleen wasn't the one doing all the work to keep Father Tim safe.

"I bet." Lucy changed the subject. "I have to say, I love your accent. Irish, right?"

"I am, thank you. Good ear—I get complimented on my 'Scottish' a lot. And sometimes my 'Scotch.'"

Lucy smiled and stuffed the wet brochures into the grocery sack. "My brother lived in Ireland a couple years. I bet he'd love to talk to you. You know, if I could ever get him on the phone."

"What brought him there?"

"He was a missionary. Loved it." Lucy started down the row of cars.

"Oh?" Molly fell in step with her. "Didn't see many missionaries in Ireland."

"Our church has missionaries all over the world—Europe, Africa, even here."

"You're not Catholic, so?"

"No, I belong to The Church of Jesus Christ of Latter-day Saints.

You know, Mormons?"

"Right, right." Molly recognized the name, but couldn't quite place it. "What kind of church is it?"

"Well, we're Christian. We believe in Jesus Christ, and that God still guides us through a living prophet—sort of like the Pope." Hope lit up in Lucy's eyes.

"Interestin'." Molly slowed as Lucy stopped. "Well, appears you're all set."

"Yeah." Lucy opened her trunk to stuff in the wet brochures and her tote. "I should go research the wholesale industry, so I can show the kids how they'll use algebra someday. I'd send a note home, but that didn't go over so well this week."

Molly couldn't imagine they appreciated Lucy's interest. But before she told Lucy the truth about the "wholesale industry," Molly realized dangerous criminals probably wouldn't dampen Lucy's zeal for her students. Would she research organized crime next? Math problems about hiring a hit man or extorting a juror?

Molly pasted on a smile. "Ah, don't bother yourself with all that. You'd do better to play Xbox or read up on the Sox."

Lucy grimaced, though Molly couldn't be sure whether it was at the prospect of video games or baseball. "I'm sure you're right. Hey, do you think you could—nah, I'm sure Father Tim is actually pretty busy." Lucy slammed her trunk shut and pressed on before Molly could offer her an appointment. "Thanks for helping with my college brochures."

"Any time. Good night!" Molly walked to her car and wished she'd ended the evening before they'd discussed Doyle Murphy's gang. Her stomach sank like a stone.

One more person she had to protect.

"Thanks so much for coming." Lisa Lonegan beamed at Zach, leading him to the door.

Zach forced himself to smile back. Although the tension from the beginning of the evening had dissipated, Lonegan had shot down a few more of Zach's attempts to talk business. He turned to Lonegan for one last try. "You heading to Brennan's?"

Lonegan raked his dark hair across his forehead. "Doubt it."

Before Zach could ply him further, Lisa opened the door. "We'll be sure to have you again soon."

"Yeah," Lonegan added quickly. "There's something—"

"Hey, Gerry," Lisa said. Zach looked to find Gerald Flynn in the hall. Flynn snapped his fingers and pointed at his sister as he passed.

"Thanks for having me." Zach waved goodbye, grabbed his umbrella and hurried after Flynn. He caught up to the mobster at his door. "I've got a minute now. What's up?"

Flynn wheeled around to scrutinize him, once again somber. "Just something I need to get off my chest. Before it's too late."

The back of Zach's neck tingled despite the sinking feeling that this was too good to be true, but he kept his expression unchanged. "You've come to the right place." As long as he didn't invoke the priest-penitent privilege by making this a confession, anyway.

The elevator at the end of the hall announced its arrival with a chime. Before the doors opened, Flynn leaned closer. "Can you meet Tuesday? Say, seven?"

Zach nodded, though his adrenaline level took a nose dive. At least he had a chance of closing the case way ahead of schedule.

"Great," Flynn said. "Your place." He ducked into his condo before the elevator doors slid apart, revealing Doyle Murphy. The underboss of the South Side barely grunted to acknowledge his new priest as he passed. Zach allowed himself a smug smirk once Murphy was out of sight. His days of freedom were numbered. Soon they'd roll up the whole crew, from Murphy down to Molly.

Zach punched the elevator button. There was still a possibility she wasn't involved, no matter how hard she'd tried to keep him from Lonegan. Right?

He'd have to test her one more time.

THURSDAY AFTERNOON, Molly knew without checking who darkened the office door. Frowning, Father Tim grabbed the chair by the extra desk and dragged it over to hers, though they both knew his basketball partners would track him down soon. "You know," he said, "I called the Lonegans to see if we could reschedule, and Lisa had no idea they'd cancelled last night."

Molly did her best to keep her hands steady over the keyboard. "Did she? Oh, now that I think of it, Cally was the one who wanted to reschedule."

"Hm. He must've changed his plans. Can't blame him—Lisa does make a great lasagna."

A lead weight landed on her heart. "Sounds like you had a lovely time."

"Yeah, I'm really surprised how nice people are here. Not like where I interned. Very cliquey."

She rubbed her elbow. He hadn't met everybody, but he'd met all the wrong people. "I'm sure we're no better than any other parish," she managed.

Father Tim gave half a smile, clearly not convinced. "I know every parish has its problems, and some are worse than others—but some are better."

He was already attached to the parish, and its mobsters. How could she tell him the truth and ruin his vision of paradise? She couldn't. "I suppose you're lucky—blessed—so."

"Hard to believe. Part of me is waiting for the other shoe to fall. Almost wish it would. It'd almost be a relief."

"Be careful what you wish for." Molly kept her eyes on her

monitor.

Before Father Tim could respond, Kathleen walked in, raising an eyebrow at Molly. Father Tim turned around. "Oh, hey, Kathleen."

"Hi, Father. Have I told you about my trip yet?" She reached her desk and held up her souvenir—a miniature baseball bat. "We visited the Louisville Slugger Museum."

"Nice."

Kathleen took her seat, a perfect perch behind her monitor to send Molly judging glares. Molly pointedly avoided her gaze. "Oh, Father, we have to reschedule the movie night. We hadn't announced it yet anyway."

"The twenty-fifth is Homecoming," Kathleen said.

"Let's see the calendar." Father Tim rounded Molly's desk as she brought up the program. "Apparently we're busy the next week, too. What does HW stand for?"

"Harris weddin'. I'll be away that weekend." She left out the detail that she was the entertainment, not a guest. She'd made it three years without telling anyone here her family performed traditional Irish music and dance, though her parents' parish still roped them into events twice a year. But with her sister moving in two months, their group would be cut in half, and all that would end.

Father Tim placed a hand on her chair, drawing her out of her moment of melancholy. He leaned over her and scrolled through the calendar. They settled on November eighth and divvied up responsibilities. She tried not to show how much she appreciated that ounce of respect. Father Fitzgerald either dumped assignments on her and ran, or micromanaged her every move.

Father Tim gestured around the office. "Anything I can do so you can work on that?"

Molly gave him the centimeter-thick stack of filing on her desk. He stepped to the cabinet behind her. "So, Molly," he began. "How'd you come to work at Saint Adelaide?"

"Job board at uni."

"College?" Kathleen corrected automatically, still focused on her work.

Father Tim shut the drawer with a pointed *clank*. He leaned toward Molly and whispered, "You were right the first time. What did you study?"

"International studies, master's." She glanced at Kathleen, who was unperturbed.

"Oh, I did international relations—minor," Father Tim added. "Undergrad."

"I suppose that's why neither of us have 'real jobs.'" That, and the "real job" she wanted most, the FBI, required US citizenship.

Kathleen stood. "Nothing wrong with our jobs," she huffed.

"Oh, no, you're right," Molly quickly agreed. "I love workin' here." Even if she was probably the last person who ever imagined she'd work at a church. By age six, she'd abandoned the schoolgirl dream of becoming a nun and never looked back. Compulsory catechism had a way of beating the faith out of you.

Kathleen handed her an envelope. "Donation for the trust."

"Thank you." Molly unlocked the bottom desk drawer, then the beige cash box inside. The spring-loaded lid leapt open, and the cash box flipped out of the drawer, slinging money and paperwork all over the floor. Sighing, Molly leaned down to clean up.

"What trust?" Father Tim knelt and collected the notes before she could smile her thanks.

"For the school, you know yourself." She held out her bank forms, and he looked up. She locked on his gaze, and in a flash of insight she saw their dangerous future. Together. Her breath and her brain seized up.

No. They couldn't—

Father Tim jerked back as if she'd slapped him. Had he felt it too?

"We keep all the donations in here?" He focused on shuffling the papers.

"Petty cash. I deposit donations twice a week." Molly barely kept her voice from wavering and her hands from shaking as she noted the mailed check in the ledger. Father Tim sorted the banknotes into the cash box. She gave him the donation, and his fingers brushed hers. At the slight contact, a tingle rolled up her arm.

Father Tim abruptly stood. Molly held her breath, hoping he couldn't see how she felt. This was anything but good.

He consulted the wall clock. "I'll let you sisters get back to work." He nodded goodbye.

Kathleen tsked. "I really think he thinks we're nuns."

Molly didn't say so, but she was pretty sure he didn't. What was she doing, fancying a priest—one she had to work with and keep safe, no less?

Basketball ran long Friday afternoon. Luckily, the public transit schedule aligned almost perfectly for a quick trip to Grant Park. ASAC Sellars was waiting by a hot dog vendor. "You're late. Red hot?" He gestured toward the cart and accepted the hard copy of the parish financials lifted from the filing cabinet.

Zach cringed at the vendor's neon green relish, but he couldn't look like he just came here to hand off papers. "Sure."

While Zach ordered and ate, Sellars thumbed through the manila folder. He hemmed over the ledgers and snapped the file closed. "Thought you said you had something." He started around the giant fountain.

"I said I might have something."

"Seems pretty clean, but I'll run it by accounting. That license plate you called in?" He handed over a slip of paper: the name of the owner of a certain maroon sedan, Kim Gallaher—wife of mobster Jay Gallaher. Typical, making sure no official documents were in his name.

Sellars lifted the folder. "Two weeks in and this is the best you got?"

Hey, getting anything in two weeks was practically a Hail Mary— and then there was his appointment with Gerald Flynn. "Someone in the parish has something on his conscience."

"I imagine lots of them do. You been handing out penances?"

Zach shook his head, focusing at the fountain in the center of the park.

"Don't let it come to a confession."

"I'll do my best to herd my guy in your direction."

Sellars's eyebrows jumped to meet his receding hairline. "You'll 'do your best'? We appreciate the help, but please don't let us distract from your priestly duties. I do still have my agent if you're not up to this job."

Since Sellars liked to tell him stuff any rookie already knew, Zach gave him some of his own medicine. "Listen, I could give this guy bus fare downtown and a good hard shove, but if he's not committed to coming clean yet, that'd just turn him back the other direction. And maybe blow my cover." Though the last point wasn't likely, a priest pushing a parishioner toward the FBI too hard might draw undue attention. Wouldn't be the first time that happened at St. Adelaide.

The tower of the fountain shot up a spray like a geyser, starting the hourly water show. Sellars stared hard at the nearest sculpture in the fountain, like it had directions. "Any idea how much this guy can give us? Any other prospects?"

Zach scrutinized the same bronze sea horse. No instructions there for him either. Flynn wasn't as connected as Lonegan, but that direction didn't seem too promising, even if Lonegan had suddenly wanted to talk right before Flynn showed up. Flynn, on the other hand, clammed up at the possibility that Murphy was on that elevator. "I'd say there's a good chance that it's not how much, but *who* he can give us."

"Turn CI? Or witness protection?"

Flynn was secretive without being skittish. But would he be willing to turn informant? Too soon to say. "I'll let you know once we talk."

"You haven't even talked to him yet?" Sellars massaged an imaginary headache. "We don't have time to lose." He squinted up at the skyline above the row of yellow-leafed maples. "He's no good to us if he gets killed."

Wouldn't be the first time something like that happened at St.

Adelaide, either.

Zach sat alone in a dark booth at Brennan's Monday night, nursing another tonic and lime. He wasn't due to meet with Flynn until tomorrow, his one hope in the case. But maybe Flynn—or Lonegan—would be willing to talk sooner than expected.

So far, neither of them had shown. Doyle Murphy and two of his henchmen, on the other hand, were ensconced in a corner booth on the other side of the bar. Murphy hadn't acknowledged him, though Zach was sure Murphy knew he was there. Zach was already on guard. Murphy hadn't become the number two man on the South Side by being careless.

Flynn stepped into the room and beelined for the bar. Zach fought the urge to pounce on the opportunity. Instead, he rolled his glass between his fingers and thumb and kept an eye on the corner booth and the bar.

Flynn didn't turn back to the booth to acknowledge his boss. He fixed his gaze on the bar's glossy wood, not looking up when the bartender slid a bottle in front of him. Relatively speaking, Murphy's booth was suddenly a frenzy of activity. The two other men on the bench slid out, and Zach could finally ID them: Miles Hennessy and Jay Gallaher. Murphy stood, too, and strolled to a side exit. His lackeys followed.

If Murphy couldn't stand to be in the same room as Flynn, the guy probably wouldn't be a useful informant for the FBI. Zach made a mental note to push witness protection when they talked.

Flynn reached in his gray suit jacket. Zach instinctively tensed, readying himself to draw his gun if the mobster pulled his—even if the guy was a potential source—but Flynn pulled out a cell phone.

Zach couldn't hear the conversation from across the bar, but whatever it was didn't look good. Flynn snapped his phone shut and shoved it back into his jacket. He sat hunched over the bar for another minute, then paid the bartender, grabbed his bottle and started for the door.

First Murphy, Hennessy and Gallaher leaving, now Flynn? Hardly seemed like a coincidence. Zach waited until Flynn reached the doors before he too settled up and hurried after him.

Zach hung back in the entryway shadows, staring out the glass doors. In the lot, a silhouette with a red hair halo—and holding a beer bottle—met with three other shadows. The redhead acknowledged each of the men around him, then bowed his head. The quartet started out of the lot.

Zach pulled a dark wool cap from his pocket and a gray trench coat from the rack by the door. The sleeves proved too short for him, but Zach was halfway across the parking lot before he realized it. Didn't matter, though—as long as it made him harder to recognize. On that note, he yanked the white plastic insert from his collar. In the daytime, he would've used sunglasses to feel more discreet, but at night they'd only draw attention and make it harder to follow.

The quartet passed under a streetlight, and Flynn took a swig from his bottle. Hennessy and Gallaher flanked him, and Murphy brought up the rear. A full escort. This couldn't be good.

Murphy stepped up and took Flynn's elbow in a firm grip. This really couldn't be good.

After three or four long blocks, the quartet cut across the street. Two of the men glanced back at Zach. Zach kept his head down and continued straight past them until the men turned down an alley between two apartment buildings. He jogged across the street in stealth mode, edging back to peer around the corner into the alley. In the light from the other end, he could only make out one figure in front of a dumpster—and with the way the man kicked at something on the ground, Zach doubted it was Flynn standing there.

His stomach clenched. He had to do something, but he couldn't go barging in. Even with his gun and the element of surprise, taking on three people who were probably also armed wasn't smart—and neither was blowing his cover. But he couldn't just let this happen.

Zach searched the ground for anything heavy and found half a brick. Odds said the police wouldn't be able to lift a useable print. He picked it up and half-ran back to the nearest darkened storefront. Right before he released the brick, he heard what sounded like two loud handclaps.

Suppressed gunshots.

The plate glass of the storefront shattered, instantly setting an alarm wailing. Pushing aside the sinking dread in his stomach, Zach grabbed his burner phone and called 911. He peeked around the corner again. Three men were standing now, arguing. Zach made a breathless report to the police dispatch—including the storefront and the gunshots—and looked for a hiding place in case Murphy and company came back this way.

When the dispatcher asked for his name, Zach hung up and detached his battery. He checked the alley—empty. The mobsters could be lying in wait, but he'd have to take that chance with some-one's life on the line. He jogged down the alley, trying to ignore a wisp of hope. Maybe he was okay. Maybe it wasn't Flynn.

As he reached the dumpster, Zach saw the shoes first. One of the victim's legs had fallen at an impossible angle—definitely broken. Zach crept closer and leaned around the corner of the dumpster. Flynn lay there gasping, red hair painted redder with blood, eyes wide open. Zach took his pulse. The thready beat grew fainter as he pressed his unsteady fingers to Flynn's neck, slipping a little in the slick blood smeared there.

Flynn caught hold of Zach's wrist, but didn't look at him. "Kristy," Flynn panted.

"I'll tell her."

Flynn's grasp grew slack and his eyes lost focus. Zach sank back against the dumpster and stared down the alley.

Had Flynn earned the mob's ultimate penalty because he wanted to talk to Zach? Or was it the other way around? Was it the story Flynn had begun to tell Zach that earned him the mob's death penalty?

Zach leaned back, his head connecting with the dumpster with a dull thud. This was why he was here—to make sure Murphy couldn't do this again. He had to maintain his cover. Even if it cost a life.

He couldn't have stopped it if he'd tried. Maybe. Probably.

But he still wished he'd tried.

Approaching sirens pulled him back to reality. Careful not to leave a trace, Zach slunk away.

Though Zach didn't know quite how he'd make it happen now, he'd stay in this parish until Murphy went down.

MOLLY HUNG UP THE PHONE again Tuesday afternoon. Two calls without success—finding Lucy for a last-minute opening with Father Tim was proving harder than wedging her into his schedule between counseling students, playing ball and visiting parishioners. Molly left a message for Father Tim to meet her at the school in five minutes, then hurried out to catch Lucy before she left.

Molly reached the car park and spotted Lucy on the far side of the lot with a tall blond man. He patted Lucy's shoulder. Wasn't he one of Father Tim's basketball players?

Before Molly could interrupt, the man guided Lucy to the driver's seat of a gold sedan. He got in the passenger's side, and they drove away.

So much for that plan.

"Molly?"

Her lungs flinched and her neck muscles tightened at the voice behind her. Doyle Murphy. She turned slowly.

"Got a minute?" He drew himself up as if to emphasize the few centimeters he had on her. A hard glint shone in his eye.

She squared those tense shoulders. "I don't really—"

"How do you like working here?"

"Grand. Were you lookin' for a job?"

He chuckled. "Not exactly."

"I am fairly busy, Doyle, so if you wouldn't mind."

"Yeah, let's get down to business. Got a proposition you'll want to hear, if you know what's good for you. For everyone."

Everyone?

A hand landed on her arm, and she nearly jumped. "Good to see you again, Doyle," came a second voice from behind her. She glanced back. Father Tim stepped closer to her—protectively close, it seemed. "Sorry to drag you away, Molly, but I need you to work on the kids' play money for the movie night."

Though she tried to breathe, her ribs wouldn't move. She couldn't leave him here with Doyle Murphy on the hunt. She backed her words with extra steel. "I'm nearly done here."

"I'll help him."

"Really, Father, I have this in hand."

"Moll." Despite the nickname, his voice carried an edge that could cut. His grip on her remained firm. He wasn't budging.

Well, neither would she. "I'll get to—"

"I want it by the end of the day."

Her rib cage remained as rigid as rock. She checked Doyle's reaction, a mocking smirk. She looked back to Father Tim. He met her gaze, and she matched the cold determination there—but the taut muscles of his jaw softened almost imperceptibly, and he nodded toward the office. A plea flashed behind his eyes.

Could he possibly know what he was doing?

Molly blinked. "You'll have to tell me what you want."

"I'll be there when we're done."

She hesitated only a split second before she backed away. Father Tim let go of her shoulder and turned to Doyle Murphy.

Her blood rushed in her ears when she reached her office, as if her pulse were finally starting again. Had she failed?

She had to tell Father Tim who Doyle really was. She turned back for the door, but the phone rang. "Hello?" Her greeting carried more than a note—a whole chord—of irritation.

"Is this St. Adelaide's?" a quavering female voice asked.

Molly made an effort to temper her tone. "It is. How can I help you?"

The caller gasped—or sobbed. "I don't really know how to do this. We need a funeral."

"I'm so sorry for your loss. Is this for one of our parishioners?" Molly sat at her desk and grabbed a notepad.

69

"Yes, this is Kristy Flynn."

She paused, reaching for a pen. "Oh, Mrs. Flynn. And who will the funeral be for?"

"It's Gerry. Last night—" Kristy broke off, dissolving into tears.

Molly's heart sank. Gerald Flynn was part of Doyle Murphy's crew—and that was most likely the cause of his death.

She glanced back at the door. Doyle had Father Tim right where he wanted him. If this was what happened to Doyle's friends, wouldn't Father Tim be safer not knowing?

Zach waited until Molly was at least halfway to the office before fully turning to Doyle Murphy. Clearly Molly wouldn't introduce him, and Zach would have to make his own way in the mob. These guys responded to power plays—and Molly resisting made it look better, even if his heart nearly stopped when she tried to stay. He didn't need to witness—or cause—two murders this week.

The mobster nodded in acknowledgment. "Nicely handled. Doyle Murphy."

"Father Tim. Can I help you with something?"

"We'll see. Getting used to the parish?"

"Just fine." Zach gritted his teeth. He did not interrupt Molly and Murphy's "business" meeting to make small talk. He hadn't waited two of his allotted weeks to chitchat.

"Let me know if there's anything we can do to help. We like to take care of our own, and they take care of us."

Sure they did. That was exactly why neighbors didn't rat out the mobsters. If they said nothing, the mobsters kept the neighborhood free of petty crime, but if they spoke up, they'd get two to the head—like Flynn.

But Zach wasn't supposed to know about that. He caught himself clenching his fists and forced himself to relax. He glanced at Murphy, then across the street. "You know, there might be something." He took Murphy by the shoulder and rotated him toward the maroon sedan once again parked there. "I haven't met a lot of the parishioners yet. Maybe you know this guy?"

"He bothering you? Want me to take care of him?"

"No, I just wish he'd gather the courage to come and face his problems head on."

Murphy cut his eyes at Zach. "Yeah."

Did he understand Zach's meaning? He had to double-check. "I know I'm new, and it takes time to build up trust. Maybe it'd be easier for him if Father Patrick was still here."

He scoffed. "The way he ended up speaks for itself." His cool tone made the casual remark seem like a threat. Or maybe it was how Zach had seen him kill a man last night. "If you're still getting to know the ropes," Murphy continued, "I'm sure Molly could help me—"

"I'll take care of anything you need. I do have to go check on her, though—you know how it is."

"Got to keep an eye on people every second, huh?"

Zach lifted his chin but held Murphy's gaze. "Some people."

Although he wanted to do all he could to pry into the mob's affairs now that he had Murphy here, Zach squelched the urge. If he appeared the slightest bit curious about Murphy's illegal activities, he'd be risking his case—and his life. Not like the mob took applications.

Looking good was the best he could hope for in this meeting. Zach took the opportunity to end the conversation with the upper hand and walked away. He hoped that was enough to make an impression on Murphy if looking drunk wasn't.

Molly was at her computer when he got to the office, but she was watching the door. The mask of determination she'd used with Murphy had cracked, and now Molly seemed drawn. "Good visit?" she murmured.

"Riveting," Zach bit off. He took a deep breath to release the tension in his chest.

71

"Father, there are some people in this parish you shouldn't get too close with." She met his eyes, somber; he stared back.

When he spoke, his voice was just above a whisper. "Like Murphy?"

Molly looked away.

"Why?"

Her gaze slowly fell, and she swallowed audibly. Zach felt himself tensing—was she about to admit something?

"I know them better than you do," she finally said. "Stay away. While you still can."

What was she saying—that it was too late for her?

Molly focused on her monitor. "I'm clearin' your schedule for Monday. We're havin' a funeral."

Flynn. Zach nodded and turned away, toward the printer/copier. The machine warmed up and spat out a sheet. A page of the kids' money.

"Found it on the Internet," Molly said. "Will that do?"

"Fine." Although he'd barely glanced at it, he put the page on the copier part of the printer and checked the paper tray. Empty. He hunted for more paper. A filing cabinet stood by the printer, in the opposite corner from the one behind Molly's desk. He tried the top drawer. Locked. "Is this where we keep the paper?"

"No, I think that's Father Fitzgerald's, or Father Patrick's." Molly directed him to the paper, but Zach spent the rest of his time in the office surreptitiously eyeing that filing cabinet.

If he couldn't make them pay for Flynn's death directly, he might still be able to make the case without him—or Molly.

By the end of work Wednesday, Molly still hadn't shaken the

melancholy from Kristy Flynn's phone call. She let Kathleen answer a
knock at the door. The setting sun cast the tall figure in the doorway
in shadow. Doyle, back again?

No, too thin. A somber young man with ash blond hair stepped
into the office—the one she'd seen with Lucy yesterday. "I'm here to
see Father T—er, Father O'Rourke?"

Molly checked the calendar. "Paul Calvin?"

Before he could respond, Father Tim walked in. "Hey, Paul. Shall
we?"

Paul nodded and followed him. Molly turned back to her computer, but couldn't focus on the bulletin. She rubbed the wood grain
of her desk.

This was all in her head. Doyle's visit was totally innocent.
Though Father Tim hadn't bothered to tell her anything about it
yesterday, and she hadn't dared to ask.

The door opened again and Molly tried to fight the dread closing
her throat. But this time Lucy walked in. "Hey, Molly, is Father Tim
around?" An uneasy smile twisted Lucy's lips, and she glanced at
Kathleen. "Still haven't been able to catch him."

"He just stepped into a meeting. Not sure how long he'll be."

"He didn't say anything about avoiding me, did he?" Lucy joked.
"I'm getting suspicious. Every time someone tells me where he is, he
disappears."

"Can't imagine it's intentional."

Lucy leaned against the door frame. "Guess I'll try again tomorrow." She puffed out a breath. "I so don't want to cook tonight. Any
recommendations? Something close, though—my GPS always gets me
lost."

"What were you wantin' to eat?"

The other woman shrugged. "I could really go for some Southern
food—but it has to be good."

Kathleen glanced up from her computer. "There's that place at
Navy Pier."

"What's Navy Pier?" Lucy looked to Kathleen, a hint of trepidation in Lucy's eyes. Had Kathleen been that mean to her?

"Oh, it's a tourist attraction." Kathleen gestured in a vaguely northeast direction. "Out by the lake. Restaurants, shopping and a pier."

Lucy hesitated. "Is it hard to get to? I'm not so good at navigating outside of my neighborhood yet."

"Sure now," Molly reassured her. "Do you know how to get to I-90?"

Lucy frowned.

"I-94?" Molly tried.

"No."

"I-57?"

Lucy's frown turned to almost a grimace. "I can really only find my apartment, the school, the seminary and the grocery store."

And yet she'd already come to the attention of the mobsters in the parish. Maybe this was Molly's chance to dig deeper into that situation. "How about I navigate for you?"

"Are you sure?"

"I am." Molly grabbed her handbag and bid Kathleen goodbye. Molly followed Lucy to her gold Mazda, and she couldn't help but comment on its dealer-pristine interior.

"In case any hot guys need a ride home," Lucy explained. "I mean—it's just seminarians that volunteer at the school. I mean, not that they're hot guys. Well, not that they're not—do you know what a bus costs? I wouldn't wish two dollar fares on my worst enemy." The fare didn't seem that high, but Lucy was vehement.

"I'm sure you haven't any enemies anyway."

Lucy sighed as if every imaginable stress crashed onto her shoulders. "I wish."

Had something happened with Murphy's outfit? Molly scanned the car park for his car as Lucy pulled to the exit. Or maybe the teenagers were tormenting her again. "I'm sure the students aren't that bad. Played some Xbox, didn't you?"

"Nah, but I shouldn't complain. I'm not the only one who has to deal with . . . 'workplace hostility.'" Lucy inclined her head toward the office.

"I do have a couple coworkers who seem to like me."

"Father Tim?"

Though she flinched mentally, Molly forced herself to smile. "I meant you."

"Oh." Lucy laughed. "Well, I hear he's nice, too. The students love him. I'm glad, after what happened with Father Patrick."

"Poor Father Patrick." Molly fingered the seat belt. Could she keep Father Tim from the same fate as Father Patrick and Gerald Flynn?

Zach took Paul, Our Seminarian of Perpetual Concern, the long way around the church building, listening to Paul's worries about his calling. Zach tried to keep his side of the conversation vague. When he'd given his life to the Lord, his calling had come on church letterhead, with a built-in end date. But Paul wasn't doubting holy orders; he just wasn't getting enough support from his parents.

They entered the building in silence, their footsteps echoing as they wandered to the front pew. "Anything else?" Zach asked.

Paul pointed out the adorer in the side chapel—Zach always forgot there was someone in the church at all times to adore Christ in the form of the Eucharist. His first slip in front of Paul. Hoping it'd also be the last, Zach led the retreat to the back of the chapel.

"I don't know how to say this." Paul bit his lip, staring straight ahead. "There's this girl."

Zach probably wasn't the best priest to be giving advice on that subject. "Okay. From before?"

"No, a teacher I met at the school." Paul slumped into the last wooden pew.

Zach joined him. "Wish I could tell you once you're ordained—" He snapped his fingers. "—it all goes away, but it doesn't." The words echoed eerily. Zach tried to lower his voice.

"I know." Paul looked down at the hymnal rack. "I just feel so guilty. I can't think about anything else."

"I think we always love the people we work with." Zach hurried to correct himself. "The people we serve. We just have to separate romantic love from . . . the pure love of Christ."

And that was a Book of Mormon phrase.

Paul stared at Zach like he could see through the cover and the collar. The collar that grew tighter each second. Was that approaching footsteps or blood pounding in his ears?

Footsteps. Paul turned around and Zach checked behind them, too. Maureen Bailey, the organist, waved to Zach and continued to the side chapel for perpetual adoration.

Paul pulled a red hymnal from the rack. "I want to stop this without hurting her. Us."

"Hm," Zach hedged between catching his breath, "you think she feels the same way?"

Paul scratched the back of his neck like that could hide the color rising in his cheeks. "I think she'd be interested, if I wasn't—you know."

His pulse almost normal again, Zach regarded the stained glass window behind the other man. Telling Paul to go for it while he still could probably wouldn't be smart. "Have you ever broken a bad habit, like biting your nails?"

"No, have you?" Paul asked gravely.

This kid really was cut out for the priesthood. "Yeah, biting my nails."

"What'd you do?"

"Took up piano." Not helpful—what was Paul supposed to do, take up the saxophone? He had a tough time picturing the constantly-concerned Paul wailing the blues.

"So . . . I should replace this habit with another one?" He mulled that over, pulling three fingers down his chin. "I could pay more attention to tutoring the kids instead of L—the teacher. But I worry this is a symptom of a bigger problem." Paul flipped through the red hymnal he still held. "I keep getting opposition from every side."

Opposition? These priestly discussions would be so much easier if he could use the Book of Mormon. Zach gathered his courage and hoped this wasn't false doctrine to a Catholic. "If we didn't have opposition in all things, we wouldn't really be making choices."

Paul contemplated the idea. "Hadn't thought about it like that." The pages of the hymnal fell shut, leaving the inside cover open. The nameplate said the hymnal was paid for by Doyle Murphy.

"I mean, think about who *doesn't* want you to become a priest. We face the most opposition when we're doing something right." Zach tried to ignore the hard rock of guilt in his throat. Watching a man get killed and doing nothing was more than "opposition."

"I guess you're right." Paul grinned. "Thanks for letting me get this off my chest." He stood.

"Any time." Zach led him to the chapel doors. "Hey, no basketball Monday. Funeral."

"Sorry to hear that." Paul bid him goodbye and headed out.

The guy wasn't the only one facing opposition. Zach wished he had someone to tell him that going up against Doyle Murphy was hard because it was right.

No, he knew that. Hadn't Flynn's murder proved that? He just had to make headway before Murphy came after anyone else. And tonight, once Father Fitzgerald was gone, Zach could see what Fitzgerald—or Father Patrick—had been hiding right under Zach's nose.

A FTER A MEAL AT A jazz-themed barbecue restaurant, Lucy paid for dinner, and Molly promised to return the favor. They left behind the hot oil smoke and vinegar tang of the restaurant for the busy, mall-like food court.

Lucy nodded, apparently coming to some conclusion. "Not bad, actually—and I'm, like, tenth-generation Southern. I should get my brother to come out and try this place. If he'd talk to me more than once a year. He'd love the live band." She gestured toward the restaurant. "He says jazz is the country's greatest achievement."

"Maybe I'll appreciate it once I'm officially an American."

"You're becoming a citizen? That's great."

"Thank you. I still have to pass my test in a fortnight." Staring at the patterned tile floor, Molly pushed away the apprehension gnawing her stomach at the thought of the impending exam.

"I hope loving baseball and hot dogs aren't a requirement. Otherwise, Immigration will be after me. But maybe my brother could bail me out. He works for the government." Lucy dodged a group of dog-collared teenagers.

"Oh, INS—I mean, ICE? Or whatever they're callin' themselves these days?" Not Molly's first choice agency, but still a possibility—if Immigration hired immigrants.

Lucy paused a moment. "You know, he's never actually said exactly where he works. But we haven't spoken since . . . before I moved here." She shook her head. "Okay, it's a sorry reflection on your life when even men related to you won't return your calls. When did I get this sad?"

Molly smiled sympathetically, though she hardly believed a cute, petite blonde like Lucy had trouble getting any man to call her. "I know what you mean."

"What, no nice Catholic guys in your life?" They slowed in front of a jewelry kiosk.

For some reason, Father Tim sprang to mind. Molly blinked away the image and pushed past the ring display. "Why, were you lookin' for one?"

"Nah, I'm all set on disastrous relationships that burn out on the first date—or before."

"Amen." Molly willed herself not to remember that moment in the office last week.

"I'm too old to make myself unhappy like this. As Charlie Brown says, 'Nothing takes the taste out of peanut butter quite like unrequited love.'" Lucy stopped at the handbag shop and touched the glass in front of a camel-colored leather clutch. "I always thought I'd outgrow this before I was old enough to be chaperoning instead of dancing at Homecoming."

"You're volunteerin' at the dance, so? You're a saint."

"All my life," Lucy chirped.

"Sorry?"

"Oh, lame family joke. I've been a 'Saint' all my life, in more ways than one—it's my last name, and then I'm a Latter-day Saint, get it?"

"Pity you're not Catholic with a name like that." Molly spied the exit and took Lucy's arm. "Come see this." She led Lucy out of the building and across a landscaped patio to the white metal railing. Molly swept an arm over the lower pavilion and Lake Michigan. The sunset's last orange-pink glow silhouetted the city's famed skyscrapers.

Lucy gasped. "Check out that view! The skyline—it's beautiful."

"The best part of Navy Pier."

They watched in silence while the sky faded to black, and the skyscraper lights sparkled in the lake's reflection.

Once it was dark, the spell wasn't quite as strong. Lucy pushed away from the railing. "You could be a saint, too, and chaperon with me." She rolled her eyes. "Just what you want to do on a Saturday night."

Molly started for the car park, but glanced back at the checkerboard of city lights. She didn't have plans, and she could see how Lucy's students acted, to see if she had anything to worry about from Doyle Murphy's gang. And that, at the least, would be worth her while. She smiled at Lucy and accepted.

If Father Fitzgerald or Father Patrick seriously thought the lock on this file cabinet would deter someone who wanted in here, he'd been mistaken. Zach surveyed Father Patrick's filing cabinet. The moon in the windows lit the office enough for him to work amid the long, eerie shadows.

Maybe another church mouse would come by to freak him out.

He laughed at himself and pulled out his lock picks. He was just glad to find a possible hiding place for the missing connection between Father Patrick and the mobsters.

Zach started on the lock. He applied light pressure on the torsion wrench, then raked the pins a couple times with the pick. The cylinder gradually turned a little, but one or two of the pins held. He pushed the pick to the back of the cylinder and used a rocking motion as he eased it out. Halfway through, the cylinder turned, and the lock popped out.

Too easy.

The priest couldn't have sprung for the expensive model? Maybe there wasn't anything important in here. Of course, if that were the case, the key would have been on the ring with the rest of Father Patrick's keys. Unless this cabinet was Fitzgerald's.

Zach pulled out the top drawer. If either priest had anything to hide, he couldn't be stupid enough to stick it right in the top drawer, but there might be something in here to indicate who owned the cabinet.

The first folder held copies of a contract dated two years ago. Kincaid Wholesalers—one of Murphy's fronts—pledged to provide "goods and/or services" to St. Adelaide Catholic Parish. A second contract in the folder renewed the agreement a year ago, but didn't yield any other information. He flipped to the last pages in both, but they were unsigned.

The next drawer held loose sheets from a day planner. The names were familiar: Murphy, Lonegan, Hennessy, O'Leary, Gallaher, Flynn. Zach ignored a guilt-kick to the gut. Notes by each name: "doubled amount." "Dropped off contract." "Took $."

But no indication who the planner belonged to. Zach didn't have much of a handwriting sample to go on—someone had cleared out Patrick's personal effects down to the shopping lists.

Then he'd eliminate known samples. Was it Fitzgerald's? He checked again. Nah. Fitzgerald's descending loops were open; these were closed.

Zach glanced at the empty desks behind him. Could it be Kathleen's? The untidy stacks on her desktop offered him plenty of exemplars. Her 'y' loops were practically check marks, like q's—aggressive and angry.

Then Molly? They'd joked about her cooking the books, but could she really?

Zach strode to her desk. Neat. Too neat? There was almost nothing on it.

The trash was more likely to yield a writing sample than her desk drawers. He raked through the garbage can: mostly paper, a candy wrapper and trash from lunch. He grabbed a couple slips of paper.

The first sample, a phone number, was angular, aggressive—oh. Kathleen's again.

"Pizza party." The second was Kathleen's writing, too.

The third, "St. Gregory's, Tuesday," was more curved. Closed descender loops. Was it the same as the day planner pages?

Zach hurried back to the filing cabinet and pulled out one of the folders, jumping back and forth between the page and the note.

The papers fluttered with his exhale. Molly's descender loops were smaller. He dug back through his Quantico training. Small descender loops meant a closed personality. Harder to get to know.

But that didn't matter. He tossed the phone message back in the trash and headed back to the filing cabinet. The third drawer was empty. The bottom drawer held a lockbox.

Just like Molly's drawer held a cash box. Coincidence, right?

Right. Molly's drawer and cash box locks wouldn't stand up to an agent with a hairpin and half a brain. The file cabinet lock was marginally better, but the lockbox was a miniature safe, with a fingerprint scanner.

Great. He had to get in there, but his tools for that were back in his room. If Jay Gallaher and his maroon sedan were watching the office—watching over whatever required a biometric mini-safe—lugging a safe out of here would definitely put Zach in the mob's sights, and not in the way he wanted.

Now what?

Molly finished her story about the misadventures of the last math teacher just as Lucy pulled into the parish car park. Their laughter died out and Lucy sighed, taking a spot and shifting into park. "All right, well, I guess I'll see you on Saturday, if that's still okay."

Saturday? Oh, the dance. "Sure now, of course it is." Molly leaned down to retrieve her handbag—but she found only the beige floor mat at her feet. "Lucy, did I have my handbag?"

"I don't remember."

"I could've sworn I brought it to the car at least." Molly frowned. "Would you mind terribly waitin' while I check the office?"

"Oh, I'll come with you."

They started for the office door, the clacking of Molly's heels echoing eerily in the arcaded hallway.

Zach jerked his head up at the sound of footsteps—high heels?—in the arched hall outside the office. This was no church mouse. He pushed the drawer almost shut, not risking the *clank-nk* of the drawer fastening.

The footsteps were coming closer. Coming to the office? Who'd come in at nine thirty?

The footsteps slowed. Was it his imagination—or his pulse in his ears—or was there a second set of feet? Either way, they were definitely coming to the office.

He could probably hide in the open in a dark office with his black clerical clothing, but he didn't dare risk it. Zach silently slipped across the room, sliding to sit under Molly's desk and wait out whoever this was.

If these people found him, there wouldn't be a good explanation for why a priest was in the office alone with the lights off in the first place, let alone hiding under Molly's desk. Could someone have seen him come in? Was this Gallaher from the maroon sedan?

Zach readied himself to draw his gun from his ankle holster. He'd pocketed his picks. The filing cabinet drawer was just open a crack. He could only pray this person wouldn't notice.

The doorknob rattled.

As she reached the door, Molly saw the problem with her plan. "My keys must be locked in there." She fiddled with the knob. It turned. She glanced at Lucy, who mirrored her surprise and dread. The door was unlocked?

Was this how it happened with Father Patrick? His murderer was still out there. Unless he'd returned to the scene of his crime. Icy fingers trailed down her spine.

Steeling herself, Molly opened the door and peered into the office. Her vision hadn't adjusted to the dark, but slowly she made out the office furniture and equipment. All in order.

Molly tried to shake off the foreboding that still pulled the hair at the nape of her neck to attention. She rounded her desk to search the drawers for her handbag.

Molly.

Even if he could cover his gun before she found him, Zach would look really suspect—and really stupid—hiding under her desk. He tried to force himself further into the shadows. Good thing she had a deep desk, and she hadn't bothered to switch on the lights, either.

But wouldn't any normal person with a legitimate reason to be in their own office after hours switch on the lights first thing? Was she here for something illegal?

She'd been here after dark on a Saturday night when Murphy dropped him off. And yesterday he'd interrupted them "getting down to business."

Zach's stomach sank like he'd missed the game-winning basket. He'd missed something a lot bigger than that.

Molly searched the top drawers on either side of the desk. She picked up the phone.

"I'm goin' to call my mobile," Molly said. To someone. "Will you listen at the car?"

"Sure," came the voice from the door. Her footsteps trailed away. A woman—who sounded really familiar. Whose voice would he recognize in the parish? Kathleen's?

Above him, Molly dialed. In the silence, she shifted her weight from one attractive ankle to the other—he'd never realized ankles *could* be pretty.

She released her relief in a sigh. "Oh, *under* the seat, of course. Be right there. Thank you." She hung up the phone and headed out of the office. The doorknob rattled and her footsteps paused. Looking over the office? Zach closed his eyes, fervently hoping she'd find nothing amiss.

He'd done something right, apparently. Molly closed the door and locked it behind her. The echo of her footsteps receded, leaving him alone in the dark to finally breathe again.

After hiding his gun, Zach crawled from underneath the desk and locked the file cabinet. He waited until he was sure Molly would be gone before he returned to the parish house. As he walked through the parking lot, he took note of the maroon sedan parked across the street. But he was more worried about the owner of a pair of pretty ankles.

He had to know, once and for all, how deep she was in. Time to either work her like a suspect or an asset—not a prospect.

The office phone rang Friday evening, and Molly checked the caller ID—the parish house. "Hello?"

"Hey, Molly." Father Tim's greeting was warm as ever. "Would you and Kathleen like some dinner?"

She glanced at Kathleen's empty desk. "I'm afraid she's already left for the day." And it was Friday. Father Fitzgerald had to be on his way to the Baileys'.

"Then would you like to join me?"

Molly hesitated a beat. No matter what she'd thought last week, she'd never cross the line with a priest, and she couldn't imagine Father Tim allowing it either. The invitation had to be innocent. "I suppose I could."

She straightened her desk, ignoring the anticipation building behind her rib cage. No need to get wound up over a handsome man—a handsome *priest*—even if he did understand her Irishisms and help her and respect her. At the parish house door, she paused for a heartbeat before she pulled her keys from her handbag and let herself in. The familiar aroma of boiling potatoes greeted her, relieving a measure of the anxious pressure on her chest.

Molly couldn't see Father Tim from the front door, but a pan clanged against the sink to give him away. She found him in the kitchen. She almost expected some sort of electric current to pass between them, but meeting his familiar eyes brought reassurance—a peace she hadn't felt since she'd discovered the office door unlocked.

He beamed at her. "Hey there. Hope you like champ."

He was cooking an Irish dish for them. The breakfast bar was set for two. That lead weight slowly lowered onto her heart again.

She was here for a private dinner with Father Tim.

ZACH BUSIED HIMSELF rummaging through the junk drawer. Molly had unfettered access to the priests' quarters. She could've admitted the murderers to the parish house and laid out the money laundering as a frame up. She could've even killed Father Patrick herself.

Ridiculous. His body wasn't in the parish house; he was outside her office. Which didn't help clear her. And that was exactly why he'd called her here—to test her.

Disarming and innocent. That was how he needed to play this. He flashed her a grin and moved to the next avocado-green drawer for a mixer or mallet or other weapon—er, utensil for mashing the potatoes. Could Molly be a danger to him?

"Just finishing up." He found a masher and held it aloft.

Molly walked behind him to take a pot from the stove. She poured the scallions in milk into the waiting potatoes. "You never did tell me how you knew I've a Dublin accent."

Zach attacked the potatoes with needless vigor, wracking his mind for a believable explanation. Was it his imagination or was the kitchen a lot smaller with her in it? "I lived in Ireland a while," he managed. "Study Abroad."

"You certainly absorbed the culture. Or at least the recipe for champ."

"I tried." He grabbed the potatoes and turned to the breakfast bar. "Go ahead and sit."

She settled onto a barstool. "And where are you from, Father?"

"Virginia." He took the stool next to her. "Would you like to say grace?"

Molly bowed her head. As she offered a short prayer, Zach sized her up. The calm on her face and in her voice as she addressed God, her hands relaxed—she'd never killed anyone. But did she know anything about the money laundering?

He echoed her amen, and they tucked into their meal. He was supposed to be assessing her, flirting if necessary, but the parish finances were the last thing he wanted to discuss.

"You're mixed up, aren't you?" she said.

Zach looked up. She pointed at his hands, the fork in his left, the knife in his right: European style instead of American. He laughed at himself. "Oh, yeah. It's easier. Erin go bragh." He gave a little fist-pump with the Irish nationalist slogan.

"*Éire go Brách*," she echoed with far better pronunciation. After all, there wasn't a more appropriate response. Especially if her father was an Irish republican terrorist.

"Was it your heritage that brought you to Ireland?" she asked.

"I'm not very Irish." Zach shrugged.

Molly furrowed her brow. "But—your last name—"

He kicked himself mentally. "One great-great-grandfather way back there. Practically doesn't count."

"Ah. Where in Ireland did you stay?"

He filled his mouth with a bite of champ to buy himself another minute. Best not to pin himself down to one lie. "All over. One of those traveling things. And you?"

"Well, I was born in Derry." Northern Ireland. Derry was no Belfast, but it had a long history with the IRA, too. "But we moved to Castleknock when I was little."

The LDS mission home was in the same suburb—but he definitely couldn't say that. "I got to visit Castleknock Castle."

"Did you like it?"

"Yeah, thanks for having me." He grinned.

Molly smiled indulgently. Was she leaning closer?

Zach resisted the urge to loosen his collar. This was not helping him figure out if she was involved in the money laundering. He shifted gears. "Sorry about the other day. I didn't like the way Doyle was looking at you, but I should've known he wasn't a threat. Hope I didn't step on your toes."

"Not at all." She bit her lip. Had he ever really noticed her lips? If her ankles were pretty, her lips—

Zach cleared his throat. "Which side of your family does the Black Irish come from?"

"Both, my grandmothers. So I'm told, anyway. I didn't really know them." Her gaze grew distant, and she fingered one of those dark curls that gave the Black Irish their name.

He tried to lighten the mood—and then he could ply her again. "Okay, I have to ask: what were your parents thinking, naming you Molly?"

Molly glanced heavenward. "It's my sister's fault. She couldn't say 'Mary.'"

"Is your family still in Dublin?"

"We all came here together: Mum, Da, my sister and her husband."

Irish terrorists in the States? Great job, Immigration. "Why haven't I met them yet?"

"Ah, they go to Old Saint Pat's." She poked at her fish. "Have you ever been?"

"No." Hopefully the church wasn't a place any real priest would make a point to visit.

"It's fantastic—a hundred and fifty years old, motifs from the Book of Kells in the stained glass and on the walls." Her enthusiasm for her native culture shone in her eyes. "You shouldn't miss it, even if you're not that Irish."

"I'll have to check it out." And time for the segue. "Y'know, it was weird—Doyle never did tell me what he wanted the other day."

"Didn't he?" She popped a forkful of green beans in her mouth without meeting his gaze.

"What was it?"

"Couldn't say."

His stomach seemed to shrink around his dinner. Why did he care so much?

Molly looked up, a defiant spark in her eyes. "Had my toes stepped on before he asked."

Zach returned her smirk, finally relaxed enough to swallow his bite of fish. He was enjoying this back-and-forth—other than the tension ratcheting across his chest. Just one more try. "Seems like something's up there. You said you know Doyle?"

"Just enough." Her simple shrug seemed to hide no guile. Either she was good—or she was *really* good. Either way, he couldn't push much harder before she shut down.

"Is he one of the people I shouldn't get too close to?"

Molly held his gaze, calm and steady. "He's one of the people you should let me handle."

And that was it. He could tell he was hitting her limit. Time to change the subject. "The school's homecoming dance is tomorrow, isn't it?" he asked.

"It is. I'm supposed to chaperon. Don't suppose we'll be seein' you there?"

"No." He sighed ruefully. "Can't be seen on a dance floor. Can't dance anyway."

Molly finished her champ and pushed her plate away. "Pity. I'll have to be content to spend the evenin' standin' in a corner."

"Nah, I bet you'll spend at least half the time out on the dance floor."

"How did you know? I've always been quite the magnet for teenage boys."

"I'm sure they're not the only ones."

A blush crept up from the collar of her off-white sweater. Zach stood and cleared their plates, though he was only half done. "Thanks for helping me with dinner. I forgot Bruce was at the Baileys' tonight."

She rubbed one finger on the breakfast bar. "Every Friday."

"This is only my third one here." He set the plates in the sink. "Can I walk you out?"

Molly had her purse before he turned around. He escorted her to her car in silence. At her green Volkswagen, they came to a stop. She stared up at him like she was trying to read his mind.

The wind drew two dark curls across her face. Without thinking, Zach tucked her soft curls behind her ear. She closed her eyes. It would be so easy to kiss her now, if he just—her eyelids fluttered and he faltered, his hand still lingering by her cheek.

Everything had its reasonable limit. Including how far he'd go in flirting to get to Molly. Er, the mob.

Before he could pull away, a woman's voice called Molly's name. They both looked to find Kathleen. "I left my glasses. Did you see— oh, Father." Her gaze darted from him to Molly and back. "Should've known. Surprised it took this long, really, the way you hang around the office."

Molly squared her shoulders. "I think it's nice Father Tim takes an interest in helpin' us."

Kathleen turned her disapproval on Molly. "I'm sure you do. Appreciate his interest, I mean." If she testified in that tone, Jesus would've sounded like the sinner.

"Do you need me to give you somethin' to do durin' work— somethin' to keep your imagination occupied, Kathleen? Because clearly it's run amok."

"Imagination?" She shot Zach another glare. "Is that what's out of hand here?"

"Kathleen." Zach kept his voice gentle, but firm—the same as he'd use with a dog. "Let he who is without sin."

She folded her arms, but averted her gaze.

"See you Sunday." He nodded to both of them and headed back to the parish house.

This was stupid—he was stupid. He was supposed to be getting information from Molly, not toying with her emotions and driving Kathleen nuts. Wasn't like he and Molly had any future. Once this assignment was over, he couldn't tell her who he was, unless he wanted to get fired and blacklisted. And he couldn't expect her to be okay with a guy who could lie to her and her parish.

No, no—that didn't matter. He shouldn't even be thinking about Molly in his real life.

Then why was he?

This was not a direction he needed this case to take.

Molly rearranged the store-bought cookies on the plastic tray. She took a bite of an overly sweet gingersnap, as if that would settle the jitters in her stomach.

Last night was all in her imagination. Hers and Kathleen's.

Guilt piled another stone on her shoulders. She took a second cookie and checked the punch station. She'd hoped a dim cafeteria festooned with stringy crepe streamers would be enough to keep her from remembering the way he'd looked at her, how much she'd wanted—

"There you are." Lucy filled a cup with punch and gave it to Molly, then filled one for herself. She waved a hand toward the empty dance floor ringed by wallflowers. "These guys are a little depressed. Lost to Saint Michael's."

"Really hurts when it's a girls' school."

Lucy smirked and checked the gym doors. "The hard part will be getting them dancing. Thanks again for coming, especially since it looks to be a boring evening." She surveyed the dance floor again. "So what's going on with Father Tim?"

Molly startled so violently she spilled half her punch. "What?"

"Still can't catch him." Lucy turned her head to regard Molly at a wary angle and offered her a napkin. If Lucy didn't know something was wrong before, she certainly did now. But rather than asking, Lucy glanced at the doors again.

"We keepin' you from somethin'?" Molly nodded toward the doors.

"Oh, just looking for . . . someone."

"Someone?" Molly let her tone tease her friend a little.

Lucy blushed. "A volunteer at the school. It's nothing. Won't go anywhere."

"You do know women can ask men out these days."

"Yeah, not this guy." She leaned closer. "He's in seminary, studying to become a priest."

Molly offered a smile she hoped would show she understood. "A James Bond/Miss Moneypenny kind of thing." Pointless and yet irresistible.

Lucy set down her punch and pressed a hand to her stomach, visibly nauseated. "Molly, Paul and I actually had *dinner* together. It was—you have no idea. We were only talking about school, but his ex-girlfriend showed up and screamed that we were on a date!"

Molly cringed. That scenario was a little too familiar—and how would she react to someone who'd dated Father Tim before he'd taken his vows?

"I'm even more confused now," Lucy said. "I wish we hadn't gone."

Molly used the same furtive tone. "I know what you mean."

"You do?" Lucy shook her head. "Of course not. You wouldn't even dream of doing—"

Molly held up a finger and made sure no one was close enough to overhear her. "Full-on priest."

"Not . . . Father Fitzgerald?" The horror in her wide brown eyes verged on comical.

"No, no. Let's just say it might be my fault Kathleen's kept you from the new priest." At the admission, some of last night's guilt lifted from her heart.

"You're kidding."

"Wish I were." Molly studied her half-empty cup. "I wonder if I've brought this on myself, as penance." Perhaps if she were more devout, she wouldn't be so susceptible to this struggle.

"I don't think God usually gives trials to punish us. The Book of Mormon says He gives us weakness so we can come to him and be humble, and the Savior's grace makes weak things strong."

Molly considered that. She wasn't terribly interested in catechism, but she'd never really got away from a basic trust that the Father and the Son were real. Could this be more than just a cross, a burden? A little more of the guilt melted away. "I hadn't thought of it that way. That's lovely."

"Thanks. I'm still not making progress." Lucy stared at the punch and hugged herself. "I can't stop wondering what if—but it's only false hope, because nothing will actually change."

"It could. Though I suppose if your man doesn't join the priesthood, you'd still have to handle the interfaith issue."

"I know. And I guess if *Father Tim*," she dropped her voice to a whisper to mention his name, "left the priesthood, he'd be out of your church, too."

Molly stared at the pink streamers fluttering overhead. That wasn't guaranteed. Then again, if Kathleen hadn't come upon them last night— "I have to be better at this."

Lucy bit her lip, then took a deep breath. "We're having this potluck thing at my church Sunday after next. There's a speaker afterward, and the topic is actually overcoming weakness. Want to come?"

Couldn't hurt—Lucy's scripture carried hope for both of them, and if it was to be more of that, why not? "Sure. What time?"

"We eat at six. I can pick you up, if you want. If you give me good directions." Lucy glanced at the door again—still thinking of Paul, apparently. She looked back and laughed self-consciously.

They both checked the dance floor. A few couples had ventured out. Molly spotted a student edging his way toward them. "Maybe he could keep your mind off your man."

"Don't think he's my type. You know, legal?" Lucy peered through the low light at the approaching student. "That's Ian. He hates me."

Ian? Molly squinted in the low light. Doyle's son ambled toward the exit.

"Hey, Ian," Lucy called. "You know once you leave, you can't come back in, right?"

"Uh, yeah." Ian fixed her with a menacing glare just like his father's. Despite her warning, he stalked out with a final glower.

"What was that about?" Molly took a sip of her punch to make her question seem casual. But how much would it take for Ian to complain about Lucy to his father?

"We can't let them back in because they might bring in alcohol or come back drunk."

Although that wasn't what she meant, Molly let the subject slide. "Should've brought my baton and handcuffs." Not that she still had her Garda equipment more than five years after leaving the force.

Lucy spotted a couple dancing suggestively and left to break them up. Molly saw another couple and did the same. By the end of the evening, she almost wished she did have her baton, but she joked with Lucy that she was pretty sure they'd kept kids out of the confessional. After a quick goodbye, Molly paused at her car in the drizzling rain. Just last night, he'd stood right here, his fingertips caressing her cheek.

No. She could work with him—and still protect him—and not lose her head. Molly straightened herself to her full height and opened her car door.

Last night was definitely her imagination.

O NCE KATHLEEN LEFT for her daily meeting at the school Tuesday afternoon, Zach headed in. This was his best chance to get the mini-safe out of the office and leave Gallaher in his maroon sedan across the street none the wiser.

But it also meant facing Molly for the first time since their dinner Friday night. Zach pushed aside that memory and marched into the office. Molly looked up from her computer with an amiable but not flirtatious smile. Now he just had to get her out of the office.

"Hey." He grinned back to sell his lie a little more. "The school has some counseling files for me. Can you go get those while I take care of this?" He nodded at the box of books and held his breath. Would she buy that flimsy excuse?

Molly scrutinized him a moment. "Of course." She left without question, giving him maybe three minutes for his task. As soon as she was gone, Zach dumped out the box of books—mostly ones he'd bought at the thrift store yesterday and snuck into the donation box at the mobsters' building last night.

He turned to the file cabinet, popping the lock on the second pass of the pick. Perfect. He grabbed the mini-safe from the bottom drawer and set it inside the cardboard box. Standing, he kicked the drawer shut and popped the file cabinet's lock in again. He peeked out the windows high on the office door. Molly was coming. He fell to his knees again to throw books back into the box.

Zach had barely covered the mini-safe with books when Molly returned bearing the folders—the files he'd requested from the school first thing that morning. She took her seat at her desk. "Almost done?"

"Most of these will end up at the thrift store." He held up a risqué romance novel—not one of his picks. "I don't think a high school library is the place for *Sinful Desires.*"

"I'd hope not." She gave him the same smile, pleasant yet platonic.

Zach collected the rest of the unsuitable books, but set aside one special find. He stood and hoisted the now-considerably-heavier box onto one hip, with *Escape the Turkmen Prison*, the prequel to the spy novel from the last set of books, in his free hand. He held up the book. "Have you read this one?"

Her eyes lit up as soon as she saw the cover. "I've been lookin' for that book for . . . ever." She accepted the tattered pulp paperback like a priceless first edition. "Thank you, Father."

"Sure thing." Zach started out of the office. He'd made it: totally work-focused. Flirting wasn't even necessary. Friday night was a fluke.

"Oh." Molly lifted the folders. "Don't forget your files."

He held out a hand. "Right, thanks."

"Want me to take the books to the charity shop?" she offered as he took the files.

"That's okay." He patted the box with the folders. "Wouldn't want to give you *Sinful Desires.*" Zach choked on his quip. Molly's jaw went slack in horror. "The book," he added belatedly. After a second of awkward pause, Zach pivoted to leave. To make his exit even clumsier, the door swung open before he could reach it and smacked into the box of books. Zach stumbled backward, struggling to keep his grip on the heavy box with the folders.

"Let me help you with that." The man who'd hit him with the door moved closer.

Zach shifted the box and its evidence out of reach, finally able to catch the other corner. "I got it, thanks." Though he probably didn't look it, halfway to a squat to regain his balance.

The stranger turned to Molly. Zach pulled himself to standing. The other man was a few inches shorter than Zach. He wasn't a known mobster, but that didn't put him in the clear. His curly bronze hair was a little too perfectly styled, his suit a little too slick and the smile he was giving Molly a little too winning.

Or did Zach not trust him because that winning smile was aimed at Molly?

"I'm Cathal Healey." He grabbed a chair and set up in front of Molly's desk, his back to Zach. Zach sent Molly a skeptical look over Cathal's head. Maybe the guy's parents had never heard the Irish name aloud, but apparently they'd missed the memo that the 't' was silent.

But Molly smiled back at the newcomer. "What brings you in, Mister Healey?"

"I'm with Stockman Developers. You know that empty lot a block over?"

She nodded. Zach readjusted his grip on the box, which was growing heavier by the second. He needed to get the mini-safe back to the parish house, but how could he leave Molly alone with this suspicious stranger?

Healey continued his pitch. "We're scouting locations for a youth center, and we figured you guys could give us a real feel for the area." He pulled a sheet of paper from a leather attaché case and slid it across her desk like a casual, five-figure bribe check.

Zach resisted the urge to scoff. A youth center in a mob-run neighborhood? Yeah, that'd keep them out of trouble. The box slid an inch lower.

"Oh, sure now." Molly picked up a pen and leaned over her desk. "We may not be a perfect fit, so." She marked the church/parish house/school complex on the map.

This didn't seem right. "Who's funding the center?" Zach asked, testing Healey's story. Molly and Healey turned to him.

"The Marcus Williams Foundation." He gave Zach the same winning grin he'd given Molly, but Healey's eyes held no warmth. "They're a community outreach NGO." Though he'd waited the exact right amount of time to answer, it still felt too slick, too pat.

Molly waved him away. "I'll take care of him, Father."

The box slipped two more inches. Maybe the guy's salesman vibe was what set him on edge. Zach bid them goodbye and headed for the parish house. Halfway across the parking lot, he dared to check the maroon sedan's usual parking spot. Was it his imagination or was Gallaher on the phone?

That night, Zach waited to check through the curtains until Father Fitzgerald left on one of his usual family visits. The maroon sedan was still parked across the street. Zach locked the front door and took the mini-safe to his room. He turned the metal box over, hefted it, tapped on it. The dull echo sounded like reasonably thick steel. Probably two locking bolts, maybe half-inch diameter. Electronic fingerprint scanner.

Unlike the filing cabinet, this had been purchased by someone who knew what he was doing. Zach retrieved his small toolkit from under the bed, replaced his lock picks, and pulled out a pencil and notepad.

If he didn't have his tools with him, of course, he would've found a way to cut the safe open without damaging its contents. Any safe small enough to carry around was usually small enough to steal and crack—literally. But this time he was prepared, as long as the last person to open this hadn't thought to wipe off the scanner.

Once the pencil was sharp enough, Zach rubbed the lead on the notepad. He blew the resulting graphite powder onto the fingerprint scanner. At an angle, the beam from his flashlight showed a good print.

Perfect. Zach grabbed the Silly Putty from his toolkit. He carefully pressed the pliable putty onto the scanner to lift the print. Low-tech indeed—though once he'd seen a TV show where they used a print photocopied on acetate to break into a lock. But now he had to be careful. If he didn't lift this right, the print would be destroyed. Then he'd have to resort to cutting the safe open, and he wouldn't be able to sneak it back without anyone knowing. Did he need to put it back? Who would check? Molly?

Zach steadied his breathing and slowly peeled off the makeshift thumb. He turned it over. The print was intact in the putty. The tension in his chest melted. Father Patrick was gone; Zach probably didn't need to worry about returning the safe. With the fake thumb on the scanner again, the lock beeped and the metal-on-metal grind indicated the steel locking bars were opened. He pulled open the door—and laughed at himself when he realized he was whistling the James Bond theme song. Between the low-tech crack and the celibate cover, he couldn't picture fiction's most famous spy in this job. Zach finally extracted the safe's contents.

Bank statements. He didn't know what he'd been hoping to find, but this wasn't it.

The statements were less telling than the contracts had been, but they were all addressed to St. Adelaide Catholic Church c/o Colin Patrick.

Between this and the information in the filing cabinet, he'd definitely tied a dead priest to a money laundering scheme. "Good work, Saint," he muttered. Zach set his jaw and started on the statements. He was on the fourth month when a knock on the parish house door made him jump despite his training. Had he locked Fitzgerald out? He stuffed the paperwork inside the mini-safe and shoved it under the bed.

Before whoever it was knocked a second time, Zach opened the door. Molly. How did she always manage to catch him—or nearly so—whenever he touched this safe? "What's up?"

"Sorry, Cally Lonegan's been tryin' to reach you—said your line was busy?"

Zach glanced at the phone behind him. Seemed fine. "Huh. Would you set up an appointment with him this week?"

A crease of concern formed between her eyebrows, but she nodded. "Indulgin' in some *Sinful Desires*?"

He followed her gaze over his shoulder again to the stack of thrift-store books on the couch next to his thrift-store Bible. "I *am* only human."

100

"As are we all." Molly lingered there another moment. "Father, I hope I haven't done anythin' or said anythin' to make you think . . ."

"Think what?" Playing dumb was the only safe option.

Molly gripped her purse strap, bracing herself. "That I see you as somethin' other than a priest."

She might as well have punched him in the gut. "I thought we were friends."

"Friends?" The blood drained from her face.

"I mean, Father Fitzgerald and Kathleen are better at lectures than jokes, and—" He sighed. "*I'm* sorry if I've done anything to make you think otherwise."

"Not at all," she choked out. "Have a good evenin'." She turned to leave. Zach shut the door on the sight of her springing step. Why did she have to come by when he was going through the statements? She couldn't know he had the safe.

Unless she had a key to that filing cabinet, and she'd checked. After all, Molly was there alone after regular business hours. All the time. He'd have to get at her keys in her desk—

Zach froze. The mini-safe had been in a drawer just like Molly's cash box. Molly's cash box held bank account documentation. Papers that account owners kept track of—terms, rates, PINs. When the account was opened. Signatories.

If those papers weren't in the safe, could they be in her cash box?

His gut tightened. No. He couldn't do that.

Zach rolled his eyes at himself. He was already bugging her computer and cell phone. Why should breaking into her desk be any different? She was a suspect. He had to think of her that way. Cool. Calculating.

She might be right—it might be her fault Father Patrick was dead.

Molly tried to concentrate on the balance sheet in front of her Wednesday afternoon, but couldn't focus on anything but rubbing her fingers over her desktop. Father Tim would stop by any minute to pick up the budget for the movie night.

Why should she be nervous? There'd been no repeat of the single incident of flirting last week. They were friends, just as he'd said last night. And a priest wouldn't lie.

No, she knew why she was worried—that meeting he'd requested with Cally Lonegan. She couldn't fix things so easily if Father Tim was the one asking for the appointment. With the mobsters even turning on themselves, Father Tim didn't stand a chance on his own. She'd have to resort to damage control, so.

Father Tim strode into the office. "Hey, Moll. Everything ready?"

She gave him the folder of flyers and decoration ideas for the movie night. "And I made you an appointment with Cally at eight."

"Thanks." He finally nodded a greeting to Kathleen.

She beamed as if Father Tim had never shown the kindness to acknowledge her. "Anything I can help you with?"

He hesitated a moment. "Sure. Do we do anything as a parish for Halloween?"

"We don't have anythin' planned until our dinner for the homeless at Thanksgivin'."

"What did you want to do, wear costumes to the office?" Kathleen snorted.

Molly looked up in time to catch Father Tim's grin. Her heart rose in her chest.

"That's a great idea," he said. "What do you think, Molly?"

"Let's—sounds massive." At her support, his smile broadened.

"Massive?" Echoing Molly's slang, Kathleen's shrill voice shattered their moment.

Not this, not now. "Oh, Father, here's another list for the . . . yokiemabob." Molly offered Father Tim the tentative food price list.

"Yokiemabob?" Kathleen squeaked. "Do you even speak English?"

Frowning, Father Tim took Molly's paper. He turned back to Kathleen, his voice carrying the same low tone of rebuke he'd used with her last week. "I understand her perfectly."

Maybe it was her imagination, but Molly received the distinct impression Father Tim understood more than her Irish slang.

Oh, she hoped not. Molly bowed her head to hide her warming cheeks as he walked out. Could he really believe they were just friends?

Zach joined Cally and Lisa Lonegan on their brown leather couch. Lisa covered her face with her hands, and her shoulders shook. Lonegan patted her knee. Two weeks had certainly changed the mood at the Lonegans'. Or maybe it had something to do with burying Lisa's brother two days ago.

"I'm so sorry for your loss," Zach offered again. Sorrier than he cared to admit. Sure, it would've been three on one—not counting Flynn—and he might've blown his cover, but wasn't a man's life worth that?

Lisa wiped her tears, straightened the stack of *People* magazines on the coffee table and murmured her thanks.

"You should go wash your face." Lonegan's suggestion was probably about as gentle as the guy ever got.

Lisa met his gaze. "Tell him."

Her husband engaged the coffee table in a staring contest.

"What do you have to tell me, Cally?" Zach leaned forward.

"It's about Gerry," Lonegan said.

"No." Lisa's voice was suddenly firm. "It's about you. Start with Father Patrick."

Zach tried to look appropriately concerned instead of excited, despite the anticipation quickening his pulse. He hadn't botched the case yet—and Flynn's death might be the last.

Lonegan jerked his head toward the back of the condo. Lisa

sniffled, stood, and shuffled away. Zach waited until he heard a door close in the back. "So, Father Patrick?"

Lonegan hesitated, then crossed himself. "Bless me, Father. I sinned."

Great. If Lonegan made this a confession, anything even as small as a clue would go out the window in court—and there was that whole authority thing. Zach allowed a nod.

"I—I tried to do this with Father Fitzgerald a couple weeks ago, but . . . I don't know."

Relief doused Zach's adrenaline rush. No break in the case, but at least he wouldn't have to give Lonegan penance or absolution. "What did Father Fitzgerald tell you?"

"Said I'm not ready yet."

"Because?" Zach scrutinized him in the silence that followed. Staring at his hands, Lonegan still bore the slump of a soul burdened by guilt. He'd tried to confess, but he hadn't repented. He wasn't ready to change. Even Zach's relief dissolved—no confessions of any kind tonight. "What did you and Father Fitzgerald decide you should do next?"

"He said I have to think about a new direction for my life. 'Make a commitment to change.'" Lonegan raked his hair across his forehead. "I just don't know if I can. Get out."

Yeah, the mob wasn't known for its cushy severance and retirement plan. "I might be able to help you better if you could tell me what exactly we're talking about."

"You name it, I done it. Except breaking my vows. Never done that. And I never killed anybody, not personally. Not directly."

Zach pulled back, faking shock. "I thought you said this was about Father Patrick?"

Though it hardly seemed possible, Lonegan's shoulders fell even further. "After what happened with him and now Gerry—I gotta stop while I can. If I can."

"What do you mean, 'If I can'?"

Lonegan smoothed his thinning hair again. "What I seen, what I done—it's all so much." He tugged at the cuffs of his shirt.

"Do you like your life? Those things you've seen and done?"

He pondered the faux wood coffee table a long time. "Thought I did. Thought it was the best life there is." He rubbed his mouth. "But now . . ."

"You want something better?"

"Don't know what I want. Don't know if I have a right to want anything, after all I took."

"Hey." Zach waited for him to look up. "We all have a right to lead a righteous life, if that's what we really want."

Lonegan focused somewhere behind Zach.

"Do you want that, Cally?"

He stared past Zach. At length, he nodded. "Guess so."

"It won't be easy, and it could take a while." Zach offered a silent prayer that Lonegan could set a world record in turn-around time. "But I know you can change. The Lord can help you—I've seen Him do it. And it *is* worth it."

Lonegan squinted and slowly shifted his gaze back to Zach. Was he pondering or doubting? "You see the Bulls' opener last night?" he asked.

"You see Rose's steal?"

Zach's "research" paid off: Lonegan's face lit up for the first time that night. "What do you think of the Bulls' chances?"

Maybe he was letting him off too easy, but Zach let him steer the conversation to basketball. If he was still questioning a commitment to change, Lonegan wasn't ready to even think about the FBI. But Zach couldn't afford to wait long until he pushed Lonegan again. He was nearly halfway to the archbishop's deadline.

MOLLY WAS FINISHING the bulletin to take to the printer Friday afternoon when Father Tim came by the office bearing two brown paper sacks. The first pretty day in three weeks, the thin fall sunlight was warm enough he could leave the door open. "Happy *Oíche Shamhna.*"

"*Oíche Shamhna shona duit.*" She nodded, automatically steadying the pipe cleaner halo on her headband. Could she ask whether he'd met with Cally Lonegan without tipping Father Tim off?

Her efforts at keeping him from the mobsters were failing worse and worse.

Father Tim flashed a smile. He placed one of his parcels on Kathleen's empty desk and handed the other to Molly. "Happy Halloween."

The sack held a loaf of raisin-speckled bread. "Barmbrack! Oh, thank you—now it's really *Oíche Shamhna.*"

"You're welcome." Father Tim glanced at the other two desks, vacant. "You know, I heard something interesting the other day."

"What's that?"

"He said Doyle gives you a deal on your rent. That's nice of him."

Molly cocked her head. "Where'd you hear that?"

"Um, Cally Lonegan."

She steeled herself against the sinking feeling in her stomach. So he had seen Cally after all. But Cally said . . . ? "He must be mistaken."

Father Tim mirrored her questioning posture.

"*You* pay my rent," she said. "I was told it came with the job. The parish has the contract." Could Cally be half-right, though?

"Oh, really?" He stepped back to lean against Kathleen's desk for a moment, until Kathleen traipsed in, her red patent leather stilettos clopping over the linoleum tile. Molly held her tongue about her co-worker's high heels and devil horns. In Ireland, that was part of the tradition, but here, some of the parish might object.

Father Tim raised an eyebrow. "Did you answer the door like that, Kathleen?"

"No," she chirped, "but I answered the phone, 'Second circle of hell, how may I direct your call?' Speaking of, did you hear what happened to Maureen?"

"What?"

"She broke her wrist. No surgery or anything, but she can't play for the rest of the year."

Father Tim grimaced. "Does she need us to do anything for her?"

"No. But she's the only one in the parish who plays the organ," Molly said. "I was about to ring 'round to see if anyone had an organist to spare."

Father Tim's blue eyes sparkled with a secret. "Don't worry. God will provide."

"A ram in a thicket?" Molly held in a laugh.

Kathleen tossed an envelope on Molly's desk as she passed. "Donation for the trust."

Molly opened her drawer for the cash box. She unlocked it and, as if it enjoyed embarrassing her in front of Father Tim, the cash box flipped its contents onto the floor.

Father Tim knelt to help her. "Sure Jeez," Molly muttered.

"Molly." Kathleen frowned, the judgmental lines on her lips pinching together. "I assume something specific brings you by, Father?"

He glanced at Molly, then turned to Kathleen. "Ah, tearin' away, actin' the maggot."

Kathleen's jaw dropped, as did Molly's—though probably for a different reason. Remembering the Irish name of Halloween was one thing; being fluent in Dublin slang was another. "Go 'way."

Father Tim grinned.

"Molly, I can't believe you'd say that to Father Tim." Kathleen scoffed. "How rude!"

Molly checked Father Tim's expression—he definitely knew the phrase was the equivalent of the American "aw, go on" and not a dismissal. And he was antagonizing Kathleen on purpose. "Has a tongue that would clip a hedge, hasn't she?" he remarked to Molly.

"Sure now, normally the office *craic* is rapid, *mar dhea*."

"Yeah, someone's on crack and it's not Maria." Kathleen completely misinterpreted the last Irish phrase—which changed the original sentence to sarcasm—and snorted.

"Kathleen." Father Tim handed Molly the last of the bank notes and stood. Drawing himself up to his full height, he towered over Kathleen. "You are always giving out to Molly," he continued, using yet another Irishism. "So what if she uses some Irish phrases? She's *Irish*."

Kathleen folded her arms across her chest. "She may be Irish, but she's in America now."

"And, what, if she wants to use Irish words, she should go back to Ireland? Come on. She's done plenty to accommodate you. It's time you did the same for her."

Kathleen shut her mouth for all of four seconds. "Thought you were dressing up, Father."

"I thought you were, too," he murmured for Molly, and slipped out the door.

Molly took a bite of her barmbrack to stifle her laugh. She hadn't had barmbrack in years. The nearest import shop wasn't far, but Father Tim didn't have a car of his own.

Kathleen discovered her brown paper sack. "What's this?"

"Barmbrack, a sweet bread with raisins. An Irish Halloween tradition. Father Tim picked it up for us."

Kathleen poked at her loaf and curled her upper lip.

"It's good." Molly took another bite of her loaf to prove it. Luckily, Kathleen turned back to her computer before Molly bit into something solid. Oh, she'd forgotten the ring baked into each loaf. Traditional barmbrack had half a dozen objects baked in to predict fortunes, though store-bought loaves generally only had the toy ring.

Molly drew a silent breath as she brushed the breadcrumbs off the gold-painted plastic. The person that found it would marry within the year. She placed the ring in her desk drawer and started to crumple the sack—but something solid was still inside. A Crunchie bar. Molly could almost taste the smooth chocolate as she slipped the bar into her desk drawer. Could he possibly know it was her favorite chocolate bar? And was she really this foolish?

Zach stepped out of the office and reminded himself he was just doing this to keep Molly close. The sheer delight in her eyes was a fringe benefit. That was all.

He'd only made it a few feet from the office when he spotted a guy with a disturbingly perfect shirt and tie, matching his magazine-cover curls. Cathal Healey waved to Zach. "How's it going, Father?"

"Fine." Zach watched Healey walk to the office door. Healey pasted on that trying-way-too-hard grin before opening the door. Zach caught sight of the one chink in the other man's armor—a pair of vertical worn patches on his belt—and Healey disappeared inside.

Zach tried to quash the self-satisfied smile he could feel coming. Molly wouldn't notice or care that Healey needed a new belt. And Zach shouldn't care whether Molly did.

Back on track in his cover, he headed for the organ manuals in the choir loft. He'd made it through a couple familiar standards when he heard the footsteps echoing up the stairwell. He shifted on the bench to make his gun more accessible, then recognized Molly's step. Had she left Cathal Healey to come see him? That self-satisfied smile tried to make a comeback.

Molly walked into view, no longer wearing the pipe cleaner halo for her costume. And no Healey. "I didn't know you played the organ," she said.

"I'm from one of those obnoxiously musical families—but we all have our hidden talents."

"I suppose you never really know people, sure." Molly leaned against the closest corner of the organ, silent a little too long.

"You okay, Moll?"

She hesitated a beat. "Thinkin' about whether to share . . . those hidden talents."

"A talent show? Awesome—or should I say lethal?" He thought he dropped the Irish slang casually, but Molly still raised an eyebrow. He pressed on. "What's your hidden talent?"

Molly looked down. Dread crept into Zach's chest. Not money laundering.

No, that would be a good thing. He leaned over until his chin almost hit the organ keys to catch her gaze. "Is it some sort of sin?" he asked in a mock-serious tone.

"No. Irish dance."

The muscles in his shoulders released, whether in disappointment or relief, he couldn't say. "That's nothing to be ashamed of."

"I amn't—er, I'm not. I just don't want to be the entertainment at every parish function for the rest of my life."

Zach nodded. "My mom still wants me to sing in church for Christmas."

"An organist and a singer, are we?"

He ran his fingers over a C scale. "I'd rather play. How long have you danced?"

"All my life."

"Should've guessed. You move like a dancer—I mean, uh—" He cut himself off with a self-conscious laugh and looked at the manuals. Flirting was one thing, but he'd blow his cover with more lines like that.

"Tell you what: I'll dance at this talent show of yours if you'll sing." She extended a hand with her offer.

"Okay." He took her hand. Her soft skin felt a little too good against his. Molly withdrew into fist a second before fidgeting with the *leiblich gedeckt* stop.

Zach tried to push past the increasingly awkward silence. "We can start on that after the movie night. Oh, tell me you chose a movie."

"I've even ordered the film."

"Fair play to you," Zach said, again using Irish slang, this time the equivalent of "Good one!"

And this time she didn't let it go. "How long did you say you were in Ireland again?"

"A school year—like eight months."

Molly squinted at him. Could she tell he'd really spent more than double that there? At least she hadn't asked where he'd studied. He'd have to watch it on the mission slang. She started for the stairs. "Oh." She doubled back, holding out a piece of paper. "Almost forgot the reason I came up. The hymn schedule."

He thanked her and turned back to the manuals as Molly walked away. But she returned within seconds. "Before I go, Father, do you know anything about Mormons?"

Zach's hand slipped and he hit dissonant chord. Grateful for his FBI training, he managed to keep his expression only mildly curious. "Why do you ask?"

"A Mormon friend invited me to an activity this weekend, and I just wanted to be sure it wouldn't be anythin' . . . 'different.'"

Molly had found the Church on her own. A priest should discourage this, right? But maybe he could subtly help her investigate. He opted for a sage nod. "Can't imagine it'd be too 'different.' Be sure to invite your friend to our movie night."

"Oh, I will. I should be off now, though—kept Cathal waitin' long enough." Molly smiled and started for the stairs with that graceful spring in her step.

She'd left Healey waiting while she came to see him, even it if was only for three minutes. Zach shook his head, consulted the hymn schedule and pulled the *leiblich gedeckt* stop. He was here for mobsters, not Molly. Besides, if she liked Healey, obviously she wouldn't be interested in Zach Saint. Even if Healey did need a new belt.

He stopped short. He'd seen that wear pattern before—all the time. Was it just out of place at a church, or did Molly have him so distracted he didn't recognize wear from a gun holster?

111

Molly. His heart crawled into his throat. Zach ran downstairs, out of the chapel, and around to the office. She wasn't at her desk. "Where's Molly?" he panted.

Kathleen copped a perfect what's-it-to-you? face. "Mister Healey took her to lunch. Or maybe I should say she took him." She looked nearly triumphant. "She drove."

Zach nodded and fought off the dread filling his gut. Whoever Cathal Healey really was, he didn't work in real estate.

It was really too late for lunch—and Molly had had Tim's barmbrack—but she tried to be polite as Cathal ordered a heavy alfredo dish for her.

How could his parents name him Cathal without even bothering to look up an acceptable pronunciation?

"I really can't imagine what else I could tell you about the neighborhood." She added a note of apology to her voice. How would the badly-lit Italian chain restaurant Cathal had chosen help them discuss the neighborhood twenty minutes away?

He beamed back at her. "I was getting a feel for the area before, talking to people on the ground. Once we narrow it down to two or three possibilities, we go in depth."

"We're one of the top choices?" Molly twisted her napkin in her lap. Did they need more impressionable youth in an area already dominated by the mob?

"Oh, absolutely. But like I said, we really want to go in depth now." He pulled a sheet of yellow legal notepaper from his ridiculous attaché. "Mind if I ask you about a few things?"

"That's what I'm here for."

Cathal read over his notes. "Let's see. . . . You've got just under three hundred students at the school, about a third of them from the neighborhood?"

"That's right."

"What else?" he murmured, tapping his lips with his fingers. "Chicago PD says the area is usually low in petty crime—but they did find a body half a mile away from the site two weeks ago. Did you hear anything about that?"

Molly nearly choked on her water. "He was from our parish." And Doyle Murphy's gang.

"Sorry to hear that. Mugging?"

She shrugged, rubbing at the corner of her napkin. Kathleen heard that Gerald Flynn had been shot in the head, execution style, and still had his expensive watch on. Hardly a typical street crime.

"And a couple months ago, you had another murder in the area. A guy named Patrick?"

Her stomach lurched. "Father Patrick, one of our priests—you know, I did say we might not be the best choice for your youth center."

The waiter delivered two plates of pasta drowning in cream sauce as Cathal laughed away her concern. "Molly, we're in Chicago. We don't expect to find a hundred-percent-crime-free area."

She speared three pieces of penne with her fork.

"But just so you know, a couple other people we talked to seemed to feel very safe in the neighborhood, especially thanks to this one guy. Sounds like a real hero." His paper crinkled when he flipped it over. "Here it is. Doyle Murphy—know him?"

"Not really. But from what I've heard, he's more like a school yard bully." Molly set aside her fork. She wasn't hungry in the first place, only going along with Cathal because he was handsome and charming. And now he was asking all the wrong questions— especially for a real estate developer.

Cathal took a few more minutes of small talk to realize Molly was finished eating. He got her alfredo to go, and she drove them back to the parish. He walked her to the office door. "Give me a call if you think of anything," Cathal said, offering his card along with her Styrofoam container.

Molly held up a hand to refuse both. "I'm more of a marinara kind of girl, thank you."

He slid the card off the box. "Then just take this. You can be our eyes and ears on the ground. For the kids."

She pursed her lips but took the card. He had better not expect her to phone. She already had enough people to protect from the mob.

S UNDAY AFTERNOON, Molly tried not to think of her own chapel—
and those minutes in the choir loft—as she and Lucy stood in
the queue for food in the carpeted gym inside the squat, stone-
façade building. Molly glanced around the room and caught herself
searching for the group of all-too-self-assured, shady parishioners she
was used to seeing. But that was impossible. Mobsters in any church
were an anomaly. Weren't they?

At a tap on her shoulder, Molly turned around to find a curva-
ceous woman in a tailored jacket. She thrust a hand on one ample hip
and looked Molly over as if assessing a rival—or meal. "You must be
new. Hannah Byrd." Her inflection revealed nothing of her appraisal.

"Molly." She looked to Lucy, who was talking to the girl in front
of them.

"Just move in?" Hannah asked.

"No, I'm a friend of Lucy's."

Before Molly could be at least civil, Lucy saved her. "Oh, guess
you met Hannah. Molly, this is my friend Susan." Lucy gestured to
the woman in front of them. They made small talk while they served
themselves and found a seat. Hannah joined them at the round plastic
table a moment later. The clatter of metal doors silenced the room.
Three fellas strode in, one holding two jars of salsa aloft. "Let's get
this party started!"

"Brian," Hannah called. "You owe me a hug."

Brian saluted with a jar. He handed the salsa off, then came over.
As he released Hannah, he ogled Molly from tip to toe, craning his
neck to peer under the table. "Who's this?" he asked.

"Molly." She tucked her legs under her chair, out of his sight.

"New in the ward?" Brian squared his broad shoulders and adjusted his over-gelled, highlighted hair, leaning closer to Molly.

She cocked her head. "The 'ward'?" She turned to Lucy. "I thought you weren't much for charity work. Are you volunteerin' with a mental hospital?"

"He means the congregation." Lucy frowned at Brian. "And it's a branch." She pointed to the food table. "Your friends are eating."

Brian left for the queue, but rather than staying with his friends, he returned with three plates of food and took the vacant chair next to Molly. An awkward silence descended as Brian devoured his tacos.

Hannah pushed away her half-eaten enchiladas. "How's your knee, Brian? He hurt it playing football yesterday," she added for the other women's benefit. Lucy covered her face.

"It's stiff, but I've had way worse." He shrugged and turned to Molly. "You should come cheer for us, too." Brian leaned in and raised his voice, drowning out Susan's attempt to change the subject. "We'd always win if you distracted the other team."

Molly tried to keep her laugh more polite than condescending.

Hannah cleared her throat. "You know she's not a member, right?"

A hunting gleam sparked in his eyes, and Brian angled his shoulders to exclude Hannah. He smiled, though it was closer to a leer. "We can fix that. Learned about eternal marriage yet?"

"No. Lucy only asked me not to judge her church by its nutters." Molly made her return smile cloyingly sweet. His appreciative leer spoke volumes—he really thought she was flirting back.

"So you're Scottish?" he asked.

"Irish," Lucy corrected. "But she'll be an American soon."

"There's easier ways to get a green card." Brian winked at her and stood. "I'm going to get some dessert. Can I get you anything?" He leaned into Molly's personal space, apparently having forgotten his several plates' worth of tacos. "I could bring you some of me lucky charms."

"I'd better visit the ladies' room before the fireside starts." Lucy stood, clearly cutting off his come-ons.

Hoping her relief wasn't evident—all right, she didn't really care—Molly leapt to her feet. "I'll come with you."

In the white tiled bathroom, Lucy hopped up to sit on the beige Formica counter, her feet dangling high above the floor. "Sorry about Brian. He's always that obnoxious, unfortunately."

"Pity he can't see your *wan* is perfect for him."

"My one what?"

"Oh." Molly tried to think of how to explain the Irish loanword. "*Wan*—woman. That girl."

"Who, Hannah?" Lucy threw her head back, her laughter echoing off the walls. "Did I tell you about how I went to a 'party' at her place last month, and it was me and her and eight guys?"

Molly grimaced. "Maybe dealin' with Kathleen isn't so bad."

"I wouldn't go that far."

"I don't know; I think Kathleen's goin' to be changin' after Friday." She launched into the story of Father Tim giving out to Kathleen.

Lucy sighed. "I wish he could solve my problems at work."

Molly forced herself to smile. Lucy couldn't mean Doyle and his crew. "Or Paul could."

"That would be my main problem."

"Don't know if Father Tim can help with that one." But hadn't Father Tim had a meeting with a Paul last week? "Wait, Paul's blond, right? Somber lookin'?"

Lucy half-nodded. "Dark blond. Tall. Hot. Almost always serious. How'd you know?"

"He came by the office for an appointment the other day. Maybe Father Tim *is* solvin' all your work problems."

The door swung open, and Susan leaned in. "We're about to get started—but Brian's still on the prowl, so be careful. He was following me around grilling me about you, Molly. Just so you know, now he thinks you're a big fan of dog-sledding and NASCAR."

They hid their snickers on the way back to the gym, where they joined the other diners filing through accordion-pleated doors to a chapel. This seemed much more church-like, albeit rather plain without stained glass or art.

They settled into an upholstered pew, and Lucy pulled a small spiral notebook from her handbag. "Better write this stuff down. I need all the help I can get when it comes to being weak."

As soon as they were seated, Brian wedged himself into the narrow space between Molly and the armrest. He leaned into her face again, still ignorant of his taco breath. "You disappeared on me."

"Oh, I—"

"I know how girls are. Always have to pee in a pack."

Lucy stifled a groan with both hands. The meeting began with a prayer—no one else crossed themselves. Brian whispered about his Iditarod dreams through the speaker's introduction until finally Hannah whipped around to shush him.

Molly focused her attention on the speaker's tales of adversity and tragedy, which made her struggles seem rather insignificant. But when the speaker moved on to quoting the Lord, something about his words resonated with Molly. She borrowed a piece of paper from Lucy to capture the ideas she'd never heard before: weakness wasn't a sin, as even Christ had human weakness, and He had experienced all sorrows so that He could comfort others.

Her own troubles were nothing compared to His suffering. She tried to remember the reference on the last scripture, but it wasn't familiar. Molly continued to note the speaker's points contrasting the causes and effects of sin and weakness.

Brian peered over to read her notes. Molly tilted the paper away from him, barely able to concentrate on the conclusion of the address, learning to accept and slowly progress from weakness. After the speaker closed, the meeting ended with a prayer.

Glancing over her scribblings, Molly followed Lucy back into the gym, Brian trailing behind them. "What'd you think?" Lucy's voice and her eyebrows rose hopefully.

"Interestin'—some lovely thoughts. You?"

"Yeah, I thought it was great. Very helpful."

Molly read over her notes once more. Twice the speaker had mentioned a common, yet unfamiliar name. "Who is this Joseph Smith? A saint?"

"Joseph Smith was the first prophet of the Church in this dispensation," Brian said.

Lucy had mentioned a prophet before—but a dispensation? A church law exemption?

"That's right," Lucy said. "We don't have saints."

"Other than you."

"All my life. Hold on, let me introduce you to someone." Lucy turned and called for some elders while Hannah cornered Brian. Good riddance.

Two young men—teenagers, it seemed—approached. In a split second, Molly was on her guard. Sure, their dark suits were a bit cliché for mobsters—but these young men stood out from the sea of khakis and pastel Oxford shirts, and they obviously had some special status here. Lucy introduced Elders Ehrisman, a lanky blond, and Franklin, a lean brunet.

Before they spoke further, both young men reached into their suit coats. Molly edged back a step.

And the room was plunged into darkness. Echoing calls to switch on the lights rang through the room along with eerie laughter.

Large hands clamped down on Molly's shoulders from behind. A cold jolt of fear shot straight down her spine. Reverting to long-ago training, she grabbed both of her assailant's wrists. Molly ducked between the arms, pivoted and twisted free. She kicked out in a blind guess at her attacker and connected.

The lights flickered back on a split second before her assailant hit the ground. Molly was too shocked to even gasp. She should have known it was him, though he'd just walked away.

Brian clutched his knee to his chest, squeezed his eyes shut and screamed.

As Zach expected, the drawer and the cash box locks yielded

easily. A hairpin from Molly's desk was close enough to a warded lock pick to do the trick. For once, Molly hadn't gotten in the way. Good thing, too. He'd already lifted Healey's card from the top drawer.

The top tray of the cash box was empty—she made one of her semiweekly deposits Friday night. Zach pulled out the tray to reveal the bank paperwork below.

He just had to see if any information here matched the account number from the mini-safe, 277135847. Zach scanned the visible tabs in the box.

The first account, a checking account—219632754.

The second account, a savings account—388763827.

The third account, a certificate of deposit—589273852.

Molly was in the clear, and Zach could get on with his investigation without involving her further. He shifted the cash box, reaching for the money tray—and saw another tab, hidden beneath the top file. Holding his breath, he lifted the top folder to reveal the tab underneath.

277135847.

Impossible. Zach read the number again, not bothering to suppress a groan. He opened the thin folder and started through the documents. First, the welcome letter, addressed to the church, care of Colin Patrick. Dated two years ago. Next, the sample checks for the account. None used. Then the sheet the ATM card came with, card gone. Zach tilted the heavy paper in the low light to reveal a reverse impression of the card number. He wrote down the card number and flipped to the last page in the folder.

Next he found a copy of the signatory card with a note in Molly's neat handwriting, "Original on file at bank." Two people were authorized to make withdrawals: Colin Patrick and M. M. Malone.

Way more incriminating than her coming by while he was working on a safe.

She couldn't have done this—and he couldn't afford to get any closer to her. Yeah, it might be efficient, but he couldn't toy with her emotions—er, blow his cover by flirting more openly. He had to get back to Lonegan.

MOLLY CLEANED HER FINGERNAILS for the fourth time in twenty minutes, trying to concentrate on anything but that antiseptic smell. Lucy frowned at the man snoring two rows over.

"Nicest hospital I've ever been in," Lucy murmured.

"Only hospital I've ever been in." Even in her few months as an active-duty Garda, she'd never had the "pleasure."

The double doors to the treatment area swung open. Lucy and Molly looked up in unison. A man in a Cubs jersey emerged with a bandaged forehead.

Lucy edged away from the busy aisle. "What's up for you this week?"

"Parish movie night on Saturday. You?"

"Tutoring, practicing. I'm singing in church Sunday. Hey, would you like to come?"

"Sure now. Would you like to come to our movie night?"

"Yeah, that sounds great," Lucy said.

One door pulled open again, held by unseen hands. Molly ignored the rising anticipation. No one appeared. The other door swung open. An orderly held it, blocking her view. She slid to the edge of her chair. They'd taken Brian through those doors over an hour ago. Had she really hurt him that badly?

Lucy rose, her hands clasped in front of her. Molly found herself on her feet, though her stomach felt like she'd left it in the seat.

She saw the crutches first. She'd crippled him.

Brian hobbled in, a hinged black brace strapped over his khakis from mid-thigh to mid-calf. He flashed Molly a wink and turned to the orderly. "That's the one, officer! Arrest her!"

She and Lucy managed nervous laughter as he clomped over to them. "Thanks for the ride, ladies."

"The least we could do," Lucy said.

He shrugged. "Well, yeah."

Molly finally dared to ask. "Is it terribly bad?"

"Looks like an ACL tear." He grimaced. "But it's so swollen they can't tell how bad yet."

Lucy clucked sympathetically. Brian didn't acknowledge her, though she was really the one who'd driven him with GPS guidance. She didn't seem to mind his oversight. "Let's get you home so you can rest up."

"I need a prescription." He gave Molly a slip of paper. "You could get it for me."

Lucy took the paper. "I'm sure your home teachers would love to help you." She led the way out. Molly tried to follow Brian, but he kept falling back to walk with her.

"You know what they say, Molly." He settled into Lucy's front seat. "You break it, you bought it." He winked. She shut his door and found herself massaging her elbow. Stupid nervous habit. What had she bought herself, indeed?

Monday night, Zach rounded the corner in the mobsters' apartment building as a doorknob rattled somewhere down the corridor. He fell back behind the corner, hidden from the door to the Lonegans'. If it was Lonegan's place, no way would Zach tip him off until he had to.

"You'd better come." Doyle Murphy's voice carried down the hall. Zach froze so suddenly his blood could have turned to ice. "They say you're going soft."

Zach puffed out a silent breath, marveling. To wield that kind of power, that he could discuss mob business openly in the halls of his building. So secure, so smug.

So going down.

"Not going soft, Doyle," Lonegan's weary voice answered.

"Better not." Silence. "One more thing. Heard you're getting close to the new priest."

Lonegan said nothing. Not daring to breathe, Zach strained to interpret the pause.

"You just remember, Cal. We've got plans for him. I don't need you screwing things up like the last priest did."

"'Course not, Doyle. Only reeling him in—for you."

Zach's ribs felt like a steel cage too small for his lungs. Was Lonegan's penitence and reluctance all part of an elaborate act to build a relationship with him?

That was fine—no, it was good. The mob was reaching out. He wouldn't have to worry about Lonegan flipping or entering witness protection. But as Zach edged his way back to the elevators, he was less worried about his case than about Cally's soul.

As soon as Zach walked into his room in the parish house, Father Fitzgerald sprang up from behind the bed. Zach jumped back—until he saw the safe-cracking kit in Fitzgerald's hands.

Zach's hackles jumped to full alert. "Why are you going through my things?"

"No, I'm not, I'm just—"

Zach crossed the distance between them and snatched his kit away. The zipper was still closed. He released half of the breath he held. Still highly suspect, even without Fitzgerald's nervous shuffling.

"I'm sorry." Fitzgerald wrung his hands. "I was only gathering up the dry cleaning, and I knocked your clock down, and I was just . . ."

Zach forced his expression to remain the same despite the fear screaming in his veins. Was Fitzgerald about to blow his cover?

Playing his part harder was his only option—for Zach's sanity if nothing else. "Did you open this?"

"No." Fitzgerald bent to pick up the suit pants on the floor. Guilt haunted the older priest's eyes—because he'd found out more than he claimed?

"You're allowed to have a personal life," Fitzgerald continued. "I don't want to invade your privacy. You had me worried with Molly and all, so I thought I . . ."

Zach drew in air, trying to calm down. "Not a big deal."

"I shouldn't have snooped. I just know what it's like to be tempted."

Zach scrutinized the older man for a moment. What was he saying—he'd had some tryst with a parish secretary once?

Whatever the old man's secret, it didn't matter to Zach. Time to smooth things over. "Jesus was tempted in all things, and I expect we will be, too, if we're trying to become like Him."

Fitzgerald pondered that for a moment, staring at the worn rug. "Better take that dry cleaning." He disappeared into his room and returned with an armload of dark suits. With a final nod, he left.

Once the door closed, Zach could finally get the oxygen he needed. Was Fitzgerald on to him, or was he just worried?

All along they'd said it was better if Fitzgerald didn't know, in case he was involved with the mob. Could that be his struggle with temptation—or why he'd gone into Zach's things? Zach turned to the mail basket, riffling through the envelopes to find the most recent cell phone bill in Fitzgerald's name. The call records showed no numbers in the mobsters' names.

Well, two could do laundry. Zach was three steps to Fitzgerald's bedroom when he realized there wouldn't be any pants pockets to search—and what was he hunting for, anyway?

Shaking his head, Zach returned to the cell phone bill. He wrote down all the phone numbers. Time to look closer at Fitzgerald.

Molly finished reading through the page on the county website for the fourth time and pushed the keyboard away Wednesday afternoon. She'd wasted her entire break from Kathleen searching for her condo's property records. If Cally was right, and Doyle owned their building, she had to get out once and for all.

But the county was trapped in the mid-Bronze Age. The best she could get from here was the property PIN. For the rest of the record, she'd have to take off work and go to City Hall.

Lucy walked into the office. "Hey, Molly. Father Tim isn't around, is he?"

"Afraid not."

Lucy glanced around the office. Kathleen's desk was empty. "That's okay." She lowered her voice. "Paul wants to talk to me about something. Don't know if I'm ready for this, so I said I had to see if Father Tim was in."

"Sorry, I haven't seen him at all this week. Wouldn't want to keep you from Paul anyway." Molly finally acknowledged the guilt tugging her heart. "Any word about Brian?"

"He posted online that he's waiting for an Irish angel to come nurse him."

"Do you think he's meanin' Hannah by any chance?"

"She's probably doing her family history now. Oh, I brought you something." She pulled a black book with gold lettering, half the thickness of a Bible, from her handbag. "If you didn't recognize a few of the verses on Sunday, it's because we actually have some additional scriptures. In case you wanted to read them again."

"Oh, thank you." Molly accepted the book and read the cover: Book of Mormon, Doctrine and Covenants, Pearl of Great Price.

"I marked some of the verses for you already, so they shouldn't be too hard to find. Maybe you can read a few and pray for me." Lucy tugged on her ponytail, looking back at the door.

Molly set the book on her desk. "I'd better pray for you first, hadn't I?" She stood, ostensibly to show Lucy out—but mostly to see if she recognized the man waiting in the sunny car park. "Yes, that's the Paul that talked to Father Tim. Oh, do you want me to try to get you on his schedule?"

"Sure, that'd be great."

"I'll see what I can do. It probably won't be till next week. Too busy gettin' ready for the movie night."

"Good luck with that. I'm looking forward to it, actually."

"Grand." Molly smiled. "Good luck with Paul."

"Thanks." She twirled one blond lock around her finger, her eyes on the car park.

Molly patted Lucy's arm. "See you Saturday." Molly closed the door behind Lucy and returned to her desk. She reread the cover to the triple combination before thumbing through the pages. With a sigh, she slipped Lucy's book into her desk drawer next to the barmbrack ring. All she really knew about the Mormon church was that it had its share of nutters, too.

But they had more than nutters in this parish.

Molly's gaze settled on the file cabinet Father Tim had asked about. Father Patrick's filing cabinet. Not for the first time, she pushed away the idea. The criminal element in the parish, involved in Father Patrick's murder?

Though he had that separate account—for money sent to the parish for the school, he'd claimed. He'd never let her see the bank statements, and never asked about donations coming into the office. She handled the other accounts; why lock those away?

Growing suspicion settled uneasily at the base of her neck. She had the account documentation. Maybe she could access statements online. Just to be sure.

Molly opened her desk drawer and pulled out the cash box. She moved the money tray for the stack of folders. She flipped open the second file, but something wasn't right—Father Patrick's account was in his name, and this information was addressed to Father Fitzgerald.

She closed the folder and scanned all the tabs. Father Patrick's account was on top. Out of order. A cold prickle ran down her neck. She always put these back in order.

Had someone else been in here? Molly rubbed at the gooseflesh at the nape of her neck.

The phone rang—the Lonegans again. Third time today. She sent the call to voice mail. Cally was part of that outfit, and he and Father

Tim were getting far too close for her comfort.

Molly glanced back at the filing cabinet just before Kathleen walked in. Could all these be pieces to the same puzzle?

She could find out.

Zach peered around the underpass late Wednesday. Could Sellars have picked a creepier place? It was night; did they really need to meet somewhere even darker?

Then again, he *had* let it sound urgent when he asked for this meeting. Zach approached the man standing underneath the overpass, discernible mostly by the dull glow of an ember between his fingers. Once Zach was a few steps closer, Sellars flicked away his cigarette and held out his hand—wearing half-shredded fingerless gloves. Zach gave him the folder of photocopied bank statements.

The ASAC used his cell phone backlight to read the contents of the folder, illuminating him like he was telling ghoulish stories around a campfire. Now Zach could finally appreciate the ASAC's disguise: five o'clock shadow, threadbare knit cap, stained coats and layers. At least he blended in under the bridge.

Sellars wasn't as impressed with Zach's work. "A month in, and this is all you've got? These withdrawals look like a typical bank account—there's no pattern here, no schedule. He's an ATM to these people."

"But they match up to the datebook. And there is one pattern." Zach tilted the folder and pointed to the line for the check written on March 13. "Some time between the tenth and the fifteenth every month, there's a check for $450."

Sellars turned to the copies of the month's checks and squinted at the page. "Made out to cash. What does the memo say?"

Zach shrugged. He'd puzzled over the scrawl on each check without success. But he didn't need to detail his failures.

Sellars pulled a paper from his pocket. "A couple of your priest's calls are to our guys' landlines, but mostly clean. How's your guilty new friend?"

Zach stared at a cement piling. "Heard him tell Murphy he's reeling me in."

Sellars nodded. "Good. And your girlfriend?"

He rolled his eyes. At least he hadn't brought up Healey. Until Zach got a bead on the guy, he wasn't about to discuss what might be a distraction.

"Keep working Molly," Sellars said. "You never know with these people."

He pursed his lips. As much as Zach hated to admit it, Sellars was right.

A S SOON AS KATHLEEN LEFT for her meeting with the school
Thursday afternoon, Molly locked the office door. Time to
find out what Father Patrick had been hiding.

Blessing her da for teaching her this skill, she fished her lock
picks from her handbag. She twisted the torsion wrench and began
tapping each pin gently. On her second pass through, the cylinder
rotated, and the lock popped out. After testing the top drawer—
success—she returned her picks to her bag.

The ringing phone startled her halfway back to the cabinet. She
glanced at the open file cabinet drawer, the doorknob, the phone.
Murphy blinked on the caller ID.

The ringleader of the whole crew, the one who'd had his greasy
grasp slowly closing around Father Tim since he'd arrived, calling as
soon as she touched the cabinet. A coincidence?

She couldn't let him think anything was amiss at the church—
who knew? He might take that as a cue to close his snare. If he
wasn't already. Her chest taut, Molly focused on breathing the
suddenly-stuffy air for a moment before she lifted the receiver.
"Hello?"

"Doyle Murphy here. I want an appointment with Father Tim."

She forced a light tone. "I'm sorry, but he's terribly busy."

"Oh, he'll make time for me." The menace in his voice drew a
shiver through her spine. He hung up before she responded. Molly
replaced the receiver and turned back to the filing cabinet. Doyle
Murphy wanted to see Father Tim. The criminal wanted Father
Patrick's replacement. All the times Father Patrick had avoided her
questions played in her mind. She knew he'd kept something from

her, but could he have been in trouble?

She yanked open the top drawer to find—a contract? She didn't recognize the supplier. Kincaid Wholesalers? Providing goods and/or services? Molly frowned. The second drawer held pages from a date-book, filled with familiar names. Parishioners. Her neighbors. From the dollar amounts indicated, somehow she didn't think Father Patrick's notes of "Murphy doubled pymt" or "Gallaher took $" were for the annual spaghetti dinner.

Wait—hadn't Kathleen once said Kincaid supplied the school's lunches? But the amounts listed here were outrageous.

It was all related. It had to be. Could Father Patrick's death be any random robbery, or was it someone searching for this? And now they were after Father Tim.

She had to do something. She placed each page of evidence onto the copier next to the file cabinet in turn. After replacing the originals in the drawer, she stooped to fetch a manila envelope from under Kathleen's desk. Before Molly could stand, the jangle of the doorknob stopped her short.

She froze to the spot. It had to be Kathleen, and she'd use her key, and then Molly could laugh at the fear slithering around her stomach.

But no key slid into the lock.

The snake of fear wrapped tighter. She looked at the tray where all the evidence lay. Something flickered past the window by the photocopier, a shadow against the half-shut curtains.

The shadow grew smaller, drawing closer. The silhouette of a man's head. Doyle Murphy? He was tall enough to reach the high window.

She was below the line of sight from the window, she told herself. He couldn't see her.

Molly was next. First Father Patrick, now her. The shadow slipped away. The python of fear slithered up to squeeze her lungs.

No. She would not succumb to these common criminals, nor to the maddening panic threatening to close in on her. She was a Garda, even without her badge or handcuffs or baton—though now she wished she had a weapon.

Any short stick would do, but where—Kathleen's miniature bat.

Molly slid the photocopied datebook into the envelope, and the envelope into Kathleen's desk. Keeping well away from sight of the window, she grabbed the Louisville Slugger souvenir off Kathleen's desk.

Molly prepped the battleground—shed her high heels, hit the lights to give her the advantage, unlocked the door and positioned herself behind it. She steeled herself to wait. If they wanted something here, they'd have to fight for it. She might not be able to win this fight, but before they got to her, she'd give them a beating they wouldn't believe.

Zach rounded the corner of the building and checked the parking lot. Yep, Molly's green Volkswagen still stood in the unseasonably warm November rain. The office lights were on when he peeked through the window, but the office was locked in the middle of the afternoon. Had she left with Healey-the-wannabe-gunslinger again? His mouth went dry.

He was supposed to be cracking her. What if she *was* involved?

Before he could answer his own question, Zach reached the office door again—and now it was unlocked. He pushed the door open a crack. The column of light fell across Molly's empty desk. The office lights were off? Had he imagined the scene through the window? "Moll?" Zach called gently. He stepped into the office and switched on the lights. He slowly scanned the room, and found her at last—behind the door, stick in hand, poised to strike.

Molly seemed to brace herself, her stance unwavering. He automatically tensed into a defensive posture, shock reverberating through him. "Holy cow, woman! What did I do?"

Molly blinked twice, and relaxed. "Father—were you the one just peerin' through the window?"

He nodded, his brow still furrowed. "I thought it was weird the office was locked. Is that why you're coming after me with a stick?"

"Hm? Oh, that's not for you." She tossed the stick—Kathleen's miniature bat—onto the empty desk with a nervous, forced laugh.

"Then who was it for?"

Molly brushed past him with an air of false cheer, until she had to stop and circle back for her shoes.

This time he didn't let her pass, moving to block her path back to her desk. "What's going on?"

"Nothing." She didn't look at him.

"Come on," he said, taking her by the shoulders. "You can tell me."

She shook her head, staring at his shirt buttons. Or his collar. Zach tilted her chin up so she had to meet his gaze—and then he saw it, the brave front in her blue eyes.

She was terrified. "Molly," he said her name yet again, still trying to reassure her, "if you don't tell me, I can't help you."

"You can't help me at all."

He leaned a few inches closer, lowering his voice. "Tell me. Let me help you."

She pulled away. "Thank you, Father, but I'll handle this on my own." She pushed past.

"Please." He'd wanted to sound insistent, but the word came as a plea even to his ears.

Molly stopped short, her back still to him. "There are things goin' on in our parish that . . . shouldn't be. That's all you need to know."

"That's all I need to know? Are you joking? If there's something bad happening in the parish, I should be the first to know. Or maybe second."

She didn't move and she didn't respond.

"What kind of things?" he asked in a low voice.

"No, I—I can't tell you."

She did know. He tried to ignore a splinter of guilt. How long ago should he have seen this? "Why not?"

"I didn't want you to know about them." Molly glanced around the room suspiciously, then finally turned to face him. "I'm not sure we should even be talkin' now."

"What are we talking about here—SMERSH or the Spangled Mob?" Despite the half-joking Bond reference, Zach knew his expression must've shown how serious he was.

She stared at him for a long moment, silently imploring him. Did she want to tell him or keep it a secret?

He watched her another second, until he saw the fear fighting behind her eyes. This was his chance. He'd protect her and he could tell her the truth.

What? What was he supposed to say? *I'm not the person you've come to know and trust over the last month; I'm an FBI agent—wanna see my badge?* Yeah, that'd go over well. He had to keep up his cover for her own good, if nothing else.

"It's the Spangled Mob, isn't it?" he tried.

Her chin lifted in slow motion, then she nodded.

His chest tightened. She knew—but was she involved?

Wasn't the answer obvious? "Why are you guarding us with a club all of a sudden?"

Molly clasped her hands. "I had to go in the cash box for some bank records and someone had been in there, and suddenly it all made sense."

"What did?"

"Certain parishioners takin' a sudden interest in the office. Ringin' over and over."

Zach squinted to play dumb. "Why would they be calling about the petty cash?"

"That's not it—can't you see? It's so much bigger than that." She retrieved the cash box, which did not perform its usual flipping act. Molly set the tray for the money on her desk and picked up the file folders from the bottom of the cash box. "I keep these in here *in order.*"

He glanced at the tabs. In his rush to put them away, he'd put them back out of order. Molly was freaking out over his stupid, stupid mistake. "Are you *sure* you put them back in order?" he asked.

"Of course, I always do."

Zach wracked his brain for an explanation. "When did you have them out last? Friday?"

"I don't know."

"When I was giving out to Kathleen?" This was one time it was okay to use Irish, to set her at ease, remind her who she was talking to—she could trust him. Even though he was a liar.

Molly considered it a moment. "I suppose so."

"So maybe you were distracted putting them back?"

She took a deep breath and released it in a shuddery sigh, sinking into her desk chair. With a weak smile, Molly took the folders back and put them away. "Well, I feel foolish."

This was his chance to see how involved she was. He dropped to his knees by her chair. "Why do you think there's a mob in our congregation after our bank records?"

"I . . ." Molly bowed her head. "Father, forgive me."

He ignored the sinking in his heart. Another confession—but how serious was her sin?

"I went through the filin' cabinet over there." She gestured toward Patrick's cabinet.

"You did?" It took little effort to appear appropriately shocked. "When? How?" And did she know the safe was missing?

"Well, after you asked a few weeks ago, I got to thinkin'. It *was* Father Patrick's cabinet, and he had that separate account, and he always gave me everythin' else, so why keep it locked?"

"How'd you get in?"

Molly pulled a set of lock picks from her purse. Zach drew back in a mix of surprise and admiration. Was it legal for a civilian to carry those around in Illinois? "Where'd you learn to do that?"

"My father was a locksmith for a while. I haven't done anythin' illegal, unless—oh, is it illegal to go in his cabinet?"

"Nah, parish property." He grabbed her chair arm, pretending to be eager. "What's in it?"

"Records." Her expression grew pensive. "Don't know what they have to do with the account."

Zach put on a frown. "Can we start at the beginning here? What's this other account?"

"A few years ago, Father Patrick said we should open another account to handle money comin' into the parish for the school. Their finances are mostly separate, now, but a lot of our donations are marked for the school. I opened the account for him, but he said he'd handle everythin' else. I never saw the bank statements and he didn't ask about the donations. I figured he'd forgotten about it."

He had to test her. Zach rotated her chair toward him. "You saw statements from the account in the filing cabinet?" Impossible, unless she put them in the safe in the first place.

"Contracts and a datebook." Molly paused, thinking. "But why would they target Father Patrick?"

"Who?"

"The people in the datebook—they're in this . . . outfit. Now, I don't know for certain, but—" She glanced at Kathleen's empty desk. "Rumor has it right after we opened this account, this outfit started supplyin' the school's lunches. But, Father, the amounts listed on that datebook—it's more than twice what the food would be worth retail. I used to handle those books; I know."

Ridiculous markup on goods run through a legitimate organization—gouging, bribes and kickbacks, sounded like. Almost everything they needed for a RICO case, if they could corroborate it.

Zach gave a low whistle. "Are you sure about all this?"

Molly lowered her gaze. "I am."

"How long have you known?"

"I only opened the filin' cabinet a bit ago," she said, gaining speed with each syllable. "After Cally Lonegan's been ringin' so much this week, I started thinkin' and then I saw the files mixed up, and I just knew they'd been in here—"

"Wait, wait, wait," he interrupted, hoping to stave off her resurging paranoia. "Cally Lonegan's been calling?"

"Yes, but—I'm tied up in all this."

He gripped her chair tighter, held his breath involuntarily and waited for her to continue.

"My name is on that account, only my name and Father Patrick's. If they want that arrangement of theirs to keep workin', they'll have to come after me for it—"

"Molly," he said, his tone firm. "I won't let them. Add me to the account and we'll take care of this. We'll end it."

The steel returned to her voice. "You don't know these people. You can't."

"Don't worry about it. Just add me." He checked the clock. Almost four. "Here, why don't you go on home? Obviously you've had a stressful day and you're probably no good to us here." He gave her a small encouraging smile.

"I can't leave. What if someone needs somethin'?"

"You'd beat them with a stick?" He patted her shoulder. "You're not in any shape to worry about helping other people. Or to stay here."

"I suppose you're right." The fear had finally begun to dissipate from her gaze when suddenly it came flooding back. "But I can't go home—they're in my buildin', now."

"Then I will go with you." Zach stood and helped her to her feet, before Molly could formulate a counterargument.

She shook her head and looked into his eyes. "You're just gettin' yourself involved."

"I don't care." Unfortunately, that was the truth—and he *should* care, since this account might be his ticket in with the less penitent mobsters. But all he was really thinking about was Molly. Zach slipped his arm around her shoulders. "Come on, let's get you home."

MOLLY PULLED ON HER JEANS and T-shirt. Father Tim had insisted she take a shower—to help her calm down, he said. And it'd helped until she got out and realized he was still there. The memory of the comfortable weight of his arms set her stomach trembling.

No, this was perfectly normal. She'd had priests to dinner before. And if he left, she'd be alone in her building with the mobsters. The mobsters she was already in the process of turning in. If they had any idea . . . Terror flickered at the back of her mind.

Father Tim could stay. They were friends. Only friends. If Father Tim could believe that, so could she.

When Molly finally ventured into the living room, toweling her hair with an old T-shirt, she found Father Tim lounging on her slate gray sectional, watching television. The delicious aroma of onions, parsley and bacon filled the air.

"You made dinner?" she asked.

"Just some white coddle. He craned his neck toward the kitchen. "Won't be ready for another ten minutes."

He'd made her an Irish stew. She couldn't ask him to leave without eating his own meal. "Anythin' good on?"

"*The Man Who Knew Too Much.*"

Molly checked the TV, though a spy movie wouldn't help her get over her scare. "Peter Lorre or James Stewart?"

"Jimmy Stewart." He finally met her eyes. His faint smile faded, leaving behind a look that was almost—Tim turned back to the television. Molly ducked back into the bathroom to rake her leave-in conditioner and curl cream concoction through her hair.

"You know," Tim began when she returned, "Peter Lorre had to learn his lines phonetically because he didn't speak English well enough for the first version of this movie?"

"You know Jimmy Stewart doesn't wipe the dark makeup off Bernard's face, he wipes on white makeup?"

"No." He looked back at her and pointed at the photographs on the green accent wall behind him. "I like your pictures. Ireland?"

Molly nodded. "Thank you. My sister took them." She glanced at the trio of large photos hung in wide white mats: skeletal trees and an ephemeral sunset reflected in a lake, the arch of a stone bridge climbing out of thin fog, frost-tipped greenery surrounding the arched doorway of an ancient castle.

"I thought Castleknock Castle was in ruins," Tim said.

"It is. That's the Blackcastle in County Tipperary."

"Family vacation?"

"Bridie was visitin' me at Garda College."

Tim gave her a look of *you're codding me.* "You were . . ."

"A Garda."

A smile tugged at the corners of his mouth. "I thought there weren't any female Guards."

"Maybe you were in Ireland a while ago; a quarter of Gardaí are women now."

Amusement still lurked behind his knowing eyes. "I just can't picture you as one of them." The movie went to commercial, and he grabbed the remote to mute the television.

"Here, so." She sat on the couch next to him and pulled a photo album from the bottom shelf of the coffee table. Tim leaned closer as she flipped it open near the middle and turned a few pages. "Graduation from Garda College." She offered him the picture of her in full uniform and watched his eyes for his reaction.

"Wow," he murmured, his mirth plain.

"What do you find so amusin' about this?"

"Nothing. But now I understand why you were coming after me with a stick."

She folded her arms. "You're lucky you called my name first. I could've really hurt you."

"I believe it." Tim tapped his fingers on the photo of her graduation. "What made you join?"

Molly hesitated. How many times had someone said her secret ambition was stupid or unobtainable? But if anyone would understand, it'd be Tim. "Eventually, I wanted to be in the NSU." At his mystified squint, she added, "They're covert Irish intelligence."

Before she could anticipate his reaction, his face lit up. "You were really doing it—not just reading and watching movies." He indicated the television. "You were really going to be a spy."

"Now," she demurred, ignoring a gratified flush, "who's to say?"

"I dunno, Moll. Today I've learned you've picked locks, analyzed documents and arrested criminals. I'm surprised the NSU didn't grab you when they had the chance."

Molly tried to downplay the blush she could feel blooming on her cheeks. "They never had much of an opportunity. We emigrated a few months after I graduated from Garda College."

"Why'd you leave?"

"My family was comin' to the States, and I didn't want to be away from them until my paperwork went through again." The full story of an IRA splinter group trying to recruit her parents was far more complicated, but it didn't make a difference now. Soon enough, she'd have her citizenship and apply to the FBI. "And why didn't you join up? Live the dream, *mar dhea.*"

Tim laughed. "I *am* living the dream—I've never wanted to do anything else."

"That's admirable." She realized she was rubbing the gray fabric of the couch and folded her hands into her lap.

He shrugged. "It chose me."

The word neither of them dared to say, that unnamed vocation, echoed in the silence. Was he thinking his profession was keeping them apart, too?

Apparently not: he shifted to prop his arm up on the back of the couch, comfortable as could be. "Remind me why you're a parish secretary these days?"

"Because Chicago PD is only interested in hirin' American citizens."

Tim glanced at the television. The commercial break had ended long ago. His gaze flicked to the remote, but he turned back to Molly. "You're going to let that stop you?" he asked.

"Actually, I amn't. I have my citizenship test tomorrow afternoon."

"You're becoming a citizen?" He leaned forward.

Molly nodded modestly. "I hope so, anyway. I wanted one last chance to get ready."

"Need any help studying?" Tim smiled—a friendly smile. Maybe this was all right.

"Sure now." She moved closer to take the photo album back.

"What's that scent?" he asked.

She slid the album under the coffee table. "What, are you burnin' the coddle?"

"No." His face grew thoughtful. "It's . . . you smell like home. I mean," he rushed to add, "this plant—flower in my parents' backyard."

Molly tucked a curl behind her ear. "Could be somethin' I use in my hair. I think the bottle says it's wisteria."

"Wisteria. That's it." He smiled at her again—and really looked into her eyes. In that sublime second, he was only Tim O'Rourke, the man with understanding blue eyes. The man comforting her and cooking her dinner. The man she loved.

Her heart slid into her stomach. She turned away. "Is dinner ready?" she murmured.

"Probably." Tim—Father Tim stood and walked into the kitchen. "Go get your study guide," he called back, "and I'll dish us up some coddle."

She hurried to retrieve the list of possible citizenship questions. And though she knew it was hardly wise for him to stay longer, Molly didn't dare say it.

Apparently she hadn't learned nearly enough from the speaker at Lucy's church. She was still weak, so very weak.

Zach slowed in Molly's hallway and glanced back at her door, the stress finally easing from his shoulders. She was innocent. He could've kissed her once he was sure.

But he'd been careful to keep his distance. They'd eaten the coddle and watched *The Man Who Knew Too Much*, then moved on to ice cream and citizenship questions.

He started away from her door. Molly would ace that test tomorrow. And as a US citizen, she could apply for the Bureau. With her qualifications, she had a better shot than he'd had. Was there some chance they'd meet up at work? That was probably the only way he could tell her the truth without losing his job.

He tried to quash the flash of hope in his heart. Molly didn't mention the FBI, and the Bureau wasn't exactly recruiting the children of former terrorists—wait, would the Guards have wanted her as the daughter of IRA activists?

Not that it mattered. He was only supposed to be flirting with her for his job.

Zach stopped at Cally Lonegan's apartment door. No wonder she'd freaked out at the prospect of returning home to half of Murphy's pack.

It was too late for a social call, but if Lonegan had been trying to reach him all week, he'd be okay with finding his new favorite priest on his doorstep.

Zach knocked at the Lonegans' door, and Lisa answered. "Father Tim. Come on in."

"Thanks, Lisa." As he entered, he realized he hadn't heard his title once at Molly's.

Lonegan slumped at the end of the couch, his oldest son sprawled over the rest of it, both engrossed in a crime drama. They didn't get enough of that in their real lives?

The show went to commercial just as Lisa shook her husband's shoulder. He grunted. "Father Tim." Lonegan rose and kicked his son's legs to edge his way past.

He settled at the kitchen table, his shoulders still slumped. Either he was angling for an Academy award, or the man was feeling the weight of discouragement. Zach pushed aside his own disappointment. It didn't matter whether Lonegan wanted to repent or not. This wasn't that kind of mission—but that meant Lonegan still wasn't ready to think about the FBI, either.

"Cally," Zach began after a long silence. "I take it this isn't good news."

Lonegan pursed his lips. "Don't see what good it does. I mean, there's Jesus and all . . ."

Zach shot him a sarcastic look. "Jesus and all?"

"Well, what would He do with a guy like me? Who done what I done?"

Zach saw his opening and offered a quick prayer this was in line with Catholic doctrine. "Who are we to put limits on the Lord's grace?"

"That's not what I mean. But if I can't change—"

"Christ didn't suffer and die to only cover our sins. He'll help us overcome them, too."

"But what if I can't hold up my end? What if I can't be any better than I am?"

Zach patted Lonegan's shoulder. "When it comes down to it, without Him, none of us can be much better than we are."

"But how?" Lonegan murmured, staring at the scratched linoleum floor. "How?"

Zach gave him a sorry smile. "Lord, how is it done?" Enos. This would be easier using the Book of Mormon, but he'd spent enough time in the New Testament lately. "Got a Bible handy?"

Lonegan pulled himself to his feet and left the kitchen. He returned to cast a dusty but well-used Bible on the table.

"The Sermon on the Mount." Zach flipped to Matthew five. "Read the last verse."

"'Be you therefore perfect, as also your heavenly Father is perfect.'" He shrugged. "You think I never heard that before?"

"Of course you have. But this time we're going to really learn it. Now, do you think God would tell us to do something impossible?"

"I don't know. . . . I guess not. I just don't see how it's possible."

Zach turned to the last chapter of Philippians and read, "'I can do all these things in him who strengtheneth me.'" He lowered the Bible. "Ten guesses who the 'him' here refers to."

"Jesus," Lonegan said in an I'm-not-an-*idiot* tone.

"And this is Paul writing, a guy who tried to destroy God's church. If Christ was willing to strengthen him, don't you think Christ can help you change your life?"

"Father, I been Catholic all my life. I believe in the Bible and Jesus, but—"

"It's time to not only believe *in* Jesus Christ but believe what He said. I could sit here all night and tell you, but that won't help you. I need you to do something for me, Cal."

Lonegan scrutinized the splashy floral pattern on the vinyl table-cloth. "I guess."

Zach half-expected his next words to be a challenge to commit to baptism. Luckily, his mouth was more loyal to his cover than his brain. "Study what the Lord says to penitent sinners. And you'll need to pray and ask God why He'd help you."

"I don't know, Father. Why would He?"

"Then ask *if* He'll help you." After a long silence, Zach tried again. "Can you do that?"

Lonegan pulled the Bible in front of him, thumbing the gilt lining. Finally, he nodded.

"I promise, if you seek Him and truly want to change your heart, He'll do the rest." Why did he always end up sounding like a missionary in these discussions? "It'll take time, and a lot of effort, but with His help, it'll come. If you're ready to change your life, He can make it happen."

Lonegan stared at the Bible for a long minute. Hope filled Zach's chest with each passing second, until he hardly had room to breathe. And then Lonegan closed the Bible and pushed it away. The set to his jaw made him seem supremely unconvinced by Zach's arguments. Zach took a deep breath and a mental step back from his frustration. Lonegan drawing him in for the mob would be a *good* thing—that much faster he could wrap this investigation up.

Just in case, Zach outlined a scripture study program, but he could only hedge his bets here for so long. If pretending he needed spiritual guidance was Lonegan's plan to reel Zach in, the man was a great fisherman.

Friday night, Zach finished his report to Sellars on Molly's innocence Friday night. Sellars adjusted his grubby coat, staring out at the drizzle falling beyond the bridge that sheltered them from the rain. "How does she know about Kincaid?" He shifted to look at Zach.

"Didn't say. The other woman in the office gossips constantly."

Sellars cast his eyes around, making the same subtle check of the underpass every ninety seconds. Nothing had changed—two real homeless men huddled around a flickering coffee can thirty feet behind Zach. Aside from the traffic overhead to mask their conversation, they were alone. The ASAC flicked the ash off his cigarette. "How does she know?"

Zach shrugged, hands on his backpack straps. "Everybody else's business is her business. Besides, you know how these things go—everyone 'knows,' even if no one *knows*."

Sellars acknowledged the point. "Accounting got back to us. Those checks that made the pattern? They're the only ones not in the appointment book."

"Any luck deciphering the memo?"

Sellars shook his head and scanned the area again, drawing on his cigarette.

Zach puffed out a cloud of condensation that made it seem like he was smoking, too. If the motive wasn't what they'd thought, where did that leave their case?

"I think they're his kickback," Sellars continued. "The last check is in July; he was killed two months later. Still can't figure out where the funds for the account were coming from."

"By the way, I like how you told me Molly's parents were suspected IRA, but not that she was on the Irish police force." Zach glanced back at the homeless men.

The men still ignored them, but Sellars lowered his voice all the same as he changed the subject. "How'd they get Patrick in this, anyway?"

"No idea. Can't figure out Lonegan's end game, and I don't see why Patrick would go along."

"If he was forced and didn't take the kickbacks, why'd it take two years to come to us?"

Zach mulled that over. "Maybe he hoped they'd come around."

"The moron." The ASAC scoffed, and made another check.

"I don't think it was stupidity; I think it was faith."

Sellars snorted in derision. "Your cover's going to your head, Saint."

Like he needed to be reminded. Or maybe he did.

"And even if you're right," Sellars said, "stupid to draw enough attention to yourself to tip somebody off."

And Zach only had four more weeks to find that somebody. He couldn't give up on Lonegan yet, either—and he still wanted to check out Healey. He couldn't abandon Molly to a gun-toting "developer."

Sellars said nothing further. Zach took the dismissal and pivoted to go. Hoping Sellars wasn't watching, he approached the homeless men and pulled two wool blankets from his backpack. He stooped to wrap a blanket over each man and hand them gift certificates to McDonald's.

"You're a saint, Father," one of the men called after him.

"From the day I was born," Zach muttered. He waved without looking back.

He really was letting his cover go to his head.

17

ZACH HAD JUST OPENED the parish house door Saturday after-noon when he spotted Cathal Healey crossing the parking lot. Zach hung back in the shadows until Healey opened the door to the school. The guy might be able to justify attending the movie night, but arriving an hour early was pretty suspicious.

Zach scanned the lot. He grabbed a pen and scrawled the plate number of an unfamiliar blue Chevy on his palm. Molly's green Volkswagen was parked in its usual stall—which meant she was somewhere in the school, probably about to be cornered by Healey.

As Zach slipped in the same door Healey had used, he saw a flicker of movement down the hall. The sound of a metal door latching echoed down the corridor.

He edged along the cinderblock wall until he reached the cafe-teria doors. He peered through the narrow rectangular window. No movement in the half-dark. Careful to keep the latch quiet, Zach slowly opened the door, slid into the room, and shut the door behind him. He scanned the room one more time, but saw only the rows of metal chairs volunteers had set up that morning.

He turned to leave—and then he saw another door to his right. Seizing the element of surprise, Zach yanked the door open. He expected a tiny broom closet; instead, he found a staircase.

What was Healey hunting for, and what did he know that Zach didn't? Zach climbed the stairs, keeping his weight on the edges of the treads to minimize any squeaks. The top of the stairs wrapped around the corner only to dead-end into another door. He steeled himself once again, though this time he opened the door gradually to creep in unnoticed. A slow swirl of dust swept through the doorway.

This time, he wasn't alone. On the other side of the room, Molly leaned between what looked like two round tabletops, one about three feet above the other. She was already threading the projector.

A warning sounded at the back of his mind. If Healey wasn't here for Molly, Zach would be smart to leave now instead of staying here. With her. Alone. Zach reached for the door handle. If he could slip out before she noticed—

And then he sneezed.

Molly gasped. "Oh, Father, you frightened me."

He smiled sheepishly. "Sorry about that. Everything okay?"

"Only settin' up."

He should go. But he couldn't walk out like that. "Your test go well yesterday?"

She held the film to the light. "It did. I'll be takin' the oath in a few weeks."

"Never doubted you for a moment." The tension in Zach's chest released at Molly's friendly tone. It wouldn't hurt to talk to her, and if she was Healey's target, the best option was to stay put. He came to watch over her shoulder. "How *do* you know how to run a projector?"

"Worked as a projectionist when I was in secondary school—I mean, um, high school."

"I knew what you meant." Zach leaned in to examine the reel. "What are we watching?"

Molly angled her shoulders to keep the film out of his sight. "You'll see soon enough." She looped it over one hand and approached the machine that was nearly as tall as she was.

"Why does the school have one of these?"

"No idea." She ran the film through the projector itself with her free hand. "I think it's been here longer than Father Fitzgerald."

"Since the dawn of time? Oh, hey, is your Mormon friend coming tonight?" Zach winced mentally at his less-than-subtle segue.

"Should be." Molly bent to thread the film through another part of the projector, her dark hair falling into her face. She shook her head twice, but her hair refused to move out of her way.

Zach parted the curtain of her curls with both hands. She quickly finished working the film through the contraption and stood—and turned toward Zach. His fingers framed her face, and they froze there.

His pulse spiked. He stared into her deep blue eyes and twined his fingers into her thick curls. They'd never been this close. Close enough to . . .

This was right. He tilted her chin up toward him. Without even trying, he closed the distance between them. In the last split-second before their lips met, the corners of her mouth gave the tiniest hint of a flinch. He made that last check for consent.

Her eyes were filled with fear. A bolt rocketed through him, landing in his stomach with a cold shock. She might as well have slapped him in the face. Zach drew back.

This was wrong. How could either of them forget for a second? Flirting with her to get to know her better—for the case—was one thing. This was another entirely.

He didn't dare meet her eyes again as he untangled his fingers from her hair. Molly knelt the second he released her, like his hands had been the only thing keeping her on her feet. She gathered the loops of film that had fallen to the ground and Zach stepped back to put some distance between them.

But he was still close enough to see her white knuckles around the film. "I am so sorry," he said softly. Her back to him, Molly nodded. Before Zach could turn away, his cell rang. He pulled it out—Father Fitzgerald was calling. He groaned inwardly. Did everyone in this parish have to have this sense of timing? "Yeah, Bruce?"

"Tim, I'm going to be late to your little thing tonight."

"Oh." He glanced back at Molly rising to her feet. "What's up?"

"I'm taking Tina Sheehan to the hospital."

Zach didn't recognize the name. "Anything I can do?"

Fitzgerald sighed. "No, it's routine—we check her into the psych ward every few months. Better to get her in now before she does something."

"Okay."

"But you enjoy yourself." Fitzgerald ended the call without waiting for a goodbye.

"Everythin' all right?" Molly's voice only quavered a little.

"Father Fitzgerald will be late."

Molly seemed to steel herself, but still avoided his eyes. "Will you be needin' help with the concessions now?"

He watched her until she dared to lift her gaze. Was she offering him help or forgiveness?

He'd take anything. "I can probably hold out until intermission."

"I'll be down, so." She gave him a shaky smile. "Have to say hello to my friend anyway."

Zach finally turned away. When he reached the cafeteria, he spotted the *Lord's Prayer* mural on the far wall, specifically the line "Lead us not into temptation."

He'd been lying to himself. He wasn't flirting with Molly for the case—clearly she couldn't help with his assignment.

He was flirting with her because he wanted to.

Not fair to either of them. Like he needed another reason to worry the archbishop would swoop in any minute.

But the archbishop wasn't the one he was most worried about.

Molly ran her fingers through her curls for the fifth time in the last twenty minutes. She hadn't dared to venture out of the projection booth.

She thought she'd be nervous seeing the mobsters now that she'd confirmed Doyle owned their building. But could anyone tell Tim had—she couldn't even finish the thought. She focused on the projector's familiar whir, but instead of *Chitty Chitty Bang Bang*, all she could see was that sublime and terrifying moment she'd forgotten the one thing that had to keep them apart.

She shook off the thought and checked the film on the platters. Spooling perfectly.

She should go see if Lucy had made it all right. Intermission was coming soon, anyway. Molly took a compact from her handbag. Her hair definitely seemed mussed, though that was probably her own fault, fidgeting with it every two minutes. She found her little bottle of gel and smoothed the top layer of her curls.

She had to face the crowd—and Tim—sometime. Molly started for the cafeteria—only to find Tim on his way up the stairs. "Molly?"

"Moths to a flame," she murmured.

One side of his mouth turned up, hinting at a sheepish grin. She'd nearly shown him how she felt already tonight; she didn't dare speak now. Hadn't they already come close enough to being burned?

"Good choice." He pointed a thumb over his shoulder. "Ian Fleming, right?"

She nodded, fixated on his collar. "Somethin' you needed up here?"

"Just wanted to make sure you're okay, Moll." Did he have to make calling her Moll so comfortable?

Before she could respond, he climbed another stair, holding out a hand for her. "I need to tell you something." His whisper carried a note of urgency.

Molly tried to move back, but her heel hit the door behind her. She couldn't do this again, not tonight. "Please, don't."

"Really." Tim climbed up a stair, leaving only one tread between them. The yearning in his expression pulled at her as though his outstretched hand were attached to her heart. It would be so easy to let him say he loved her, to finish what they'd started.

"Tim—Father." She focused on a point on the wall. "Friends do not . . . do *that.*"

"Friends." His tone betrayed his hurt, as if he could even be "friend-zoned."

"You were the one who said—"

"I know." His hands fell to his sides. Tim grasped at the empty air and finally backed down a stair.

Molly took a hesitant half-step forward. "Father, I . . . I was only comin' to see if you still needed help with intermission."

"Oh." As he turned away, the same regret keening in her flashed in his eyes.

In that instant, she almost reached for him, asked him to tell her everything—anything she could do to keep him from looking that way because of her. "You know I—"

Tim stopped short, his back to her. What good would it do for her to say the words?

He waved her off and walked down the stairs. She descended behind him. At least things couldn't get worse downstairs in front of everyone.

When Zach led Molly back into the cafeteria, on screen Truly Scrumptious was starting her song about her feelings for Caractacus Potts, "This Lovely, Lonely Man." Exactly what they needed to make the cramped quarters of the concession stand even more awkward.

Like magnets aimed to repel one another, they retreated to opposite corners to prepare the snacks, making a conscious effort to keep their backs to one another. Like that would somehow make them forget—or even less aware of—what had almost happened.

The movie rolled to intermission, and the kids who'd earned their play money in Sunday school lined up. As soon as he got a break in filling orders, Zach turned to the back of the booth to fill a few more bags of buttered popcorn.

"You made it!" Molly's voice rang out. Her Mormon friend. She was happy to see him. "I suppose you'll be wantin' to meet him, so? Father Tim?" Molly called back to him. He turned around slowly to find—Doyle Murphy? Murphy returned Zach's confused frown. That couldn't be who Molly meant. Zach looked down at the short woman waiting in front of Murphy—and froze.

"This is Lucy Saint," Molly finished.

He didn't really hear her name through the rush of blood pounding in his ears. But he didn't need the introduction—he'd know the woman standing across the table anywhere.

His little sister.

Lucy scraped her jaw off the floor. "Z—"

"Sweet sister Lucy!" Zach jumped in before she could finish his name in front of Molly—and Murphy.

"Actually, Father," Molly interjected, "Lucy is the Mormon friend I've been tellin' you about, and the teacher you're meetin' with on Monday."

If he weren't in a profound state of shock, he would've been relieved Molly's Mormon friend wasn't a guy. Instead, Zach was struggling to speak and act in a way that at least looked normal. "Of course. Since when do you live in Chicago, Luce?"

Was he so out of touch during his last case that he didn't know his sister had moved a thousand miles from home and changed careers?

Still staring slack-jawed, Lucy hadn't recovered yet—and he needed to make sure there was no mistake. "I guess even you should call me *Father* Tim now."

"You two . . . know one another?" asked Paul—what the heck was the priest in training who'd come to him for advice doing here? He took a protective step closer to Lucy and looked uneasily from Zach to his sister. Zach could feel Molly giving him the same disconcerted gaze.

"Lucy and I go way, way back. Don't we?"

Lucy filled her tone with sarcasm. "Oh, is that how you'd characterize it, 'Father Tim'?"

"Didn't I ever talk to you about joining the priesthood?" He glanced at Murphy. He didn't seem to be paying attention, but it was impossible to tell with these guys.

"In all the discussions we've had about the priesthood, this was not what I pictured."

Zach allowed himself a small laugh, which he hoped sounded casual. "Listen, I'd love to catch up, but we'll have to talk later."

"Now seems like a pretty good time to me." She folded her arms across her chest.

He checked on Molly, who'd been silent far too long. She stared back at him, her lips set in a hard line. Zach turned to his sister and lowered his volume. "You're holding up the queue, Luce."

Lucy noted the children behind her clutching their tickets, patiently waiting for their candy and popcorn. Though she didn't seem huffy or flouncy as she walked off, Zach recognized his sister's sulky stalking. Paul trailed after her, bewildered eyes still wide.

But before Zach had time to think all that through—or give the long-suffering children their treats—another grown woman cut in front of Murphy. Zach shook his head and returned to finish with the popcorn.

"Hello, Father! Remember me? Emily?"

"Hi." He glanced over his shoulder. Everything about the blonde screamed cheap, although her dyed hair and her skin-tight clothing had to be expensive.

"Thanks for inviting me. This is so fun!"

Had he invited her? Maybe—he'd only mentioned this activity to everyone in the parish. Emily turned on an artificial smile. "It's so good to be back at church again," she told Molly.

Zach watched Molly in his peripheral vision. Her expression softened almost imperceptibly—something only someone who knew her way too well could notice. "Well, welcome back." She gestured at the now quite long line of children still waiting behind Emily. "If you'll excuse—"

"Oh, dear, aren't you cold?" With her supernatural ability for detecting a moral threat to a priest, Kathleen bustled over to cast a meaningful stare at Emily's strapless shirt.

"No, I'm fine, thanks."

"Excuse me," Molly said firmly. "The children have been waitin' patiently."

Emily checked behind her and finally she understood. "You guys need any help?" She might have been addressing both of them, but her attention was fastened on Zach.

"We're grand, thank you," Molly answered for him.

Emily waited for Zach to respond. "Yep, we're all set."

Kathleen took Emily's elbow to drag her away. "Have you met my son Teddy? I know he'd love to get to know you." She was no less subtle than Emily.

"No, I haven't met anybody but Father Tim." She winked at him and finally allowed herself to be led off.

"Oh boy," Zach muttered. Between Molly and Lucy, he really didn't need yet another woman complicating this case. But he had little time to think about any of those women as he hurried to fill the children's orders along with Doyle Murphy's. Molly slipped out to restart the movie. The people in line quickly returned to their seats once the movie re-joined the flying car mid-plummet—and the mishaps of a pair of inept spies.

Zach settled into a folding chair behind the table, but he couldn't focus on *Chitty Chitty Bang Bang* once he spotted Paul on the back row. Next to him, Lucy turned back to glare at Zach every few minutes. At least she had the sense not to confront him now.

What was she doing here? Last he heard, she was still living in Norfolk. Or was it Virginia Beach? Newport News?

They used to be close, but after practically his whole life became classified information, talking to his family had gotten harder and harder. When was the last time he'd spoken to Lucy? He'd definitely called for her birthday in February—eight months ago.

The third time she turned around, he smirked and waved at her, though he doubted she could see him in the dark. Okay, so maybe he wasn't so good at keeping in touch anymore. But the FBI should've seen this. Hadn't they checked the personnel files? What would he tell Lucy? And Sellars?

Of course, they also hadn't seen fit to tell him Molly was a Guard—

What could he say to Molly about anything that happened to-night?

Zach rubbed his eyes. This was *exactly* what he needed. He'd have to explain this to Molly somehow—and tell Lucy enough to keep her quiet.

After the movie ended, Zach managed the final rush of con-cessions customers and made sure the cleanup was underway. He took care of the food, packing up candy bars and tying the extra pop-corn bags shut. Molly was nowhere to be seen.

Lucy, unfortunately, was. Zach tried to escape to the projection room, but Lucy cornered him. "Hey, uh, 'Father,' we need to talk. Now."

"*Not* now—I have to clean up, and I have early Mass tomorrow."

Lucy lowered her voice. "I'm sure you want to ensure my full cooperation?"

Zach laughed, but shot pointed looks at Paul ten feet away, Father Fitzgerald and Cathal Healey walking into the cafeteria together—and Doyle Murphy approaching Molly. What could he want with her? Zach had to get over there. He glanced back at Lucy. "Don't we have a meeting Monday?"

"I've been trying to meet with you for weeks."

"Monday, then." He kept his tone light—and his focus on Murphy looming over Molly.

"You better not slip out of this one, buster." Lucy punctuated her warning with a poke to his chest. Paul bid him a hurried goodbye, affording Zach and his sister a second of privacy.

"Slippery," Zach whispered, "and wise as serpents." Lucy didn't seem to get the quote from Matthew, but he slipped away from her without looking back.

18

MOLLY TRIED TO KEEP her heart rate steady despite Doyle Murphy closing in on her. He didn't know she'd discovered the datebook. He couldn't. Would he ask for—no, demand—a meeting with Father Tim again?

"Hi, Molly." He smiled as if contemplating the many ways he could have her killed. "I take it you're the mastermind behind all this?"

She nodded slowly, hoping he meant the movie night, and not . . . well, nothing else made sense, but the fear threatening at the edges of her thoughts gave no heed to reason.

"Did you have something planned for the leftover food?"

Molly finally found her voice. "Em, no."

"Could we take it down to the soup kitchen?"

"Sure now." The vise around her rib cage disappeared once Doyle turned away. Before he could change his mind, Molly backtracked out of the cafeteria.

But as soon as she reached the stairwell back to the projection room, someone behind her grabbed her elbow. She gasped and jerked away from— "Tim?"

"What did he want?" His eyebrows knit together in concern before the stairwell door shut behind him, plunging them into shadows.

"Doyle?"

"Did he say something about . . . ?" He pointed in the direction of the office.

"Of course. He said—" She slipped into her best Chicago accent. "—'Nice little shindig. By da way, if you say anything you'll swim wid da fishes.'"

Tim ignored her joke. "I won't let them hurt you."

These people killed Jim Mulligan. They killed Gerald Flynn. They killed—no, even Doyle Murphy wouldn't have killed Father Patrick. But how could Father Tim stop them? He stepped forward and Molly finally met his gaze again. His intense eyes searched hers—he had something to say.

The same mix of feelings from their last intimate moment washed over her, the cruel hope and the gnawing dread that exactly what she wanted was happening.

"I should explain about Lucy," Tim said.

Why did he have to choose that topic? She folded her arms and tried to ignore a rising tide of jealousy. "You don't have to explain yourself to me, Father."

"I guess I don't. But I will if you want me to." The caution in his eyes now was the same guard he'd raised earlier when he'd spoken to Lucy.

She certainly didn't want to confirm her suspicions. "Why should that matter to me?"

After a second of silence, Tim clamped his jaw, acknowledging her point with a curt nod, and walked back out the door, leaving her as weak-kneed as Doyle Murphy had, though for a far different reason.

Zach started off with a normal knock, but after being ignored a few times, he was pretty much pounding on Lucy's apartment door. It'd taken him half an hour to hack into the school's computers, find her address and walk here. She had to be done with Paul by now. Wasn't like he'd be interrupting them making out or—or her telling him who Zach was.

"Come on, I know you're home!" He banged on the door again.

"What do you want, Zach?" Lucy called through the door.

He immediately checked over his shoulders. No witnesses, but just to be safe . . . "It's Father Tim." He tried the knob. "Just let me in."

Lucy still didn't open up. "Are you alone?"

"What kind of question is that? You think I brought my friar friends?"

"What was I for Halloween in third grade?"

Zach threw up his hands. "Lucy, this is stupid."

"If you were the real Zach, you'd know."

"If you were the real Lucy, you'd know I don't remember." What had Lucy liked when she was little? "Were you Hello Kitty?"

Lucy groaned through the door. "No!"

"Maybe that was Tracey. Or was it your lunch box?"

"Try Barbie Princess Dream Castle."

She was tormenting him on purpose. "Fine. Guess I'll see you Monday."

After another minute, she sighed. "Wait." The deadbolt scraped and Lucy opened the door, but blocked him from entering. He didn't really care—he hadn't spoken to anyone in his family for months. But when he tried to hug her, Lucy pushed him away. "I don't feel comfortable hugging a priest."

Zach aimed a sarcastic smirk at her. He pulled out the plastic insert that formed the white square of his clerical collar and stuffed it in his pocket. "Better?"

"I guess." Though she was obviously still mad, she gave him an awkward hug and finally let him in her apartment.

"Like I haven't been a priest since I was sixteen." Zach glanced around her place. Typical Lucy: open yet cozy, with tons of—did she have to have so many family photos on display? And if she was friends with Molly— "Has Molly been to your place before?"

"Why?"

Zach paced around the room, snatching up the framed photos of their family over the years. "Put these away and don't get them out."

"What's your problem?" Lucy yanked the photos away. "You don't want Molly to see what a dork you were in high school?"

He grabbed them back. "What do you think this is, a game?"

"You're the one playing dress up." Lucy stuck her hands on her hips like he owed her an explanation.

"Think about it." This would be much easier if he only could tell his family he worked for the Bureau.

Lucy rocked onto one hip, her whole posture daring him to make her believe *that* one. "Are you pretending to be a spy or something? Give me a break."

What was so incredible about that—especially since it was true?

"You really believe it, huh?" she choked out amid gales of laughter.

Zach resisted the urge to flash his gun or badge. He wasn't about to lose his job over his obnoxious little sister's teasing.

After a ridiculously long time, Lucy noticed that he hadn't joined in her still-uproarious laughter. She stopped mid-hoot. "Wait—you're serious? You're not making this up?"

Apparently his cool demeanor about the situation wasn't convincing enough. "No, I really do like pretending to be a priest. No one bugs me about when I'm getting married." He shifted the photos in his hands and rolled his eyes.

Lucy fell back a step. "And you make money doing this?"

"It's my job."

"But I thought you worked for . . ." Realization flickered in her eyes. She finally got it. "Do Mom and Dad know?" Lucy's voice was hushed.

Zach moved closer. "You can't tell them—you can't tell anybody."

"Okay . . . wow."

"Absolutely no one. Not a word."

"'Kay." Silence reigned while she contemplated the new reality of her brother—whom she apparently still thought was a first-class dork—as a top-secret government operative. "What are you doing as a priest impersonator?"

"I can't say much—only that it's an intelligence gathering assignment." Kind of.

"Intelligence on the Catholic Church?"

He ignored the question. "Tell me you didn't tell Paul."

Lucy shook her head. "Is this why you never return my calls?"

"Usually. Sometimes I just don't want to talk to you."

She sank into the couch, ignoring his jibe. "Wow."

That was all they would say on that topic—and not just because Lucy was thoroughly stunned. Zach changed the subject and settled on the couch next to her. "So when did you move to Chicago?"

"A headhunter recruited me a few weeks ago. Said he'd heard about my work in the outreach program." Shock still filled her eyes. "Since when do you live here?"

"I'm still based out of D.C." He set the family photos on the couch next to him. Awkward silence settled over them. "How's the school?"

"Uh, good, I guess. Most of the kids hate me, I think." She cringed. "At least some definitely do and the rest don't care."

Typical teenagers. "Still teaching math?"

"Yep, to the upper grades."

Like any good brother, Zach reveled in the perverse joy of tormenting his sister. "Any of the kids you want me to talk to, put the fear of God into them?" he joked.

"Uh . . ." Though they were—probably—safe inside her apartment, Lucy glanced over her shoulder. She was really thinking about it. "I don't know who your people are, but maybe you could tell them something for me."

He raised an eyebrow. "What?"

"Wait here." She headed to the back for a few minutes of noisy rummaging, then returned and offered him a piece of paper.

Zach took the letter and read over it. *You ask too many questions. Curiosity killed the cat. Keep quiet and this blows over,* and then, a couple inches lower, *You are being watched.*

He jerked his gaze back up to her standing over him. What had she done?

"Actually, this is what I wanted to talk to Father—well, you—about. I think some of our students are involved with the mob. Or at least their fathers are."

He hemmed noncommittally, disguising his surprise. "You watch too much TV. This is probably a student prank." Come to think of it, that made more sense than Murphy getting bent out of shape over a math teacher giving his kid a college pep talk.

"No, really." She wrung her hands, earnestness brimming in her wide brown eyes. "This one clique of kids at school has always been weird to me. They hate the idea of college, and their parents aren't any help, either."

Zach suppressed an impatient sigh. Lucy rambled when she was nervous—but did she really think there was some other reason for him to spy on this parish and school?

She pressed on. "Ian Murphy and Brandon Lonegan told me straight out they weren't going to college, they were going to work in the family wholesale business. Then, the next day—" She broke off abruptly and reached for her ponytail.

"What, Luce?"

Lucy looked down. "I sent a note home to get their parents excited about college, show them how useful it would be in the wholesale business, I hoped. I got that on my car." She pointed at the letter.

"Sounds like you should steer clear of those kids."

"Gee, thanks, Zach, couldn't figure that one out on my own. I was going to write back to invite them to tea."

He mock-scowled. "Don't think I forgot the Word of Wisdom."

She groaned at his joke. But this might be more serious than Lucy could know. If only he had the official authority to fire her or make her leave. Or even unofficial authority—but the last time she'd done something because he said, she was in diapers.

He had to try. "If you want my opinion—"

"Don't remember asking for that."

"—you should get as far away from people sending you threats as you can. Like, I don't know, back to Virginia."

"No way!" Lucy's shout seemed to take even her aback. She continued in a more subdued tone, "I'm just getting through to some of these kids—DeWayne, Carlos—the other day, Janelle O'Leary even asked me for a letter of recommendation. I can't leave now."

Zach clamped his lips into a grim frown. He couldn't fire or force her out, but if he could maneuver her away from the mob and make sure she left their kids alone, maybe she'd be safe. Time to admit nothing and deny everything. "Please tell me you haven't tried to infect other people with your case of the crazies."

Lucy scoffed and plopped into the creaky rocking chair. "Actually, I was giving Paul—I mean, a volunteer at the school a ride home that day, so it's a little late for that."

It wouldn't have taken him this long if he hadn't been so shocked to see his sister, but finally it all came together, along with the perfect opportunity to change the subject completely. "So *you're* the teacher."

"Saint Adelaide's has twenty-four teachers on staff, as you would know if you actually attended to your priestly duties. Oh . . . I guess you really don't have any."

"Of course I have priestly duties—like counseling conflicted seminary students. Like Paul Calvin."

Lucy dropped her folded arms along with her pretense of disinterest. "How do you know him? What did he say to you?" she asked, her voice full of both eagerness and dread.

"Let's see." He waited as long as he could—until Lucy looked about ready to throttle him. "He feels guilty for being 'so attracted' to you." He grinned. "Priest-wrecker."

"Now I know you're making this up." But her blush said otherwise.

Zach's grin grew broader. He kicked his feet up on the ottoman. "And you like him too. That's adorable."

"Almost as cute as your crush on the parish secretary?" Her retort rang with a note of triumph. She straightened her shoulders. Her chair gave a loud squeak with her movement. "I know all about that one, bro."

He pretended her jab didn't metaphorically knock the wind out of him—and managed not to entertain any of the hundreds of questions he might ask someone in Molly's confidence.

"And anyway," Lucy continued, "I'm not crazy. Paul was there. He knows."

"Sounds perfect for you. I'm sure you'll be very happy together in the mental institution of your choice."

Lucy scowled at him. "I'm not going to dismiss this and neither is he."

"You don't think so?"

"He followed Ian and his buddies to a bar the other night. Definitely sounds like organized crime is involved here."

Great. The last thing he needed was amateurs ruining this case. "I'm telling you, go back to Virginia."

"And I'm telling you, Zach—"

"Please—Father Tim. Can't have you slipping up in front of my parishioners." Especially the ones who'd kill them both if she did.

Lucy groaned. "Father Tim then. We can't sit by and let these kids get dragged into this—this mob!"

And getting dragged in was exactly what Zach wanted to do. He sat up straighter and put on his best somber expression. "Listen, Lucy, seriously. I have no idea what you're talking about."

"Then maybe you should talk to Molly. She seemed kinda freaked out whenever I brought up the wholesale industry."

Lucy was more right than she knew. Molly had been terrified when she thought she was next—and he'd promised to prevent that.

"Or maybe it's just the stress of working side by side with you," she teased. Lucy smiled wickedly. Did he detect some perverse joy of her own at bringing up Molly again?

Zach kept his gaze level. "Probably best not to talk about me with her. At all." Especially after what he'd almost done tonight.

He glanced at the family photos still next to him on the couch. "How are Mom and Dad?"

"Fine. Mom's finally sewing that dress for Annika."

Their niece needed a dress? He nodded like he knew and cared about a ten-year-old's wardrobe. "You could tell them you got an e-mail from me and I'm doing good," he suggested gently.

"Okay." Lucy bit her lip. "Can I ask you something? I mean, about my students."

"You can ask, but I don't have to answer. I may not be a real priest, but I still have to respect priest-penitent privilege."

She nailed him with a sarcastic glare. "You know anything about a Tommy Mulligan?"

Zach folded his arms across his chest. What, because he was with the FBI, he'd run background checks on everyone she met?

"You do, don't you?" Lucy's eyes lit up. "Tell me, Zach. Tommy's one of my students, and I want to reach out to him, but nobody will tell me the whole story."

"Have you heard of a little thing called the Internet?"

"Yeah," she snapped. Then it dawned on her. "You think the truth is out there?"

What was this, *The X-Files*? "Some of the facts probably are. I'd better get back." He stood and held out his arms. After a moment, Lucy gave him a real hug.

"Remember," he said at the door. "Father. Tim."

"I got it." Lucy met his serious stare with one of her own. "I can't believe you're doing this."

"Me neither." Zach bid her goodbye and headed out.

Could this get any more complicated?

19

MOLLY SWITCHED OFF THE LIGHTS to the cafeteria and turned to leave, but once again, Doyle Murphy blocked her way, standing in the door. It was too late for her to casually change course, and no one was around to save her. Doyle's hands settled onto his hips—he expected to get whatever he wanted from her.

"Did you get the food you were needin'?" She kept her tone light.

Doyle snorted in amusement. "Where's Father Tim?"

She looked over her shoulder, but the dark cafeteria was empty. "Haven't seen him for the last hour."

"Guess I'll go hunt him down." Doyle started down the hall.

Ice coated Molly's heart. "Oh, were you still wantin' an appointment with him?"

Doyle turned back. "You know, maybe you're the one to talk to."

"Sure now." She gave him half a smile.

He took two paces toward the car park, then looked back at Molly. She clamped down on the fear roiling in her stomach and fell in step with him. He walked her through the car park to the parish office. "Glad we're finally working this out."

Molly's heart slid down a centimeter. No. She wouldn't be party to a mob's plot. She was a Garda.

That was right. She was a Garda. Molly held her head higher. She could handle this. "I think we'd better not talk here."

"At home?" Doyle folded his arms. "When?"

"Tuesday. Eight." Molly seized her keys and her opportunity to end this encounter. "Can't have anyone in the office after hours, you know yourself."

He nodded slowly, examining her as if his hooded eyes could gauge her honesty. She slipped into the office and locked the door behind her. Molly settled into her chair and leaned back to stare at the beams on the sloped ceiling.

Father Tim had no idea what he was up against. Even Molly only had the evidence from the datebook, and rumors to go with it, to guess what these men were capable of.

As much as this outfit's power and impunity terrified her, she was still better equipped to face them than Father Tim was. She had to keep Father Tim safe.

Because she loved him.

Molly sat up in her chair. She couldn't let herself think that. Already tonight—

What had they done? There was no undoing it, no denying it. Perhaps no stopping it.

She flinched at her own thought. Of course she could stop it. She could control her feelings and save Father Tim from ending up like Father Patrick. That was why she was protecting him—he was her priest. Not because of the knowing light in Father Tim's eyes, or how he'd defended her and her Irish culture, or how he remembered silly things like barmbrack and Crunchie bars, or how much she'd wanted him to cross those last centimeters tonight.

Molly turned to her desk. She had to stop thinking about that moment. She slid open the top desk drawer. Between the barmbrack ring and Lucy's book lay the Crunchie bar. She tore into the gold and purple wrapper and took a bite of the chocolate bar—but either the quality of imported sweets had declined or ... hadn't Lucy said something about disappointments in love and one's sense of taste?

She glanced down at the book Lucy had given her. Hadn't she also said something about weaknesses becoming strengths? Molly set aside the Crunchie bar and picked up Lucy's book, thumbing through until she found a highlighted verse.

And if men come unto me I will show unto them their weakness. I give unto men weakness that they may be humble; and my grace is sufficient for all men that humble themselves before me; for if they humble themselves before me, and have faith in me, then will I make weak things become strong unto them.

Molly read the verse three times. Humility and faith. Could it be that simple? A calm assurance began to fill her chest. She turned to the next page and read on.

As promised, the following afternoon Molly returned to the squat building with a stone façade to hear Lucy sing. Trying to ignore the jittering undercurrent of nerves, Molly settled in the blue upholstered pew next to her friend. Molly still didn't know what to expect from Sunday services—sacrament meeting, as Lucy called it—at the Mormon church.

The organ and piano by the pulpit reassured her that the music wouldn't be too different. Or at least not a rock and roll band. As the services began, the phrases from Lucy's book echoed through Molly's mind.

While the meeting had far less ceremony than Mass, the congregation was quiet enough to add a solemn air to the plain chapel. Lucy had explained the stillness: the congregation was composed entirely of unmarried adults. Molly wasn't sure if it was rude to ask why there were no children or married couples among them.

The speaker, Lucy's friend Susan, finished her remarks. She returned to her seat behind the podium, and Lucy flipped open a green hymnal and gave it to Molly. "This is what I'm singing," she whispered, tapping the pages. "Verses four, five and seven."

Molly glanced down at "How Firm a Foundation." The minister announced Lucy's song as she walked to the pulpit. Though the hymn was familiar, Molly had never heard this tune before. Lucy's clear soprano and the new melody set the words in a fresh light:

When through the deep waters I call thee to go
The rivers of sorrow shall not thee o'erflow
For I will be with thee, thy troubles to bless
And sanctify to thee thy deepest distress.

When through fiery trials thy pathway shall lie
My grace, all sufficient, shall be thy supply
The flame shall not hurt thee; I only design
Thy dross to consume and thy gold to refine.

The soul that on Jesus hath leaned for repose
I will not, I cannot, desert to his foes:
That soul though all hell should endeavor to shake
I'll never, no never, no never forsake!

Lucy and her accompanist gathered their music in the profound hush—a palpable reverence.

But the peace was short lived. Brian noisily struggled to his feet—and crutches—and hobbled to the podium. He was well into a series of jokes by the time Lucy reached Molly in their pew. Then Brian spotted her, too.

Molly tried to maintain a mask of polite interest despite the resurging wave of guilt. Brian shifted his comedy routine to the crippling incident, concluding with the diagnosis: an ACL tear of at least moderate severity, which might require surgery to fix. Brian aimed his snake-oil-salesman smile at her and started his address. Molly stared at her knees.

He redeemed himself, however, in his conclusion with a reference to the verse she'd studied last night. "When Moroni says he's not up to his task," Brian continued, "the Lord shows him that weakness can become a strength. And the Lord's strength is sufficient for all of us."

Although she had no idea who Moroni was, something about Brian's message brought back that same feeling of peace and reassurance she'd had while reading last night and pondering the text of Lucy's song.

Truth be told, she hadn't much cared about church until she needed a job from one. Nominal belief had got her through her Catholic education. But somehow, this feeling went beyond that. What did that mean?

Brian's gaze settled on Molly. "Brothers and sisters, I know God will make us strong. He will lead us to become better until we're the best we can be, the souls Christ will sanctify at the last day." He closed his address, and Molly joined in the chorus of amens.

After the prayer, Molly and Lucy tried to make their way out of the chapel, but the entire congregation seemed to cluster around them. Molly assumed they were approaching to compliment Lucy's performance, and many did—but several came up to say hello to Molly and to welcome her. Not the treatment she expected after nearly crippling a parishioner last week.

At the chapel doors, the teenagers perplexingly called elders met them. "We're so glad you came." The blond about her height, Elder Ehrisman, pumped her hand. "Molly, right?"

She nodded.

Elder Franklin joined in. "How'd you like sacrament meeting today?"

"Very well, thank you."

Brian limped past Lucy to place a hand on Molly's arm. "Want to learn more?"

She pulled away. "I—ah." She glanced around. Lucy, Brian, the missionaries and everyone within earshot seemed to lean in eagerly. "That is, I hadn't thought about it."

"How about an appointment, elders?" Brian offered.

The boys' faces lit up. Lucy stepped forward. "Only if Molly actually wants to."

All eyes turned to Molly again. What was she getting herself into if they all reacted so dramatically to this? "All right," she said slowly.

Elder Franklin had his datebook out before she even finished her sentence. They made an appointment for Tuesday night.

Brian winked. "I'll clear my schedule."

Molly nodded and hoped her smile didn't appear too uneasy as they shared enthused handshakes all around—Brian's the most enthused of all.

She bid Lucy goodbye and walked to the car park, trying to dismiss her new bout of anxiety. It wouldn't hurt anything to learn a little more about Lucy's church. Obviously these were good people—good Christians. Even Brian, obnoxious though he was, sincerely believed.

But what would Father Tim say?

Zach locked the parish house and headed out. Once he was out of range of the church, he pulled out his phone and dialed into his Bureau voicemail. Without a secure Internet connection—and with Sellars always on the warpath—Zach had called in Healey's plate to his D.C. office late Saturday night. By Monday evening, they should've reported back to him.

The first message reported Cathal Healey as the registered owner of the blue Chevy. Zach barely had time to be disappointed before the second message—from the same clerk—began. "This your idea of a joke?" the clerk asked. "Illinois Bureau of Motor Whatever just made fun of me for running one of our own plates. Thanks a lot. What am I supposed to tell Chicago when they call?"

Zach's stomach sank. On autopilot, his fingers deleted the message. Was Cathal Healey Sellars's pet agent? Why would the ASAC send in another agent?

He reached the stop just as his bus arrived. And then he realized the maroon sedan he was now used to seeing parked across the street hadn't been there today. With these guys sending Lucy death threats, and her a no-show for their scheduled meeting that afternoon, he had to make sure she was okay. He boarded the bus and dialed her number.

"Hello?" she answered after four rings.

"Luce? It's me." He took a seat in the middle of the half-full bus.

"Zach—Tim—whoever you are," she spat out. "Where were you today?"

Zach frowned. "Figured you canceled. It wasn't on my schedule when I called the office." He wasn't quite ready to face Molly again, though she'd sounded fine talking to him.

"Are you kidding? You left me at Father Fitzgerald's mercy. I couldn't talk to him about the mob, so I made up something about tightening the dress code. The guy is a control freak."

That might explain why Fitzgerald had taken the meeting. The bus turned right, and Zach switched seats, popping on a watch cap as a disguise. "In this parish, he only qualifies as a quirky character."

"He sort of grilled me about you, actually."

Zach silently groaned. What would he have to add to his cover's legend? "Tell me you didn't say anything embarrassing, Luce. I have to live with the guy."

"What, you think I'd tell him about the girl you played kiss tag with in second grade?"

He glanced around the bus and lowered his voice even more. "She played; I ran away screaming. If you have to humiliate me, at least get it right."

Lucy sighed. "I said we knew each other growing up and lost touch after college."

That worked. Good cover, especially from an amateur. "Nice. Lying to a priest."

"Better than lying about being one. Was that all you wanted?"

He hesitated a beat. Could he admit he was worried about her, or would that scare her even worse—or tip her off? "Just wanted to make sure you're not avoiding me again."

"I'm not the one doing the avoiding." The irritation level in her voice climbed, but she backed down. "I'll prove it. What can priests do for fun?"

"What, Paul hasn't given you the full run down?" He could just see the flabbergasted expression on her blushing face. He smiled and looked out the window. Almost there.

"Are you trying to change my mind about being nice?"

"Okay, okay, I won't mention him again." Zach tugged the chain to signal his stop.

The bus had slowed to a stop by the time his sister spoke. "How about dinner Wednesday?"

He needed to see Lonegan that night, but it was far easier to agree now and cancel later. He hung up a block before he reached the meeting point. Sellars slumped on the sidewalk outside the all-night diner. The guy sure knew how to pick 'em. The greasy spoon was the kind of dive Zach would probably never dare enter unarmed. From the looks of the place, he hoped Sellars was carrying underneath that homeless getup, too.

On the other hand, it was probably better than meeting out in the freezing rain with the raw hollow feeling at the back of his throat. Getting sick would be less than ideal, especially with Sellars's prized pet poised to poach his assignment.

"Evening, Father," Sellars greeted. Zach motioned for Sellars to join him in the restaurant and they slid into a booth.

"What's troubling you, my son?" Zach didn't bother hiding the irritation in his voice—if Sellars would let him do his job, Zach would tie this whole case up in due time.

Of course, the "in due time" part was exactly why Sellars was siccing Healey on him. The older agent stared at his menu. "Your girlfriend contacted us. Sent in the appointment book."

What? Then again, he shouldn't be that surprised. "Guess you didn't need me after all. Two agents is overkill anyway."

Sellars's gaze barely flicked away from the laminated menu. "Hope you like pancakes."

Zach scanned the street through the window and his reflection and the drizzle outside. Like one of his parishioners had followed him across town. Okay, that wasn't outside the realm of possibility—but he didn't have to worry. No one would know who Sellars was. And if they were going to suspect anyone's cover, it'd be Healey's, with his transparent cover. "You know," Zach said, "a heads-up is the minimum respect you could give any professional."

"Heads up, Saint: your time's half up and I needed someone else on the ground. Consider him plan B."

"If he's not more subtle, you'll need a plan C. And you should probably tell him Molly's innocent." And Zach's territory.

Sellars sipped his coffee. "I'll decide what I tell him, when I tell him. We have to be sure your girlfriend's not guilty before we go broadcasting it. She has to walk me through the case."

"The *whole* case?"

"As in blowing your cover?" Sellars smirked. "If she needs to know. We'll see." He unwrapped his silverware from its paper napkin. "Figured out where the deposits to his account came from. Patrick drained some old savings accounts out of state."

"So the money wasn't coming from the church or the school, or being laundered?"

"And I really doubt Patrick was giving them charity." Sellars scoffed.

Then why was he paying them? Zach nearly asked it aloud, but Sellars would tell him finding out was his job. Or worse, Healey's job.

"Good news is, this seems like a reasonably good circumstantial case," Sellars said.

"What's the bad news?"

Sellars laid down his fork and knife and leaned across the table. "We've had 'reasonably good circumstantial cases' against these guys before. They've gotten out of them."

Zach pursed his lips. From what he'd seen, these guys weren't remarkably brilliant, but maybe that was part of their cover.

Sellars pressed his fingers to his temple. "I'm not going to Justice this time without somebody to connect the dots on the stand, testify to something—Patrick's murder, a pay off, blackmail, anything. We need someone to roll on Murphy, or you need to hurry up and get reeled in already."

A waitress delivered their food—two huge pancakes, three strips of bacon and a pile of half-cooked hash browns for each of them. Zach started on his pancakes while they were still warm. "Some advice," he began once the waitress was gone. "Next time you send someone deep undercover like this, review *all* the personnel files from the whole organization."

Sellars looked up from his plate. "Now what?"

"My sister just got hired as a teacher at the school."

Sellars glanced around like he was waiting for the punch line. "You suggested her."

Wait—was he serious?

The headhunter that recruited Lucy. This had Sellars's sloppy handwriting all over it. "I was joking. She doesn't know what I do— I'm a class C," he added under his breath, leaving off the "covert agent" part of his job title.

The ASAC's jaw dropped in slow motion. Good thing Sellars was between bites. He recovered, muttering curses. "Could've sworn you were B. Does she know?"

"Now she does. Lucky for you, she's keeping it quiet—she has to." Zach pulled Lucy's letter from his coat pocket and handed it over.

Sellars read it. "Are you trying to make this about you, or does it just come natural?"

"She was trying to get their kids to go to college. Apparently they're not interested."

Sellars pocketed the letter. "Hm. She might be useful to us."

"Useful how?"

"Someone's done a better job drawing out our friends than you have." Sellars set aside his fork to tap the pocket where the letter now rested.

"First you send in another agent without telling me, now my baby sister is bait?

The ASAC aimed a cool glare at him. "I'm not saying you should put her in the line of fire. Sometimes we have to make a sacrifice for a case. Like you did with Gerald Flynn."

Zach stared out the window, ignoring the bitter taste of guilt.

"That's how much I want this, too," Sellars concluded. "Don't let this get personal."

Zach sighed and finished off his food. How was using Lucy as a lure supposed to make it *not* personal?

*Z*ACH UNLOCKED THE PARISH HOUSE DOOR. Once again, he was home just before midnight. Between late nights with the FBI and late nights nudging Lonegan in their direction—not to mention the long, rainy walks home—he was ready to fall into bed and stay there for a week.

Father Fitzgerald stood in the living room, his arms folded, his glower ready. Zach's brain jumped to defensive mode. But something was awfully amusing about this scene. Zach had never—okay, well, very rarely—had his father catch him breaking curfew, and even then his dad didn't look as much the "bad cop" as Fitzgerald.

"Did I do something?" Zach finally asked.

"Did you?"

He sighed. "As much fun as I can tell this guessing game will be, I'm tired." Zach started toward his room.

"How do you know her?"

That stopped him. "Who?"

"Miss Saint. From the school."

This paranoia of his was getting ridiculous. Zach definitely hadn't crossed any lines with Lucy. Gross. "We grew up together. What's the big deal?"

Fitzgerald stalked toward him, which would've been more threatening if Zach wasn't half a foot taller than the other priest. "I saw you with her."

"What, in the cafeteria?"

"At her apartment."

Zach's eyebrows shot up. That was a little different—and apparently he wasn't the only priest/spy in the parish. "You followed me?"

"You took off your collar."

He didn't have time to memorize all 1752 canon laws, but Zach was pretty sure that was okay. Fitzgerald jabbed an accusing finger into Zach's chest. "What have you done?" His voice was dangerously low. If he was this mad, maybe an affair with a parish secretary wasn't his secret.

"Nothing, Bruce." Zach pushed his hand aside. "Catching up with an old friend."

"And you can't do that wearing a symbol of the priesthood?"

He took a deep breath. Fitzgerald had no idea how ridiculous— and disgusting—this idea was. "She didn't know I entered the priesthood. It's strange for her to see me wearing a collar." After a few seconds of the old man's hard glare, Zach tried again. "Come on. What am I going to do, lie to you?"

Fitzgerald's frown softened, but quickly rekindled to full fury. "And tonight?"

"Cally Lonegan's," he lied. "Working with him."

"Oh." His glower left completely. "Thank you. I was afraid I'd lost him."

Zach shrugged. "That's what I'm here for."

Fitzgerald nodded. After a minute, Zach started to walk away.

"I'm sorry, Tim."

"Thanks." Zach shut his bedroom door behind him. This would be easier without Fitzgerald getting in the way. And Lucy. And Molly.

When this was all over, he'd definitely dis-recommend this kind of scheme to the Bureau.

Zach realized he was tapping his foot and forced himself to stop.

Couldn't let his nerves show his first time back at the mobsters' hangout since Flynn died.

He slid his empty glass side to side on the table. Was this a good idea? Sure, Lonegan hadn't returned his calls, but he could've camped out in the hallway. And make every other mobster in the building trip over him. Right.

Zach settled back against the fake leather booth. At least at Brennan's he could hide in the shadows, even if Murphy and two of his lackeys were in the opposite corner of the bar. They hadn't glanced Zach's direction. Lonegan hadn't shown in the last three hours, which fit with Murphy rebuking Lonegan for going soft. Made things tougher for Zach, though.

A waitress came by to trade his empty glass for a full one. He sipped the root beer and scanned the bar again. A man walked in, but as he reached the end of the dark entry hall, he turned back to the door. Even in the low light of the bar, his curly brown hair gleamed like bronze.

Zach shook his head. He did not want to see Healey tonight. Had Molly mentioned this place to him? Doubtful. He must've been talking to other people in the parish.

Or Sellars had shared Zach's information with him.

Zach pushed away the rest of his drink. Healey finally walked in, nodding to the bartender. The bartender acknowledged him like he was a regular. Was this not his first time here? He took a seat at the bar, facing Zach, though Healey didn't seem to notice him.

What was he hoping to accomplish here? Murphy wouldn't believe a real estate developer would hang out in the local bar to get a feel for the neighborhood. Zach certainly didn't buy it.

The side exit door latched just loudly enough to pull Zach from his thoughts. He checked Murphy's booth. The lackeys were gone. Murphy moseyed over toward the bar—toward Healey. Zach gulped his soda to stop the sinking feeling in the pit of his stomach. It didn't work.

Murphy took the stool next to Healey. Though Zach couldn't hear their conversation, it didn't seem like the first time the two were meeting, either. Healey pasted on his too-perfect smile and shook

Murphy's hand, then held up two fingers to the bartender to order them both drinks. Murphy waved the bartender off before he could fill the order.

Maybe there was nothing to worry about. Murphy wasn't smiling, but he also didn't seem as upset as he had when he'd met Zach. Or maybe he was more upset about Flynn's big mouth at the time.

Murphy said something, and Healey's eyebrows lifted. He craned his neck to see the door, then turned back to Murphy and nodded.

Zach's glass slipped from his fingers and skittered a couple inches away before he caught it. This wasn't déjà vu.

He tried to think of some alternate explanation. Maybe Murphy owned the lot. No, Zach had checked the tax records; Stockman Developers already owned the lot. Either the Bureau had purchased it as part of Healey's cover or they'd lifted the name of an actual development company from the records. The first option was safer—nobody could call the real company and blow Healey's cover.

Healey and Murphy rose and headed for the door. Zach stayed put for a few tense seconds, then slowly lifted his foot. He pulled up his pant leg under the table and grabbed his gun. He slid his gun into his front pocket, left a few bucks on the table and finally followed Healey and Murphy. They weren't in the entry. Zach borrowed a disguise from the coatrack—a long black jacket and a baseball cap.

This was already too similar to his last visit to Brennan's. Zach stooped his shoulders and checked the parking lot through the glass door. A group of four men passed out of the streetlight on the far side of the lot. Zach hurried into the sharp cold to keep them in sight.

When the foursome stopped at a busy crosswalk, Zach ducked into an alley, hunching over to conceal his height, and keep warm. They weren't taking the same route as last time, but Murphy kept a grip on Healey's elbow just like he had Flynn's.

The traffic light changed, and Murphy, Healey and the henchmen started across the street. Changing his disguise, Zach stuffed the baseball cap into a pocket of the jacket and started after them. When Zach reached the corner, Murphy glanced back. Zach bowed his head and kept his shoulders stooped—and turned to continue around the block instead of crossing the street after them. By the time he dared to look back at Murphy, the traffic signal had changed, and the building across the street blocked Murphy and company from sight.

Zach crept back to the crosswalk, keeping to the shadows. He could just peer around the building to see Murphy. He and his men turned and disappeared at the far end of the block.

Hand in his pocket to keep his gun from bouncing around, Zach jogged across the street, paralleling Murphy's route. He reached the next corner just as Murphy appeared at the other end of the block. They continued straight across the street. One more block would bring them to the same street as the church.

Another murder at the church? Zach swallowed to get his heart out of his throat. This didn't make sense. What message could they send by killing Healey at St. Adelaide?

Zach replaced the ball cap and hurried across the empty street, again parallel to the mobsters' route. At least it'd be completely unsuspicious for Zach to show up at the church.

But at the end of the next block, they continued straight across the street instead of turning for the church. Zach waited to see which direction they went next—left. Toward him. Should he cross the street and run into them or wait to see if they did something incriminating?

From this distance, he couldn't see Murphy's or Healey's faces, and he couldn't hear any conversation. But Murphy's grip on Healey's arm still sent a menacing message.

Before Zach stepped out from the shadows, the four men across the street stopped in the middle of the block. Murphy let go of his quarry, and Healey walked into the vacant lot.

The vacant lot Healey was asking about. Had Murphy discovered Healey's identity this easily—and what did that say for Zach's cover?

Murphy and his lackeys watched Healey from the sidewalk. Murphy thrust his hands on his hips. Was he reaching for his gun? This was Flynn all over.

The two other mobsters followed Healey into the weeds. Healey was barely visible pacing through the dark lot. Killing him here would send one message loud and clear: stay away. Did he know what was coming? Was he armed?

Zach couldn't let this happen again, especially not to a fellow agent. He started across the street, not waiting for the signal, focused on the men in the lot. The second he reached the sidewalk on their side of the street, he heard the men laughing. Was that good or bad? He gripped his gun in his pocket.

Murphy, angled away from Zach, raised an arm and signaled for his men to come in. The shadowy figures in the field converged. He didn't hear a struggle or any sign of alarm, but when they emerged from the weeds, the henchmen held Healey between them. Healey didn't look happy, but he didn't look too scared, either.

His eyes grew a little wider as Murphy moved closer, his chin jutting forward like he was delivering a threat. Zach remembered to take off the ball cap, in case they'd noticed the guy in the hat following them, and stuffed it back in the jacket pocket.

"And if anything goes wrong." Murphy's voice was almost too low to hear as Zach approached. He didn't want to startle Murphy, but if Healey wasn't directly in danger, then they'd both want to hear Murphy's threat.

But Murphy didn't finish aloud. He shuffled to the side one step, holding open one jacket lapel. Zach saw the glint of metal at his waistband before Murphy let the jacket fall closed. Hennessy and Gallaher released Healey, and Healey reached for his back pocket.

Was he reaching for his credentials? What, would he arrest Murphy for brandishing a weapon, *maybe* a class-C felony?

Before Healey could pull anything out, Zach began whistling as loudly and off-key as he could. All four men turned to him.

"Oh, hey, Doyle." Zach nodded to each of the men. Would they ask why he was coming from the opposite direction of the church?

Murphy lifted his chin. "Just the man I needed to see."

Zach's palms grew clammy. He hadn't interrupted this to trade places with Healey.

"Actually," Healey said, "Father Tim and I were going to go over plans for the youth center curriculum."

"Great idea," Murphy said. He turned from one to the other. "Let's talk it over at my place."

"Okay," Healey agreed a beat too quickly.

"Sure," Zach said. But he had to get this coat back to the bar so its real owner wouldn't notice—and get his gun back into his ankle holster so the mobsters wouldn't see it.

Luckily, the mobsters walked them back to Brennan's. Zach made an excuse about settling his tab and headed inside. After ducking into the bathroom to holster his gun, he traded the long black coat for his shorter navy jacket and hoped the mobsters wouldn't notice.

They didn't say anything as Murphy herded Zach and Healey into the backseat of his black Audi. The henchmen took a separate car—a certain maroon sedan—and they started for the mobsters' building.

How could Zach—or Healey—bluff through a youth center curriculum discussion? And what did Murphy hope to gain from this?

"IT'S A COMPREHENSIVE gospel studies curriculum." Zach settled back on Murphy's green faux-suede couch. He'd adapted the early-morning seminary and Institute programs to a Catholic setting—and so far, no one had called him on it.

Healey frowned. "No offense, Father, but we need something a little less . . . religious."

Zach let his shoulders sink.

"Pity," Murphy said, rising. "Thanks for coming by, Cathal. Jay'll take you back."

Both lackeys stood, and so did Healey. Zach glimpsed the trepidation in his eyes at being alone with the mobster. Zach didn't like the guy, but he wasn't about to abandon him to his fate with these guys. "Can you take me, too?" Zach asked.

Gallaher looked to Murphy. "Actually," Murphy began, "you—"

"Brennan's is right by the parish. Hate to make multiple trips." Zach tried to keep his expression steady despite the nausea creeping into his stomach. They hadn't said Healey's car was at the bar. He shouldn't know where they were going.

Murphy set his jaw; Zach held his breath. But either they were slow on the uptake or didn't realize they hadn't mentioned it: Murphy jerked his head to give them permission to leave. The henchmen led Healey and Zach out, and Murphy brought up the rear.

Zach didn't care if Murphy came along, as long as Gallaher didn't take Healey somewhere alone. Who knew what might happen?

They waited for the elevator in uncomfortable silence. Finally, the elevator chimed and the doors opened to reveal Molly. She scrutinized the quintet. "Evenin'."

"Hi, Molly." Healey was first to respond. "Just discussing plans for the youth center."

Zach groaned inwardly. Did he have to sound so eager to talk to her? Either Healey really liked Molly or he was still nervous, anticipating a question she might not have asked.

Molly got off the elevator, staring at Healey. "Were you, so?"

"Yeah," Zach said. He caught the closing door and practically shoved Healey aboard.

"The five of you were?" She turned to eye them.

"What, we don't care about the neighborhood kids?" Murphy scowled.

"I didn't say that."

Murphy glanced at his watch. "You ready for our meeting?"

Zach moved across the elevator to hold the Open Doors button. He had to hear this.

The heavy metal door to the stairs clanked. Molly looked over, out of Zach's line of sight.

"Hey, Molly!" called an unseen man. "We're here! And we brought pizza!"

"Brian. So you did." She gave Murphy an apologetic smile.

"Hi," said another man out of sight. "We're—"

"I'm afraid I've another engagement," Molly cut him off, turning to step between him and Murphy.

Murphy scrutinized the men over Molly's shoulder, then Molly. "We had an appointment."

Zach had to help. He punched the Close Doors button. "See you tomorrow, Molly."

"Appears you've somewhere else to be as well," Molly said.

Murphy and Gallaher hopped into the elevator car. Before the doors shut, Zach glimpsed Molly's expression, concern and anger. Maybe he'd avoid the office tomorrow.

"Feds?" Hennessy murmured. Zach monitored Healey in his peripheral vision; Healey didn't flinch.

Murphy chuckled. "Undercover as teenagers?"

Who were Molly's visitors that saved her from Murphy—and why was she meeting with the mobster?

Molly frowned at the elevator doors. Didn't Father Tim understand? Why was he with Doyle?

"Who was that?" Elder Ehrisman asked.

She looked to Lucy. What if Murphy came back to meet with her?

"A neighbor," Molly said. She started for her apartment. "Shall we?"

The missionaries' lesson started familiarly enough, with God, Christ, the Bible and its prophets. But the rest of their belief system implied the religion she'd practiced from birth wasn't the one true faith.

The one true faith? Had she ever believed it? Truth be told, there wasn't much she did believe anymore. Of course, at no point did anything sound unreasonable or outlandish. It all made perfect sense. And that was the problem.

Half an hour into their meeting, Molly shifted on her gray sectional to accept Elder Ehrisman's offered book and tried to ignore the uneasy feeling growing in her middle. She read the highlighted passage inviting her to pray about the message of the Book of Mormon. She'd been too distracted Saturday night to consider the implications of a new book of scripture.

A double knock sounded. Doyle. Molly leapt to her feet to answer. Elder Ehrisman, Elder Franklin, Brian and Lucy all gawked at her like she was mad. She pointed to the door.

"That was my cup hitting the table." Lucy picked up her empty glass from the end table and wiggled it. "Sorry."

"Right." Molly handed the book back to Elder Ehrisman, sinking back onto the couch. "Sorry. You were sayin'?"

"You can ask God if it's true." Brian jumped into the discussion for the fourth time. At least he could act somewhat normal as long as they focused on religion. "And if the Book of Mormon is true, Joseph Smith was a prophet. 'And by their fruits . . .'"

Molly realized she was rubbing her elbow. From what little she'd read of it, the Book of Mormon was at least an uplifting book. But did it matter—did she really have to ask *that?*

"Molly." Elder Franklin filled his voice and his wide brown eyes with sincerity. "Will you pray to know the Book of Mormon is the word of God?"

Surprise cleared every thought from her mind. After their extremely obvious hints she *could* pray about the Book of Mormon, she didn't expect them to come right out and ask.

Elder Franklin pressed on. "He'll answer you, I promise. I know the Book of Mormon is true."

She nodded, trying to ignore her clammy palms. God answering her? Hard to imagine. And what would Father Tim think?

But what could it hurt to pray about it? And if she did get an answer . . .

"Will you, Molly?" Elder Ehrisman echoed his companion's question.

Again, Molly looked at the expectantly hopeful light in the faces of the quartet surrounding her. She tucked her hands under her tweed skirt. "All right."

Lucy, Brian and the missionaries all broke into instant grins, Brian's the widest. He threw an arm around her shoulders and squeezed. Molly waited two long seconds to free herself. She forced a smile as they bid the elders goodbye. Brian stayed to hem and haw about his lame knee and the nursing he needed—until Molly asked him to help clean. He left in under a minute.

Lucy pulled her long blond hair back before collecting the water glasses. "Hey, what happened to my meeting with Father Tim yesterday?" she asked in a suspiciously blithe tone.

"I've no idea. Have you not seen him?"

"Not since Saturday. Sorry I stormed off like that, I just didn't expect to see . . . him."

Molly balled up the unused napkins a little tighter than needful. "He didn't seem too surprised. You know him better than I, though."

"No, no, he's only a casual acquaintance. Really." Lucy put the used paper plates inside the empty pizza box.

Sure she would say that. Molly simply nodded.

"What'd you hear?" Lucy leaned forward with urgency. "I mean, what'd he say?"

"He hasn't said a word about it since." Molly checked herself. Was she actually glad to report something that might hurt Lucy? She had no reason to be jealous.

"Honestly, we were never more than friends. Sometimes not even that—we fought a lot."

Casual acquaintances who fought a lot? "Sure." Molly picked up the pizza box and stuffed the napkins inside. "I'll walk you out."

After a silent, awkward elevator ride, Lucy tried again to convince her in the car park. "Really. There's never been anything between me and Za—zat man."

She protested too much, especially with that odd accent. Molly stopped scanning the cars for Doyle's black Audi and cocked her head.

Lucy bit her lip. "I'll prove it to you: come with us to dinner tomorrow. We're going to C, where I had dinner with Paul?"

Molly turned back to her friend. The idea of tagging along wasn't appealing—but neither was not knowing what they were doing in a romantic restaurant. "All right."

Lucy laughed in nervous relief. Molly threw away the rubbish and waved goodbye to Lucy, but she couldn't ignore the uncertainty turning her stomach sick—and for once it wasn't Doyle Murphy's fault. Which of her commitments worried her most?

Zach was about to call his sister to cancel dinner Wednesday night when his phone rang—Lucy. He'd barely gotten out a greeting when she launched into her breathless story. "Zach! I didn't know who to call. I mean, the police wouldn't actually believe me anyway—"

"Whoa, slow down. What's going on?"

"I don't recognize the driver, but it's a maroon Mercury. Following me."

He'd wanted to downplay the mob to Lucy, but he couldn't pretend this threat wasn't real. Zach realized he'd slid to the edge of the parish house's worn couch, his stomach buzzing. He managed to keep his voice calm. "Why do you think he's following you?"

"You think I'm stupid? Every time I make a turn, he does too."

"For how long?"

"Since I left school."

Zach checked the clock. School ended two hours ago. Had she stayed late, or had she been driving all this time? "Okay, they say you shouldn't go home if you're being followed."

"Who told you that one, 'this little thing called the Internet'?"

Classic Lucy, sarcasm at the worst possible moment. "Don't go anywhere alone. Stay in a public place."

"Like the restaurant? Don't tell me you forgot dinner at C tonight."

She hadn't said anything about going *out* to eat—but it'd give him the chance to make sure she was safe. "Just running late."

Zach only reached the parish parking lot before he nearly ran into Lucy's seminary-student crush. Paul had been snooping around the mob too much, too. If Lucy was on their list, Paul could be next. He shook Zach's hand with a solemn nod of greeting.

"What are you up to tonight?" Zach asked.

Paul ruffled his blond hair. "Nothing, really."

Zach cut to the point. "You should come with me. I'm meeting Lucy for dinner. You know, priest, girl, restaurant—awkward?"

"Don't want to intrude." Paul rubbed the back of his neck. Speaking of awkward.

"I insist." He half-dragged Paul to the bus stop. "You know where C is?"

"Sure. Right on this route."

For once, something was going his way. He hoped it wasn't the last time tonight.

Lucy was waiting by a fake-plaster wall when Zach and Paul walked into the restaurant twenty minutes later. "Hey, Luce. Look who I ran into on the way here."

She bared her teeth in an expression closer to a grimace than a grin. "Hi." She tugged a lock of her blond ponytail.

"Hope that's okay." Paul glanced at each of them.

"Of course," Lucy said. "You solved the mystery, after all."

Now what did they do? Zach pretended he hadn't heard, scanning the restaurant for the best tactical position—er, table—in the atmospheric lighting.

"Any problems finding the 'place,' Father Tim?" Lucy asked.

"None." He hadn't seen the maroon car, and with Paul there he couldn't search the lot. But neither could Paul and Lucy. Better to keep them out of trouble than save them from it.

Smiling, Lucy craned her neck past him to the door. "Hi, Molly."

Zach groaned inwardly. What had Lucy done?

The perky hostess stepped forward. "Is this all of your group?"

"Just a minute." Zach grabbed Lucy's arm and dragged her into the vestibule between the sets of double doors. "What are you thinking?" he asked once the glass doors swung shut.

"What were *you* thinking? You brought Paul here to watch me squirm."

But what she'd done was somehow okay? "Are you kidding me? Running into him on the way here is totally different from inviting her in advance. Which of us do you hate?"

Lucy rolled her eyes. "Quit making this about you. Not everything is, you know."

"I forgot, it's about you—as always."

"How could you do this to me?"

Way to prove his point. "You know, there's a remote chance you two could be together, but Molly and I don't even have that."

"Yeah, right." Lucy kicked at the fake cobblestone floor in a show of impatience. "You know I wouldn't get married outside of the temple. And P.S., he's taking a vow of celibacy."

Zach cleared his throat and pointed to himself. "Can't imagine what that's like. Do you have any idea what this is doing to her?"

Lucy scoffed and pointed at herself, too. "Believe it or not, I do." She tried to sneak a glance at Molly and Paul fidgeting inside the restaurant. "Listen, she's one of the best friends I have here. She was acting weird about us seeing each other Saturday. I want to prove we're just friends."

"Friends? That's pushing it."

"Fine. Go home. Let her think there's something between us you don't want her to see, and leave us all to the mercy of these criminals."

He looked to the nearly-dark parking lot. If Gallaher was out there, maybe this was the best place for Zach, and for his case. He closed his eyes in resignation. This could not end well.

Molly kneaded her elbow through her jacket, watching the animated argument through the glass doors. Casual or not, if they fought like this, Lucy and Tim's relationship couldn't have lasted long. But that didn't matter. She'd handle her jealousy, and dinner together wouldn't help anything. Molly pushed open the vestibule door as Father Tim reached for it.

"Ready?" he asked.

She shook her head. "Wouldn't want to be a third—fourth wheel. I'll just be goin'."

"Molly," Lucy and Father Tim said in identical imploring tones.

She waved a hand as if she could brush aside their concerns like cobwebs. She edged to the exterior doors—and saw Jay Gallaher's maroon sedan rolling through the car park. She made eye contact with Father Tim. Did he recognize—

"You should stay." His tone and his nod were equally firm.

"Then I'll go." Paul tried to squeeze between them.

"No, no." Molly spun him one hundred and eighty degrees.

Father Tim clapped a hand on Paul's shoulder. "Nobody has to leave."

"That's right, our table's waitin'." Molly took Lucy's elbow and hoped the gesture came off as friendly. They finally followed the confused hostess.

Whatever Father Tim had discussed last night with Cathal, Doyle and Jay, he finally seemed to understand the danger. Molly and Tim released their captives at their table. Paul held out a chair, but once Molly let go of Lucy's arm, Father Tim pulled Lucy aside again.

"Where'd you park?" he demanded, his voice tense, and well above a whisper.

Lucy glanced at the doors. "Strip mall across the street."

Tim released her, the tension in his jaw slackening. Lucy allowed Paul to scoot her to the table, and Molly took hold of the contemporary spindle-back chair by Lucy's—the seat with the best view of the front doors.

"Um, Moll." Tim pulled out the next chair over for her.

"Oh, thank you, but I'd rather sit here."

He motioned for her to step away from the table. She folded her arms, but obliged him. She was careful to keep her volume low enough to avoid attention. "I need that chair."

"Not a good idea."

He knew she'd been a Garda, and she certainly knew the mobsters better than he did. Couldn't he see why she needed the best tactical position? Molly put on her you're-more-likely-to-win-at-the-lottery look. "I'll be takin' the seat."

Tim checked on their audience. Paul hovered by Lucy's chair. They both stared, waiting. Tim swept a hand in their direction. "If it's that important to you," he said, his whisper as begrudging as his invitation.

Once they were all seated, Paul asked the second most obvious question. "Lucy, how do you and Father Tim know each other again?"

"We were really close neighbors," Father Tim supplied.

"Same floor." Lucy didn't look up from her menu.

"Quit it, Luce." He turned back to Paul. "We grew up on the same street."

Molly had to loosen her fists to pick up her menu.

"Hey, Moll." Tim dropped his nickname for Molly as easily as Lucy's. "They have cockles and mussels."

She checked her menu and joined in Lucy and Tim's polite laughter. The joke dispelled a little of the tension knotting in her shoulders.

They placed their orders and moved to a more comfortable topic—favorite movies. But once the check was paid and they filed to the doors, the easy conversation was all but gone.

How many of them were wondering whether Gallaher was still out there?

Tim took Molly's jacket off her arm once they reached the vestibule doors. He slid the coat onto her shoulders, leaning close enough to whisper. "He has to be gone by now."

Molly tried to ignore the feather-light warmth of his breath on her neck. "He'd better be." They both glanced at Lucy and Paul. Paul mistook the cue and leapt to help Lucy with her coat, although she already had it halfway on. She reached for the second sleeve, but the much-taller Paul yanked the collar of her navy coat up, moving the armhole out of Lucy's reach.

"I got it, thanks." Lucy pulled her coat free. Once she'd shrugged it on, she turned to smile at Molly, though her smile petered out somewhere north of her lips. "No dessert?"

"Not tonight," Father Tim answered. "Work in the morning."

Lucy stared at the doors with trepidation and fiddled with her coat buttons. "Never heard you say no to free food. I seem to remember you eating pizza from a dumpster."

"College doesn't count, and you threw away a whole pizza in the box."

"You two went to college together, too?" Paul frowned, echoing Molly's own dismay. Why did Tim and Lucy always have such a strange undercurrent of tension?

"Saw each other on breaks," Father Tim said. "Our parents are very close."

Lucy snorted. "I'll say." She turned to Molly. "Isn't the rectory on your way home?"

Molly glanced at Father Tim. Her flat and the parish house were in opposite directions—but she had to protect at least one of the people with her. "Sure now."

"Actually, it's closer for you, Luce," he said. "And the seminary's not too far from Molly's."

He knew where Lucy lived? Heat leaked into Molly's veins, bypassing her protective instincts. "The parish house isn't that far out of my way."

"Yeah," Lucy said, staring at each of them in turn. "It's basically all the same."

"Molly." Father Tim's voice carried the intense determination she'd only seen from him once before—when he'd ordered her away from Doyle Murphy. "It's better this way."

She readied her best resolute stare, but Tim pulled his cruelest trick. His decisiveness wavered, revealing real care in his blue eyes.

Her gaze faltered of its own accord. "I suppose you're right."

Father Tim led the foursome out of the restaurant. By unspoken agreement, he scanned the right side of the car park while Molly scanned the left. The lot was packed, but no maroon Mercury. She checked with Tim; he nodded the all clear.

But the clamp around her heart was still tight.

Oblivious to the danger, Paul and Lucy were already at the corner. Molly hurried to join them, but her heel hit a lifted pavement crack. She teetered until Tim caught her elbow and steadied her with a hand on her waist. Molly seized his arm to regain her balance, then raised her gaze to his—and stopped.

His face—his lips—were centimeters from hers. If either of them even thought of leaning in—her stomach plummeted. Tim's eyes searched hers. Her breath came in short gasps; blood rushed to her cheeks.

Paul cleared his throat. "What was Lucy like when she was little?" he asked.

Tim released Molly so suddenly he almost pushed her backward.

What had she nearly done—again? Molly turned to Lucy and

Paul. The constant furrow of concern between Paul's eyebrows seemed even deeper under the streetlight. Her back to them, Lucy surveyed the car park. Tim reached them. "Shorter, if you can imagine."

His answer was too late to dispel the awkwardness, even if Lucy hadn't noticed. She scowled and punched Tim's arm, hard. "I'm over there." She pointed across the street.

"And I'm here." Molly pointed down the aisle. With a glance at Father Tim and Lucy, Paul started for Molly's car. Molly stepped off the curb and willed herself not to look back.

She was a fool for staying tonight, even if she'd managed to keep her friends safe.

ZACH GRIPPED THE DOOR HANDLE and his seat belt, but he was still reeling from that second almost-kiss.

Like the first time hadn't been enough.

No—it wasn't enough. Because it didn't really hit him until tonight, the reason he felt so bad: he was falling for her.

"What is your problem, you freak?" Lucy shouted over her car stereo.

"I don't know what you're talking about." Zach snapped the stereo to off. Lucy hadn't seen that moment with Molly—right?

"Um, if you'll recall, the whole point of tonight was to make sure Molly *doesn't* think there's something going on between us."

He'd probably convinced her of that. The look in Molly's eyes as he'd held her flashed in his mind. A cold fist punched into the pit of his stomach again.

Definitely falling.

"What was with trying to take her chair, anyway? Like it actually matters. You didn't *have* to sit next to me—way to make that one seem normal."

"You're the one that brought a gangster with you. Did you want the person with the gun to have the best shot or the second best shot?"

Lucy jerked around to stare at him. "Gun?"

Zach kept his gaze steady and strengthened his tone with steel. "Moving on."

"Then you insist on riding with me, and practically shove Paul into her car." She shook her head and hit the steering wheel.

"If you wanted your alone time that badly, you should've said something." He checked the side mirror. No one behind them.

"I tried—I mean, that's not the point. What if the people that followed me—?"

"Molly will keep Paul out of trouble, and she can hold her own." But, Zach realized, he hadn't believed that up until the second he'd said it. He'd almost liked the way she'd stood up to him, rising to the challenge.

"Yeah, well, one way or another, I'm sure neither of us have to worry about our love lives after tonight. Good job."

Could Molly doubt after that moment?

Lucy pulled into the parish parking lot. "Later."

He nodded and got out of her gold sedan. No way could he let Molly wonder if he was only leading her on. But how could he tell Molly? Halfway to his room, it hit him—a code. Weren't all Guards required to speak Irish? He'd promised he'd sing at the talent show, and he'd learned songs in German, French and Italian before; he could learn one in Irish. Maybe if he impressed the Bureau and the archbishop, they'd let him sneak back for one last night.

Zach picked up his pace, though he probably couldn't find a traditional Irish song called "It's Okay If You Like Me, I'm a Spy."

Molly stayed in the office for lunch Thursday. She didn't dare go out and run into Father Tim. How could she face him after last night?

But she also had something to do. Several times already, Kathleen had casually mentioned she'd spoken to Cathal Healey that week. If Cathal was hanging out with Doyle and Kathleen, he had to have heard what kind of people he was dealing with.

Molly locked the office door before she opened her drawer. She searched every pocket of the organizer—but Cathal Healey's business card wasn't where she'd left it, on top of the barmbrack ring.

She sank back in her chair. Could she have thrown it away and forgotten? No, she'd remember that. She'd wanted to toss the card in the rubbish the minute he'd given it to her, but she'd hung on to it just in case.

Molly sat up again. Cathal had moved on to chatting up Kathleen, and Molly could only imagine she'd regaled him with all the gossip Molly had worked so hard to keep her from telling Father Tim. She used a letter opener to force the feeble lock on Kathleen's desk and raked through the disarray.

If Kathleen had Cathal's card, Molly couldn't hope to find it in this mess before Kathleen returned. Molly racked her brain for the name of his company. Stockton? Saxon?

Stockman. She returned to her computer and searched the Internet. One Chicago listing came up. Molly crossed her fingers and dialed the number. A man's voice answered after two rings. "Hello?"

"Is this Stockman Developers?" she asked.

"Uh, yeah, Cathal Healey speaking."

That was a little . . . convenient. Why was his number listed as their public contact number? She pushed aside the unsettled feeling in her middle as they exchanged pleasantries.

"Did you think of something else we should know about the area?" Cathal asked.

"Nothin' specific, but . . . I wanted to be sure you realize that if you're wantin' to keep children out of trouble, this isn't the right neighborhood. After the people you've met with this week."

Cathal was silent a long moment. "I see. Any reason you'd say that?"

Molly rubbed the wood grain of her desk. "Just rumors, Cathal. But better safe than sorry, don't you think?"

He agreed a bit reluctantly. Molly ended the call quickly as she could, though she wasn't sure he was convinced.

Why would Cathal Healey answer the publicly listed number for the company? Unless . . . perhaps it wasn't a real company at all. But did that make him an undercover LEO or a rival mobster?

She didn't have enough time to puzzle that out now. Molly dialed

Father Fitzgerald's mobile. After their greetings, she broached the subject. "Father, I'm afraid I need to move out of the parish's condo."

"Oh? Why's that?"

Molly groaned inwardly. She hadn't figured he'd ask—why hadn't she prepared an excuse so at least Father Fitzgerald could remain ignorant of the mobsters? "My parents. I'd feel better if I were closer to them."

Father Fitzgerald accepted that better than Cathal had taken his excuse. "Is this your thirty day notice?"

"It is." She'd hoped to be out sooner—but if she moved out too far before her deadline, Molly was sure to draw more suspicion. Even a cursory check would show her parents were in perfect health.

She was stuck with Doyle and company for a few more weeks.

Though he muscled through the congestion Thursday, when Zach woke Friday, he couldn't breathe, he couldn't move without aching, and he couldn't go back to sleep. Light streamed through the window of his small, sparse bedroom—mid-morning. He'd missed Mass.

With two weeks till his deadline, Cally Lonegan contemplating repentance, and Healey assigned to breathe down his neck, Zach didn't have time to get sick. Between fits of coughing, he heard an insistent knock at his bedroom door and called for them to come in.

"Oh, he lives." Fitzgerald smiled at his own joke. "I told you to pace yourself."

"Good morning to you, too." Zach sniffled for emphasis, though he probably didn't need to with his raspy voice. "Sorry I missed Mass."

"That's all right; I can do it on my own." Fitzgerald stepped out of the room and returned with a glass of orange juice.

Zach took the cup and tried, unsuccessfully, to clear his throat. "Why didn't you wake me up?"

"I tried." Fitzgerald pursed his lips. "You coughed in my face."

"Sorry."

"You need to stay home today. Obviously *someone's* telling you something."

Zach almost choked on his orange juice. Stay here with Fitzgerald all day? "No—I have to—" He stopped to cough, but after several seconds of continued hacking, Fitzgerald resumed the conversation without him.

"I'll take care of all that today. You rest. You've been running yourself ragged, Tim. You had to know this was coming."

Zach pointedly looked away and climbed out of bed. How did Fitzgerald always make him seem like a sulky teenager? He followed the older priest into the living room and found the cold medicine above the fridge.

"I know you're eager for the work, Tim, but if you wear yourself out, you won't be doing God any good."

Zach blinked at him slowly and drank the bitter green medicine. "I'm not wearing myself out."

"What time do you usually get up?"

He shrugged. "Six."

"And you're walking everywhere, aren't you?"

"I don't mind."

Fitzgerald folded his arms. "When do you get home?"

"Midnight, one."

"The archbishop isn't too happy with your schedule."

Zach groaned inwardly. Fitzgerald settled at the bar and flipped through his paper. "A wonder it's taken you this long to get sick."

Zach turned away and rolled his eyes.

"One way or another, Tim, you're going to have to slow down."

If he didn't know better and if Fitzgerald didn't sound so casual, he'd take that as a threat. Zach headed back to his bedroom to wait for Fitzgerald to leave for the day.

Molly gathered the bulletin from the office Friday and started to leave. But as she straightened the pages, she realized the top sheet wasn't hers. "Legacy accounts," read the header. She stopped on her way to the door. The names on the list included Flynn, Lonegan and Murphy.

"Oh." Kathleen stood. "I forgot I printed something."

Molly handed over the paper. "What's this?"

"You know—the kids attending the school on the trust account. I wanted to see how many of them attend Sunday services."

The trust account? A chill of realization swept over her. But before she could fully process that, the door swung open. Molly held out her foot to stop it. For one irrational second, her stomach plummeted—it was Father Tim. Could she face him after Wednesday night?

But Father Fitzgerald came into view. "Oh, Molly, didn't see you there."

"That's all right." Her breathing steadied, and she moved toward the doorway.

"What can we help you with, Father?" Kathleen smiled.

Father Fitzgerald glanced from Kathleen to Molly. "Actually, I need to speak with you, Molly. About Father Tim."

She stopped short. Clammy fear crept up her neck, and she could feel the blood draining from her face. She should've left sooner. How much did Father Fitzgerald know?

"I need you to clear his schedule for the next few days."

Molly nodded, more surprised than relieved. "How long exactly?"

"Depends on how long he's sick."

"He's sick?" Kathleen interjected.

Father Fitzgerald sighed. "Might just be a cold, but if he doesn't get some rest, it could become something much worse."

Tim, ill? Molly caught herself reaching for her elbow. "I'll cancel his appointments through Tuesday, as soon as I run off the bulletin."

"In the future, no matter what Father Tim says, let's keep him under a hundred hours a week."

"A hundred hours?"

Father Fitzgerald shook his head sadly. "Yes. He's up by six, and he's out after midnight half the time."

That wasn't her doing. "Now, I haven't—"

"I was trying to ease him into this. I know how easy it is to take it all on at once—the zeal of starting out. Guess I didn't warn him enough."

"It's not your fault." Kathleen pinned Molly with an accusatory smirk.

"I tried to get him to take even an hour off, some leisure time," Father Fitzgerald said. "He was always too busy. Let's try not to over-schedule him so much in the future. Everybody needs time off."

"Father Tim has leisure time." Molly mentally winced at her defensive tone, especially when Kathleen and Father Fitzgerald turned to her. Eager to escape their scrutiny, she started toward the still-open door.

"Basketball with the students?" Father Fitzgerald propped up a skeptical eyebrow. "Two hours a week isn't enough, and it's too cold now anyway."

"He has other time off," she insisted, doubling back.

Kathleen rolled her eyes. "Five minutes in the office doesn't count, either." She echoed Father Fitzgerald's reasoning with a note of incrimination, as if it were Molly's fault Father Tim worked himself to death. "You really need to go easier on him, Molly. He's allowed to have a personal life."

"He has one."

"Oh, really?" Kathleen's haughty tone was even more mocking than usual.

"Wednesday he went to dinner with—friends."

"One night?" Kathleen scoffed. "You don't have to give everyone and their dog an appointment. Think about him for once. When is the last time you let him have time to relax?"

Was she really saying this was Molly's fault? "Last week we had dinner and watched a movie." The second the words were out, her brain screamed to call them back. The heat sapped out of her defiance, replaced by a cold surge of nausea. She steadied herself on the doorknob.

"You and Tim went to dinner and a movie—together?" Father Fitzgerald asked slowly.

"No, it was at . . ." Her rejoinder snagged in her throat. This wasn't any better. "My flat." Molly looked from Father Fitzgerald to Kathleen. Surely this was the final tidbit Kathleen needed to power the parish gossip mill about Molly and Tim for the next six months.

Some defense that had been.

Molly held up the bulletin to explain her reason for leaving, but she doubted they were fooled.

If only she'd escaped a minute sooner.

When she returned from her errands, Molly let herself in the parish house, ducking the chilly rain and her misgivings. She was only here to repay Tim's kindness—and prove everything between them was platonic.

From the corner of her eye, she saw Tim jolt upright. "Oh, Molly. Wasn't expecting you." He tugged the cuff of his track pants down and slouched into the couch. Even when he'd played basketball, she'd never seen him in anything but clerical clothing. Tonight, he wore a tracksuit emblazoned with "W&M." As if she needed another excuse to forget his vocation.

She tried to focus on anything else. Tim was pale, his eyes faintly rimmed with red, and his voice hoarse. "You *are* ill, aren't you," she said. Molly emptied the grocery sack on the counter, then opened the chicken soup. "You've been workin' yourself too hard."

"Do me a favor, Moll. Leave the lecturing to Father Fitzgerald."

"As soon as you take time off so he doesn't come after me for overworkin' you again."

Tim grimaced vaguely. "Sorry."

She stuck the soup bowl in the microwave. "How much medicine have you had?"

"Don't worry, I'm not ODing. I think." He laughed, but his mirth dissolved into coughs. Molly patted him on the back, but it didn't help.

Once his coughing subsided, Molly warmed up the soup. Tim accepted the bowl with thanks, and Molly settled in the worn chair that might've once been green, taking the remote from the rickety coffee table. They were silent save for the spoon's clang on the bowl. Molly scrolled through the television program guide—and tried to think of anything but being alone with Tim.

She settled on a '60s spy movie. Michael Caine was watching a film brief, exchanging a glance with an attractive woman.

"You know this one?" Molly asked. *The Ipcress File?* She laid down the remote.

"Never seen it." Tim watched the set for a while, but when she glanced at him again, he was staring at her. "Going to confession tomorrow?" he asked.

She nodded slowly, apprehension already constricting her chest.

"What happened wasn't your fault."

So they *would* discuss it. "Is that your way of offerin' absolution?"

"You know I can't do that. But you don't have anything to be absolved of."

Molly focused at her hand rubbing her other elbow. Just the reminder she needed. He was a priest and forgetting that—or worse, ignoring it—was wrong.

"It was my fault." Tim waited until she looked up. "I was the one trying to—"

"I didn't stop you."

His gaze returned to his bowl. "You did. I saw it in your eyes. You

202

knew it was wrong."

"It was," she whispered, her vehemence surprising even her.

"Yeah." Tim paused. "I'm sorry."

Had he already confessed? She could hardly imagine he'd said Mass with this on his conscience. Little wonder Father Fitzgerald had been upset at her spending time with Tim.

They lapsed into silence as Michael Caine's Harry Palmer cooked for Jean Courtney. In a minute, she'd decline to join him for the meal. The romantic storyline in this movie was hardly a subplot. How did she only seem to see those parts?

"Thanks for dinner." Tim set his bowl on the coffee table. Molly took it to the kitchen.

She came to stand behind the faded couch with its black-and-neon crocheted blanket. "I should probably go."

"Guess so." Tim turned to her. Neither made any move for the door. "I won't ask you to stay."

But his eyes did that as clearly as if he'd said the words aloud.

Molly returned to the chair, willing herself to stare only at the television—decidedly not Tim. They passed half an hour in companionable silence before Molly finally broke down and turned to him. He was fast asleep. She tugged the tacky afghan over his shoulders.

A knock at the door made her drop the blanket as though it burned—as though she'd been caught playing with fire. Tim didn't stir, so Molly answered to the door.

Doyle Murphy stood on the porch. Molly gasped instinctively. He rocked back on his heels, folding his arms as though he was in charge. She gripped the doorknob and shifted to block Doyle's view. "Father Tim isn't feelin' well," she said. "Can I help you with somethin'?"

Doyle took on a cat-with-cream air. "You work with the school, right?"

"I don't. If that's what you're needin', Father Tim won't be much help, either."

"Hm." Doyle's gaze shifted over her shoulder. "What if I told you I could give you what you want most?"

Molly fought off a smirk. "What do you know about what I

want?"

"You, Father Tim, together, without anybody saying a word. A blind eye."

Her insides reacted first, though her gut couldn't decide whether to be alarmed or elated.

But nothing Doyle Murphy or anyone else did would make that right. "Off you go, now."

She was already shutting the door when Doyle responded, "Fine. Do it the hard way."

Molly leaned against the closed door. Even the deadbolt didn't make her feel safer. But Tim slept on, oblivious. On the television, Courtney took Palmer's hand and kissed him before she let him leave, the end of the romance in the movie. Because she had to let him go.

Molly's heart grew cold. She switched the television off and collected her jacket. This had to end. They might be friends, but she'd never have a place in his life beyond that. Time to stop fooling themselves.

Across the car park, Doyle's black Audi peeled out. All right, perhaps she had no place in Tim's personal life, but until Doyle was truly gone, she couldn't leave it either. Molly walked into the drizzle alone.

AFTER THE MASS POSTLUDE SUNDAY, Zach hurried down from the choir loft to see Molly. But even the cold medicine couldn't dampen his instincts when Zach heard his cover's name carry through the vestibule in a conspiring murmur from the chapel. He pressed himself against the vestibule wall where he could listen unnoticed.

"And then," continued the first speaker—Kathleen? "Molly said they went on a date!"

"A date?" The second speaker, a man, didn't lower his voice as much.

"Dinner and a movie at her place—can you believe it? It's like living *The Thorn Birds.*"

The man gave a low whistle. "All I ever hear is what a saint he is."

That wasn't an allusion to his real identity, was it? Though Zach was already as still as possible, he stopped breathing a brief second.

"Well," Kathleen said, "he's a good guy. His heart's in the right place, I think."

"Not worried about his heart. But come to think of it, I heard him say she was beautiful."

The gossipers moved into view—Kathleen and Doyle Murphy.

"Did I tell you about the time I caught him attempting to flirt? Embarrassing to watch." Kathleen took Murphy by the elbow and leaned in to launch into her next tidbit.

"I heard," Zach began in his own furtive whisper, "he even gossips."

Murphy and Kathleen jerked around. "Oh, Father, I—" Kathleen choked out.

Zach pushed off the wall and approached the pair. "I don't care what you say about me—but dragging Molly into this? Aren't you the closest friend she has in this parish?" She bowed her head, but he wasn't done yet. "Did you think about what your overactive imagination would do to her reputation?"

"I—Father, I—I mean—" She surrendered into silence.

He patted Kathleen on the shoulder. "'Go and sin no more.'"

She nodded and hurried away.

"Certainly know how to handle your people," Murphy said once the echo of Kathleen's footsteps faded.

Zach kept his gaze level. If that were true, Kathleen never would've said those things in the first place.

"But Kathleen's the least of your worries." Murphy took two paces toward Zach.

Zach folded his arms, fighting back his defensive reflex. "Oh, really? Why's that?"

"You'll see. Soon enough."

"Doyle?" came a timid call. A short woman with the heavy-lidded eyes that came from years of submission shrunk back a step from the exterior doors. "Are you ready to go?"

Doyle watched Zach a moment longer. "Yep. Got everything I need. Just you wait."

Zach let them go, refusing to rise to Doyle's bait. As soon as Doyle was out of sight, Zach grabbed his phone and dialed Lonegan, but there was no answer.

If Kathleen had given Doyle everything he needed, then Zach wasn't the only one in danger.

Molly was wrapping up her work Monday when Father Tim came to the office. He appeared about as ill as he had Friday night, but without the languid listlessness.

She busied herself with the last email check of the day to keep herself from remembering everything they'd said that night or her decision not to go to confession Saturday. "Afternoon, Father. I cleared your schedule today, and I moved your school counselin' to tomorrow. Other than a few dinner appointments, that's everythin' for the week."

Father Tim took on a skeptical expression. "I'm not an invalid. I can do more than one thing a day."

Molly glanced at Kathleen. "We're supposed to make sure you don't overwork yourself while you're recovering," Kathleen said. She seemed to address Father Tim more gently today. If that was how she treated someone on the mend, maybe Molly should play the convalescent.

"Father Fitzgerald acts like no one's ever been sick before. This was his idea, wasn't it?"

"Apparently he thought you were at death's door."

Tim smiled weakly. "Yeah, it was touch-and-go for a while. Watch out, the Chicago cold epidemic will claim more lives before the year is out."

"We're glad to see you in good spirits, at least." Kathleen returned his smile, though hers was oddly empty.

"Owe it all to good soup." Tim turned up one corner of his mouth. "Hey, Molly, I need to get on that account. Can we go by the bank?"

Molly's hands balled into fists. After she'd caught him palling around with Doyle and his ilk this week, she had no intention of adding Father Tim as a signatory. He still didn't seem to understand the gravity of the situation. She was trained to handle criminals.

She willed her fingers to relax. "They'll be closed by the time we get there, and I have to get to rehearsal."

"Tomorrow then." He didn't meet Molly's gaze as he left.

She released a breath she didn't know she was holding. One last thing to take care of. She picked up the phone and dialed Doyle Murphy. His wife Claire answered. Molly introduced herself and silently wished her good luck would hold. "I need to leave a message for—" She checked on Kathleen, busy sweeping an armful of paper into the waste bin. Was she listening, too? "—your husband," Molly finally finished. "Father Tim's just getting over something, and he won't be able to keep their appointment. We hope you understand."

Claire made some noise of assent, and Molly bid her goodbye. She'd bought him another week. "See you tomorrow, Kathleen." Molly collected her handbag and started for the door, almost late for her family's dance rehearsal. She'd only made it to the car park when her mobile phone rang.

The missionaries. Molly rubbed her lip, contemplating her mobile. They'd already rung her twice this week to remind her of her commitment to pray about the Book of Mormon. She still hadn't, and they were meeting tomorrow. Though she really didn't need another reason to feel guilty, Molly pressed the button to ignore the call.

She got into her car and stared at the steering wheel. Her life had been just fine two months ago. Now she was driving herself mad trying to keep Father Tim—and her heart—safe. And then she'd promised to pray about the Book of Mormon, when she'd always been taught the Bible was the only book of scripture.

But who was she to disregard what might be God's word? After all, reading that book had been the only thing that felt right—that brought her any sort of peace—since Father Tim arrived and made all of her prior refuges unsafe.

Molly waited until Kathleen left for the day, then went back to retrieve the book from her desk. She only had a little time until dance rehearsal, but she'd given her word, now, hadn't she?

Molly traced the grain of the faux cherry conference table, waiting for the first of her two nerve-wracking appointments Tuesday. At least the missionaries hadn't asked her to take two hours off work for their meeting tonight, as the FBI had.

At last, the door swung open. An African American in a dark suit ill-fitted to his girth entered and shut the door behind him. Assistant Special Agent in Charge Reginald Sellars introduced himself and shook her hand. "Thanks for coming in."

"Of course."

Sellars slid a manila folder across the table. Molly accepted but didn't open it. She slipped back into the familiar power structure of law enforcement as though she'd never left. "What can I do for you?" she asked.

"We need a little more information. We have an agent on this case full-time—"

"You?"

Sellars smirked. "Aside from me."

"Perhaps it'd be easier for me to speak to him."

"Don't worry about that." His smirk deepened into full-blown amusement.

Molly fixed him with a look to take him down a notch. Did he think she was that ignorant? "I know how these things go. Wouldn't it be simpler for me to speak to your agent, instead of havin' him hear it secondhand?"

"You're right." Sellars leaned back in his chair. "But that's not going to work for us now. So, about these pages?" He flipped open the folder.

"I'd really like to speak to your man."

Sellars simply grinned. "I bet you would. But I promise to take good notes for him."

Molly pursed her lips and turned to the pages from the datebook. "What do you want to know?"

"Why do you assume organized crime is involved here?"

She didn't need the datebook for that. "I can read, Agent Sellars. Everyone knows what they're up to—and you do, too, if you've an agent on the case already."

"Then what are they after?"

"I've been thinkin' on that, and I may finally have it." Molly reached for her handbag and pulled out a sheaf of folded paper. "I'd almost forgotten about this—not part of my job—but there is a bit of money associated with the school." She gave him the papers.

Sellars studied the top page. "What's this?"

"The school's trust. Been goin' nearly thirty years, since the parish first decided they wanted a school. Some smart investin' has made it basically self-sustainin'. It covers grinds—tuition—for charity slots and any of the original investors' children and grandchildren, which is how Doyle's son ended up enrolled."

"This number right?" He pointed to a spot on the page. "Thirteen million?"

Molly nodded. "Thought that might attract their attention."

"One more thing—we have some bank records that don't match up with this appointment book. There's a monthly charge for $450 we can't trace."

Her stomach sank. It was true then. "That'd probably be rent on a condo. For parish staff."

"Ah." Sellars thumbed through the pages. "We appreciate this information."

She knew a dismissal when she heard one. She stood and started for the door, but doubled back before she walked out. "Would your man happen to be Cathal Healey?"

Sellars lifted his gaze slowly. His expression remained unchanged, but Molly saw the shadow that flitted behind his eyes. "Who?"

"No one." Molly strode out. With the evidence in the FBI's hands, Father Tim would be safe for good—and she might not have to worry about Cathal anymore, either.

Zach headed to the parish office Tuesday evening. Day three that Lonegan didn't answer his phone. Zach puffed out a cloud in the chilly air. He'd had little excuse to stop by the office since Molly lightened his priestly load, but now he had a legitimate reason: he promised to protect her from the mobsters. With Lonegan avoiding him, he still needed Molly's signature to get his name on the bank account to seem like he was cooperating.

But once again, Molly was making his job anything but easy. He steeled himself for the coming conflict and opened the office door. Molly stood behind her desk, pulling on her green jacket. "How was your counselin' today?" She picked up her purse and rounded her desk.

"Oh, you know." Zach laughed, his voice still husky from his cough. "Half the kids are only there to get out of class and the ones that really need it won't come."

She shook her head pityingly and maneuvered past him to the door.

"Ready to head to the bank? They're open late today."

"Sorry, I've an appointment this evenin' and I can't be late." With that, she stepped out of the office, closing the door behind her.

He frowned and looked to Kathleen. "Has she done that to you before?"

"What, walk out while I'm talking to her?"

"No—it's still quarter till."

Kathleen checked her watch. "She usually stays late. But I think she's earned fifteen minutes off." She turned back to her game of computer solitaire.

Zach nodded absently. Something wasn't right. She didn't answer yesterday when he said they'd go to the bank today, and she ended the conversation when he brought it up. Was she trying to get out of putting him on the account? Was she up to something?

Frowning again, Zach turned to Molly's desk, dragged her phone over and picked up the receiver. He hit the redial button. Before he hung up, a familiar phone number registered on the phone's display. Doyle Murphy's.

Molly was a signatory on the account. She refused to add Zach.

She called Doyle.

She was taking them on all by herself. Dread and fear clamped down on his chest.

"Later, Kathleen." Zach strode to the parking lot, but Molly was already gone.

How soon could he get the Bureau's transcript of that call? It'd take days.

Sellars's counsel came ringing back to Zach's ears: *don't let it get personal.* But if Molly was taking those mobsters on her own for his sake, he hadn't let it get personal enough.

Molly rounded the corner from the elevators and stopped short. Two skinny teenagers in suits stood at the Lonegans' door, shifting as if they'd knocked and were waiting for an answer.

And yet the jitters she expected to beset her heart didn't come. Instead, her pulse kept steady with the calm she'd felt when she'd knelt to pray last night—and the confidence she could get them away from the Lonegans.

"Oh, elders." Molly reached them. "Wrong flat."

"We were just—"

"Early." Molly led the elders to her flat, but they didn't cross her threshold.

Now what had she done? She stood just inside the door. "Are you not comin' in, so?"

"We're not allowed to be alone with sisters," Elder Ehrisman said. "Have to wait for Brian."

"Oh." Was that why he insisted on coming? Odd as the practice sounded, perhaps it was wise. If Father Tim had that rule, maybe they wouldn't have had anything to worry about.

Well, they'd still have one thing. She resisted the urge to peer into the hallway to see if the Lonegans had answered the door.

"Did you get a chance to pray?" Elder Franklin ventured.

"I did."

"That's great!" He grew more serious. "Did He answer you?"

"He didn't appear to me, if that's your meanin'."

"That'd be a great story, wouldn't it?" Elder Ehrisman laughed.

Elder Franklin didn't. "But do you feel like He answered your prayer?"

Molly fiddled with the doorknob and considered the question. At least she didn't have to discuss this in front of Brian, even if they had to stand in full view of Murphy's pack until he arrived. "Didn't hear a voice or anythin'. But . . . I had the same feelin' from readin' your book."

"And what feeling was that?"

"I don't know—a deep calm. Something I've needed lately," she added in a lower tone.

"God can speak to us with a feeling of peace, definitely." Elder Ehrisman nodded.

Elder Franklin picked up where he'd left off. "Heavenly Father often answers our prayers through the Spirit, and we sometimes call the Holy Ghost the Comforter."

Before they could speak further, Brian's voice rang out down the hall. "Hey, guys! Hey, Moll!" Somehow, that nickname was endearing from Tim but annoying from Brian. He pushed past the missionaries to throw an arm around her shoulders. She automatically tensed. "Shall we?"

She should have been relieved to let the missionaries in, and stop worrying that the Lonegans would find them. But being around Brian was just another kind of uncomfortable.

Lucy arrived five minutes into the lesson on Jesus Christ. Molly was somewhat familiar with this topic—although when she'd said that, Elder Franklin and Elder Ehrisman had been alarmed instead of amused. After that, though, the lesson was lovely—hard to go wrong on that topic, though a few points were once again not quite what she'd always learned.

"Molly," Elder Ehrisman concluded, "will you follow Jesus' example and be baptized by someone with God's priesthood authority? We're having a baptism service two weeks from Friday. That's December fifth."

Had she heard that correctly? She shook her head to clear the shock at the invitation—and the warm peace filling her chest. "Oh, I—I just can't—and I've already been baptized." She glanced at Lucy; her friend avoided her gaze, focused on a strand of her blond ponytail.

"Well," Elder Ehrisman said, "we believe priesthood authority is restored in the LDS church, and it's really important to be baptized with the right authority."

"Of course it is, but this is all just—I'm busy that night."

"What are we doing?" Brian interrupted.

"Parish talent show." Molly barely acknowledged him.

"Ooh, a dog sledding demonstration?"

What—oh, Susan's made-up interests for her. Molly exchanged an amused glance with Lucy. "Can we stick to the lesson, Brian?" Lucy shot him a censuring look.

"Is there a reason you don't want to be baptized?" Elder Franklin refocused the conversation on Molly. He wasn't letting her off easy.

"Elders." Lucy stepped in as though treading on ice. "We don't want to rush anyone."

"No, no," Elder Franklin agreed. "But earlier, Molly was telling us how she felt when she prayed about the Book of Mormon. Right, Molly?"

She nodded again, careful not to look at Brian's or Lucy's reactions.

"That peace is a gift of the Spirit, and being baptized and receiving the Holy Ghost can give you that gift all the time. Isn't that something you'd want?"

Molly held onto both her elbows. Weren't there some sort of prerequisites for this? Like actually believing in . . . anything? "I can't make a decision like that on the spot. You do realize what you're askin'. My family's been Catholic since they learned the Trinity on a shamrock."

"It's a big change, but you can do it with Christ. Think about it,"

Elder Franklin said. "We still good for another lesson next week?"

She hesitated a moment. "I suppose."

When the missionaries left, Molly watched to make sure they didn't go canvassing her neighbors. Suddenly she wasn't sure learning about Lucy's church was so harmless—for any of them.

ZACH HUNG UP the parish house phone Thursday. For the fifth day in a row, nobody at the Lonegans' would answer his calls. Now he'd have to go back to Molly. This wasn't the way to keep her safe.

But as soon as he walked into the office, he regretted whiling away Wednesday watching Robert Ludlum movies. Molly's eyes were bloodshot and puffy, her mascara smudged. He checked if they were alone—Kathleen was there. She'd been crying, too.

"What's the matter?" he asked.

"You haven't heard?"

Zach glanced at each of them for another clue. "About what?"

"Father Patrick." Kathleen cut off a sob with the back of her hand.

Molly motioned Zach closer, then turned her monitor toward him. She brought up the WGNtv homepage and clicked on a headline under Breaking News: "Second Alleged Victim of Slain Priest." The photo captured his attention first: Doyle Murphy, his son Ian, and Lonegan's son Brandon, on limestone steps. Zach tried to skim the article but was quickly drawn in.

> When St. Adelaide Catholic Church buried their slain priest, Father Colin Patrick, the suburban Chicago parish thought the worst was behind them. That was until this week, when two teenagers in the parish came forward with allegations the late priest molested them.
>
> "We regret Father Patrick's death, but people need to know there was way more to this tragedy,"

said Doyle Murphy, father of the first victim. "No matter how much you want to trust someone, if something's wrong, follow your gut."

Zach straightened, deadweight settling on his chest. Could this be the real reason Patrick was murdered? Molesting a mobster's child had to be a quick route to certain death.

But coming forward with these accusations in an unsolved murder case was a lot dumber than Sellars said these guys were. Then what was going on?

"It can't be true." Kathleen's declaration carried the finality of a death sentence. "They weren't altar boys."

He folded his arms. "I don't like it either, but we can't go blaming the victims."

"She's not speakin' metaphorically," Molly said. "They weren't altar boys. I've never even seen them at services. I suppose they do go to the school, though."

"You just . . ." Kathleen sighed. "You think you'd know something like this was going on. If he was capable of this."

"If there's one thing I've learned, it's that you can never tell what people are capable of." Zach watched Molly for a long moment. Her gaze wandered over her desk, lost. Was there something he could do, something he could say to help her?

No, anything to comfort her might distress her more coming from him. He shook his head sadly and left for the parish house.

Had Cally Lonegan lied to him? He couldn't have known Father Patrick abused his son and not been in on a plot to kill the priest. And the first time they'd met, Lonegan said it had something to do with Father Patrick.

Or maybe Brandon didn't go to his own father, telling Murphy instead. Might explain why Lonegan wasn't in the photo. But—for once—Kathleen was right. Wouldn't somebody have had some idea this was going on before it escalated to the level of murder?

Zach found Father Fitzgerald sitting at the parish house's breakfast bar, pondering a bowl of soup in solemn silence. Fitzgerald knew. Apparently the parish rumor mill was running like clockwork.

"Have you heard?" Zach asked, though he knew the answer.

Fitzgerald nodded.

"Why didn't you tell me?"

"What was there to tell? Colin made some terrible choices; I hoped you could make better ones without making an example of him."

Fitzgerald fixated on his bowl, but his eyes remained unfocused. The slump in his back, the hollow stare—far from shocked or even surprised, he was resigned to the facts about Father Patrick.

"How long have you known?"

Fitzgerald stirred his soup in silence for a minute. "Ian told me in September."

"After Colin died?"

He shrugged. "It's all a haze."

"But when he was alive, you didn't have any idea—"

"No. None whatsoever."

So this was that terrible secret Fitzgerald was keeping. Zach waited for Fitzgerald to look at him. "You've known for two months and you haven't said anything?"

"I tried counseling the boy and his family, but what good would it do to tarnish the memory of the dead for everyone else?" Fitzgerald rubbed a hand over his face. "Oh, Colin. How could you—how could anyone—?"

Zach sank onto the stool next to Fitzgerald. How could he have missed this?

Zach flipped on the TV at noon Friday, but he couldn't bring himself to see if local networks picked up the press conference Fitzgerald and the archbishop were holding.

This just didn't make sense. How had he not seen this? Had Murphy found out about the abuse and forced Father Patrick to make the deal with the mob? Or maybe Ian or Brandon had murdered him, and the mob was covering.

A knock at the door jolted Zach from his thoughts. Maybe it was Molly with the news—and he could see how she was holding up. He hurried to answer.

Doyle Murphy jerked his chin in greeting.

Like this was his fault, a shard of guilt lodged between Zach's ribs. "Doyle, I'm so sorry. Father Fitzgerald's still downtown—"

"No, I want to talk to you. Walk?"

"Sure." Zach grabbed his coat. What was Murphy doing here while the archdiocese was apologizing to his family? Or were they done already? "Were you at the press conference?"

"Yep."

Zach shut the door behind him. Unsure how to continue, he let the conversation lapse as they walked to the end of the block. At the corner, Murphy stared straight ahead. What could he want to say? They crossed the street in silence.

At the end of the second block, Zach shoved his hands deep into his coat pockets. Was he going to have to start this conversation? Murphy concentrated on the crosswalk signal. What did he expect Zach to do?

By the end of the third block, Zach wished he'd sat in on a course in grief counseling at the seminary. No words could help Murphy, who still wasn't looking at him.

"Got something I want to talk to you about," Murphy finally began on the fourth block. "A business transaction."

Zach slowly turned to stare at Murphy. Was he completely out of his mind? Business, now?

Murphy took in his shock. "Obviously you've been following the news."

"And obviously business should be the furthest thing from your mind."

"Business is always on my mind."

The hairs on the back of Zach's neck stood at attention, and not because of the cold. Zach silently berated himself. How could he have relaxed his guard with Murphy? He'd forgotten who he was dealing with. He kept his eyes on Murphy and mentally reviewed the lay of the land. A cluster of older women strolled half a block behind them. A man and a woman passed each other on the opposite side of the street.

Murphy gestured to his black Audi. Zach's mind jumped to full alert. An ankle holster wasn't accessible enough to do much good, but he kept his right hand free. While Murphy rounded the car, Zach scrutinized the backseat for any hint of movement. He could only see his reflection in the tinted glass, bewildered and wary.

He braced himself and yanked open the door. The backseat was empty. Murphy was already waiting in the driver's seat. Zach quickly sat and pulled the door shut. The gray interior smelled of stale cigarette smoke, but he pretended he didn't notice. "What about your business is so important that you're coming to me now?" Zach asked.

"You're the one in charge of the school, right?"

Zach nodded, though it was only partially true.

"The kids need their lunches."

What was Murphy getting at? "Why don't you just say what you mean?"

"I supply the food for the school, but my contract is up for renewal."

The contracts in the filing cabinet. "Well, Doyle, we have to check out our options, of course, but if you're the best deal—"

"That won't be necessary, Father."

Zach feigned curiosity. "Oh?"

"It's not our prices that make us your best option."

"What, your competitors are selling tainted food?" After a pause, Zach tried again. "Hey, I want to help our parishioners out, but we can't bankrupt the school to do it."

Murphy tapped his fingers on the steering wheel. "You've heard about Ian and Brandon."

"Again, I'm sorry." But he was growing less sympathetic every second he sat in the mobster's car talking "business."

"You wouldn't want to be in Father Patrick's position if he were alive, would you?"

"No." At the hooded look Murphy shot him, Zach chose to play dumb. "What's that got to do with it?"

"Just something you might want to consider before you go trying to change things."

Then the full implications hit him—it was all a lie. A perverted power play to show Father Tim what they were capable of. Killing a priest, getting their sons to lie about him molesting them—what weren't they capable of?

He could feel the indignation rising in his chest, but Zach took a long moment to gather his composure. "The archdiocese would have to be pretty stupid or pretty desperate to ordain someone so degenerate he'd start abusing his parishioners' kids in two months. And it might seem a little suspicious if that priest happened to target the same families as their last one—who ended up murdered."

"You think that's the only way it could go?" Murphy laughed derisively. "No, Father, for you, I have something else in mind. You know Molly Malone?"

He pursed his lips. He'd played right into Murphy's hands. "Rings a bell."

"Now, what's the penance for breaking a vow of celibacy?"

Zach's fingers tightened on the edge of his seat to fight back a rising tide of anger. He was trained to keep his cool. Not let things get personal. "She'd deny it."

"What wouldn't she do for you? She's in love with you."

Zach stilled his tapping foot and rolled his shoulders to release the tension. Murphy couldn't possibly know that, no matter what Kathleen told him. He was baiting him.

It was working.

"But," Murphy continued, "I saw the two of you together. So did Jay Gallaher. You can't refute eyewitnesses."

"Just like you can't refute boys who say they've been molested by their priest."

"We understand each other?"

Nerves gnawed at Zach's stomach. He willed his fingers to release the gray upholstery. He'd flirted with Molly so she'd target him, not so the mob would target her.

Was he thinking like an FBI agent or a man trying to protect Molly?

"Or do we have to air all the parish's dirty laundry? Because believe me—" Murphy leaned forward and lowered his voice to just an edge of danger. "—it'll get a lot worse. We'd hate for something to happen to her."

Zach chewed his lower lip. Much as he hated going along with anything a mobster proposed, maybe if he gave Murphy enough rope . . . "Send me the paperwork."

"Knew you'd see it our way." Murphy offered him a piece of paper with a dollar figure and an account number—277135847. Father Patrick's private account. "Transfer this account into your name. Things'll go smoother."

"Father Patrick's, I take it?" He didn't need clarification, but Murphy didn't know that.

He nodded. "You'll have the contract on your desk Monday. I'll give you a lift home."

"Rather walk." Zach opened the car door, but before he stood, Murphy offered his hand. Zach ignored it and got out of the car. He was a block away before the tension in his back muscles began to dissolve—and he realized what he'd just gotten.

Father Patrick had been extorted. Father Tim was soon to follow in his footsteps. And Zach didn't only have evidence. He was a witness. Heck, he was practically a victim—and so was Patrick.

He had to talk to Sellars.

"Not enough," Sellars said once Zach related the threat from Murphy Saturday night.

"What do you mean, not enough?" Despite Zach's efforts to keep his voice down, there was still a hushed echo through the frigid shadows of the ASAC's favorite underpass. "You've got your witness—me."

Sellars stuck his fingers under the brim of his worn out cap to massage his temple. "Great. We go to trial, Murphy argues entrapment and gets off."

"This is obviously not entrapment."

He snorted. "I know that and you know that, but you just try making a jury see it with lawyers like his. Best case, we get Doyle Murphy for a few years."

"You're not seeing the big picture." Zach rubbed his hands together. "This extortion attempt could be evidence of the extortion against Father Patrick. That's two counts—that's racketeering. And extorting Father Patrick could be why they murdered him."

"And Murphy will argue Patrick molested his kid, and the jury will nullify. Or he'll say Ian killed Patrick, but Murphy's willing to take the fall for his son, and the jury will still nullify."

"We still have him on the deal with the school."

"Do you really think we sent you in there to nab him for school lunches?" Sellars scoffed. "His lawyers would have a field day."

Zach pulled his jacket tighter. "You give Murphy's lawyers a lot of credit."

"Seen 'em in action." Sellars took out a pack of cigarettes.

"But even they can't refute an agent as an eyewitness. We'll get him on that at least."

Sellars shook his head. "We're not settling for only Murphy. I want them all."

"Getting greedy, Sellars. Bird in the hand?" Zach glanced around the empty underpass. Good thing the homeless men who lived here weren't out on a night this frigid.

The older man sighed. "Rookie mistake. Thought you were 'made for this.' Or was that Healey?" He focused on lighting his cigarette.

Frowning, Zach bounced on his heels to warm up. He was no rookie. What mistake?

"We *need* them all. The mob isn't like a snake—cut off the head and the body dies. If we take out Murphy, there's ten more like him waiting in the wings."

"Maybe he'd flip on them."

"Tried that. We let him buy his freedom testifying against guys who turned out to be peons. Not this time." Sellars shook his head again. "Now he's the second-in-command for the whole South Side. We're not going to deal unless he gives us his boss—the don."

"And how do you expect Father Tim to make that happen?"

Sellars placed emphasis on each word of Zach's title, but kept his voice low. "*Special Agent Saint* will dig Murphy a hole so deep he won't know which way is up. Roll up everybody so he can't flip on anyone *but* the boss—or Special Agent Healey will have to come back."

He pursed his lips. Not helpful. "I can handle this. But I need more time."

Sellars puffed on his cigarette and said nothing.

"Just a little."

"I'll talk to the archbishop. You get your guy into protection; I'll get the paperwork."

Zach saluted. Lonegan wasn't taking his calls since the news about Ian and Brandon. Might be faster to drag Murphy in than Lonegan—and he only had eight days left.

Z ACH PAUSED BEFORE THE CONCLUSION of his homily Sunday to scan the congregation for Lonegan again. Though he didn't want to preach false doctrine and he'd had to say *something* about the accusations against Father Patrick, Zach was most nervous about using his first talk in Mass to push Cally Lonegan to turn on the mob. With only one week left in the parish, Zach and Molly were the mob's target, and he still wasn't sure Lonegan even wanted out.

No sign of him among the parishioners. Doyle Murphy, however, was right down front.

Zach continued his sermon about the sinner returning to God. "It's not easy to change—it never is. In the Sermon on the Mount, the Lord counseled if our hand or our foot or our eye causes us to stumble, we should remove that body part and cast it away."

He took a deep breath and reminded himself to speak more slowly and clearly at the most direct part of his message to Lonegan. "Obviously He was speaking figuratively, since I don't know many people whose hands or feet randomly lead them into sin without some input from the rest of their bodies. Instead, as we change our lives, we have to cut off possessions, habits or *people* very important to us. But it's better for us 'to enter into life halt or maimed, rather than having two hands or two feet to be cast into everlasting fire.'"

He paused for one last scan. No Lonegan. Zach finished his sermon with a last scripture on offering a broken heart and a contrite spirit and hurried back to the choir loft during the Nicene Creed. He'd gotten too used to wearing the simpler choir dress he could wear when he was just the organist instead of the full complement of Sunday vestments he needed to preach. He managed to wait until he reached the stairway before he unceremoniously hiked up the heavy ceremonial clothing to give his feet clearance to take the stairs two at a time up to the choir loft.

He double-checked the loft to see if Lonegan had snuck in there. Maybe he didn't want to be seen in the congregation after his son's accusation that week. Still no Lonegan.

After Father Fitzgerald concluded Mass, Zach played a short postlude and rushed down to greet the parishioners in the vestibule, searching the crowd one last time for Lonegan.

"Father Tim?"

Hoping the woman addressing him would be Lisa Lonegan, Zach turned. To his surprise, a sheepish Kathleen stood there, shifting her weight from foot to foot. "Just wanted to thank you for your homily." She looked away, again shuffling.

He nodded, then craned his neck to scan the passing parishioners for Lonegan.

Kathleen moved closer and lowered her voice, but still didn't make eye contact. "I'll be more careful about what I say."

He tried not to gape at her. "Oh, I didn't—I hope I didn't offend you."

"No, no. I . . . I know better than to gossip. You were right. We have to cast away bad habits."

He converted his amusement into a sympathetic smile. "Glad to know the Spirit moved you today."

She bid him goodbye while he looked over the stragglers. Still no Lonegan. How long had it been since they talked last? Could he have changed his mind about wanting out? Zach headed through the chapel to get his phone from the sacristy. With every step, the knot in his stomach twisted tighter. If Lonegan's son was going along with the extortion scheme, could Cally *not* be a part? If Murphy was making his move for Father Tim, maybe Lonegan was done "reeling him in." Maybe Zach had run out of chances.

He grabbed his phone from the drawer and dialed Lonegan. Five . . . six . . . seven rings—no answer. Zach tossed the phone onto the vesting table.

Now one of them was in real trouble.

A manila envelope dropped onto Molly's desk Tuesday when Kathleen returned with the mail. Addressed to Father Tim, no return address. Molly slid the papers out and read over them. One phrase caught her eye—and then the blood chilled in her veins.

Kincaid Wholesalers. Doyle Murphy's crew. They wanted Father Tim's signature.

Could she get away with shredding this?

No one would know. Father Tim wouldn't miss it, and Doyle Murphy would have to go through her. She still had sole access to that account.

"Hey, Moll." Father Tim walked in, oblivious to the threat she held. She clutched the paper tighter. He stepped closer, eyebrows arched in mild curiosity. "You busy?"

"Only paperwork. Records." She avoided his gaze as she grabbed her keys from the top drawer. She unlocked the lower drawer and thrust the contract on top of the cashbox. Before Father Tim could lean over her desk, she shoved the drawer shut and locked it.

Father Tim didn't seem overly concerned. He turned away to sift through another box of donated books. But the vise around her ribs didn't loosen. She still had to ask him about the Mormons. And Kathleen serenely filed her nails at her desk.

"How's the talent show coming?" Tim asked after a moment.

"We had good acts sign up, but a lot have backed out." Molly glanced at Kathleen. Her daughter was the latest cancellation. "Grace said she can't do it, either. One of her backup singers has a schedule conflict."

"How many does that make?" Kathleen asked.

"Four. At this rate, we won't have anyone left."

"Except for you and me." Tim finished sorting the books and

started reloading the box.

"Do you want to go first or will I?"

"You can. I have something special planned." He gave her half a smile. "You speak Irish, right?"

Kathleen cleared her throat; Molly ignored her. "*Tá.*" She nodded. "We'll have you as the closing act, so." She silently prayed it wouldn't be "Molly Malone" in Irish.

"Bet I could get Lucy to sing, too—one more act you know won't back out."

Molly folded her arms to rub her elbow. She didn't want to give him an excuse to talk to Lucy, but being jealous was ridiculous. Father Tim turned back to the box, and they lapsed into silence.

"Have you heard from the Murphys or the Lonegans this week?" Father Tim's solemn murmur broke the stillness.

"No." Molly matched his low tone.

"Any word on their lawsuit?"

Molly waited for Kathleen's reply. "No."

A somber silence fell over them again for a few moments, broken only by the muffled rhythm of Tim stacking the books.

Until the door swung open and in limped—Brian? Molly groaned inwardly. Someone else she needed to have a delicate conversation with.

"Hey, Moll—whoa, who died?" He looked from Molly to Kathleen with their twin expressions of grim solemnity.

"The last priest," Tim supplied.

Brian startled and stepped around the door to see Tim kneeling by the box of books. "And you're, what, his apprentice?"

Tim slowly rose to his feet. Molly couldn't help a bit of gratification as Brian had to crane his neck to look up at Tim once he stood at his full height. "I'm his replacement."

"Uh, yeah." Brian turned to Molly. She caught a glimpse of the sarcastic smirk he must've given Tim.

"Is this your boyfriend, Molly?" Kathleen finally spoke up.

Brian's eyes lit up. "You've been talking about me—or this?" He patted his knee brace.

Molly gritted her teeth. He didn't need encouragement.

"I was thinking we could get an early dinner this week." Brian jerked his head in Tim's direction. "You don't need his permission to leave, do you?"

She glanced at Tim. "Technically you *are* my employer, aren't you?"

"What am I going to do, chain you to your desk?"

Brian scoffed, arranging his highlighted brown hair. "Come on, Molly."

Molly again looked from the man she could hardly stand to the man she couldn't have, unsure what to say. She pulled on her coat and silently begged Father Tim to find some reason to object, even the flimsiest pretense of a task for her. He lowered his gaze, but gave her the smallest nod of assent. He was right—they both were.

Molly shut down her computer and grabbed her handbag. "Bye now."

"You ever been to *C*?" Brian asked as the door shut behind them.

The restaurant where she had dinner not a week ago with Lucy, Paul, and Tim—Father Tim. She put on her gloves to buy herself time to answer. Was it ironic or fitting to follow the strangest double date in history with the most uncomfortable date she'd ever been on?

They reached his silver SUV. Brian made no move toward the door handle—and when Molly did, he leaned a hand on her door. She didn't dare look at him, but at the edge of her vision, she could see him waiting, a smirk on his lips, but hunger—and intent—in his eyes.

Was he serious? How could he possibly think they were at a place, metaphorically or literally, where she'd kiss him? She choked on a laugh.

Just as Brian started to lean in, Father Tim's voice carried across the car park. "Have fun, Moll!"

The interruption was perfectly timed: Molly ducked underneath Brian's awkward advance. "See you tomorrow!" She maneuvered around Brian while he was recovering his balance. "You know, I'm not really interested in goin' out."

"Oh. Okay. I'm sure the missionaries can meet us at my place early." He pulled his mobile from his pocket. Before Molly could clarify that she meant she wasn't interested in going out at all, ever,

Brian continued. "That priest of yours has quite the sense of timing. How can you stand him?"

"We're friends." Father Tim wouldn't have interrupted Brian's attempted kiss on purpose, would he? She'd have to thank him later. "And speakin' of friends—"

"Guys can't be 'just friends' with hot girls." He shook his head. "Even celibate guys."

Her ribs shrank a centimeter. "Brian," she murmured. "I know you're not Catholic, but we can all respect the priesthood."

"Oh, yeah. Sorry." He smiled. "You make me want to be better. I want to marry someone just like you."

Molly opened her handbag to search for her keys to hide her shock. They'd never even been on a date. She'd seen the man all of five times. What could he mean by "just like you"—female?

Suddenly this evening didn't seem a much better idea than an evening with Tim.

Father Tim.

MOLLY FROWNED AT THE DIAGRAM Brian had drawn to accompany the missionaries' lesson in his high-end bachelor pad. The center circle represented Earth, with continents, a sea monster, and stick figures of the missionaries on the South Pole, holding copies of the Book of Mormon—and Brian and Molly on the North Pole, holding hands.

She'd waited for any opportunity to end her time with Brian, but the lesson had flowed with dizzying smoothness. Elder Ehrisman finished his description of the afterlife. Brian slid the diagram over the glass-and-brushed-nickel coffee table to add three circles in a column after the judgment bar.

Molly interrupted the missionary. "Three heavens?"

"Kingdoms. Telestial, terrestrial, celestial," Brian listed, labeling them. He drew flames in the bottom corner of the paper. "And outer darkness, but you don't need to worry about that."

"God rewards us according to what we did while we were here being tested." Elder Ehrisman indicated the Earth circle. Molly eyed the drawings of her and Brian. She was certainly being tested.

Brian was surely not her sorest test, though.

"I think Catholics believe you have to be part of God's church and be righteous to go to heaven, right?" Elder Ehrisman said.

She wasn't expecting a quiz on the catechism. "I suppose."

"But really, it comes down to Christ's atonement. We could never be good enough to deserve even the lowest reward without His atonement to make up for our sins and make us better."

Molly mulled over Elder Franklin's words. She must have been taught this sometime, but what did that mean?

"What questions do you have about what we've taught?" Elder Ehrisman asked.

She blinked at the unexpected phrasing. If they'd just asked if she had any questions, she probably would've said no. But it seemed like much more of a lie to have to actually say she had no questions. "What does it mean that Christ's atonement makes us better?"

"Oh." Elder Ehrisman and Elder Franklin exchanged a glance; Elder Franklin gestured for the other to take the question. "Well, obviously, part of the Atonement is to make up for the sins we repent of. Another part is to feel all the pains and sorrows we feel. And another is God's grace, like a blessing of help and strength."

Molly realized she was staring at the table again. She needed strength; that was certain. "How do you get that?"

"Christ gives it to us when we have faith and repent and try our hardest to obey the commandments."

"And what if we can't keep the commandments?"

"We can all try." Elder Ehrisman met her gaze with a strange mix of pity and hope. "It's not like we'll be perfect on the first try. All of us need His grace because of Adam's fall, and because we're human. Weakness is part of the deal."

So was there or wasn't there any help—or hope—for her? Especially if faith was required?

"Does that answer your question?" Elder Franklin asked.

She nodded automatically. She half-listened to Elder Franklin's prayer—he asked for her to find peace and understand God's plan for her. Once the missionaries had left, Molly made an excuse to leave, though Brian insisted on walking to her car.

This had gone on far too long. "I'm sorry, Brian, but really, I'm just not interested."

He glanced around as if looking for a frame of reference. "In the lessons?"

The question derailed Molly's train of thought. Obnoxious though he was, Brian did seem sincere about his beliefs. "I know I can help." He threw his arm around her shoulders. "Do you know the Book of Mormon's the word of God?"

Molly fiddled with her coat button. The missionaries had never asked her outright, and she'd been content to leave her impressions as feelings of peace and comfort, without letting herself think of their implications.

"I think that . . . it is." As soon as she said it, that same serene solace filled her more powerfully than ever.

Brian noticed the change, or was satisfied with her answer, judging by his knowing smile. "Then what's keeping you from the Church?"

At that second, she had none of her normal objections. What if she joined the Mormons?

And then logic reared its head. How could she break with her family's beliefs? She'd have to leave the church, leave her job. Leave Father Tim. "This is askin' a lot—givin' up practically my whole life." And didn't she have to believe? And not be so weak?

"Listen, why don't we talk about it over dinner?"

"Thank you, no."

He'd already started limping toward his car, but he turned back. "No?"

"That's right. No, thank you." She could almost hear her mum chiding her, so Molly added, "I'm sorry."

"It's okay. I know how snappy girls get when they're hungry. Let's go eat."

She set her jaw. Had she really worried about his feelings? Molly stood her ground. "I amn't hungry."

"Oh, okay. Are we still on for your talent show?"

What would it take to get through to him? "We'd be glad to have you come," she said, subtly emphasizing the *we*, "but you must know I really don't see this goin' anywhere."

She ducked into her car to end the conversation, but Brian laughed. "Don't worry, I'm not expecting much. Not like you're a professional dancer or anything. See you Friday!"

Not a professional—? She'd been a world-ranked champion and retired before the man could shave. Before she "snapped" at him again, Brian shut her car door. Still flabbergasted, Molly watched him hobble away. He was really that mad—absolutely crazy. But his brush-off wasn't what made her feel so unsettled as she pulled out and started for home.

How could this belief feel so foreign and yet sound perfectly logical? Why was she still entertaining the idea of joining the Mormon church?

Faith. The answer was so simple and yet so hard. Sure, she believed in Christ, believed in His atonement.

She found herself slowing out of habit as she passed the church. The lights in the priests' brick cottage were on.

If anyone could put her mind to rights, it would be Father Tim. And a doctrinal question would be a perfectly safe reason to seek him out—who better to talk to than her priest?

She turned into the car park and hurried to knock on the door. Father Fitzgerald answered. "Molly? Are you all right?"

She clutched her handbag tighter. This was the opportunity she wanted. "I'd like to speak with you, if you have the time."

"Of course." Father Fitzgerald escorted her into the parish house. Once she'd settled in the shabby armchair of indiscriminate color, he waited patiently for her to begin.

As if she knew where to start. "Father," she finally said, "how does Christ's atonement work?"

Father Fitzgerald raised his bushy silver eyebrows. "Not quite what I expected." The priest settled back in the couch. "There are a number of theories, but I'm guessing you're not here for a theological debate. What aspect of the atonement are you wondering about?"

"How does His atonement make us better?"

"That's one of the mysteries of God, really." Father Fitzgerald studied her for a moment, his expression verging on consternation. "Why do you ask?"

She sorted through the words to find the best way to tell him. Perhaps if she went back to Lucy. "A friend said something to me about how Christ's atonement helps us when we're weak."

"Certainly—think of the novenas, all the devotions, the Hail Mary. We always pray for help from God and from all the saints to strengthen us."

Molly focused on the black-and-neon afghan behind Father Fitzgerald. She knew every prayer, though she hadn't exactly used them lately. That didn't seem to be what Lucy and the missionaries meant, but Molly couldn't quite put her finger on the words to articulate the difference.

"How about this?" Father Fitzgerald began. "Try something like studying the scriptures or adoration for half an hour, perhaps the Stations of the Cross. You might even try witnessing of the faith. To help you have the spirit of Christ."

Witness of the faith? That would require having real faith. How could any of those things help her when she had to face Father Tim? "What if I'm still weak?"

Father Fitzgerald grew quiet. "We're all weak, Molly. We're human. We're tempted by lust and anger and pride. God won't tempt us above what we're able to withstand, so we have to overcome our temptations. And if we don't . . ." His voice trailed into a hollow echo. Molly glanced at him. Father Fitzgerald's eyes were empty, as if he'd retreated into the cavern formed by his hunched body. He had no more help to offer. She thanked him and left.

The last thing she needed was yet another source of turmoil.

Zach swallowed another groan. Whether Lucy was mad that Zach was between her and her "unboyfriend" Paul or she just liked to annoy him, he'd endured ninety minutes of her sniping between ladling gravy onto the volunteers' plates. Working alongside parishioners and other volunteers, the mobsters were serving the indigents already filling the long tables in the school gym.

Zach deposited a scoop of mashed potatoes onto the Gallaher boy's plate, and ignored Lucy's dig about the girl he'd had a crush on in middle school.

"Speaking of crushes," Lucy murmured, eye-pointing toward the next in line: Molly.

"Shut up," Zach hissed back. He dished potatoes onto Molly's Styrofoam plate, but when she tried to move on, he didn't let go. After a second, Molly cast a meaningful glance at the bustle around them—Lucy serving gravy, Paul doling out rolls.

Zach leaned over the pot of potatoes. "I have a mission for you."

"What kind of mission?" She bent forward, mirroring his intimate posture—and his amused smile.

He lowered her plate, allowing them to draw close enough to speak without being overheard. "I need to talk to Cally Lonegan."

"He's not here."

"Wouldn't be much of a mission if he were." He broadened his grin a split second. "I want you to find out if he's avoiding me."

Molly narrowed her eyes with an undertone of flirting. "Secretary, Father, not spy."

"Even Miss Moneypenny got pulled onto the job sometimes."

"But Miss Moneypenny wasn't Bond's secretary, it was—"

"Miss Ponsonby and then Miss Goodnight."

She gave him an oh-you-think-you're-so-clever look, like he was the man who knew too much about the world's most famous spy.

"And you're not my personal secretary anyway, Miss Malone." He nodded at the table where Jay Gallaher and Miles Hennessy were taking a break from serving Thanksgiving meals.

Molly cast another glance around them. The delay was beginning to hold up the line—and attract attention.

"And I'm tellin' you, Father—" She raised the plate and her voice for anyone within five feet to notice. "—we can give them more than that!"

Zach pursed his lips in a show of exasperation, but kept the smile in his eyes and slapped more potatoes onto the plate. Molly made for Gallaher and Hennessy with her trademark springing step.

Lucy elbow-nudged Zach. "Smooth, Captain Obvious," she said, waggling her eyebrows in Molly's direction. "Why don't you kiss her and get it over with?"

"Shut. Up." He gave an exaggerated look around. Couldn't she be more careful? Maybe not—to her this was more of a game than a hunt for a mob and a murderer.

"Sensitive," she muttered.

Zach tilted his head toward Paul. He wasn't the only one with a secret flame.

"All right, Scrooge. Where's the holiday spirit?"

"Why don't you work on your own problems, spinster?" The instant he said it, regret stabbed his gut. Lucy slowly set her spoon in the gravy pot, then shoved past Zach. Why did they always end up bickering like kids?

"I better see if she's okay." Paul dropped the bag of rolls onto the table.

Noble, but Zach kind of had something to say to her. "No, I caused this, so I'd better fix it. Man the potatoes."

He followed his sister past the table where Molly sat chatting with Hennessy and Gallaher, and found Lucy a few feet outside behind a tall hedge, alone, crying in the cold. Like she was trying to make him feel worse. "Lucy."

She turned her back on him. "Go away. How could you say that to me?"

"Luce—"

"It's not fair for you to call me a spinster. That's just so . . . hateful."

"You do realize I'm four years older than you and still single, right? Pot, kettle, black?"

Lucy shot a glare over her shoulder. "Is that supposed to be an apology?"

"Fine. I'm sorry, Lucy." Yeah, it was a low blow. But did she really have to tease him about Molly—in the same room as the people who'd kill them both without a second thought? "I need you to be more careful. It's one thing in front of Paul, but the rest of the parish—"

"More careful about what? I didn't say anything loud enough for anyone to hear. *You're* the one who needs to be careful. Your badge doesn't give you a license to be cruel."

He scoffed. It was always about her, wasn't it? "Yeah, you're right. If I end up dead because you blow my cover, I'll die happy knowing I haven't hurt your feelings lately." Their older siblings were right: Lucy could get away with murder.

She sniffled and sulked in silence.

"Look at me."

Lucy aimed a sullen scowl at him.

"I know this seems like playing dress up to you, but this isn't a game." He leaned closer to emphasize his point. "You know how dangerous this could be."

She gave a one-shouldered shrug. Zach seriously considered leaving her out there in the cold until she got it through her brain that if anyone here thought he was anything other than a priest, he'd be in serious trouble, and not only with the Bureau.

How could she possibly not get this was dangerous? She'd received a threat from the mob herself, and it seemed pretty traumatizing—she had to be in denial.

He couldn't walk away from his own sister. "All right, you want to tell me what's really going on here?"

"All of a sudden I'm the expert on the situation? I thought you were the only one who was allowed to know what's going on."

Zach folded his arms across his chest, which had the added benefit of a little extra warmth. "Come on. This is your chance to tell me why you're acting like you hate me."

"Like you care."

"I'm here, aren't I? I could've let Paul come to you—maybe I should've."

Lucy whirled around. "This is the first substantial conversation we've had in four years. You were my best friend, Zach."

His heart stopped for a split second. He glanced around to see if anyone heard her slip. They were alone. His sister noticed her mistake and grimaced. "Sorry."

He nodded. "Guess it has been a while." Had this been bugging her all this time? "I'm sorry. Really." Zach held out his arms and Lucy reluctantly yielded to a hug.

Somehow, he'd violated a cardinal rule: to protect her, he had to get his sister to trust him. He'd assumed that was a given, and he was wrong. "What have I missed?"

Lucy sighed. "Where do I start?"

Molly waited for the two mobsters to acknowledge her question about Cally. Though she wanted to keep Father Tim from their outfit, they were all worried about the Lonegans. All except Miles Hennessy and Jay Gallaher, apparently. Miles finally stopped shoveling pie between his thick lips to snort. "What, don't they have enough problems?"

"Miles, we're all concerned for them. Maybe Teresa's talked to Lisa?"

He shook his head. "Try their lawyer."

"Talk about closing ranks," Jay Gallaher jumped in. "Nobody's been able to talk to Cally ever since."

"I can't imagine what it's like dealin' with this." Molly searched their faces. "Father Fitzgerald and Father Tim really want to reach out to their families, offer them the support of the parish."

"Y'know, they're just . . . I dunno." Jay propped his sharp elbows on the table. "Doyle's still talking to us, but Cally's taking it hard."

"Which is why it's so important we talk to him and his family."

"Good luck." Miles bowed over his plate.

Molly nodded and stood. Father Tim would be reassured he wasn't the only one getting the silent treatment from Cally—and her mission was accomplished.

Pity. An "undercover mission" was a bit of a thrill, though she wasn't sure whether it was spying or working with Tim that made her fingers tingle with excitement.

But when she got back to the pot of potatoes, Paul greeted her.

"Hi, Paul. Have you seen Father Tim?"

Paul's gaze snapped to the side doors. "He's outside."

Molly frowned at the trepidation in his tone—and the fact that Paul was now the only person left at their serving table. Lucy was gone, too. "He left you here alone? I needed to speak with him."

Though she hadn't meant she'd go after Tim, Paul tossed the ladle into the potatoes. "I'll go with you." He rounded the table, and Molly followed him to the side doors.

Molly opened the metal door that led outside. Before she released the handle, alerting anyone nearby to their presence, voices carried from beyond a tall brick enclosure a meter away. Paul and Molly froze to listen.

"Moving here has been way harder than I expected." Lucy—had she been crying? "I'm just . . . lonely. You're here, but it doesn't count because we have to keep everything a secret."

Paul glanced at Molly, the unease she felt evident on his face, too. *Everything?*

"I'm sorry things aren't like they used to be," Father Tim said, "and there might not be a whole lot I can do to change that. But I do love you—you know I always will."

Her stomach dropped. That declaration should be hers. Not that she necessarily wanted to hear it, but—

"I love you too," Lucy said, unknowingly twisting the knife. "And I'm really not trying to get you in trouble or make you lose your job."

"Thanks. I'm not—okay, I *was* trying to hurt your feelings. But I'll try not to do it again."

Paul shrank back into the building and Molly followed, careful not to let the door latch make a sound.

"That was probably . . . nothing." He nodded, confirming his own shaky conclusion, as they reached the main hall. "She was upset and he was just concerned, as a priest."

"He isn't *her* priest." Molly's good sense beat out her jealousy, and she stopped short—she was standing only meters from other parishioners. She didn't need to badmouth Tim in front of everyone, no matter how he was hurting her. She checked the nearest table. Miles Hennessy and Jay Gallaher stared up at her in silence.

The metal doors swung open behind her, but she didn't look back.

"Back to work!" Lucy announced. "You guys holding up without us?"

Molly still didn't turn around. "Grand, as always." She returned to the beginning of the food service line without looking at Lucy or Father Tim.

She knew she was a fool for falling for a priest, but she didn't realize she was quite that big a fool.

ZACH FROWNED UP AT the white stucco apartment building Friday night. If Lonegan's neighbors weren't mobsters, Zach would still be banging on his door. But neither of them needed extra attention from Murphy and their ilk—and apparently Lonegan didn't want Father Tim's attention either. As Zach finished sticking the GPS tracker on Lonegan's car, though, his phone rang. He tried to contain his rising hope.

Doyle Murphy. Zach glanced back at Lonegan's dark windows. Just in case, he stepped into the shadows of the Dumpster pen to answer the phone. "Yeah?"

"You must've forgotten to tell me you're on the account. Got the contract, right?"

"Haven't seen it. Better have your secretary send over another."

Murphy snorted. "You're on the account, then?"

"It's been a short week—the bank closed early on Wednesday, and I didn't have a chance before that." And he had no actual intention of following through—but now that Lonegan was incommunicado, he might have to. More evidence couldn't hurt.

"Don't drag your feet," Murphy said.

"Yeah." The taut irritation in his voice was a little too real. He shouldn't antagonize the man, but he didn't have to sound eager to be extorted.

"Be a real shame to bring Miss Saint into this."

A flash of panic at his name subsided quickly—although threatening his sister wasn't any better. He peered over his shoulder to check Murphy's windows. Was he watching the lot? No shadows on the blinds. "Lucy?"

"How many different rumors do you think it'd take to get back to the archbishop?"

That was probably supposed to be the convincing part of Murphy's argument. Instead it just made the mob's posturing even more ridiculous. He was only supposed to be here two more days anyway. "Come on. If I deny it, what's he going to do? Pawn me off on Cleveland?"

"Oh, that's right. I heard you like to play games. Well, this isn't basketball, kid."

"Tell me again why I shouldn't go to the feds?"

"Hey, you know, do what you gotta do. But remember, rumors aren't the only option. We wouldn't mind taking care of Miss Saint, too."

Zach's ribs tightened a notch. He might only have another couple days here, but Lucy and Molly would still be there to face the consequences. "I'll go to the bank Monday."

"You have the paperwork." Again, Murphy maintained his casual tone.

Zach hung up without saying goodbye. Should he tell Lucy? He might be able to remind her this wasn't a cloak-and-dagger game.

Half an hour later, he reached Lucy's building—and a movement in the shadows by her front door drew his attention. Two figures skulked in the dark there.

His pulse throbbed in his temples. They were already starting on her.

If he surprised them and any of them made a noise, Lucy might open the door and get dragged in. He hurried to the back of Lucy's ground-floor apartment, popped open her scarily-insecure window and climbed in.

Then he realized arriving through her bedroom window would alarm Lucy as much as a scuffle outside her door. Sure enough, when he opened the bedroom door, Lucy was crouched in the hall. She jumped up, but Zach clamped a hand over her mouth before she screamed.

"It's only me," he said. Their gazes locked, and alarm traded places with annoyance in her eyes.

He dared to release her. "What's wrong?" she whispered. "Are they here?"

"Don't know. But they're trying to get to me through you." Zach strode past her to the living room. He wanted her to understand how serious this was, not have a coronary.

"How did you get in here?" she demanded, running to keep up.

He shushed her. Lucy held her tongue, and then they heard it—scratching at the door. Whispering. His sister's eyes grew wide. Oh yeah. She got it.

Zach drew his gun and pushed Lucy behind him. "Hide, would you?" Lucy kept back against the wall. He mentally braced himself, gripped his gun tighter, and reached for the knob.

He threw the door open, revealing—two teenage girls? The girls reared back and shrieked in unison. Zach shifted to hide the gun behind the door.

"Hey, Lucy?" he called over his shoulder. He turned back to the girls. "Can I help you?" Then he saw the paper hearts on the door. Not the kind of heart attack he was trying to prevent.

"We're trying to surprise Lucy," said the girl in the *I can't . . . I'm Mormon* sweatshirt. "Is this the right place?"

"Yeah, she's just—" He glanced over his shoulder again.

Lucy stepped up. "Oh, look at my door!" She forced a smile.

"We don't want to interrupt anything." The second girl gaped at Zach.

"This is really sweet of you." Lucy managed to convince the still-stunned girls to leave in less than a minute. As soon as the door shut behind them, Zach sighed and rubbed his temples. He didn't need those girls undermining his warning to Lucy.

"Glad I have my big brother to save me from a heart attack." She flopped onto the couch.

"You need to watch yourself."

She nailed him with a yeah-right look. "What, another random act of kindness in my future?"

"If you see anything suspicious, go somewhere safe and public and call me right away."

The sarcasm in her expression softened. Lucy looked away and pulled at a strand of her hair. "Maybe I shouldn't tell you about Tuesday."

"What?" He leaned forward, showing more of his concern than he wanted to.

"Probably nothing—just . . . Ian Murphy stayed after school." His little sister stared up at him, her brown eyes wide with innocent fear. "Something about you and not having to take my crap much longer."

He couldn't tell her they threatened to kill her. Half the truth would be enough to keep her safe. "They only said they'd start rumors about us."

"Rumors? What would they—oh." Lucy threw herself back against the couch and groaned. "I swear, if one more person thinks we dated—"

"Who said that?"

"No one—well, not in so many words. But Father Fitzgerald's been all freaky about it, and Molly acts like I'm a leper whenever you come up, and then yesterday, Paul actually—oh, great." She nodded slowly. "That'll make next week at work *fun.*"

"What will?"

"She and Paul overheard us talking yesterday." Lucy shook her head. "The part about how we still love each other. Apparently they got the wrong idea."

He made a show of gagging. "Gross."

"No kidding. Actually, Paul warned me you were 'playing the field.'"

"As a priest?"

She shrugged. "He said he'd seen it before. You'd never let it 'get out of hand,' but you'd string me and Molly along forever." She grabbed a blue throw pillow and tugged at its corners.

Zach groaned. Had Paul told Molly that, too? "I suppose one day, we'll look back at this and laugh. You know, if we both live that long."

"Just like we'll laugh about whatever Leah and Kristi say when they corner me at church tomorrow? What am I supposed to tell them?"

"You're taking the Catholic discussions? Harboring a fugitive priest?"

She gave him a sarcastic smirk. "That'll go over well."

"That I'm in town for a costume party?"

"And you're an old prison buddy?" Lucy tossed the pillow at his face.

He swatted it away. "Say I'm a friend and leave it at that. Can't risk anything else getting around."

"And hopefully they won't see you at the grocery store. Wait, do you shop?"

Zach rolled his eyes. "No, I subsist on donated food."

"You're a regular martyr to the cause. A real saint."

"All my life." He started for the door, but stopped short. "Oh, I need a favor."

Lucy sighed and dragged herself to her feet. "Now what?"

"We're having a parish talent show and we need your help." Especially if he was getting yanked this weekend.

She snorted. That was her entire reply.

He searched for the dorkiest talent he could think of. "Okay, great, I'll put you down for yodeling. Thanks for helping us out."

"When is it?"

"The fifth—next Friday—and you wouldn't have to do much. I'll get your boyfriend to come." He grinned, though he didn't really intend to drag Paul there.

"I don't have a boyfriend." She pushed past him to grab the doorknob. "The answer's no."

"Come on, Luce. We've had a bunch of people back out already, and now Grace Carver can't do it because her backup singers have a conflict, and I thought I could depend on you for help." A little guilt trip couldn't hurt.

Lucy let go of the doorknob. "Zach, you know I hate doing talent shows."

"Please? I told Molly you would."

She huffed out a breath. "Fine, but only for her. And you're not getting a Christmas present, or a birthday present next year—this is it."

"Like I could come for Christmas."

"And you have to do something for me. Remember that college fair I wanted to do Tuesday after school? Tell Principal Hickburn you approved it."

Zach didn't remember, but wouldn't say so. As long as it wasn't another background check. "You got it." He glanced at the contemporary-style clock in Lucy's kitchen. If he didn't get back, Fitzgerald would get suspicious. "Better go."

"Stay safe." Lucy looked away.

Did she understand? This could be his last chance to warn her—or see her—unless Sellars had talked to the archbishop. "You'll be careful?" he asked.

"Yes." She gave him a halfhearted hug before practically shoving him out the door.

So much for not letting it get personal.

Molly reached her flat Saturday afternoon and balanced her grocery sack on her hip. She fished in her handbag for her keys—but stopped short at the voices approaching down the hall. Cally Lonegan, more sloped-shouldered than usual, rounded the corner. He nodded to her.

This was her chance if she wanted to fulfill the "mission" Father Tim had given her two days ago. The day he told another woman he loved her.

Molly doubled back to her neighbor. As much as Father Tim's conversation with Lucy hurt her, it didn't change the fact that Cally could probably use a friend—and a priest—like Father Tim now, and he'd asked her to do this for him. "How are you gettin' along, Cally?"

He nodded again.

"We're all sick at heart about what's happened."

"You shouldn't be. We'll deal with it ourselves."

Before she could come up with an appropriate response, Doyle Murphy stepped from behind Cally. He lifted his chin in greeting to Molly.

How could she tell Cally Father Tim wanted to meet with him and tell Doyle he was too busy? Both of them had to be going through the same torment now. She shifted her grocery sack to her other hip and steeled herself. "We're worried about both of you."

Cally looked to Doyle as if asking permission to speak to her. Doyle lifted one eyebrow and one corner of his mouth in a hint of odd amusement. What about their situation was funny?

Molly looked back to Cally. "Father Tim's especially concerned."

"Figures." Doyle folded his arms across his chest.

And it figured a mobster like Doyle Murphy was incapable of actually caring about his own son. Molly focused on Cally. "You should come to Mass tomorrow. It's the beginnin' of Advent, you know yourself."

Doyle snorted derisively. "We'll see."

"Really, Cally." What had Father Fitzgerald and the archbishop said in the press conference? "Might help you find healin' and peace, especially with Christmas comin'."

"We'll think about it." He glanced at Doyle again; Doyle glared back. Before Molly could press Cally for something concrete, he turned to his flat, leaving Doyle and Molly alone.

"Father Tim's all worked up over Cally, eh? Any particular reason—other than . . . you know." He waved his hand. His son's accusation and the lawsuit were nothing?

"Other than that?" She scrutinized Doyle, and he returned the hard stare as though he could measure her mettle. But he'd already misjudged her, and so far she'd managed to stay ahead of him. The shredded Kincaid Wholesalers contract and the appointment book now with the FBI were proof. "Father Tim wouldn't go revealin' anythin' confidential, Doyle. Even if he did, I certainly wouldn't make the same mistake."

"Sure." Doyle's tone conveyed the full weight of his sarcasm and he continued to his door.

Molly shook off the lingering uneasiness that followed any encounter with Doyle Murphy. It didn't appear Cally was avoiding Father Tim on purpose—in fact, Doyle looked to be the one pulling the puppet strings. She'd fulfilled Father Tim's mission. Apparently another woman receiving the declaration Molly had longed for—and dreaded—didn't change the fact that she'd do almost anything Tim asked.

Maybe this was for the best. She had an even better reason to let him go, to see him as only her priest. Once she reported to him tomorrow, of course. And maybe then, if she could really see him as a priest, she could ask him about overcoming weakness.

Though it seemed he was already trying to help her do that.

The deadline, the first day of Advent. That meant no organ, so Zach was at the front of the chapel for Mass again—and expecting someone from the archdiocese to drag him out any minute.

After the first Mass cleared out, Zach bid the last of the parishioners goodbye and scanned the parking lot for a Bureau sedan. He started back into the church to help collect bulletins left in the pews—but he didn't make it past the vestibule. Molly stood by the heavy wooden door in the exact spot he'd occupied two weeks ago as Kathleen and Murphy gossiped about them. Molly beckoned Zach over.

She glanced around, her stealth laced with enough cool composure to be utterly convincing, even to a professional spy. "Never got to report back to you Thursday."

"What'd you find out?"

"If he's avoidin' you, it isn't personal. No one's spoken to him all week."

"He all right? Has anyone seen him?"

Molly moved a little closer. "I saw him in the hallway yesterday."

"Any idea how long before he'll talk to me?"

She tilted her head toward him and lowered her voice. "I'd keep my eyes open."

What could she have said to make him come to church? "Nice work, Malone."

Molly snapped to a palm-out salute—though her wry smile undercut the formal gesture. "Now, I don't plan on bein' your permanent spy."

"I don't know, Molly 'The Mole' Malone has a certain ring to it."

She laughed. "But really—I can't be sneakin' around for you forever. You're goin' to have to talk to him yourself."

"I will. I just want to make sure—" A footfall behind Zach stopped him short. Was Lonegan here already? Zach turned to find Father Fitzgerald and his favorite reproving look.

How much had Fitzgerald heard? Zach mentally reviewed the conversation. Had the priest come in before or after "I can't be sneakin' around for you forever"?

"I'll see you tomorrow," Zach bid Molly before heading into the chapel proper. He winced at her expression—the longing in her eyes, like she wanted him to stay one more minute to talk to her.

Fitzgerald had to have seen, too. "Tim." His most authoritative tone echoed off the arched ceilings.

Zach wheeled on him. He hoped his sarcastic scowl said all he needed to.

"What are you doing?" Fitzgerald demanded.

Zach didn't bother to play innocent. "Whatever you heard was out of context."

His chest thrust out like a bantam, Fitzgerald stalked forward into Zach's personal space. "And there's some context where that interaction is perfectly fine?" he shouted.

The echo rang through the chapel. Zach leveled him with a cool glare. "You're overreacting. She was checking on Cally Lonegan for me." One thing he wouldn't miss after today: Fitzgerald. Zach strode away, leaving the other priest in the aisle, confused and fuming.

MONDAY MORNING, Zach got the call: the archbishop had given him one more week. Like that would be long enough to make a difference. Still, he had to try. Zach didn't give Molly the option of saying no to a bank run today. With that contract still missing and Lonegan refusing his calls, the only way to build a case against Murphy was to seem like he was cooperating.

Molly gripped the steering wheel hard enough to leave nail marks in the plastic. Whatever she'd wanted to say to him yesterday, she wasn't now.

"Father?" She hesitated before she finished her question, staring straight ahead. "How does Christ help us when we're weak?"

Oh, great. A doctrinal question. Zach turned to her, choosing his words carefully. "What do you mean?"

"A friend—Lucy told me that God gives us weakness so that we can become strong. Do you think that's true?"

Oh man. Not just any doctrinal question. Zach adjusted his seat belt, but it didn't make it any easier to breathe. This was too fine a line to walk. She had to be asking him as her priest. "Well," he said slowly. This definitely wasn't covered in his seminary training— Catholic or Mormon. "I guess we see examples of that in the scriptures. What brings this on, Moll?"

She stopped at a red light and focused on the beige steering wheel. "Suppose I should've told you sooner."

Zach shifted awkwardly in his seat. "You've been talking to Lucy?"

"Well, Lucy, Brian—the fella who came by last week—and their missionaries." The traffic light changed, but Molly still stared at her hands.

"You've got a green light."

She looked up at him, clearly surprised. "Father?"

He pointed to the traffic signal.

"Oh, of course."

"You have a green light for the missionaries' lessons, too, if you want."

Molly drew a deep breath. "You wouldn't tell me not to?"

"It's your choice." As a priest, he probably should object. This moment was fast becoming the most difficult conflict between his cover and his real life. He still didn't expect God to bless him in this assignment, but Zach said a quick prayer for the right words.

However, he did not say the first words that came into his mind: *I'm Special Agent Zachary Saint, and I know the Church of Jesus Christ of Latter-day Saints is true.*

"I don't see any harm in understanding your friend's beliefs." The second response was a little more appropriate.

"That's just the thing—I don't understand them. How does Christ help us overcome weakness?"

It took Zach great effort not to turn away. What was Catholic doctrine here? "When we turn to Him for help, asking Him in faith."

"Have you done that?"

"Sure."

"About . . . ?" Molly gestured at the two of them.

She thought he meant something about their relationship? "I, um—"

"Sorry, that's too personal, isn't it."

"That's all right." He steeled himself. "I probably should. It's a process, though, not an overnight thing."

Molly kept her attention on her driving, but her expression grew contemplative.

He hoped he'd handled that okay. His job was supposed to be rooting out corruption in the church, not leading its members . . . anywhere.

This wasn't his doing, though. He only needed to keep it that way for six more days and let Molly follow her heart—when it came to the Church, anyway.

Zach scanned Brennan's parking lot that night, a last ditch shot in the dark. The GPS unit said Lonegan was here. Sure enough, his blue Ford was on the far side of the lot. Zach headed for the bar entrance. But as Zach neared the door, one man lumbered out alone. Zach squinted under the single streetlight. Was that Cally?

The man raked his hair across his forehead and shoved on a knit cap. Yep. Lonegan all right.

"Cally!" Zach called, still ten feet away.

He expected the other man to scowl or maybe try to get away, but instead Lonegan raised an arm in greeting. Was he actually smiling? "Father Tim. How you been?"

"Little worried about you." He reached Lonegan and offered a sympathetic frown. "How are you and Lisa holding up?"

Lonegan shrugged. "Same old. Why?"

"I mean . . . after Brandon and Father Patrick."

"Oh, that." Lonegan scratched the back of his neck. "We're doing better than you'd think."

Zach nodded. Did he know the truth? "On your way out?"

"Yep, just had to stop in to talk to Doyle. You going in?" He jerked his head toward the entrance.

"Actually, I was looking for you."

Lonegan glanced around the parking lot. "Want a ride?"

"Sure." He seemed sober. Zach followed Lonegan to his car. Once they were on the road, Lonegan shook his shoulders like a weight was dropping off him. "Father, I gotta tell ya—I really didn't think you had a clue."

Zach shot him a mock-glower. "Gee, thanks, Cal."

"But you were right!" Lonegan drummed the steering wheel. "I thought about what you said, about believing Jesus, and I started reading, and—" He broke off, grinning so broadly he couldn't continue.

"What did you learn?" Zach found himself leaning forward, too, echoing Lonegan's eagerness.

Lonegan raised a hand like the sheer size of his understanding awed him. "I can't even tell you. I know it. I don't know why—I mean, I don't understand it—but He'll do it."

"And if Christ will do it, then—"

"Then I can do it," Lonegan interjected.

Zach savored the pride of satisfaction. But was this too good to be true? "Exactly, Cally." Out of habit, he shifted to check the side mirror—and found headlights behind them. Lonegan turned left and the headlights followed. "Hey, Cal, I think Father Fitzgerald has a meeting at the parish house tonight. Why don't we go back to your place?"

"You got it." Lonegan drove past the church parking lot. The headlights stayed with them.

"So, what helped you get it?" Zach hoped he didn't sound too distracted.

"Like you told me, Father—I listened to what He said."

"Sounds like you got a lot out of the Bible."

"Yep." Lonegan took a right. The headlights were still on their tail.

Zach stayed focused on the mirror. "Do you know what's next?"

"Already started. I was just talking to Doyle."

That could be bad. "What about?"

"About getting out. I'm done. Finished. Free."

Zach eyed Lonegan, then glanced in the side mirror again, concentrating on the hood of the car behind them. Was it his imagination or was that maroon?

Zach propped his ankle on his other knee to bring his holster within reach. They passed under a streetlight. Yep. The car following them was a maroon sedan.

Lonegan really might be finished. They both might be.

He pulled into his building's parking lot. The maroon sedan pulled in behind them.

In less than a minute, they were parked and getting out. Zach watched the sedan drive past. A coincidence, or had they had another near-run-in with Gallaher?

Lonegan opened the back door to his car and fished out a fast food bag. "Lisa'll jump all over me if I don't toss this."

Zach waited at the car, and Lonegan headed to the Dumpster pen. They were forty feet apart when Zach saw the car round the middle row of the lot—a maroon sedan. Zach's blood pressure inched higher. He started for the Dumpster, but his feet weren't moving fast enough. "Cal!"

"Yeah?" He turned around.

The sedan began to slow, the driver searching the lot. Zach picked up his pace.

Lonegan opened the Dumpster and tossed his trash in. The lid slammed shut, alerting the driver. The sedan sped up, closing the distance to Lonegan.

"Get down!" Zach tried to run, but it suddenly seemed like the Dumpsters were a mile away, and he was trapped in a bad movie's slow-motion. Yet Lonegan barely had time to look at him as Zach charged across the car's path.

In the corner of his vision, Zach saw it—a dark cylinder emerging from the back passenger window.

"Gun!" At full speed, Zach tackled Lonegan. They hit the concrete; the first gunshot hit the Dumpster. The metallic echo was swallowed by a second shot. Zach could barely hear the engine gunning and wheels spinning as the assailants made their escape.

"Cally, you okay?" Zach rolled off him and helped Lonegan sit up. His eyes wide, Lonegan nodded. He released a shuddering breath.

"Let's get inside before they try again."

Still in shock, Lonegan nodded again. Zach dragged him to his feet and pushed him into the building. What if another trap was waiting inside?

No. Murphy couldn't have had time to organize a backup plan. But Zach kept his hand free to draw his gun until he and Lonegan sank into Lonegan's brown leather couches.

"What was that about?" Zach huffed.

A shaken Lonegan shook his head. "Maybe I shouldn'ta talked to Doyle."

"You and me both."

"Hm?"

Zach glanced at him. How much could a mobster obviously on the outs know about that plot? "He came to see me, actually. About 'business.'"

Lonegan sighed heavily, and tugged at his frayed shirt cuffs. "So you know."

"Is this what you've been involved in? Extortion? Price gouging? And—the church?"

"I shouldn'ta let them drag my kid in. He even liked Father Patrick." He massaged his forehead like he could scrub away that memory. "We all did."

"What kind of 'business'?"

"Wholesale."

Zach suppressed a laugh. Not quite what he meant. "Are we talking organized crime?"

Lonegan rubbed his face. "You see why I thought this'd be so hard?"

"Yeah, I understand." He waited for the other man to meet his gaze. "Are you sure you want out?"

"Little late to rethink that." Lonegan puffed out a sigh and looked to the ceiling. "What am I gonna do?"

It *was* too good to be true—but Zach was willing to take that chance with the adrenaline still in his veins. He leaned in and kept his volume at a whisper. "I know people at the FBI."

"What do you mean?"

"If you're getting out, don't let Doyle and them get away with what they've done to you and Father Patrick." Zach shifted closer on the couch. "Witness protection."

"But . . . we'd lose everything—our home, our friends—our family."

"Your friends and family are the ones making your son lie, the ones who just tried to kill you. And who knows what else they're into?"

In the silence, Lonegan fidgeted, tugging at the cushion corner. "I do," he finally said.

"Put them away, Cally. Save this parish."

"I don't know." Lonegan shifted, the leather couch crinkling beneath him.

Zach contemplated his hands. He wasn't supposed to let things get personal with Molly and Lucy—but with Lonegan, this was exactly why he'd befriended the guy. "Doyle's going to say. . . I've been doing inappropriate stuff. Excommunicable stuff."

"Nobody'd buy that."

"And they would've bought it about Father Patrick? You know how Doyle operates. He's got people ready to lie about it." Zach sighed. "He's even threatened to kill more innocent people—teachers at the school. You're the only one that can stop this."

Lonegan's gaze grew distant for a long moment. "Can they really keep us safe?"

They'd do a better job than Zach had tonight. "They've never lost anyone following the program. I'll call my friends. The Marshals might even be able to start the process tonight."

"That fast?"

"Yep." Normally it'd take days or weeks, but Zach had it on good authority that if Lonegan was sure about this, they'd extract him and his family at a moment's notice.

Lonegan nodded slowly. "All right. Make the call."

"Thank you, Cally. I'm pretty sure they'll want to pick you up tonight. We'd better stay inside until they get here."

Lonegan skewered him with a sarcastic glare. "Think I learned my lesson."

Zach managed to rein in his satisfied smile until three hours later, when the Lonegans were in protective custody and Zach on his way home. He grabbed his burner cell and dialed Sellars's office. Naturally, after eleven o'clock on a Monday night, the voicemail picked up.

"Sellars," he said, "mission accomplished."

The case was effectively finished—or it would be once they got Lonegan's full statement in forty-eight hours. Zach only had two regrets: not officially closing Father Patrick's murder, and . . . Molly.

Zach was still trying to ignore the tug of regret the next afternoon. He ventured over to the school to make sure Lucy's college activity hadn't attracted any angry fans. He was sidetracked, however, by a Hispanic seminarian volunteering to read the Christmas story for the talent show Friday night.

"Ricardo," called someone behind them. Zach and the seminarian turned to find Paul, flushed and frowning. Once he saw Zach, the crease between Paul's eyebrows grew deeper, and his blush grew even darker.

Paul took Ricardo by the shoulder. "Can we go?"

"Of course." Ricardo shook Zach's hand and started to leave with Paul.

"How did the thing with Lucy go?" Zach asked.

Paul whirled around, his eyes wide. "What?"

Zach pointed to the cafeteria door. "Lucy's college fair thing?"

"Oh." He looked around like the linoleum tile held the answer. "Fine."

"Very well," Ricardo commented. He subtly watched Paul, concern in the wrinkle of his brow.

Paul met Zach's eyes and opened his mouth to speak. But as soon as he started, Paul shook his head and turned away. "We'd better hurry. Don't want to miss the bus."

Why was the kid so evasive today—and was it a coincidence he freaked out when Zach mentioned Lucy?

He'd better find out. "It's raining out there. Want a ride home?"

"Thank you, Father." Ricardo accepted without glancing at Paul. "I'll see if Lucy's ready to go."

"No!" Paul's shout echoed in the hallway. Zach blinked, and Ricardo stepped back in stunned silence.

"I mean." Paul rubbed his neck. "She'll probably be a while, and we have to get back to study."

Zach definitely wouldn't let Paul get away now. "Wait here." He hurried into the cafeteria. He scanned the thin crowd for his sister, but she was nowhere in sight.

"What's up, Father Tim?" DeWayne got up from the nearest table, jerking his chin in greeting. "Been looking for you."

"Sorry, can't talk. Have you seen Miss Saint?"

DeWayne nodded toward the stage at the end of the room. Zach found Lucy behind the black curtain, sitting on the floor, crying. He dropped to one knee next to her. "What happened?"

Her head jerked up, and she tried to scrub the tears from her cheeks. "I—Paul—" She buried her face in her hands.

What had he done? Zach wrapped an arm around her shoulders. "Should I shoot him?"

"No. Unless it's to put him out of his misery. And you shoot me first."

"Should I go get Molly?"

"I—" She took a deep, ragged breath. "I just want to be alone."

He nodded. "I know this isn't a great time, but can I borrow your car?"

Lucy narrowed her puffy eyes in incredulity. "You're unbelievable." But she waved a hand at a canvas bag on a desk by the curtain. He found her keys and headed back to the hallway.

"I'm sure Father Tim is too busy," Paul was saying as Zach arrived.

"Nope," Zach said, coming up from behind. "I caught a terrible cold running around in the rain. I'd hate to see you two getting sick before the talent show." He winced at his tone, false and bright. He'd rather give the kid the third degree until he admitted what he'd done to Lucy.

Zach held up the keys. "Lucy loaned me her car."

Paul's eyes grew wide again. "Is she okay? Did she say any-thing?"

"She was kinda busy." Zach opened the door for them.

Paul led the way, trudging to Lucy's gold car like the condemned approaching the guillotine. He reached for the passenger door, then thought better of it and got in the backseat. Ricardo took over as navigator. Zach monitored Paul's sulking slump in the rearview the whole ride to the seminary.

Zach parked by the brick dorm and exchanged a glance with Ricardo. Zach pointed at himself and Paul, to signal he'd try to talk to him. Well, his real goal was to try not to shoot him, but whatever Ricardo got from the gesture was close enough. He made an excuse about Latin homework and hurried off, leaving Zach and Paul in the parking lot.

"Everything okay?" Zach asked.

"Finals are next week. I'm sure he wants to study." Paul shrugged.

Zach laughed a little. "I meant with you. You're acting weird. Nothing to do with Lucy?"

Paul pondered the asphalt for a long moment. "Did you ever do something you couldn't undo—something so terrible there was no taking it back?"

Something terrible he'd done to his baby sister. Zach set his jaw, but his pulse still pounded. "What?" he demanded, his voice tight. Was Paul being dramatic, or was this way more serious than he'd realized?

"You wouldn't understand. Even I don't understand how we could do this." Paul sighed and turned away.

Zach grabbed his shoulder. "If you hurt Lucy," he said through clenched teeth, "I swear, I'll—" Paul met his gaze. The raw pain in the younger man's face stopped Zach short.

"I know. But I'll probably beat you to the punch." Paul backed away, and Zach let him go.

But what had he done to Lucy? First regrets, and now this? Did everything have to fall apart?

Zach was set to corner Lucy in the hallway and force her to tell the full story, but he'd only handed her keys back when Cathal Healey approached them. "Hey, Father. Got a minute?"

Zach didn't bother hiding his groan. Did Healey know who he was? Lucy, her eyes still red and puffy, took the opportunity to duck back into the cafeteria. Zach signaled for Healey to follow him to the parish house. Once the other agent was inside, Zach shut the door and locked it. "I've got to hand it to you," Healey started.

Zach held up a finger to silence him. "Bruce?" he called. No answer. "Hand what to me?"

"I thought you two had to be totally oblivious to let this kind of stuff happen in your parish."

"Oh yeah?" So he didn't know who Zach really was. He did his best to bite back a triumphant smile and leaned against the door.

Healey shook his head. "How'd you get Lonegan to come in?"

"I only suggested it, really. He was ready to come clean."

"Bringing down Doyle Murphy's crew," said the other agent. "Bet you're relieved."

Zach raised an eyebrow.

"I mean, now you won't end up like that last priest. I mean, assuming that's what actually happened. Didn't come up in Lonegan's preliminary interview."

Something twisted in Zach's gut.

After Flynn died, Lisa said Lonegan's change of heart had to do with Father Patrick. Could Cally Lonegan have held back something about Father Patrick's death? Zach had no idea. It had never come up again. Father Patrick's murder might never be officially solved now.

"Well, good job, Father." Healey stepped forward and offered a hand.

Zach opened the door and shook Healey's hand. He waited until Healey was on the doorstep before leaning closer. "Oh, and Special Agent Healey? The 't' in Cathal is silent—and you should invest in a gun belt."

Healey whirled around, his eyes wide. "What are you—?"

He shut the door on Healey's denial. Zach knelt on the couch to peer through the lace curtains. Healey stared down at the scratches on his belt, frowning.

Zach waited for Healey to shuffle off. As soon as the coast was clear, he could go track Lucy down. His gaze gravitated to where he'd parked her gold sedan—gone.

He sighed and sank into the couch. He'd call her, but ten bucks said she wouldn't answer. But that might not be his biggest problem. If Healey was right, somehow he'd forgotten the whole reason he'd been able to come to the parish.

Maybe it'd all come out in Lonegan's formal statements. Zach was supposed to stay in the parish until they made all the arrests; he'd have a few more days to figure it out. And maybe he'd get a chance to bid Molly a proper goodbye.

But even that thought couldn't take the edge off the anxiety eating at his gut in earnest.

T HE ELEVATOR DOORS SLID OPEN, revealing her floor. Molly's rib cage constricted. Everyone in the building knew the whole Lonegan family had disappeared. Hardly seemed like a co-incidence after what Molly had done for the FBI.

Did her neighbors know about her role?

She started down the corridor, fixedly staring past the mobsters' doors. Just as she reached her flat, a door swung open. Molly raked through her handbag. Where were her keys?

Footsteps padded over the carpet. In her peripheral vision, Molly glimpsed a shadowy figure approaching. She seized her keys, but they slid from her clammy palms.

"Molly?"

She jumped. Her handbag tumbled to the ground.

"Uh . . . hi?"

She knew that voice. Molly finally dared to check. Father Tim stooped to pick up her keys and handbag, raising a half-mocking eyebrow. "You okay?"

"I am, only a bit—"

A deadbolt down the hall scraped open. Molly snatched the keys, jammed the right one in her lock and pulled Tim inside.

"I know it's none of my business," Father Tim said once the door closed, "but you might want to consider moving."

Molly gave half a laugh. Already done, but Tim didn't know that. "Give me a raise so I can afford rent in the area or the commute."

"Done."

"Can I get that in writing?" she joked. "What brings you by?"

Tim frowned solemnly. "Jay Gallaher was arrested tonight. Kim's mom called us."

One knot around her heart loosened. She wasn't happy because his family was upset—but she certainly felt safer.

If the arrests had begun, she wasn't the only one who was safe. Tim didn't need her protection anymore. Perhaps this was the last thing holding her back, and now she could finally believe.

But even if she believed, could she really leave her family's church, leave Tim?

She flinched at her own thoughts. Was she really hesitating because of her futile, futureless feelings for him?

"You okay, Moll?" He peered at her in concern, as if he sensed her thoughts.

Molly nodded. "I've just been thinkin'."

"Of . . . ?"

She collected her courage. "The Book of Mormon. That is, I'm thinkin'—I don't know. How can I leave—?" She broke off, but couldn't keep herself from looking to him, filling in that gap.

"I don't see what I have to do with it."

Molly jerked her head up. Could he pretend not to care?

"Don't get me wrong," he continued quickly and in earnest. "I'm concerned for your soul, Molly. Really. But this is a personal decision—I mean, obviously I believe there's only one true church on the earth."

She lowered her gaze again.

Tim pressed on. "But I can't make you believe anything. I think God's more concerned with where your heart is and not which church ends up with your records."

"What are you sayin'?"

He looked to the ceiling for help. "I'm saying . . . it'd be wrong for you to leave the church over me. But it'd be just as wrong to stay in the church for my sake, too. When it comes down to it, Molly, the choice is yours. It comes down to what you believe."

That was the problem. "I want to believe what they've told me—that Jesus can make me stronger."

"You're one of the strongest women I've ever known. Living here, working so hard to protect the rest of us from these people. You're a

Guard, for heaven's sake."

Molly held onto her elbow. "You of all people should know how weak I am."

Tim placed his hand on her shoulder. She barely dared to meet his blue eyes filled with searching urgency.

He was that concerned? Then he did care.

"Molly, I have to tell you—" A knock at the door cut off Tim's insistent whisper. Was that going to be the declaration she'd longed for? He closed his eyes and released her shoulder.

Molly checked the peephole. "Teresa Hennessy." She opened the door.

"Hi, Molly. Do you have Father Tim's cell—" Her gaze shifted to behind Molly. "Oh." She looked from Tim to Molly and back again, disbelief flickering in her gaze. "Ohhh."

"Did you need something?" Tim asked.

"Just wanted to let you know about the Gallahers. Jay—"

"Was arrested. I heard."

Teresa nodded, still scrutinizing each of them in turn, obviously jumping to the worst conclusion.

"Okay," Tim said slowly. "I'm gonna go. See you tomorrow, Moll."

"Good night, Tim."

He edged past her and left. Teresa watched them both warily until Molly shut the door.

Her empty apartment seemed to echo the silence. Had she expected Father Tim to smooth over all her problems? She was no closer to a decision on anything.

Zach inhaled the musty smell of the curtains and the tangible tension backstage before a performance. Technically, he shouldn't be here anymore, but he wasn't leaving without saying goodbye. His gaze drifted to Molly, gorgeous even in her exaggerated stage makeup. Her family was the center of attention, with their sparkly costumes, their noisy shoes and her father's uilleann pipes—but his green tartan kilt seemed to draw the most interest.

Zach steeled himself. Her family might understand his song, but after he'd blown his chance to tell her last night, he had to sing. She deserved some closure, even if it was just the assurance she hadn't imagined this, that if circumstances were different, everything would be different.

But he had all night to wait. He shook off a wave of nerves. He had to do this.

Two minutes to show time, Zach caught Lucy peeking around the curtain. Looking for Paul? That made two hopeless Saints. "Heads up," he told her. "You're the act one closer."

"Who am I singing with?"

He cocked his head. "No one?"

"You said someone was quitting because she needed backup singers."

"Grace? You're her replacement. The whole act."

Lucy started to say his name, but stopped in time. "You didn't say I'd solo!"

"But—I didn't—can you still do it?"

She fumed a moment, fists clenched, then huffed in resignation. "Fine. You owe me."

He searched for something they'd performed together. "You know 'Crazy,' right?"

"I know *you*, don't I?"

Zach ignored the jab and raised his voice for all the performers. "Show time!" he announced. After introing Molly's act, Zach hopped off the stage to grab a front-row seat. No way was he watching this performance from the wings.

The lights went dark for their entrance. First the uilleann pipe droned, and then the lights raised on the four dancers. The tune began, and the quartet pivoted and began their dance.

Despite keeping her arms rigid and her smile fixed, Molly's dancing was more than a well-executed tap routine. She leapt and clicked and spun like she was born to move that way. Too soon, the quartet returned to their starting positions, and the music wound down. Good thing the kids were next—no adult would follow that performance. But the kids' acts mostly went well, and the hapless magic show . . . well, it went. For the last number, Zach took his place at the piano, and even he couldn't tell Lucy'd only had thirty minutes to practice the Patsy Cline standard.

At intermission, he found Lucy backstage with Molly, already in her street clothes, though still wearing her stage makeup.

"Hey, you didn't ruin the show." Zach clapped a hand on Lucy's shoulder. Molly instantly focused on his hand; Zach pulled away.

Oblivious, Lucy turned to him. "Wish I could say the same for you."

"That doesn't count for our deal." Molly's smile said she was straining to keep their conversation light. "You promised to sing."

"I can't go on after you." Zach teased.

"I had to," Lucy grumbled.

"Did you volunteer to open?" Zach muttered back.

"I didn't volunteer at all."

Molly shifted uncomfortably, searching the backstage crowd for an escape. "As long as it isn't 'Molly Malone.'" She slipped away to talk to her parents, and Kathleen made a curtain call.

"Don't let her leave before I go on," he charged Lucy. "Get her in the front row."

After an awesome puppet show—"The Old Testament in Three Minutes"—Zach broke down the O'Learys' set through the next acts. If he'd been with Lucy, they would've kept a snarky commentary running about the blonde from the movie night and her continual key changes.

He was next. Zach peeked through the curtain. The two women sat on the front row.

Nerves set into Zach's stomach. His anxiety had nothing to do with singing—and everything to do with *what* he was singing.

Kathleen led the applause for the second-to-last act. "Now, for our finale. You know him, you love him—some of you more than others—Father Tim, singing 'Moll Dub'!"

Zach took the stage. "Thanks, Kathleen—but it's actually called 'Moll Dubh.'" He emphasized the second word, pronounced more like "doov." The way Kathleen said it probably wouldn't translate as "Dark Molly."

He stepped back from the mic, took a deep breath that didn't faze his nerves, and searched the front row for Molly. But her seat and Lucy's were empty. Lucy let her leave?

Was he making a declaration to no one?

Molly waved to her parents pulling out of the snowy car park. Huddled against the cold, she hurried back to the building. At the doors, she passed Emily, the tone-deaf blonde—leaving with Brian, without a hint of a limp. He didn't notice Molly's gawking. Lucy caught her two paces inside the building.

"Was that Brian leavin' with that blonde?" Molly asked.

Lucy sighed. "Paul's crazy ex. Brian loved her song. Quote, 'Catholic girls are hot.'"

"Did I tell you he laughed when I said our relationship wasn't goin' anywhere? And said he wanted to marry me or someone just like me?"

Lucy joined in her laughter, and regret laced through Molly. How had she let Tim, a man she couldn't have, cost her a friendship with Lucy, who truly understood what she was going through? Besides, whatever Lucy and Tim had had, it'd been over for years. Right?

"Lucy, I have to ask—I heard you say you loved Tim, and he loved you."

"Like a brother," Lucy insisted. "That's all. Promise."

Molly nodded slowly. That *would* explain the odd rivalry between Lucy and Tim.

"Oh, his song!" Lucy grabbed Molly's wrist and dragged her back.

Tim was onstage, singing in Irish—and he had an incredible voice: clear, ringing and warm, better served by a recording studio than a cafeteria. The song was familiar, but not "Molly Malone." She'd thank him later. Molly and Lucy crept to their chairs. Despite their stealth efforts, their movement attracted Tim's gaze. His eyes met hers and held—a gasp seized in her chest.

Tim kept singing. Molly was still good with Irish, and she should've understood the meaning—something about a bird—but she was too caught up in staring back. Halfway through the refrain, the Irish words translated themselves in her mind. Could he be saying this? *Dark Molly of the glen has my heart.*

The way he was looking at her, there was no question. He was singing about her—to her—*she* was Moll Dubh. She had his heart. Her ribs turned to ice around her lungs, but all she could do was watch Tim.

Molly blinked, and his song was over, the houselights up, the stage empty. She stood, craning her neck to search for him. Finally, Doyle Murphy stepped aside, revealing Tim, his back to her.

As if he could sense her gaze, Tim wheeled around. Molly could only imagine her expression: shock, joy—horror. She had her declaration, and it was all she'd ever have.

She backed away. Tim—*Father* Tim—started toward her, but a row of chairs stopped him.

Molly ran. To the hall. Out of the building. Through the falling snow. She didn't stop until she let herself into the office, not bothering to switch on the lights. She wanted—needed—to be alone.

Molly pulled out her mobile and looked up the lyrics to "Moll Dubh."

She's Dark Molly of the valley, she's Dark Molly of the spring
She's Dark Molly more ruddy than the red rose
And if I had to choose from the young maids of the world
Dark Molly of the glen would be my fancy

Me without a wife, I won't be all my life
And Dark Molly in youth just blooming
Lifeless the song of the bird that sings alone
On a mound by the edge of the moorland

Dark Molly of the glen has my heart in her keeping
She never had reproach nor shame
So mannerly and honestly she said to me this morning,
"Depart from me and do not come again!"

She'd thought she wanted this. But there was no more naïve denial, no pretending that because they didn't voice their feelings, they hadn't done anything wrong.

Molly yanked out the top desk drawer, but Lucy's Book of Mormon was at home. The organizer held only the plastic ring from Tim's barmbrack. How could she have let herself hope?

That'd been it all along. She'd clung to a ridiculous hope Tim could be with her, and everything would be right.

Molly rolled the ring between her fingers a final time before dropping it into the waste bin. She hugged her knees to her chest. Tears fell, but she didn't care that she'd streak stage makeup on her face and jeans.

She wished she'd never met Timothy O'Rourke. Father Timothy O'Rourke.

A knock came at the door. Molly sucked in a breath. Did she dare answer?

ZACH WAITED OUTSIDE the parish office in the brutal cold. Molly's car was in the lot, and the office curtains glowed blue. She'd all but run away from him, and he followed as soon as he could—not as soon as he wanted. Now she wouldn't open the door.

He wished he could comfort her, tell her now—kiss her and make this all real. Why hadn't he just taken the five extra seconds to tell her the truth last night?

Like that had ever been realistic. What could he say? "Surprise! I love you, and it's okay because, P. S., everything you think you know about me is a lie"? Right. He wouldn't ever be allowed to tell her the truth, and telling her would only hurt her more. Even the impulse to tell her was selfish.

She loved someone who didn't exist. She wouldn't leap into Zach Saint's arms—someone who'd lied to her and mocked her church for months. If he loved her, he had to leave her alone. That was as much closure as either of them could hope for.

Zach finally turned away and trudged into the parking lot's ankle-deep snow. Did he always have to be such an idiot?

Headlights swung into the lot and headed for him. Zach instantly tensed, ready to run or draw. Then he recognized the driver: Sellars.

Here it was. His time was up, and he was being pulled out. Some goodbye he'd given Molly. Sellars pulled up to him and gestured for Zach to hop in. Zach leaned down.

"On our way," Sellars said into his phone. He tapped the screen and pocketed it. "Murphy's holed up. His favorite priest is coming to talk him down."

"Who, Fitzgerald?"

Sellars pressed his fingertips to his temple. "Just get in."

Zach obeyed, and in minutes he was at the white stucco apartment building. He should have known. Murphy's place.

Molly's building.

"All right," Sellars called as they got out of the car, "we got him." He pointed to Zach.

"No go," said a plainclothes cop, probably the ranking local officer on the scene. "Murphy's got a hostage."

Zach's stomach fell like he was on a roller coaster. Could it be Molly? The office computer might have been left on, and Murphy was at the talent show tonight. He could've snatched her any time.

If it was Molly, she'd figure out he wasn't a priest pretty quick—and he wouldn't lose his job for telling her. She wouldn't be too happy with him, but maybe she could forgive him if he saved her. He just had to save her.

He *would* save her.

"He's going in," Sellars insisted, jerking a thumb in Zach's direction. Was the ASAC throwing him to the wolves here, or did he finally think Zach could do his job?

The cop raised an eyebrow, probably less at Zach's collar and more at the gun and holster he was strapping on his belt.

"What do we know about the hostage?" Zach asked. "Male, female? Sure it's only one?"

The cop glanced at the building. "*Your* guys chased him in."

"Are we sure it's not just his family?"

"Don't know."

"Well, get those agents over here." Zach pulled on an FBI jacket and made sure it concealed his weapon.

Finally, a short guy with huge arms approached. "You wanted to see us?" One of the first agents on the scene. He, too, eyed the collar.

"Did you get a good look at the hostage? Is it his wife or kid?"

"Never made it in." The agent lifted a massive shoulder. "Murphy only said 'she.'"

That ruled out Ian at least. "Could be anyone—or no one?"

"He said he'd kill her if we went in. Didn't want to try him."

Zach nodded. "How desperate is he? Is this the hill he wants to die on?"

The agent thought a moment. "He threatened her life twice if we didn't back off. He's in the corner—unless he wants to climb down the fire escape, there's nowhere else for him to go."

Not good. Zach waved the other agent away and took the burner phone from his pocket. He offered a silent prayer Molly would answer.

The phone rang three times and went to voice mail. Could she be the hostage? "Molly." What could he say? "Don't go home. Get somewhere safe right now and stay there." He hit end.

Sellars clapped a hand on Zach's shoulder. "You're a go. Get in there." He shoved a McDonald's bag at Zach. "It's what he ordered."

Zach approached the building, and an FBI hostage negotiator fell in step with him. "You ever done this before, Reverend?"

Zach resisted the urge to correct his title—his cover's title. "Something like this." He kept his tone light. He'd been in armed standoffs before—okay, once—but he'd never been in a hostage situation.

And nothing where the hostage meant this much to him.

Zach and the negotiator reached Murphy's floor and slowed. They made their way down the hall, keeping to one gray wall. The hostage negotiator pushed Murphy's door open, but neither of them dared move into view—and the line of fire—without warning the guy first.

The other agent tapped the fast food bag. "Bringing food establishes a psychological dependence on us." Like Zach needed the clarification. The negotiator turned to the door. "Doyle? Can you send someone for your food?"

Murphy scoffed. "Right, so you can pull something? You bring it to me."

"I'll take it," Zach whispered.

The negotiator shook his head. "Too dangerous, Reverend. He could take you—"

Zach flashed his badge. "Did you think the jacket was standard issue at the seminary?"

"We're sinking that low, huh?" The other agent pinched the bridge of his nose. "Well, remember, make him see the light at the end of the tunnel. There has to be a kernel of truth in everything you say. Make his crimes sound small, but don't pretend he can get off completely; he'll know that's a lie. If anything goes wrong, we'll go tactical in a heartbeat. SWAT's on the stairs."

"Is there a signal?"

"'Rabbit.'" The negotiator raised his voice to call into Murphy's apartment. "We got someone here who wants to talk to you."

"I'll bet."

"Doyle, it's me, Father Tim."

"Back off, Father, this doesn't concern you."

Arms raised in a surrender pose, Zach stepped inside the open door—and stopped. The hostage cowered on her knees in front of Murphy.

Lucy.

"Nice jacket," she said shakily.

What was she doing here? He amended his last prayer and turned to the man holding his sister at gunpoint.

Molly collected the last paper from the printer tray. It was done. Almost. She folded the paper in thirds and slipped it into an envelope. Now she just had to deliver it.

She labeled the envelopes—one for Father Fitzgerald, one for Father Tim. Tim's told him everything he needed to know: she understood his message, she wished things were different, but they weren't. Everything he needed to know—except that she loved him.

He didn't need to know that.

And he didn't need to know he was the reason her letter to Father Fitzgerald cut so deeply into her heart: her immediate resignation.

Molly squared her shoulders and faced the door. But she couldn't force her feet to move.

What if she just slipped the letters under the door, or left them in the mailbox?

Molly tucked the envelopes into her handbag. The flap of one envelope slid along her finger, slicing into her skin. She sucked in air through her teeth, then popped her finger in her mouth. She checked the wall clock. Quarter of ten. She wouldn't bother him tonight—if she could even gather the courage to face him again.

No. Even if she didn't dare to say the words, she needed to give the message to Tim in person. It was the least she could do for him.

She looked over the office. She could collect her things Monday. After she gave them her letters.

Time to go home. She collected her handbag and remembered her coat was still in the school, probably locked there. She'd have to hurry to her apartment, so. Molly hugged her arms tight around herself and stepped out into the cold.

"Got your Big Mac." Zach shook the greasy bag. He'd managed to edge a couple feet into the room, but Murphy wasn't exactly rolling out a welcome mat.

Murphy narrowed his eyes and brandished his flashy silver revolver. "Didn't I warn you about going to the Feds?" Behind Murphy, his wife Claire whimpered on the couch. Their son Ian slung a protective arm around his mother.

"They called me. They wanted me to make sure you, Claire, Ian and Miss Saint were all okay." Zach pitched his voice for the hall to apprise the negotiator of the full situation.

The mobster still hesitated.

Zach shook the bag. "Do you want your food or not?"

Murphy finally waved for him to come in. Zach gave Murphy the fast food before turning to his sister. "You all right, Lucy?"

Her only answer was a sob.

"Luce." He slowly approached to kneel by her.

Murphy settled at the white tiled kitchen island. "Back off, Father." His mouthful of hamburger undermined his threat.

"Hey." Zach waited until Lucy met his gaze. "'Thine adversity and thine afflictions.'" He hoped Lucy remembered the rest of the Doctrine and Covenants verse: *shall be but for a small moment.*

She pursed her lips despite the tears glistening in her eyes. "I don't know how that collar's affecting your brain, but remember how Joseph ended up?"

Martyred at the hands of a mob. Shot to death. Zach glanced at Murphy's gun.

"You've said your piece," Murphy called. "Now get away from her."

Zach stood. "You know, Doyle, it's not too late."

The mobster rolled his eyes and chomped away at his burger.

"You haven't done anything we can't walk away from here," Zach tried.

"You don't know anything about what I've done."

Zach folded his arms across his chest. "I do have some idea. The school's trust."

Murphy waved the last bite of his Big Mac. "That's nothing."

"Right, sure. So we all walk out of here, and what will they do?" He laughed. "I mean, school lunches? Who could go down for school lunches?"

"Not me." Murphy crumpled the wrapper and tossed it over his shoulder into the kitchen, then started on the next burger, still holding his gun.

"Exactly. Come on, Doyle, I know these people. We can all walk out of here, just start with a show of good faith. Send out Ian."

Murphy snorted. "Ian's going with me."

Practically glowing with defiance, the teenager nailed his father with a hard stare.

"Then send Lucy."

"She's my bargaining chip."

Zach remained focused on Murphy and slid his hand into his jacket for his gun. Too soon to draw, but if he pushed Murphy—he had to get Lucy out. "I'll take her place."

"No." He tossed the last bites of his second burger in the bag and stood. "Nobody's going anywhere," he said, jabbing the counter with each word.

Lucy cowered away from him. Zach stepped closer to maneuver himself between her and Murphy. Murphy contemplated the countertop. "This isn't how it's supposed to be."

"It can all end now."

"Yeah, if I'm willing to go to jail."

Lucy grabbed Zach's ankle. He glanced down, but she didn't look at him. He checked the direction she was staring, but the empty white wall held no answers. He turned back to Murphy. "These people cut deals all the time," Zach said. "And it's better than the alternative, isn't it?"

"You ever been in prison?" Murphy barked a laugh and shook his head. "I did everything right. Played all my cards right."

"Of course you did."

"Quit encouraging him." Lucy released his ankle long enough to punch his calf. Zach concentrated on keeping his heart rate under control and not kicking his sister in response.

Murphy ignored her. "It's still going to work out. You've got nothing."

"Even more reason to talk to them. You haven't done anything we can't walk away from, and nothing else will stick."

"What do you know, anyway?" Struck by sudden inspiration, Murphy wheeled on Zach. "You. You did this."

Lucy's nails dug into his skin. Zach wrapped his fingers around his weapon's grip. "Come on. Me?"

Murphy would not be soothed. "This all happened after we talked to you."

"Doyle," Zach tried again in his best let's-be-reasonable voice.

"You just said you know them. You called them, didn't you?"

Murphy's voice dropped to a calculating growl. He circled toward Lucy.

Zach pulled his gun from the holster, but kept it beneath his jacket. "Hey, now."

"Didn't you?" Murphy turned his gun on him.

"Doyle." He kept his voice calm despite the fear freezing his lungs. "Lower your weapon." Lucy's claws had to be drawing blood by now. He shook loose and stepped out of range.

Murphy came even with Lucy. "This isn't basketball, kid. Prove this isn't your fault."

"Dad." Ian rose from the couch, leaving his mother cowering alone. "What are you going to do? It's bad enough to say that crap about Father Patrick—you want to shoot a priest, too?"

The distraction gave Zach the chance he needed. "Rabbit!"

Murphy whirled on him. Suddenly it felt like it would take SWAT years to get there. Murphy took aim again—at Lucy.

Zach didn't even have to think. He charged straight at Murphy. The mobster looked up. Panic flashed in his eyes, and he tried to target Zach. But he didn't have time before Zach plowed into him.

A gunshot rang out.

Finally, SWAT men poured through the door and around Zach, poised to use their confuse-and-subdue tactics. Hands pulled Zach up, patted him over for wounds. He couldn't take his eyes off Murphy. The man was face down in cuffs before Zach fully registered what happened.

He'd done it. He'd taken out a mobster. In nine weeks, no less. And he'd saved Lucy.

Or had he? Zach looked around for his sister. She was nowhere in sight. He craned his neck to see past the agent shouting in his face. The guy grabbed Zach by the shoulders. "Are you okay?"

Zach pushed past him. Of course he was okay. They'd just checked him out. Murphy had missed him.

What about Lucy? "Where's the hostage?" he called.

Sellars stepped into the room. "Gotta admit it: you were made for this job."

"Maybe we should wait before we make that call. Where's the

hostage?"

Sellars pointed over his shoulder with his thumb. "They ran her downstairs. Ambulances in the parking lot."

"Is she okay?"

"I—I dunno." Sellars held his temple. "Haven't heard."

Zach pushed past the ASAC and ran for the stairs.

Molly reached her block and slowed. What were all these people doing here so late—and film crews? And—

Red and blue lights. At least three police cars flashed their light bars beyond the gathering crowd.

It was finally happening. They were finally being arrested. All of them. Molly came to a full stop and craned her neck to see past the press. Was Special Agent Sellars here? Had her information helped?

She hoped so. She inhaled, the feeling of triumph filling her lungs. Father Tim was safe now. Forever. The thought was a minuscule Band-Aid on the open wound in her heart. Now she really could leave him.

Molly watched a moment longer, but she couldn't see anything beyond the crowd. Then she'd leave the police to their work—and she'd join their ranks as soon as she could. Molly started for her parents' house. At least she wouldn't have to spend the weekend alone.

Zach reached the parking lot and almost crashed into Ian Murphy. The teenager paused in front of Zach, gaping. "I can't—" Ian shook his head. "I can't believe my dad would try to kill a priest. I'm so sorry."

"Thanks." Zach patted him on the shoulder, then shoved past him. Where was his sister?

Outside, the parking lot swarmed with law enforcement—cops, FBI, SWAT, plus EMTs and ambulances grinding the snow on the ground into messy slush. A huge mass of onlookers stood just outside the police perimeter, with local news crews forming miniature oases in the crowd.

Zach turned his back on the cameras and scanned the faces of people within the perimeter. He stopped someone in SWAT gear. "Where is Lucy Saint?"

"Zach!" Lucy pushed between two cops, a smear of blood down one cheek. She dropped the blanket around her shoulders and threw her arms around his waist.

Zach pulled her off to examine her wound. "Can we get an EMT?"

"Quit trying to be a hero." She waved a hand at the approaching medic. "I'm fine."

The EMT raised an eyebrow. "You're covered in blood, miss."

"No, I'm fine," she insisted. "There's not a scratch on me."

"Don't listen to her." Zach shook his head. "She's in shock."

The medic shone a light on Lucy's temple. With an impatient frown, she submitted to his exam.

"Nope," the EMT said. "Not a scratch." He disappeared into the nearest ambulance and returned with a wet towel.

"Told you so." Lucy took the towel and wiped at the blood with a smug lift to her chin. "He grazed Claire Murphy."

His own wife. Zach shook his head and addressed the medic, pointing at his sister. "Treat her for shock."

Lucy pursed her lips but trailed behind the EMT to the ambulance for an oxygen mask. Zach grabbed the blanket she'd dropped and joined his sister on the ambulance bumper. He wrapped the blanket around her shoulders. "We're going to need a statement."

She nodded.

"You sure you're all right?"

She lifted the oxygen mask. "I'm *fine*, Zach. I'm not in there anymore. Anything's better than that. Well, almost anything."

He didn't dare ask, but she answered the obvious question anyway.

"Remember that time we had to share a room? I was seven, you were eleven—it was the longest six months of my life?"

Zach scoffed. "You could be a little more grateful, you know? Or did I not just save your life?"

"While you are obviously my hero—" She paused to dramatically roll her eyes. "—I knew they wouldn't send you in without a vest."

"What if he'd shot me in the head?" He glared at her until the EMT stepped between them. Zach took that as his cue to leave. "I have a lot of paperwork." He stood.

"Zach?" Lucy called after him. He doubled back. "Thank you. Seriously."

"Yeah, well, I won't be getting you a Christmas present, or a birthday present, either." He sighed, releasing the tension in his chest. "Glad you're okay." He started away again.

"Wait, where are you going?"

"I don't want to talk."

"I was just held at gunpoint for an hour, Zach. You don't have to say anything."

He stared at her in silence for a few seconds. He hadn't forgotten that she was more than a foot shorter than him, but somehow the streaks of blood still on her face and the oxygen mask made her seem even tinier than she was. Or would she always be seven years old to him?

Lucy waited almost a full minute before she began the conversation on her own. "Ian Murphy changed his mind about college. Claire saw me at the talent show and asked me to come over afterward to discuss their options. Kinda wish I'd said no."

"No kidding."

"Speaking of college, did you hear? Duke and Kentucky are scouting DeWayne."

"Ian *and* DeWayne. Your college thing worked." He scanned the crowd. No Molly.

"Not for everyone. Brandon Lonegan yelled at me right after. I started bawling, Paul tried to make me feel better, and . . . we kissed."

Zach grimaced. "Explains why you two freaked out."

"Knew it couldn't end well."

"Still sucks. I'm sorry." He finally joined Lucy on the bumper again. Being with his little sister was almost as good as being alone, even if she wasn't the person he wished he were comforting.

Really? Somewhere in his heart, he'd actually hoped Molly was being held hostage by a murdering mobster just so he could have some chance with her? She didn't deserve that. And he didn't deserve her.

Lucy hugged her knees to her chest, like she could make herself even smaller. "Still think you won't be coming for Christmas? We're meeting at Tracey's—it's less than six hours away."

He wished. "No. I'm going back to D.C. Probably ASAP."

She nodded again, then finally rested her head on his arm. "I'm glad you were here, at least."

He tucked his arm around her shoulders. "Me too."

Zach glanced back at the stucco building. Even if they'd just—maybe?—arrested Father Patrick's murderer, one more person still wouldn't get closure.

31

S ELLARS MANAGED TO GIVE ZACH a minute to say goodbye to
Lucy when they dropped her off at her apartment, then they
headed out. "We can put you up in a hotel downtown," Sellars
offered.

So he could just disappear on Molly? "I have some things to take
care of at the church."

Sellars nodded, quiet. He said nothing on the drive back to the
church. In the parking lot, he turned to Zach.

How could he tell Molly goodbye? His stupid plan tonight had
backfired; he couldn't leave things like that.

He could leave her a note. No idea what he'd say, but at least it
was an idea. "Um, it might take me a while to wrap things up here.
Why don't you come back in the morning?"

Sellars slowly lifted one eyebrow, then pressed his fingers to his
temple on the same side. "If you really want."

"Yeah." Zach got out and trudged through the snow to the parish
house. He shook his head and shut the front door behind him.

"Timothy." Father Fitzgerald stood by the coffee table, clenching
and unclenching his fists. His posture matched the reproving tone of
his greeting. Like it hadn't already been a long night, here Zach was
again like a curfew-breaking teen.

Fitzgerald jabbed a thumb in the direction of the school. "What
was that?"

Zach was sorely tempted to tell him to mind his own business.
"What?"

"Am I blind or just stupid?"

"Bruce, what are you talking about?"

"You think I didn't see what you did at the talent show tonight?"

Right. That. Zach played innocent. "Sang a song?"

"What did it mean?"

Zach shrugged. No way Fitzgerald could've known what he'd sung. "It was hard enough to learn to say it."

"Then why were you staring at Molly the whole time?"

"Because it's an Irish folksong?" Zach reined in the urge to roll his eyes and started for his room.

Fitzgerald gave no heed to his explanation. "And why did Teresa Hennessy tell me she saw you leaving Molly Malone's at ten o'clock last night?"

Why couldn't Teresa have gotten nosy five minutes sooner and seen his arrival, too?

"What are you doing, Tim?" Fitzgerald moved toward him and ticked off his complaints on his fingers. "You're out till midnight or later every night again, you have this proclivity for women's apartments—have you even been meeting with Cally Lonegan?"

Zach gave in and rolled his eyes. He did not have the patience for this. At least he wouldn't have to put up with Fitzgerald anymore.

"Answer me!"

"Keep your cassock on. Nothing happened."

"That poor girl probably thinks she's in love with you, or you're in love with her."

Molly had to know that, but Zach clenched his jaw to keep himself from firing back. Glowering, Fitzgerald closed in on him. Zach fell back on reflex, checking possible escape routes—door behind him, his room to the right, the hall to the side door to the left. He took a step to the side to keep from getting cornered against the door. Not that he had any reason to worry.

Right?

"You can't do this here." Fitzgerald punctuated each word of his fierce whisper with a jab to Zach's chest. "How dare you betray their trust—*my* trust—*God's* trust?"

"I haven't done anything." He leaned forward, matching the older priest's emphatic tone with an extra note of defiance.

"You've done too much already." Fitzgerald clamped onto Zach's shoulders. "I won't let you do this to them!" His eyes seethed with rage. His fingers dug in, inching closer to Zach's neck. Zach's throat instinctively constricted.

He wrenched himself free of Fitzgerald's hands. "Get ahold of yourself." Zach pushed the older man away, but instead of falling back, Fitzgerald lunged at him. Zach sidestepped the attack. He grabbed Fitzgerald's arm and twisted it behind the priest.

"I said calm yourself," Zach growled. Fitzgerald struggled to get free; Zach pinned him against the door. He held Fitzgerald there, counting each pant. After a dozen gasps, Fitzgerald's labored breathing changed from incensed to injured.

"Let go." Fitzgerald grimaced, and his free shoulder twitched with the pain.

Zach released him and backed away, his mind still racing through the nearest escapes. "What are you thinking, attacking me?"

Fitzgerald swallowed hard, gaze on the ground. "I'm sorry." He took a deep breath. "Don't know what came over me." He stood there a minute, then slunk away under Zach's wary gaze.

No way was he staying in a house with someone with that kind of rage issue. Zach strode from the parish house. He'd take his chances with the drafty chapel over one more night with Fitzgerald in the next room.

He sank onto a hard wooden pew, the last of the adrenaline draining from his muscles. He could still see Fitzgerald's eyes and their unbridled fury.

And then the pieces fell together so smoothly they made an almost audible click.

Zach hopped up. He paced the chapel aisle twice, trying to unthink his conclusion. Because that had to be wrong.

One way to be sure. He let himself into the cramped sacristy and locked the door behind. He didn't have a secure connection, and the ASAC would ream him out for this, but he didn't have time to worry about that. Zach dialed Sellars.

He picked up on the third ring. "What?"

"I need to talk to our guest."

"Why?"

Couldn't Sellars just cooperate? "Have to ask him something. Now."

Sellars hesitated, then grunted. "Hang on, I'll get the number."

The wait felt like forever, but within fifteen minutes, Zach was calling Lonegan. Someone—a U.S. Marshal?—answered the phone. "Yes?"

He hoped this marshal was familiar with the case's paperwork, and thus, Zach's name. "Special Agent Zachary Saint, FBI, to talk to Cally." He held his breath, though odds were low anyone was listening, electronically or otherwise. "Pertaining to an ongoing investigation."

"One minute."

Zach leaned against the low dressing table with his vestments. On the phone, a television in the background grew louder, then the marshal's distant voice: "Phone."

"Hello?" Lonegan—or whatever his new last name was—asked tentatively.

"Cally, it's Father Tim." He rushed on before Lonegan could respond. "The first time I came over to your house, Lisa said this was about Father Patrick."

"Well, yeah. I mean, what they were gonna say he did—he's a priest!"

Zach frowned. "You don't know anything about what happened to him? It wasn't your people, or Ian or your rivals?"

"No, no. You'd know if it was. They don't exactly do things quiet."

He forced a note of relief into his sigh, though he was anything but reassured. "You have no idea who killed him?"

"Thought it was a robbery."

"So did I," Zach murmured. "I'll be seeing you." He tucked his phone in his pocket and surveyed the cluttered sacristy where they dressed for Mass every day.

The archdiocese was sending his replacement in less than twelve hours. Would that be long enough to make sure he was right?

Molly checked on the sealed envelopes in her handbag and stepped into the chapel far too early the morning after the talent show. The letters were not why she was here, more composed, at dawn, though she was finally ready to give Tim his—as soon as she was done serving as a last-minute substitute for perpetual adoration. And then she'd tender her resignation letter to Father Fitzgerald.

The older priest brushed past her in the aisle, barely acknowledging her. She could wait to give him his letter. She climbed the marble steps to the side chapel and signed the book on the podium. With a nod to Kathleen, leaving from her turn at adoring, Molly took her place in the adoration chapel. The soft overhead lights glinted off the gold leaf of the sunburst statuette that held the wafer of the Host. Above, the crucifix motif in the blue-toned window was still dim.

An hour of perfect solitude to search for the peace she needed. Molly settled into the leather chair back and tried to think of the Lord. She stared up at the white and gold altar. Father Fitzgerald had suggested adoration, but how was this supposed to help?

Molly closed her eyes and made her breathing deep and even, trying to recall the feelings of reassurance and peace she'd had only days ago. But all she could see was Tim gazing at her as he sang his song. Her body might have been in the chapel, but her mind was still rooted in the cafeteria.

She was weak.

Should she give him her letter now? It was early, but he was probably up.

She opened her eyes again. The stained glass window glowed with the growing light. But as the only adorer, she had to stay in the chapel—and so far, it wasn't bringing her the solace she needed.

What was the scripture Lucy had first shared with her?

Something about coming to the Lord in faith and humility, and He'd make weak things strong. He would strengthen her weaknesses.

Maybe He already was. Weren't the letters in her handbag tangible proof?

She smiled slowly. He could make this right.

But her focus was short-lived. A soft sigh echoed in the chapel behind her. She didn't have to turn around to recognize him, but turn she did. Father Tim sat on the steps to the sanctuary, slumped forward, his head in one hand.

An aftershock of the ache she'd felt the night before rippled through her. He was suffering as much as she was.

"There you are," came a voice from the far end of the chapel. Father Fitzgerald walked down the aisle to the foot of the steps. Shouldn't a priest have a bit more consideration for the adorer twenty feet away? Then again, with the chapel's acoustics, he probably wasn't speaking that loud. "About last night—"

Father Tim cut off his statement with a sharp, dismissive chop.

Father Fitzgerald leaned closer to peer into Tim's face. "You look terrible. Did you sleep in here?"

"No." He stood. "I mean, I was here. But I didn't sleep. Bruce, there's something I need to tell you." Father Tim sighed and looked down. "I'm no priest."

Molly's heart nearly sprang from her ribs, but her stomach dropped. Was he leaving the priesthood—to be with her?

"Oh, my son." Father Fitzgerald moved up a step. "What have you done? Is it Miss Saint?"

Father Tim—or was it just Tim now?—pulled back in obvious surprise. "I wouldn't touch Lucy with a . . . pole of any length imaginable, ever."

Father Fitzgerald lowered his voice to an imploring whisper. "Tell me it's not Molly."

"Again?" Tim shook his head. "You, Kathleen, Teresa Hennessy— why is it nobody thinks I'm capable of behaving when there's a pretty face around?"

Father Fitzgerald's eyebrows drew together. "Why is it you *act* that way whenever she's around?" He climbed another stair, finally making him taller than Tim.

Molly shifted in her chair. How many times had Father Tim and Father Fitzgerald had this conversation? Was this the reason he was leaving the priesthood?

"Glad to know you hold Molly in such high regard, too." Tim climbed the steps to tower over Father Fitzgerald.

Father Fitzgerald abandoned any attempt to keep his voice down. "You're the one in a position of authority. It'd be totally understandable if she fell when you abused that trust."

"If you can't believe I have a tiny scrap of self-control, at least give Molly some credit."

"Self-control can only do so much when you insist on putting yourself in temptation's way. Both of you." Father Fitzgerald circled Tim—like a vulture.

Molly had never heard Father Fitzgerald use such a condescending—or angry—tone. She hardly recognized either of her priests, the way they were acting. Clearly something was going on here beyond the argument.

"Why don't you just admit what you two have done and make it easier for us all?" Father Fitzgerald demanded.

"What we've done?" Tim turned to face Father Fitzgerald, still circling. "I could never—do you have any idea what that would do to her?"

Father Fitzgerald continued his circuit, closing in on Tim. "Then stop trying to find out. Don't you understand what it means to make a vow?"

Tim held up a hand, visibly biting back another argument. "This is irrelevant."

"Irrelevant? Your sacred obligation is irrelevant?"

"I don't have a sacred obligation! I've never received Holy Orders. I. Am. Not. A. Priest."

The room began to rotate, and Molly grabbed the back of the chair. A cottony hollow filled her chest. Never received—?

Father Fitzgerald's volume crescendoed. "You're not a priest?"

"You heard—"

Father Fitzgerald ripped the white insert from Tim's clerical collar. "You'll be excommunicated!"

"Probably would be, if I were Catholic."

"You're not even—?"

"Federal agent." Tim pulled a notecase from his jacket and flashed a badge.

Father Tim wasn't a priest. Molly's lungs closed on themselves, forcing out all her air. This couldn't be happening. She tried to stop the spinning, to swallow, to *think*. Federal agent?

Tim's voice barely reached her through the blood rushing in her ears. "When exactly did Ian tell you Father Patrick abused him?"

"I told you, I don't remember exactly."

"September thirteenth?"

The day Father Patrick died? She fought off the onset of shock, but her breath still came in short, silent spurts. She dug her nails into the back of the leather chair.

"Yes." Father Fitzgerald's voice was only a pained pant.

"Is that why you killed him?"

Molly drew a noiseless gasp. No. This had to be a nightmare.

Father Fitzgerald drew back, stopping short of the stairs. "What are you—?"

"You confronted him, didn't you?"

"I—I—"

"Come on, Bruce. Look at how you reacted to me flirting with Molly."

Fitzgerald shook his head vehemently. "That isn't the same."

"No, it's not. There's no way you could let Father Patrick do that kind of thing here."

Father Fitzgerald stumbled backward off the stairs, but caught himself. "I don't know what you're trying to say."

"You found out about Ian." Tim turned to Father Fitzgerald, his back now to Molly. "And you came and strangled Patrick with his stole."

"But—"

"Maybe you thought, if you stayed here, you could make it up to the parish. To God." Tim advanced on Father Fitzgerald. "You'd never do it again, right?"

"I didn't—I couldn't—" He broke off and pivoted away.

"But, you see, the thing about anger is once you give in, it only gets easier to do it again. That's why you attacked me."

Father Fitzgerald threw up his hands. "No, that was a mistake."

Tim grew even more acerbic. "And killing Patrick wasn't?"

"If you would just listen!" He clenched his fists together.

"See what I mean about anger? And once you kill, there's no going back."

Father Fitzgerald grabbed at Tim, but Tim blocked Molly's view of the exchange. "You don't understand," Father Fitzgerald shouted. "Colin molested Ian! For *years*! And who knows how many other innocent children! Such a sin, such a betrayal—"

"He deserved to die?"

"Yes!" Father Fitzgerald thundered.

Father Tim wasn't a priest. Father Fitzgerald was a murderer. Molly couldn't begin to wrap her brain around this.

The echo of the priest's voice slowly died. Tim's shoulders fell. "He didn't, Bruce."

"What?" He pulled back a step, into Molly's line of sight, his brow furrowed.

"Doyle Murphy was extorting him, and he made all that up to force Patrick into it."

What? Father Patrick was innocent—and Father Fitzgerald was guilty. And Father Tim was an undercover federal agent. Molly's head swam.

"But . . ." Father Fitzgerald looked around as though he'd lost his way without any hope of finding it. "Why would they say that after he died?"

"To show me they meant it. They wanted me—had people ready to say I was sleeping with Molly. Which, by the way, I didn't do, either."

Father Fitzgerald's jaw dropped, and the dread in his eyes re-kindled. He glanced to where she sat in the side chapel. Tim whipped around to look, too. He met her gaze, and realization dawned in his eyes, along with horror.

Physical pain tore through the numbness to sear into her chest.

Molly shook her head—how could he?—and his gaze fell in shame.

"Come on, Bruce. The police are outside." Tim took Father Fitzgerald's arm and pulled him toward the aisle.

"Who'll take care of the parish? Not you, I hope."

"The archdiocese is sending a replacement for me. Do you want him to get here before or after the squad car leaves?"

Father Fitzgerald allowed himself to be conducted out of the church, leaving Molly in a stupefied silence.

Tim wasn't a priest at all. He was a federal agent.

And he was gone.

She turned back to the altar and settled back in her chair, the leather upholstery sighing for her.

He had to know what he'd put her through over the last two months—and that was all for nothing? She would have understood if he'd told her. He *knew* she would've understood, and he still hadn't told her.

No, he'd lied. And lied. And lied.

Did he really feel anything for her, or had it all been designed to provoke Father Fitzgerald into a confession?

By the time the next adorer arrived, anger had begun to gnaw at the edges of Molly's shocked stupor.

She was a fool, and he'd certainly played her for one.

The parish house door fell shut behind Zach for the last time. His replacement, Father Gus, knew as much as he needed to: Fitzgerald was in Chicago PD custody and Doyle Murphy and his gang were in jail.

And he'd been wrong—again—about tying up all the loose ends. How could he have been so stupid? He always forgot about perpetual adorers in the chapel, but couldn't he have at least looked around? Habit more than hope took him past the parish office. He should've told her last night. Or at her place the night before. Or the first time he saw her. No matter what it cost him. What had his selfishness cost her?

Zach stopped at the end of the arched hallway. Beyond the bare maple tree, Sellars waited to take him away from here. Away from her.

Like she deserved.

Zach stepped out toward the skeletal maple, and Molly rounded the corner. They locked eyes and froze. This was his chance. He had to tell her the truth.

"Molly, I—"

She held up a hand to cut him off. "I don't care." Tears shone in her eyes, but her voice was firm.

Zach broke their gaze, nodding. She clamped her mouth shut and waved him aside. He started for Sellars's car again. At the sedan, he took one last look back at St. Adelaide, his case, his job, and his home for the last two months.

He'd been so worried about this assignment—worried he was betraying his faith, worried he was making a mockery of the Catholic Church, worried he'd mislead faithful members. But in the end, he'd done some good. He'd helped Cally. He'd found Father Patrick's murderer. He'd freed the parish and the school from the mob.

In fact, there was only one person he hadn't done right by. Molly still stood at the corner of the church, hugging her heavy green coat close around her. She stared back at him, and the wind tugged her dark curls into her face. Couldn't he try to tell her one last time?

"Hurry up," Sellars barked from the car.

He couldn't explain this. Even trying—it was just him being selfish again. As he got into the car, the look on her face said it all. He could've told her the truth a thousand times, but her answer would still be the same as Moll Dubh's to her suitor in his song last night: *Ó imigh uaim 's nach pill go brách orm.*

Depart from me and do not come again.

32

MOLLY SHOVED THE LAST of her moving boxes into the corner of her parents' living room, and the house fell silent again. When her parents told her they'd be spending Christmas with Bridie and her children in their new home across the country, Molly had known she'd be alone for the holiday. But not this lonely.

Was Tim alone now? Did he have a family?

Molly shook off the thought and puffed out a breath. It had been almost three weeks. She wasn't supposed to be thinking of that liar.

She opened the box and pulled out—a secondhand Bible. Father Gus had brought it by the office, saying one of the priests had left it. She couldn't open it to settle the nagging matter of religion and faith, and she couldn't bring herself to donate it yet. Just like she couldn't bring herself to delete the last voicemail Tim had left her, warning her to go somewhere safe while they were arresting the mobsters.

Did that mean he really cared about her? Was that one thing she could trust about him?

No. It was only part of his cover. Even if he did care—she couldn't let herself think that—but even if he did, it didn't change anything.

She was trying to forget him, but he just kept popping back up.

A knock at the door helped distract her. Finally. Molly stuffed the Bible back in the box and found Lucy on the front step, her usual smile thin and tired. Perhaps things hadn't gone much better for her and Paul. "Hey, Molly." Lucy came in. "How are you holding up?"

"About as well as you appear to be."

"That bad, huh?" Lucy made a minimal effort to grin. "Ready?"

"You're sure this isn't intrudin'?"

"No, no, not at all," Lucy said, "we don't have to mention . . . you know, everything, and I've already screened the guest list. You'll be like part of the family."

"If you're sure it wouldn't be a bother."

"'Course not. And I need the help driving." Before Molly could protest again, Lucy grabbed her travel bag and lugged it to the car. Molly collected her suitcase and followed.

Spending Christmas with someone else's family might be awkward, but better than sitting at home. Quiet. Alone.

They settled into their seats, and Lucy dug through the center console a moment. She came up with a note card she offered to Molly. "The missionaries wanted you to have this."

"Oh, thank you." Molly tucked the list of Bible references in her handbag, and her fingers brushed an envelope. Her letter to Tim.

If Lucy had known him as kids, she must've known who he really was all along. Molly finally mustered the courage to ask. "You knew, didn't you? About 'Father' Tim?"

Lucy lifted a leery eyebrow.

"Federal agent," Molly murmured, her heart squeezing in her chest.

Lucy sighed. "Couldn't exactly fool me. I mean, you know we're—"

Molly held up a hand. "You know, I don't want to talk about him. Any of it."

"Sorry." Lucy slipped an arm around Molly's shoulders. "Well, at least Brian won't bother you anymore. Apparently he eloped with Paul's crazy ex. Good luck—I mean, did you hear her song at the talent show?"

"No." Molly willed herself not to think of another talent show performance.

"My favorite line was 'Although you'll be a priest, my love will never cease.' At least Paul will be relieved. If he finds out."

Molly cocked her head. "Won't you be tellin' him?"

Lucy's weak smile faded altogether. "We're not actually speaking anymore."

Then they were as bad off as Molly and Tim—no, just Molly. She gave Lucy's shoulders a squeeze.

"Hey, um, do you mind if we make one stop first? I thought the temple might help us feel better before we go."

That neogothic skyscraper downtown? "If you say so."

"Here." Lucy handed over her mobile. "Man the GPS, please?" Lucy rattled off an address—not downtown—and Molly entered it for her. The GPS voice took over, and Molly closed the app. She moved to set the mobile in the cupholder, but accidentally opened another app first. Before she could close it, she realized she was reading the scripture verses on the screen.

"Would you mind terribly if I used your mobile?"

Lucy grabbed the charging cord and offered it to her. "Go ahead."

Molly pulled out the card Lucy had just given her and set about reading those verses. The list kept her occupied the whole drive, until Lucy pulled into a parking space. Molly looked up. Though it wasn't even five o'clock, the sun had set during the drive. From this side, only the black roof of the huge A-frame building was visible through the row of bare trees.

Lucy opened her door. "Come see." She hurried down the walkway. Molly trailed after with a more measured step, still pondering the verses she'd studied. What would she find here?

She came through the trees to the wide, well-kept round patio in front of the temple. The whole circle glittered with Christmas lights, but nothing so bright as the temple itself. Spotlights shone up on the white spires and the gray marble patchwork of its triangular façade.

Molly lifted her gaze to follow the lights and spires heavenward. She was still so weak—so broken.

Yet the peace of this place was palpable. Maybe she'd been over-thinking it all this time. All she had to do was believe, and He could make weak things strong.

Though she wanted to forget everything he'd ever said, Tim's advice echoed in her thoughts: *the choice is yours.* Not the last millennium of her ancestors'—hers.

And she wanted to believe. She stared at the sky a moment longer, then lowered her eyes to the temple. A tangible warmth seeped into the vacuum that had occupied her heart. This was where she wanted to be, where she needed to be. The moment she admitted it, serenity settled over her like a down comforter. A peace she hadn't

felt since before Tim—

Molly held her breath. She waited for the keening ache that had been her constant companion to return.

But it didn't.

"Tim," she whispered, testing it again. The pain hovered beneath the surface, but for now that was enough. The Lord had taken her pain and given her peace. He was strengthening her, and He would continue to strengthen her. Just as He promised.

Lucy made her way back around the patio and joined Molly, gazing up at the gray marble of the majestic building for a silent moment. Lucy shivered. "Ready?"

Molly smiled. "I am."

Molly held her scarf over her hair, protecting it from the falling snow, while Lucy knocked at her sister's door late that night. The gray slush made Christmas Eve dingy in the tidy neighborhood.

The door swung open, and the aromas of Christmas—hot chocolate, evergreens and pie—spilled out. In the doorway, two women opened welcoming arms. Judging by the blond hair, these were Lucy's mother and sister. "Lucy!" cried her mother. "Now we're all here."

Lucy kicked the snow from her shoes and stepped into the marble-tiled entry. "Mom, this is Molly, the friend I told you about."

"Molly." Mrs. Saint greeted her warmly, her short bouffant shaking with her enthusiasm. "Merry Christmas." Even with the Southern twang, the standard American tiding didn't sound right to Molly's ear.

"Happy Christmas," she returned.

Mrs. Saint's smile didn't waver. "That's right, Lucy told us you're

Irish." The plump woman showed them to a sitting room. "We loved Ireland. How did you meet Lucy?"

Before Molly answered, Lucy's mobile buzzed. She pulled it out and frowned. "I actually need to take this." She glanced at the other women. Each of them nodded permission, and Lucy slipped out the front door.

"We worked together, in a way," Molly finally answered Mrs. Saint's question.

"I'm Tracey, by the way." Lucy's sister, nearly as tall as Molly, gestured at herself.

"You can call me Debbie," Lucy's mother said.

"Pleasure to meet you both." Molly surveyed the room decorated in dark red and cream, a Christmas tree in the corner trimmed to match. "Your home is lovely."

"Thank you," Tracey said. "Here, I'll take your coat." Tracey held out a hand. With a nod of thanks, Molly shrugged out of her jacket, and Tracey left to hang it up.

Debbie took Molly's arm. "Where in Ireland are you from?"

"Mostly Dublin."

Debbie conducted her out of the sitting room and down the hall, approaching the boisterous sounds of the family at play. "Dublin was wonderful! I'm sure Lucy mentioned her brother was a missionary there."

Molly nodded. Lucy had dropped hints about her brother until Molly told her about Father Tim. Tim.

It didn't matter what she called him. Thinking of him might not hurt as much anymore, but she still needed to stop thinking of him.

"Well, good news—he surprised us today! He hasn't spent Christmas with us in years. Here, let me introduce you," Debbie offered. They came into a room with another tree with children's handmade ornaments. Ten feet away, a very tall man stood with his back to them, surrounded by a giggling knot of pajama-clad children, competing with a stereo playing cheery carols.

Did everything have to make her think of Tim? This was exactly how they'd met, her coming up behind him only to have him turn around and turn her life on its head.

"Zachary!" Debbie called. "There's someone here I'd like you to meet."

He looked over his shoulder. Was it the powerful memory of the first time she'd seen him, or her imagination—or did Zachary's deep-set blue eyes, hair, everything look just like Tim?

Molly reeled, staggering back until she almost stepped on Debbie. His jaw dropped. "Molly."

She recognized his voice, though it was only a whisper. This *was* real. Her stomach grew cold and tears welled up. They stared at one another, locked in place. In the sudden silence, the stereo's jazzy "Happy Holidays" blared as if trying to drown out the awkwardness.

After a long second he turned, breaking their gaze, and strode from the room. Unsure which way to go, Molly stumbled into the quickly-blurring dining room. She reached the table and swiped at the tears on her cheeks. It finally made sense. Lucy said she'd loved him like a brother—bickered with him like a brother—because he *was* her brother. Why hadn't Lucy told her? Why had she brought her here? Lucy knew she didn't want to see him. Didn't she?

"Molly?" Debbie's gentle query came from behind her.

Unable to reassure Debbie any other way, Molly waved her off and glanced around for another escape route—the back door. She'd probably freeze to death before she had herself calm enough to return, but at that second she didn't care. She needed to be alone to think this out. Molly unlocked the back door, braced herself against the cold and stepped onto the terrace.

But she didn't even know what she was trying to muddle through.

Zach found the right number and called as he reached the front door, though he doubted Sellars would answer at night on Christmas Eve. He swallowed to fight his rising blood pressure. This was impossible.

Covert? Compartmentalizing? Ha. Molly was in the middle of his real life—his family.

He opened the door to find Lucy on the front stairs, also on the phone. Lucy took one look at Zach and jumped. Before she could say anything, he glowered and pointed at her. "Remind me to kill you later," he muttered and shut the door between them.

Zach climbed the stairs to pace the beige carpet. Could this cost him his job? His call rolled to Sellars's voice mail.

What would happen if he went back and willingly told Molly the truth? It wasn't his fault she was here, that his cover and his real life had collided one last time. He wasn't supposed to call Molly or seek her out, but he couldn't run and hide if he ran into her on the street. She might not have known his real name, but she already knew his job. They couldn't fire him.

But his job wasn't what he worried about most.

How could he face her? Unless he disappeared, leaving Lucy to explain to everyone, he couldn't avoid it—avoid her. But nothing he said could make this right. Zach pocketed his phone and headed downstairs. He met Lucy, also off the phone, walking in the front door.

"Lucy." He used his best warning tone. "You got some 'splainin' to do."

"Thank you, Ricky Ricardo." She pursed her lips.

"Is it me or her you hate?"

Lucy put on her patented wide-eyed innocent act. "I thought she knew about us—and *you* said you weren't coming."

"I shouldn't have to clear my itinerary with you. I have a right to see—" Zach broke off. Lucy's innocent expression had faded into a silly smile. She couldn't be that happy about tormenting him. "What's wrong with you?"

"Um." Lucy ducked her head in a futile effort to hide a rising blush. "Paul just called. He realized he doesn't have to be a priest to serve God."

"Well, hooray for you. You get a merry little Christmas, and Molly and I get nervous breakdowns." Zach craned his neck toward the living room. "What can I say to her?"

Lucy scoffed. "Maybe try the truth?"

"Didn't go well last time."

She ignored him. "Listen, Zach, Molly seems interested in the Church—"

"Really?"

She nodded, beaming. "I really don't want you messing that up. I mean, having you around would ruin anyone's Christmas—"

He smirked. "You want to make this up to us?"

Lucy nodded as they reached the befuddled group of adults at the end of the hallway. Zach gave Lucy his wickedest grin. "You're dating a Catholic priest?"

He looked past his now-shocked family, searching for Molly. His mom pointed him to the back door before asking Lucy how serious her relationship was.

Someone—probably his mom—had draped both his coat and Molly's over a dining room chair by the door. Two mugs of hot chocolate with marshmallows *and* whipped cream steamed on the table.

Lucy had said she wouldn't get him a present, but she might've brought him exactly what he wanted, even if he barely would've admitted it to himself. Or maybe it had been someone else orchestrating things down to this moment. He glanced heavenward with a quick prayer for luck—and thanks.

Zach collected the coats and cups and steeled himself to step into the cold. He could finally do what he'd wanted all along—tell her the truth no matter what it cost him. And he'd be lucky if she didn't slap him. No, he'd be lucky if she cared enough to slap him.

No. This wasn't about him. This was what he owed to her. He'd spend their weeks together focusing on what he wanted. He had to put Molly first. He'd give her what she deserved—the truth—and then go. Like she wanted.

And yet the hope still rose in his chest as Zach opened the back door.

33

MOLLY DIDN'T LOOK behind her when she heard the door open. She tried to douse the hope lifting her heart, to cling to the pain he'd caused her, until her whole chest ached as though she'd held her breath too long.

If it was him at the door, what then?

"Molly," his voice ventured as softly as the falling snow.

It was him. She took a deep breath and waited as long as she could—an unimpressive two and a half seconds—before turning around. Tim—Zachary stood behind her, her green coat draped over his arm.

"Are you tryin' to tell me to go?"

"I won't ask you to stay."

Just what he'd said when he was ill a month ago. And now, as then, he was lying. The look in his eyes—she scarcely dared to check—begged her to stay. As if she could've torn herself away. "I am a fool, amn't I?" Molly laughed at herself.

"I don't think so." Zachary crossed the terrace and set two mugs of hot chocolate on top of the snow on the table. He held out her jacket. Molly begrudgingly turned around and allowed him to help her put it on. The chill stopped creeping through her Aran sweater, but she didn't feel any warmer. She retrieved her gloves from her coat pockets and tried in vain to force her freezing fingers into them.

He took the gloves and helped her with those, too. Her hands were so numb, she could barely feel the warmth of his skin. He held onto her gloved hand a heartbeat longer than necessary; she pulled away. She wouldn't let herself be dragged into that again.

He contemplated the deck. "If you wanted to do this inside, I wouldn't object, you know yourself."

Using an Irish phrase wouldn't be enough today. "What, in front of your family? No, thank you kindly."

"Lucy's distracting them." Zachary threw on his own jacket.

"Still a no. You know you look nothin' like her."

He picked up a mug and pressed it into her hands. Why was she letting him do these things for her? "She's adopted," he said. "And sorry, by the way. I told her I wasn't coming."

"Are you incapable of tellin' the truth? Lucy looks just like your mum."

He nodded. "She thought you knew we were brother and sister."

They regarded one another in silence for a long moment. Couldn't he see what he'd done to her, the keening ache in her heart?

Zachary brushed the snow off a chair and sat. "How do you want to play this?"

She scoffed. "How can you be so cold?"

"*I* never said I didn't care."

"Yes, Father—Tim—whoever you are." Molly opened her arms to indicate the slushy gray garden. "*This* is how little I care. Comin' out here to freeze because I've seen you again. You're one to talk."

"You know I care."

"I don't know anythin' about you." She reined in her anger enough to keep her voice down. "You're not a priest; you're not even Catholic."

"I believe the Bureau's logic was 'no good Catholic would do it, and no bad Catholic could.'"

As if telling the truth now made up for it. Exasperated, she rolled her eyes. "How could you put me through all that for nothin'?"

Zachary lowered his gaze. "I'm so sorry. If I could've told you—I almost did anyway."

"Sure now." She took a long draught from her mug to cut off her sarcasm.

He stood and picked up his hot chocolate. "When you were freaked out about the mob. After the movie. When you said you were talking to the missionaries. At your apartment that last time."

Molly tried to remember those conversations. Only the last was clear enough: the final private moment they'd had together, him clasping her shoulder, saying he needed to tell her something— something she'd thought she wanted to hear.

This wasn't what she'd expected. She shivered, pulling her focus back to the freezing present and the man in front of her.

"I'm covert. Even my family doesn't know what I do."

He was that covert? And he'd still almost told her? She ignored the twinge in her chest.

"Remember in *Catch Me in Zanzibar*, how Frank runs into Katya in Stone Town and she's happy to see him?" Zachary half-smiled hopefully.

She turned away to keep herself from falling for that smile again. "And remember how I said that book wasn't very accurate?" And Katya later tried to shoot Frank.

"I told you how I felt before I left." He waited until she met his gaze. "I'm so sorry, Molly."

She bit back a sarcastic retort, but let the sentiment show in her eyes.

Zachary took a deep breath. "I never meant to hurt you."

"But you did." She spun away and took another sip of her thick hot chocolate. Couldn't he see how deeply his lies cut?

"Please look at me."

Molly fixed him with a suitable glare.

He came to stand a meter in front of her and stuck out a hand. "Hi, I'm Zachary Tyler Saint. I'm from Virginia, and I like basketball and my job, which I might lose for talking to you."

Molly ignored his hand and the twinge of guilt at his last statement.

"Fine, I'll do your part," Zachary said. "You're Molly Malone, you're from Ireland, and you like traditional dance and spy novels."

She leaned against the railing. So he knew one or two facts about her. So what?

"Okay, my turn again. There's one more thing you should know about me." Zachary contemplated his hot chocolate for a long time before meeting her gaze again. "I'm a horrible, selfish person, who told himself flirting with you would help his case, but in reality, I was lying to myself, too. I flirted with you because I wanted to. Because I'm in love with you."

Molly turned to the back garden, clamping down on the excitement racing through her veins like sweet, pure adrenaline. He was a liar; he'd just admitted it. Sure, he'd only done it because he had to for his job, but that didn't mean she should believe him now. She set her mug on the snow on the railing to rub her hands over her arms. "I don't even know you."

He came to lean against the porch railing next to her, facing but not looking at her. "But you know *me*, Moll. We're only missing some details."

"Details." She sighed and shook her head. "Your name, your religion and your occupation are all details?"

"Even my family doesn't know my occupation, but you know all that now."

Could it be that easy? Could it really be possible?

Zachary cleared a place for his mug by hers on the railing. "If you want me to leave, I will."

He was willing to give up his first Christmas with his family in years—for her.

So what? A frigid gust blew a burst of fresh snowflakes between them.

"I understand if you hate me," he said. For the first time, she recognized the pain in his voice.

She couldn't let him think that. "I don't hate you, I just . . . can't believe anythin' you say."

"Yes, you can. Molly, you wanted—you wanted *me* then. Didn't you?"

She stopped her hand halfway to her other elbow and closed her eyes. Her heart and lungs squeezed in her chest. How could she answer that question when he was standing there staring at her with those same knowing eyes—the ones that had known her from the first moment they'd met? How could she pretend she didn't want him then, that she'd never felt anything? At last, she nodded.

"And now?"

Of course she still wanted him. She wanted it so badly that it cut her heart all over again just to look at him. She kept her back to him, watching the snow blowing on the house. Finally warm, she pulled the collar of her coat up to keep the wind out.

In a low voice, Zachary began to sing. Why did he have to choose this song? He started with the chorus—about her. *If I had to choose from the pretty young women of the world, Dark Molly of the glen would be my choice.*

Molly wheeled around. Zachary's gaze locked on hers. The pain was still there—but more than that. A familiar longing—one she could fill.

He kept singing the verse that began "Me without a wife, I won't be all my life."

Then the reason that look was so familiar struck her—he had the same look in his eyes at the talent show. And she felt the same way.

He'd tried to tell her.

Zachary continued with the next verse, Dark Molly telling her suitor to leave. Could she tell Zachary to leave her again? Her heart twisted in a knot. She had a second chance. They both did. And the choice was hers.

Could she let him leave again? Molly squeezed her eyes shut at the thought, forcing out a tear. He *was* the same person. It was in his eyes. She turned back to face him and the yearning in his eyes, a yearning she knew all too well. He loved her, and not just as part of an act. She dared to inch closer to him as he began the next verse.

"Is go ceillí, múinte, cneasta a dúirt sí liom ar maidi—"

"Tá a fhios agat go bhfuil grá agam duit," Molly provided a last line for the verse.

Stopped mid-song, Zachary creased his brow. Oh, he didn't really speak Irish.

"Ah, the song says 'Dark Molly of the glen has my heart, she never had any disgrace; so . . .'" She reviewed the last line he'd sung. "'So sensibly, politely, decently, she told me this mornin'—'"

He nodded. Obviously he knew the meaning of those words; that had to have been why he'd chosen the song. "And you said?" he finally asked.

The vise around her heart crept open. "You know I love you."

The smile began at his lips, but in a split second his entire countenance sparked with hope. He tentatively reached out to twine one of her curls around his finger. "Moll, I meant it then, and I mean it now."

"I know."

Zachary brushed the snow from her hair, then combed her curls behind her ear. He searched her face intently, his fingers lingering at the back of her neck. She knew that look, too.

He was going to kiss her. Her pulse raced in her throat. She tilted her chin up.

Sure enough, he began to lean down the next instant—but as he had before, he hesitated at the last second before she closed her eyes. "I love you, Molly Malone."

"I love you, too, Zachary Saint."

"Say that again?"

Would he really make her wait longer for something he'd teased her with for months? "I love you?"

"Well, yeah, that part, but—say my name?"

His real name, one without a title and calling that would keep them apart? Gladly. "Zachary Saint." His name—his real name—sounded as free and easy as laughter.

His smile barely registered in her mind before he finally bridged the gap that had separated them for so long, and kissed her.

Dear Reader,

Thank you so much for reading *Saints & Spies*! This book is a true labor of love: it took *seven years* to bring it to you, and a major detour where a trade publisher accepted it, but we couldn't agree on their contract. Now it's finally in your hands! I hope you enjoyed it as much as I enjoyed writing it and sharing it with you.

I've done all I can to make this book as enjoyable as I can for you. Can you do me a quick favor? If you'd be willing to review this book online, it would help me secure advertising spots and spread the word about this book. Additionally, if you send me a link to your review, I'll send you an invitation for a free review copy of my next novel. You can email me your link (or for any other reason! I love hearing from readers!) here: Jordan@JordanMcCollum.com.

Looking for more to read? *Saints & Suspects* is out now, and the third book in the series will be coming soon! In the meantime, if you haven't already, check out my other series, Spy Another Day. Join my reader's group and you'll get a free ebook to get you started in the series! You can join me here: http://jordanmccollum.com/newsletter/

Thank you again for all your support, and I hope to entertain you again soon!

Jordan McCollum

Acknowledgments

THE STORY OF HOW this book came about is the story of making a writer. Once upon a time, this book was a funny idea Sarah Anderson and I came up with. We both wrote feverishly, her on Lucy and Paul's story, me on Zach and Molly's. We finished the novels in under two months.

Eventually, after many, many critiques and rewrites, a publisher offered me a contract for my novel. When they refused to negotiate on certain terms, I tearfully had to turn it down.

Now, seven years after I first started writing this book, it's finally coming to readers as my fifth novel, my seventh work of fiction, my tenth book. The vast majority of everything I know about writing, I have learned from this story, from tearing it apart and putting it back together again, from refining and polishing it, and from the amazing people who made this possible.

As this was once going to be my first published novel, I received an extraordinary amount of encouragement, feedback and help from so, so many people.

My patient husband, Ryan, has endured hours of writing time, plotting, discussion and agonizing over this book. He was the first person to hear the plot and encourage me to write it. Our children, Hayden and Rebecca at the time I drafted this novel, and now with Rachel, Hazel and Benjamin as I'm publishing it, have also been very patient, as I spent way too much time with imaginary people instead of them. My parents, Ben and Diana Franklin, have taught me to love reading and writing from a young age, and along with my sisters Jaime, Brooke and Jasmine, they have believed in and encouraged me.

My friends Kim Tran and Erin Brown have also supported my writing for more than a decade, and other friends like Lynne Kelson and Megan Mitchell have been there to cheer me on through the submission process.

I'd like to give a special thanks to Marnee Blake for being the first reader of the full manuscript and my Catholic consultant. An amazing number of others have also helped by reading the full manuscript, among them: Holly Horton, Diana Franklin (AKA Mom), Christine (C.K.) Bryant, Cindy Ricks, Stephanie Black, Julie Coulter Bellon, Deana Barnhart, LisaAnn Turner, Nikki Wilson, C. Michelle Jefferies and Rachel Hert. Each of them offered encouragement, advice and critiques to make this book better.

In this latest iteration, Ranée S. Clark provided invaluable feedback to *finally* fix the timeline problems that have plagued me from the beginning, so I could finally feel confident sending this out into the world. Kierstin Marquet, Emily Gray Clawson and Ben Franklin (AKA Dad) also gave final feedback, and naturally, Sarah Anderson gave it one last read-through before it was ready for you.

Sarah M. Eden gave me fantastic advice on writing an Irish character, and Aisling Doonan kindly consented to read a complete stranger's book and offered excellent help on perfecting my Irish and Catholic phraseology, since she's both Irish and Catholic. Jenn Wilks provided editorial feedback, but any errors here are not her fault. I'm blaming gremlins. Or lazy fingers. Or possibly one of my children. (The two-year-old likes to "help" me type.)

Finally, I must thank my friend Sarah Anderson once again. We have written together for fifteen years, and without her, this book—and especially Lucy and Paul—never would have come to life. She walked with me through every word and gave me her support, feedback and ideas daily.

And of course, the source of all inspiration, talent, time and effort is my Heavenly Father, and I'm eternally grateful to Him for these blessings.

About the Author

PHOTO BY JAREN WILKEY

AN AWARD-WINNING AUTHOR, JORDAN McCOLLUM can't resist a story where good defeats evil and true love conquers all. Her first four novels, the Spy Another Day series, were all voted as finalists for the Whitney Awards, a juried prize. In her day job, she coerces people to do things they don't want to, elicits information and generally manipulates the people she loves most—she's a mom.

Jordan holds a degree in American Studies and Linguistics from Brigham Young University. When she catches a spare minute, her hobbies include reading, knitting and music. She lives with her husband and five children in Utah.

Made in the USA
Las Vegas, NV
16 June 2023

73471165R00177